goodbye

THE

VOID

INFINITE

BETWEEN

AND

GOODBYE

HELLO

A NOVEL # Hello SAMMY D.

Cover Designer/Illustrator: Sophia Del Plato

ISBN: 979-8-9851805-2-7 (paperback)
ISBN: 979-8-9851805-3-4 (ebook)

Follow the author
www.svdbooks.com

Other books:
Count to Six

❀ Created with Vellum

To all the people that make us look dumb for falling in love with them.
To all the people that show us we're never dumb for falling in love.

Always. Remember. This.

The infinite void sucks.

♥ —Sammy

1

SPARKS

"This party's boring as hell," Lydia says. "Why the hell do we even come to work parties anymore? Forced fun is never fun. And it's so fucking *hot* on this boat." Lydia pulls her black dress away from her body as if it will be any cooler than having the thin, almost non-existent fabric against her. Her mouth-of-a-sailor contrasts her glittering earrings hovering above her straight back and four inch heels that make her regal compared to the other Bank employees on the boat that she rivals in height and who don't wear any shimmering jewelry. Chris swirls the remnants of his ice cubes and pepsi around the tall, narrow glass. He's limited himself to one drink at work events ever since that first Christmas party.

"Because forced fun is what businesses think will make their employees love working there," Chris says. "Besides, free food, drinks, and music on a fancy yacht on a lake is something we'll never be able to afford otherwise." He side-eyes Lydia. "Also, there's sure to be cards somewhere on this boat."

Lydia looks around and taps her foot unconsciously at the mention of cards. 'But is it worth this heat?" She downs a quarter of her beer. 'If I wanted to drink shitty beer, I'd just go to a dive bar. I'm not going to complain if the bank buys that shitty beer, though."

Chris raises his empty glass and clanks it together with Lydia's and Austin's.

"I'm ready for this party to end so I can go crash in bed," Austin says. "I hate feeling obligated to stay at work after working a full day. It's Friday."

Austin's suit is one of the few on the yacht that rivals Lydia's regalness. His slim blue suit makes him contrast with the crowd of mostly black and white, and his bright pink bowtie only adds another target on him to look. His handsome features are curated as much as Lydia's, the effort enhancing him beyond his coworkers' normalness. Holding the position of Human Resources Director doesn't hurt his ability to stand out, either.

"I agree," Lydia said. "Let me go home and eat my way through a Doritos bag while watching *Murderers Who Walked Free*."

"Why do you always watch those murder shows?" Austin asks. "Why can't you just cry to *Gilmore Girls* like the rest of us?"

Chris laughs while sipping the melting ice cubes. Coworkers surround them on the yacht's deck: some eat through little plates of appetizers, some lean on the railing as the vessel speeds across Lake Champlain, while others stand in circles laughing at exhausted work stories that weren't funny the first time they were told. Chris despises anything work after work, but a free yacht excursion is a free yacht excursion.

Dresses and black suits plaster the deck, forming the illusion that everyone who works at the Bank is at all elegant. Most would rather join Lydia at a dive bar for shitty beer, even if they had to pay a few bucks for it themselves. Dancing between the guests are servers who retain the air of serving fancy people even when they see some of the guests devolving to their college days, competing to see who can down a beer quicker. More than one of the servers eyes the guests with jealousy.

"How long does this party go for?" Chris asks. "I have to go home at some point to let Keith out."

"Why did you have to name your dog Keith?" Lydia asks. "That's a man's name, not a dog's."

"What's the difference?" Austin says.

"Not the point," Lydia says. "I feel so weird calling a dog Keith. Why couldn't you name him Riley or Luke or Charlie? A normal dog name."

"Keith loves you," Chris says, "so leave his name alone."

"And I love Keith, which is weird to say because it sounds like I'm talking about a man, and Lord knows I've never felt that way about a man."

"You've said that to men before," Austin says.

Lydia waves her hand. "I say a lot to men. And so have you, if we're broaching *that* topic. Men need confidence boosts sometimes. Honestly, a dog has more confidence than a man."

Chris sets his empty glass on a passing server's tray and asks for water. It is surprisingly easy to forfeit multiple alcoholic drinks at work events. Austin's ears perk up the moment before Chris says 'water.' Austin has stopped him from ordering a second glass of wine before, and Chris is thankful for that. Everyone needs a best friend like Austin.

"There goes Harris chasing Martha *again*," Lydia says. "He's pathetic. Men like him are why I'd rather date a dog named Keith."

Chris snickers as he watches Harris lean on the railing, holding a tall beer glass as the wind whips back his hand and flips his suit coat open, revealing his emerging 29-year-old beer belly; Chris shivers at the thought of their ages. If it weren't for Harris's full head of thick hair and endless energy, he would have looked 10 years older. Martha drags her billowing hair from her face as her dress flaps around her legs. She gazes across the lake while offering Harris inconsistent nods; treats thrown to an unknowing puppy that encourages his bad behavior. She drowns in money from her dead husband but she hasn't dated since he died 4 years ago. That hasn't stopped Harris from trying whenever he's between girlfriends, which is more often than not. Martha told him she didn't date men a decade younger than her but Harris saw her money and saw a woman who denied him and vowed persistence until she accepted a date.

Lydia calls a server over for her third beer. The young server dashes away when she gives him a wink. Chris feels bad for him though the server should be a little smarter than to expect a woman in her late-20s at this type of event to be even mildly interested in a college-age server. Chris' attention drifts away as booming laughter resounds from the lower level at the boat's rear.

"That beer can't get back here fast enough," Lydia says.

"What are you up to this weekend?" Austin asks Chris. "I've got something to show you."

"I'm working Saturday morning but I'm free the rest of the day," Chris says.

"Ok, I'll pick you up from the office at noon," Austin says.

"Hey Harris. Did Martha turn you down again?" Chris asks.

"Every time," Harris says. He found his way over to his three friends when Martha grew tired of nodding dispassionately and Harris realized his words missed entirely, whereas before they at least were considered.

Lydia rolls her eyes. "Maybe not all women want to go home with you."

"How absurd," Harris waves a hand.

"Because you're the best catch this side of Lake Champlain," Lydia says sarcastically.

"As long as you understand," Harris says. "At some point you won't be able to resist me as well."

"Did you ever think that maybe women want a man with direction and stability?"

Harris laughs. "I won't let a woman tie me down like that. I'm still enjoying my youth and my 20s."

"Something tells me you won't stop 'enjoying your youth' even into your 30s," Lydia says.

Harris slops some of his beer onto the deck. Austin waves across the deck and exhales with a heaviness that could anchor the yacht where it was.

"This is why I hate work events. I've got to keep face with Este and Alex. Why does the CEO even invite his children to these parties? I'll chat with y'all later. Hopefully."

He inhales before marching toward the twins waiting for him near the deck's makeshift bar. They have a drink ordered for him when he arrives and greet him with hugs and laughter. Austin's greetings rivals their authenticity and heart. Chris loves that about his best friend.

Chris and Lydia lean on their mini high-top table while Harris searches the deck for someone to hit on, as if he hasn't worked his way around the entire office multiple times already, and as if he wasn't turned down by nearly everyone. Chris admires his persistence. Circles of condensation from their cups dot the round glass table top like tattoos rippling in the wind.

Another booming round of laughter echoes from the back of the boat, the layers of fake laughter obvious beneath the genuine chuckles. Chris thanks the waiter for his water but holds the glass on the sides where the server's fingers hadn't touched. Lydia gives the young man another wink, making the college kid blush. Chris shakes his head but the server is oblivious to everyone except Lydia.

Harris perks up when he spots one of the people that had

gone home with him after a previous work party. As she walks down the deck's steps to the lower level, Harris gives chase, leaving Chris awkwardly leaning on the table, waiting for Lydia to finish flirting with the boy.

"Wait," Lydia says, cutting off the server, "what did you just say?"

"I'm sorry that it took me a while to get your drink. The people playing poker downstairs had a large drink order."

Lydia touches the waiter on his cheek, her palm already sweaty as she thinks about cards downstairs. "Thanks honey. Here's a tip." She hands him a $10 and lingers on his eyes for a moment long enough to enrapture him. She looks at Chris. "Those bastards started without me." She rushes toward the stairs Harris disappeared down. Chris follows reluctantly.

The lower deck is packed compared to the sparse, half-empty tall tables above. The clumps of tightly packed and laughing people dot the deck and leave barely enough room to walk between them, raising Chris's anxiety. Chris sometimes forgets the hundreds of people that the Bank of Burlington employs in its seven-story tall downtown building that the locals decried when it was built a decade ago.

Lydia grabs food off a passing server's tray. "I wish they'd start carrying around more desserts."

"You've already had a slice of cake and two cookies," Chris says.

"And it's not enough," Lydia clarifies as she eats a cannoli.

They pass coworkers laughing for all the reasons Chris actively chooses to avoid them: making fun of the way another is dressed or someone's too-thick Southern accent or an older coworker's struggle to learn some program to the same level as their 20-year old counterparts. He sips his water and ignores the laughs. As Lydia dives into the sea of formally dressed coworkers, Chris takes a deep breath.

They weave between dresses, ties, and the rare out-of-place polo. A few people wave as they pass and try to start conversation, but they both pretend to not hear anyone, which isn't a far stretch given the wind and the deafening chatter on the deck. Lydia clutches her beer so it can't be knocked out of her hand and focuses straight ahead on the doors leading to the interior deck and the poker game. She weaves with unparalleled skill through the crowd, almost dancing around coworkers and through the small windows they leave open between them.

Chris struggles to pass between any of them but he also doesn't want to be here so he pursues Lydia at all costs. If the space between people is too tight to pass between, he holds his breath and makes sure only his jacket's sleeves touch them, then makes a mental reminder to wash all of his clothes as soon as possible. Someone's hand brushes against his by accident as Chris pivots to avoid touching someone else. The thick sweat on their hand paints Chris's. He searches for a bathroom to wash it off but there are none on the outer deck. He hopes there's one inside. He waves at a few coworkers he passes. Most are friends he's been out with for drinks or known since they all graduated college together.

"Lydia! Lydia! Where have you been? We've been looking for you." Chris sighs as Greg struggles through the dense crowd. He's surprised Greg is even able to spot them through everyone, but Greg's superpower is he can find anyone he wants whenever he wants to. "The guys are idiots. You've gotta come over and tell them about that loan and that asshole of a CEO."

"Work is done," Lydia says, "I don't want to keep talking about it. Now if you want to talk about the serial killer documentary released last weekend, I'm down."

"Stop being a buzzkill and just come over to back me up," Greg says.

"Again, work is done. Plus, it's poke time."

"Why do you have to be so difficult?" Greg says.

Lydia looks longingly at her half empty glass. "Why do you have to be a pain in my ass?"

"Waste of time," Greg says. "I'm glad the guys talked me out of dating you last year."

"Well fuck you, too," Lydia says as Greg waves his hand and stomps away, quickly drowning in the tsunami of people. "What an asshole. I should never have gotten on this damn boat. Netflix released the finale of *My Boss's Killer* and I have to wait until tomorrow now to watch it. There's so much I could be learning from it. What a waste of time tonight is. Let's just go inside to play some poker."

Chris shuffles behind Lydia as they weave through the crowd, bending at angles he wasn't aware his body could move to avoid touching anyone.

"Isn't gambling is a bad way to deal with stuff?"

"Well, I can't watch my serial killer shows so what else do you expect? I can't exactly go around killing people on a boat I can't get off of."

Chris wonders if she would kill people if she could get off the boat. Lydia's anger fuels her through the crowd and around the clumps of suits and dresses, most of which wave or say hi to her with shallow overtones. Lydia's stomping and shrieks of 'hello' are nowhere near the friendly tone she carries at work. She would have shocked her coworkers if most weren't a drink or two deep.

The crowd grows denser as Chris chases his friend through it; he's not sure if he sweats more from the anxiety of having to touch so many people or from the heat. Just as many people wave and greet Chris. He waves back and wants to stop to keep face with all of them but also doesn't want to separate from Lydia, so he shouts that he'll see them Monday and scurries after Lydia. Being the only sober one doesn't make his task of weaving between a sea of drunks any easier.

Though the door is along the wall Lydia and Chris hug, they are forced to leave the wall when a crowd of people refuse to shift aside. Two men block Lydia's path but a brief shriek from her scares them into parting. Chris trips as he tries to quickly squeeze between them. He fumbles to stand up straight and chase Lydia.

A group of women circle Lydia and Chris, prohibiting their march toward the yacht's cabin door. Lydia groans loudly and faces the women with disgust. Chris would prefer to avoid these women but Lydia isn't one to forfeit a potential fight. He loves her defiance and strength but sometimes wishes she knew which battles were worth fighting.

"Well hi!" Mona says loudly, the fourth wine glass in her hand speaking for her. Lydia scoffs at how easily Mona loses control when drunk. "We wondered if we'd see you two. The gay one isn't with you?"

Some red spills over the deck when Mona waves her wine glass too quickly. The three women with her giggle away Mona's spilled wine as they sip from their own glasses that teeter dangerously close to also spilling.

"The field guys are here tonight," Leah says. "They always send the hottest ones into the field. It's too bad we rarely get to see them." Her above-average height makes her eye-level with the men around her, though she tries to make herself smaller and less intimidating when one talks to her.

"I don't understand why corporate invites them," Mona says. "They're the reason we were kicked out of the ballroom at last year's party."

"Yeah, but a yacht is so much better for a summertime party than a college ballroom," Leah says. "I miss college parties sometimes but then I look at the extravagance of this yacht and the handsome men in suits around us and I forget all about those dingy houses and cheap beer."

"Those are not days I want to go back to," Erika says, "far too many nicknames that don't need to make a return."

"Some people still say them to you," Mona says with a sip of her wine and a smirk.

"How are you two enjoying the party?" Erika asks, ignoring Mona.

"We were trying to get inside the cabin until you got in our way," Lydia says.

Chris appreciates her honesty, though his friend's impatience often ignites her short temper. Chris searches for an exit from their conversation but the four women surrounding them don't let people go until they're done with them. Chris would have preferred to talk to any of the suits or dresses around them over this group.

The fourth woman sips her wine while looking around the deck, casually ignoring the conversation but desperate to be involved. Brenda's recent employment at the bank and her just-as-recent relocation to Burlington has made her desperate to cling to anyone that offers to talk to her. She rivals the other women in intelligence and looks but her anxiety displays itself in the wine that can never grow still in her glass, in her uncertainty at what to say, and in her attempt to stay in the good graces of these three. Chris once tried talking to her but Mona's influence permeates to everyone.

"Dessert?"

A waitress cuts through the four women like they don't exist. Her tiny infinity necklace reflects blindingly in the sun. She carries a tray full of thin slices of cake that couldn't satisfy anyone. Lydia refuses all dessert unless it is unhealthily large.

The waitress's interruption separates two of the women far enough that Lydia weasels her way between them, ensuring an escape. Chris shifts as the waitress throws her tray around, causing the four women to back up farther to avoid the sugar being teased. Lydia grabs Chris' hand and pulls him out of the square of death, breaking free of the women and continuing their path toward the yacht's cabin. Chris is thankful for Lydia's help escaping but he wishes she hadn't touched him.

"We'll see you Monday!" Mona calls after Chris and Lydia. "Don't have a repeat of a few years ago!"

Chris breathes a sigh of relief when he and Lydia finally stumble through the edge of the crowd and into the yacht's spacious cabin. He breathes easily with room to move without touching anyone, then sees the bathroom sign next to the center of the cabin.

"I hate that bitch," Lydia says without caring how loud she is.

The cabin is mostly empty except for the far end, where three people sit around a table full of empty glasses and six others who sit around a separate table, a deck of cards already dealt for poker. Near the door is a busy bar with people coming with empty hands and leaving with fresh drinks. They all go back to the deck and Chris can't blame them: the sun is gorgeous across Lake Champlain and the breeze is warm. Some of the cabin's windows are cracked open but the breeze is non-existent inside and the air is stagnant.

"Thank God," Lydia says when she sees poker. "Don't listen to Mona about two years ago. She just wants to hang it over your head because you're better than her. She's always been a petty bitch." She starts through the cabin as Chris goes to the bathroom.

Halfway across the cabin, two of the people playing cards shift and call for the bar's server, who rushes over despite the crowd waiting for their drinks at the bar; he knows who tips best.

The server disappears from the poker table as Lydia and

Chris arrive, but within a minute he's back with Lydia's favorite drink and a glass of water for Chris. Two players shift for Lydia to sit, leaving Chris to pull up a chair and look over her shoulder, though he doesn't get close enough to be touching anyone. He doesn't mind staying out of the poker conversation and using it to hide from the party.

Bowls of chips, nuts, and pretzels cover the table, along with a picked-over bowl of trail mix with mostly raisins left. Piles of bills and coins, a drink, and two cards sit in front of each player. As usual, Derrick deals. Lydia is upset that he's across the table because she'll have to crane her neck to see the flop. She peeks at her two facedown cards as carefully as someone diffusing a bomb.

"We're surprised it took you so long," Derrick says.

"Little is a buck, Big is two bucks," Josiah says next to her. "You've missed the two hours of coins."

"I'm not here to gamble on coins," Lydia says. She sips her drink. "Thanks for this, by the way." She pulls some bills from her clutch and throws two on the table. "Let's play, fuckers."

Lydia brashness contrats with her reserved college self. Sometimes it shocks Chris but he's mostly gotten used to it. Chris relaxes in his chair and sips his water like a child while everyone casually drinks their whatever-alcohol-over-the-rocks or fancy mixed drinks. When he first gave up more than one drink at work events, he was bothered by everyone still drinking around him, but over the last few years he found it easier than he expected to stop caring and accept how things were. He would give up a second drink for the rest of his life if it meant avoiding another mistake.

Lydia stops acknowledging anyone not playing poker until she either loses all her money or Chris shakes her out of her poker trance. Chris could wait out the rest of the yacht ride watching poker and not be bothered by anyone. There aren't many co-workers Chris actually dislikes, but there are many he'd rather avoid after working with them for 8 hours. Too many are little bug bites that never stop bothering you once they say hello. He learned in his first post-college job that your time is yours when work stops paying you, and he isn't being paid to be on this yacht, even if it is forced fun. The largest benefit from sitting around the card players is that they barred work talk from the table.

To Lydia's right, Jeanne folds after the flop, but Josiah to her left calls Lydia's raise. Jeanne turns to Chris, disinterested in watching the rest of the hand.

"How's Keith?" she whispers.

Jeanne loves visiting with Chris's dog almost as much as Chris loves talking about him.

"He's good," Chris whispers in return. His walls collapse immediately when Keith is brought up. "I've had to crate him over the past few days because he's been sick. It's been a nightmare cleaning up after him. Yesterday he wasn't as sick so I'm hoping we're in the clear soon."

"Did he eat anything weird?" Jeanne asks.

"Who knows. There's a park near our apartment and he might've gotten into something there. How are your cats?"

Jeanne turns back to the table as a new hand is dealt. She looks at her cards and pushes forward the big blind.

"They're fine, same as always," she says.

Their conversation pauses while she works through the hand. Chris has watched so much poker that he's picked up which hands beat which hands and understands what a flop, river, and turn mean. His statistical brain even picked up a little of the probability based on what's in Lydia's hand and what's turned face up. Being able to figure out probabilities intrigues Chris but he doesn't like to throw away money as easily as Lydia.

"I don't understand why you keep adopting cats," Lydia says.

"They tear up your furniture and you've had to replace your curtains every year because of the holes they put in them."

Jeanne shrugs. "Sometimes something comes into your life and you love it so much that the little things that happen just don't bother you that much."

"I'd rather just be surrounded by my plants until I find someone responsible enough to not break my things and take care of himself," Lydia says.

"Cats more or less take care of themselves, though they do break things sometimes," Jeanne says with a laugh.

"I'll stick with being single." Lydia threw in double the big blind, forcing the rest of the players to opt out. "Oh come on, how am I supposed to win money if you bitches all drop out when I throw in some more money?"

She collects what was already thrown in and leaves it in a rough pile in front of her while Derrick shuffles.

"By the way, we have a hike planned for two weeks from now," Jeanne says to Lydia. "It'll be peak number 29. Same crew as usual."

"Count me in," Lydia says as she watches Derrick deal. "Did you actually rent a campsite this time or are we going to have to sleep in a field again?"

"I learned my lesson. We'll be in a park with a couple of sites," Jeanne says. "You're never going to let that go, are you?"

"How could I?" Lydia says. "My shoulder is still messed up."

"Drama queen," Jeanne says.

"Maybe when I've taken enough money from you, I'll get over it," Lydia says with a grin.

Chris sips his water as the women ignore him and disappear into their hiking conversation, which they pause while playing each hand. He is used to melding into the background when with the poker crew. Eventually, each would greet him or say something, but none would talk to him for more than a few minutes when poker and money were on the table. Being with the poker crew - even if being ignored - meant avoiding everyone else.

Poker lasts most of the night. The sun starts to set when Chris escapes his trance and looks out the cabin's windows at the shoreline. The piles of money haven't shifted too much, though two players did have to pull out their wallets to continue playing at one point. The waiter returns with fresh drinks when any of the poker player's glasses are empty, and out of pity they bring water to Chris when his is gone. Nobody asks the servers for anything, but when one of the poker players holds up a $50 bill, Chris understands. An open bar means large tips, which this poker group has no trouble offering. They rotate whose turn it is to tip, though they always skip Chris, which he appreciates.

A bellow of laughter breaks into the cabin as the door leading to the deck opens against the weight of a group bursting through it. They aren't overly drunk, though they shout and move about as if they are. Chris shrinks next to the poker group, who ignores the outburst entirely, as if the world beyond their tables and chairs is non-existent.

Two women lead the pack and order drinks from the bar first. One is a coworker, Devon, the second-best in their department after Chris, while the other is a woman Chris has never seen. They talk casually as the rest of the group orders another round of drinks. Chris shrinks further but a hand on his shoulder tells him that they found him.

"How are you, Chris?" Devon says. "I wondered if you were here or if you skipped tonight to take care of Keith."

"Who's Keith?" the second woman asks.

"My dog," Chris says.

"You named your dog 'Keith'?" the second woman asks. "That's a strange name for a dog."

The second woman is professional yet average, though she

speaks without a quiver in her voice or a falter in her calculations that makes her more spectacular than those around her. Her dress pants and button-down stands in contrast with Devon's lightweight dress, which is as light as possible because of the heat wave cooking Burlington. The second woman doesn't seem bothered at all by the heat.

"He's a good boy," Chris says.

Devon introduces them to move the conversation forward.

"Marissa is one of the board members," Devon says.

Chris's posture perks and he briefly glances sideways at Devon but keeps his gaze on Marissa. He had only met one other board member, and that was by accident during orientation years ago. Social visits were not something the Board did despite constant feedback that the employees wanted to see them more often at work events.

"Devon's been filling me in about your department and the excellent work you've all been doing," Marissa says. "You've been here for quite a while."

"Yes, 7 years back in June," Chris says. "I started a few months after graduating."

"This is a poker game," Lydia says when she loses a hand. "Can you take this conversation somewhere that's not here?"

Chris bites his tongue and holds his breath as Devon glares at Lydia - who hasn't turned from the table - but Devon ushers Chris and Marissa out a side door onto a narrow walkway along the side of the yacht that connects the front and back. A few people walk back and forth but they find different ways around the boat when they see Marissa.

"Now we won't be bothered by *those* people," Devon says. "So, Chris, how is that new account with the State going?"

"We don't need to talk about your experience with the Bank," Marissa says. "We were built on the ideals that we need to form relationships with the community and that we should serve communities that care as much about themselves as we do. So, Chris, tell me about your connection to Burlington."

Chris glances at Devon and sees in her sharp glare that something more is happening. Though she ranks below Chris on their division totem pole, she is the one who brought Marissa to him. He needs to find out what this is about, but Marissa is probably too smart to not notice him digging for information in a conversation. For now, he will wear the business mask like an expert.

"Other than connecting businesses with each other through the Bank, I'm also involved with the Players and I volunteer a lot with the community garden."

"You're involved with the garden?" Marissa asks. "My family donates to it."

"It's amazing what something as simple as a community garden can do to boost a community's morale," Chris says. "It's grown in such an amazing way over the past two years. This summer the Bank actually donated enough to cover the supplies we need."

"Ah, so you're the reason that we received that donation request," Marissa says. "We wondered which of our employees were that invested. We don't often receive requests that are so grass-roots. Usually the requests are for tens of thousands donated to a school or to some politician."

Chris nods. "Thank you for approving the donation. Grass-roots are a great way to support a community."

Marissa relaxes against the railing and sips her drink as she converses with Chris over the different volunteer organizations around Burlington with parallel missions to the community garden. Marissa listens with all the intensity of someone who cares and none of the air of someone on the Board. Chris proceeds hesitantly with all the concern of someone waiting for the other foot to drop and none of the confidence of someone having a genuine conversation.

Chris becomes so lost in their conversation that he walks away an hour later with the sun fully set. Devon gladly ushers Marissa away with a wink at Chris. He watches them leave with Marissa's business card in his hand, her number scribbled quickly in a calligrapher's perfect penmanship on the back.

He remains on the side deck alone, soaking in the quietness of the walkway and reveling in the peacefulness and escape from his co-workers. The sparse green Vermont shoreline with only the random lake house lit up in the dark is nothing like the busy New York City shoreline of home, littered with cement and steel buried beneath never-ending honking and cars that drown in light. Ahead he sees the outline of the few tall buildings in Burlington, with the Bank of Burlington standing tallest. Its founders wanted it to stand out, and made sure its height did just that, despite cries from the residents and the Mayor that wanted to preserve Burlington's beautiful history. The Bank's founder argued that it would only rival the University's tallest buildings, and the permits were granted. Money speaks.

Lights flicker to life like fireflies along the shoreline as Burlington grows closer. The wind from the boat's speed cools him after the oppressive sun cooked him all day, refreshing him as they sail toward the dock. A few people start using the side walkway again, some waving as they pass but most thankfully leave him alone. Seeing someone lean on a boat's railing and stare at the mountains of Vermont beneath a starry sky is a sensation everyone from the area respects. Chris appreciates the understanding, an experience he doubts he'd receive back in NYC. His family may miss him, but he doesn't miss anything of home except for them.

Austin leans on the railing next to Chris silently. Had it not been for the wind carrying the faint scent of his body spray,

Chris would have been lost in his shoreline trance and never knew his best friend had appeared. They stand in silence for a few minutes, Austin joining in the admiration of the shoreline and the approaching batch of lights that is Burlington, including the Bank standing taller than the rest of the city with its top three floors lit up in red, white, and blue. The last colors from the sun clinging to the day disappear quickly behind the western shore, turning the last red and orange in the sky to a dark blue that rivals black.

"I'm glad this party is almost done," Austin says. "Did someone check on Keith tonight?"

"Yeah, my neighbor," Chris says distractedly. "Hopefully they played with Keith a bit, too." He stretches and groans. "Damn I'm so tired. I'm going to crash when I get home."

Austin snickers. "Are we really that old?"

"Late twenties hits different. We're 29 now. You're almost 30. This extended workday is awful."

"We're *both* almost 30," Austin says. "Hopefully you had some fun tonight. Who knows when we'll be back on a yacht. I didn't expect the Bank to spring for one, but I'm not going to complain. Drinks go down so smoothly when you're drinking them on a fancy yacht."

"You'll have to cherish that feeling for me," Chris says.

Austin is quiet as the yacht navigates the harbor toward the dock. Everyone is gathered near the back of the vessel, where the crew waits to jump off and tie the yacht off before lowering the walkway. Harris is among those near the front of the crowd, some female co-worker hanging on him as much as he is her.

Austin's arm is close enough to gently press against Chris' when they sway from the floating yacht. They've been best friends for a decade and have no issue sitting side-by-side and touching or sleeping in the same bed. You aren't best friends for that long without being naked around each other at least once, at which point everything else is comfortable. Besides, Austin has a boyfriend and Chris has no interest in men. Despite the other headaches in life, Chris is calmed when Austin chills in silence next to him.

The side of the yacht bumps against the dock, sending a small splash upward though only drops reach the deck. Chris and Austin watch the crew tie up the yacht and then attach the bridge for the partiers to depart. Neither Chris nor Austin move until half their co-workers are off.

"Is Kyle picking you up?" Chris asks.

"Yeah, the twins ended up convincing me to drink one too many," Austin says. "He insisted on picking me up anyway and pushed me to just let loose. He thinks I've been too preoccupied lately."

Chris laughs deeply, loving his friend for his obliviousness. "You're *always* preoccupied. I may be a stick in the mud at work but you are obsessed."

Now it's Austin's turn to laugh, and Chris joins him. After a decade of being friends, Chris appreciates that they can still laugh like they did in college when one of them tripped in their messy dorm room, can still feel like their friendship is smooth and fresh rather than the robotic, stale friendship he sees in so many others.

"The new house is quite a bit," Austin says. "I'm so excited for fires on the back porch overlooking the lake and long Euchre nights where we kick ass and to decorate for Christmas and to buy a full sized bedroom set. Damn, it's exciting to have my own house."

Austin steadies himself on the railing; he isn't drunk enough to not be able to stand, but he is drunk enough that a bobbing boat unsteadies him.

"Has the boy moved in yet?" Chris asks. He hesitates and gives his best friend a sideways glance.

Austin shakes his head furiously. "Nah no no no, nah. This is strictly still mine. I've only been dating Kyle for 8 months. I love him but I want some time in my house before it becomes ours. I'm sure he'll spend a lot of time there, anyway. Oh my god what if he tries to take down my decorations once we're living together or if he doesn't put the couch throw pillows back exactly how they should be? I'll break up with him." Austin hesitates. "Ah, now I see. Yeah, I might be a little high maintenance. That is what is going to drive him away."

Austin leans against the railing and rubs his face in his hands. Chris gently knocks his friend's side.

"Kyle is a great guy. And there isn't anything about you that would cause him to break up with you. So stop worrying and walk off this boat with me and tell me more about how crazy you are."

Austin stands up straight - placing a foot behind him to steady him - and then steps forward and begins the short walk to the back deck. He and Chris rival each other in height though Austin's slight drunk-walk is all the more obvious because of Chris's completely sober stride. Austin regales Chris with all of the details of the closing as they wait with the last of their coworkers to depart. Austin leans an arm on Chris's shoulder as they stand with nothing near them to lean on.

The waitress wearing the infinity necklace from earlier walks past with empty glasses clenched between her fingers and more wrapped between her arms and body. Chris notices her strong walk that doesn't slow as other staff mistakenly cross her path. Within seconds she's back out of the cabin door with her hands and arms empty, walking past the thinning group of Bank employees toward the front of the yacht. She flicks an eye momentarily in Chris's direction though her stride doesn't lose its determination. Chris sweats, though not from the warm night.

"I'll be right back," he says to Austin, removing his friend's arm from his shoulder.

He walks toward the front of the yacht where the waitress gathers a dozen empty glasses from one of the tables placed strategically around the yacht's stern. Her meticulous motions to grab each cup are as precise as if she were a robot and grabbing each cup is a coded motion.

"We're no longer serving drinks," she says when Chris approaches, though she doesn't look up.

"I, uh, I'm not interested in a drink," he says.

"The kitchen is also closed," she adds, though she slows down her cup gathering.

The momentary glance she steals toward Chris gives him the confidence he lacked seconds ago.

"I saw you earlier," Chris says. "You saved my friend and I from that group of women."

The waitress moves the cups around like a con artist hiding a pebble beneath them. "Those four women looked like the kind to trap people. I saved a few people from their grasp. You're welcome."

Chris chuckles. "I appreciate it. I noticed your infinity necklace. It's pretty."

The waitress pulls a pad of paper and a pen from her pocket, scribbles on it, then rips off the top piece and returns the rest. She gathers the cups in her fingers and arms again with the torn paper somehow between two free fingers. She walks toward Chris, who steps out of her way.

"This is my number," the waitress says, waving the paper with her two fingers, causing some of the glasses to *clink* together. "Text me your address and I'll be there after work."

Chris stares at the paper in shock but grabs it quickly. "Thanks."

The woman walks away without another word.

Chris watches her go until she's inside the cabin. He hurriedly returns to Austin's side and waves the paper at Austin.

"Who's that from?" Austin asks as they step off the yacht, regaining his land legs.

"One of the waitresses," Chris says. "I went to say thank you for saving Lydia and I from *those* four but before I could ask her on a date, she gave me her number."

Austinn shakes his head. "Harris is an awful influence."

"Not all of us can be in happy relationships like you," Chris says.

Kyle waves from the parking lot, his head peeking over the SUV's roof. After a brief hi to Kyle, Chris begins his short walk back home to see Keith, who by now has been staring at the door for over half a day, waiting for Chris to walk through it.

2

IT'S A HOOKUP

After a short walk to his downtown apartment, Chris is greeted by Keith wagging his tail from the couch with one paw delicately crossed over the other. The thump of his tail on the couch thunders around the open living room and kitchen, which are separated by a rectangular island and Keith's food and water dishes.

Keith shifts so there is room on the couch. Chris collapses next to him and Keith immediately lays his head on Chris's lap, looking expectedly up. His tail stops wagging until Chris's fingers reach behind his ears. Chris lifts his feet on the coffee table and pulls out his phone and the paper the waitress gave him. He punches in her number and writes a text with his name and address.

"Don't look at me like that," Chris says to Keith when his dog rolls his eyes at the paper in his hand. "I'm single. It's a hookup. Leave me alone."

Keith sighs as Chris hits send, then remembers he never said his name and sends a follow up that he's the guy from the yacht.

His phone vibrates almost immediately with a response that she'll be off in a half hour and on her way. Keith shifts to extend across two cushions and push Chris against the armrest. Years of sharing a bed with Keith has taught Chris how to be comfortable with minimal space. Some nights Keith pushes Chris right out of bed but manages to keep the blankets on the bed for himself. Somedays Chris wonders why Keith thinks he runs the house when he doesn't pay the bills.

Chris texts the waitress back and then waits. The annoying wall clock his mother shipped to him back in college ticks from the kitchen like a club track the DJ turned up too high and the few cars that drive by rumble like semis. Keith's snoring adds to the mix to complete the latest club sonata. Chris wonders how his dog falls asleep in a millisecond and also how his legs can be so strong while sleeping.

His legs grow anxious as tingles crawl up and down them. He glares around his untidy apartment and stands, groaning as he starts a quick clean before the waitress arrives. Untidy is an unfair description, though there are enough things out of place that he is annoyed and doesn't want to look like a slob when she arrives. In truth, he doesn't want to resemble Harris, though he flew past Harris's baseline when he got one decoration: the wall clock in his kitchen. He puts the keys on the hook rather than leaving them on the coffee table, folds the blanket for the first time to drape it over the back, rushes to the kitchen to wash that morning's cup and bowl, and then inspects the space. His couch and chair have dog hair on them but once Keith has claimed an area, there is no hope for it to be clean. His coffee table is cleared for the first time in a few weeks and his shoes are not lying around the door, also a first in too long. He wonders how long it's been since he's had a hookup over, but he's happy to know he can still do the 5-minute cleanup.

His bedroom is already neat except for last night's boxers and tshirt, which are thrown carelessly on his bed, though that is made. The pillows rest against the wall because he never got around to purchasing a headboard. Austin's influence has made his apartment grow up in certain ways but not others. Chris grimaces at the black marks left on the wall by the pillows and wishes he had purchased a headboard.

Keith watches from the couch, his head on the armrest, his droopy eyes full of judgment.

"Listen, I know I should have kept my apartment tidier," Chris says, turning on the window AC unit, which grumbles on reluctantly. "I don't need you judging me over there."

Keith scratches himself, then rests his head again against the back of the armrest.

"You are the laziest damn dog I have ever seen yet you sit there and judge me like you own the place. What do you contribute to the bills? Nothing, exactly."

Keith raises one ear.

"I don't need your sass. This is just a hookup. So stop judging me for that."

Keith looks toward the coffee table, where Chris' phone vibrates. Chris springs to the couch and opens the waitress's text, asking how to get into his apartment. After some directions and hearing a car pull up alongside the building, he stands behind the couch and leans on its back, breathing two deep breaths out. He's glad he turned on the AC because his apartment's temperature suddenly spikes and he sweats. Was he always this nervous when hooking up?

She knocks on his door and he bounds for it, then takes a deep breath as he opens it. She's still in her waitress uniform and wears the tiredness from work on her face and in her lackluster smile. He closes his apartment door as she walks inside and takes in his apartment.

"Well this is quite clean," she says.

"What do you mean?"

"I highly doubt your apartment was this clean before you came up to me on the boat," she says.

"Well it was, I didn't do, this is, what do you, how it-"

"Don't hurt yourself," she says, "it looks nice. If you did clean up, thanks."

Keith stares curiously at her and in disbelief at Chris. Otherwise he is motionless on the couch as he watches the waitress take off her shoes.

"So, um, this is my place," Chris says.

"I suspected as much," the waitress says, "otherwise this would be very awkward for the occupants."

Chris walks toward his bedroom, uncertain what else to say, but the waitress stops and holds her hand out to Keith. He smells it in disgust when the sweat permeates everything, though she runs her fingers along his head and scratches behind his ear, which makes his tail wag.

"That's Keith," Chris says, recovering from his route to the bedroom by turning to go to the kitchen. "Want a drink?"

"What kind of name is Keith for a dog?" the waitress says. "A beer would be good."

She settles onto the couch and Keith rotates to lay his head on her lap. Chris scowls at him from the kitchen and grabs two beers from his fridge, popping their tops before bringing one to the waitress. He sets it down on a coaster - Austin's influence again - before holding his own as he sips it on the chair. The emptier the bottle becomes, the less irritated at Keith he is for warming up to the waitress so quickly.

"It's weird to have someone bring me a drink," the waitress says. "Irony."

Chris wishes he had something more intelligent to say. He isn't sure if he should ask the waitress to come to his bedroom, if he's supposed to remove Keith from her lap to take his place, if

they're even going to hook up at this point. Who sits on the
couch and has a conversation when the plan was to hook up?
Was that even the plan? He swigs his beer while she matches
him. Chris tosses around what to say but each is insufficient and
reminiscent of what one adolescent virgin would say to another
when both are trying to act like they've been there before.

Sweat bristles on her face and Chris realizes her beauty
doesn't need to be accentuated by makeup at all; she's naturally
pretty. She is as stoic as she was on the yacht, not letting a twitch
break through the mask as she sits erect, prepared to jump up
and answer a call to action. Black jeans and a black shirt makes
her look shorter and smaller, though she is only 2 or 3 inches
shorter than Chris. She stares at Keith in silence for the first half
of her beer, her eyelids struggling to stay open and her eyes
avoiding Chris at all costs. The one time her eyes met his, he
swore her mouth twitched downward as one eye watered,
though her hair covered her face.

"So how was work?"

He feels like an idiot but she isn't phased. Chris notices her
infinity necklace again.

"It was alright," the waitress says.

"Do you work most nights?" Chris asks slowly, searching for
each word and not knowing what he is going to say next.

The waitress sips her beer. Chris wants to lean back as casually as he can, but in the shadow of her perfect posture he maintains a respectable one. His phone vibrates on the coffee table
but her stare holds his attention. He's unsure if the extra sweat is
from the AC not cooling down his apartment or if it's from her.

"Not most nights," she says.

She waits for whatever he has to say next, though she doesn't
glare nor tap her foot in expectation. She patiently holds her
beer loosely like Chris, letting the beads of sweat roll over her
fingers. She lifts her foot and puts it dangerously close to Chris's

foot on the coffee table. Her toes magnetize to his and she gently brushes them against his foot in sporadic movements. He doesn't flinch or pull his foot away or feel disgusted by her touching him. A breath he held since she walked into his apartment escapes. How does he feel clean with her touching him?

"What's your name, by the way?" he asks.

"Taylor."

Chris taps his beer in anticipation of more but she doesn't offer anything else, so he takes a quick sip.

"I'm sorry about hitting on you while you're working," Chris says. "That's not a norm for me."

"It's an occupational hazard of being a female and a waitress. Usually only creeps hit on me."

"Hopefully I don't seem like one of those creeps," Chris says.

She shrugs and her eyes peek over her beer as she takes a sip. Chris isn't sure what to make of the mask molded from sweat and tiredness on her face.

"So you're a big banker man?" Taylor asks.

"Nah, I just work at the Bank."

He takes a long swallow of beer to try to stop his shaking leg. Her toes caress his feet like silk. She watches him rather than respond.

"I work on business accounts." To fill the gap of silence, he continues, "Though on the yacht one of the board members pulled me aside for a while."

Taylor's raised eyebrow is reminiscent of Keith when he expects something of Chris. Everybody hates banking. Keith most of all. The expectation to explain his job is a first.

"I'm, uh, I..."

Chris mulls over how much to say, what terminology to use, tries to guess where the line is that will peak Taylor's boredom. His past dates had turning points where talk about the Bank ensured a second date wouldn't occur. He is only on his first beer, but his infrequent drinking makes one beer enough to help him let go of his rationale to forget where that line is. Chris drains his beer past halfway. Taylor's gaze makes him sweat more but her impassiveness entices him to tell her everything.

"It's for, uh, on the yacht a peer introduced me to one of our board members and we had an hour long conversation about non-banking things. It was quite odd. I'm not sure what it means or why it happened, but I suspect when I get to work on Monday that I'll hear something more."

Chris refocuses on Taylor and forces himself to stop. That seems like a good place to let her say something to not drown her in dull Bank talk.

"What do you think it was about?" she asks.

Chris inhales deeply and runs a hand over his head. Has the hookup game changed that much that you have a full conversation before fucking? He didn't think a couple of months was that long.

"Oh, it's all just a lot of financial jargon and contracts that's probably quite boring."

Taylor shakes her head slowly, her short hair bobbing. Contrasting with her firm posture, her shaking head is gentle and reaffirming. Unwavering eyes give Chris the encouragement to continue without fearing her rising halfway through and leaving without a word, Keith following her because he, too, is tired of hearing about Banking, and because he just wants to leave.

Like a diver jumping off a 30 foot platform, Chris inhales deeply before explaining the details of his job, breaking the topic's surface with barely a ripple disturbing his cadence. Without missing beats of his story, Taylor asks for clarity at certain parts and repeats back information, fueling his eagerness to divulge everything. He explains the intricacies of initial meetings to contracts to services provided to retaining clients before moving onto predictions for why the Board member wanted to talk to him. Taylor hangs onto every word like she's watching a long-awaited movie; Chris gladly writes more of the script to fulfill her interest.

Her shiny, silver necklace stands out above her black v-neck, the infinity shape discernible from across the coffee table like it is inches from Chris' face. He notices it briefly as it catches light but Taylor's attentiveness to his job explanation pulls him easily back into telling his story and forgetting about the necklace.

Taylor finishes her beer before Chris finishes his story. He's not actually done, but after rambling for a half hour, he realizes what he's done and wants to stop monopolizing the conversation around the dry topic of banking. Taylor keeps up with him during his monologue, matching his excitement with her own. Never before has anyone so easily encouraged him.

"I'm sorry I rambled for so long," Chris says. "People don't often ask about my job. Banking tends to be a boring conversation topic."

"I can talk about waitressing if you think that's more intriguing than banking."

"Are many jobs that exciting?"

"There's much more exciting things in life than just what we do for work," Taylor says, "but that doesn't mean that work can't be exciting, too."

Chris's burst of laughter draws Keith's irritation. "You are fascinating."

"I suppose that's a compliment," Taylor says. Not a hint of joy has crossed her face all night. "Your accent is from Vermont."

"I moved here a decade ago for college and got the Bank offer shortly after, so I stayed. I guess I've lost my Long Island accent a bit but I haven't picked up a northern one, either."

"Long Island," Taylor says. "Not what I expected."

"I'm glad I can subvert one of your expectations. Where did you think I was from?"

"Boston."

Chris's guffaw could have been used like a weapon to slay an army of a million Bostonians. "There's not a worse insult you could have pulled out against me."

Taylor shrugs. "What about Burlington made you want to stay? It's quite a bit smaller than Long Island. There's not much here."

"Then why are you still here?"

Taylor sets her empty beer on a coaster and continues scratching Keith behind his ear, who seems so content he could lie there forever.

"I'm sure it's more beautiful here than on Long Island," Taylor says.

"So you're familiar with Long Island?"

"Familiar enough. Why'd you stay rather than move home?"

Chris ponders 'familiar enough'. He wants to ask for her to explain in the same way he explained his job, but her college degree in avoiding anything focusing on her tells him he won't get far. Instead, he focuses on what she said about Burlington's beauty.

The city's beauty, the landscape, the unclogged air, the view from the top of the Bank, the familiar feel, the downtown hominess that is enough of a reminder of home: how do you explain all of that when you've never said any of it out loud? How do you explain the essence of home a place gives you? Chris fumbles over how to communicate it all to a stranger but is at a permanent loss of words to do so. So he says it exactly as it runs across his mind - as an endless train of thought.

Taylor listens as he explains, letting him travel down tangents without interrupting. She listens to his love for the nature around them and the issues with a handful of his family, his fumbling over how to say that he misses home but can't explain why the thought of living there is abhorrent. Chris disappears into his own world as he explores so much of what he has never said, and Taylor lets him. Another half hour of their night is consumed by his second monologue, though she doesn't respond immediately when he finishes.

"Sorry," he says with a laugh, "I don't usually ramble like this. I'm not sure what's gotten into me."

Taylor shakes her head. After the beer, her posture no longer intimidates him.

"Don't be sorry. Burlington is pretty."

"What about you? Are you from Burlington?"

"No."

Chris waits for a longer response but Taylor just pets Keith. He wants to be drowned in a sentence longer than a handful of words, but she seems intent on keeping her end of the conversation short, which makes Chris desire more. It's not just wanting to hear about her life; it's also wanting to be let behind her solid expression and jail-bar covered eyes, the way she has let him say whatever up to this point without interrupting and without getting bored. It's the way she's shown interest in him. He wants to return that feeling to her.

"When did you move here?"

"A few years ago."

She offers nothing else. He fumbles with how to follow up her vagueness.

"Do you come downtown a lot?" Chris asks when the silence stretches longer than he's comfortable with.

"Sometimes."

She relaxes on the couch and Keith shifts to snuggle his head more into her. She seems distracted but doesn't pull her phone out or make a move to leave. She even ignored the few dings from her phone since arriving.

"It's nice downtown, especially Church Street," Chris says. "You should start coming downtown more often."

"Perhaps," Taylor says. "How is living downtown?"

"Convenient with the Bank so close. And living just off Church Street makes everything I need so close. Work is close, socializing is close, stores are close, nightlife is close. I really like it."

"Must be interesting to live so close to everything," Taylor says, as detached as she could be without walking out of his apartment.

Chris ignores her nonchalant attitude. Her fingers casually sift between Keith's fur and she finally relaxes after nearly two hours of being prepared to jump up to fight at a moment's notice. Now lounging, a new wave of attraction contrasts the demanding physicality of her stern posture. Before she resembled a statue of a soldier, but now she resembles a lonely person waiting expectantly for something to dissolve the loneliness, though she can't quite put her finger on what that thing is. Her allure wraps around him like a net twisting around prey.

"I assume that if you don't come downtown often then you live near the outskirts of Burlington?" Chris says.

"I don't live close enough to walk here," Taylor says. "How long have you lived in this apartment?"

Her curt response isn't cold or aggressive; she simply provides an answer to his question and then pivots. She doesn't wait to respond or glare at him for asking; she only watches him calmly with a slight smirk on her face that isn't manipulative or vengeful, and is very likely from the beer. Despite her responses, Chris is compelled to continue the conversation. He wants to know more about her but her wall is fortified.

"It's coming up on three years. Sometimes the street is noisy and the tourists around my apartment's entrance can be annoying, but I like the proximity to everything. I guess living near downtown reminds me of home, to some extent."

Taylor nods, her eyes like lasers. Even in not responding, Chris knows she listens to every word.

"I don't miss home that much, but living in a place that feels similar to it makes it easier to be away permanently. I don't have my parents or siblings here, but I have the feel of home. Sometimes, when the waves on Champlain are strong enough and crash into the shore and the traffic is dense with honking, it reminds me of home. It's a weird comfort thing." Chris pauses as he brings himself mentally back to his living room. "Sorry, I'm not sure why I just said that."

"You're fine," Taylor says with an even voice. "It's hard when you miss home."

Chris nods because he's still stuck in memories of home and his friends left behind when he moved permanently to Burlington. Taylor stares as he processes through the times he and his friends ran through his parent's neighborhood the night before Halloween to ding-dong-ditch houses, the time he and his siblings spent the day on the beach on Long Island to watch storms roll across the ocean, the moment he wandered NYC alone between skyscrapers that felt like they stretched to Heaven and the blacktop that surrounded him like a swarm of ants encroaching on all sides.

"I decided when I was 16 to move out of the City," he says. Taylor doesn't stop him. "I was exploring the City alone for the first time and stumbled into Central Park. I'd been there before with my family but we were always told to stay close to my parents and we never stayed there long. We rarely left the City because my parents couldn't afford vacations paying for our house. Central Park was an escape from the cement and blacktop and a safe haven from the quick pace of the City. The

City was too much and Central Park let me escape it. That's when I knew I wanted to leave the City one day."

"So you chose Burlington."

"I wasn't sure where I was going to end up, but Burlington had the City feel while being close to mountains and a lake, really all of the nature I wanted."

"Are you happy here?" Taylor asks.

Chris's smile breaks out.

"You seem happy here," Taylor says. "It's a nice enough city."

"You don't seem happy here," Chris responds.

Taylor shrugs in that nonchalant way that intrigues him and makes him want to understand what's happening behind her mask. She stands and grabs his hand. Neither of them say anything as she leads him to his bedroom and closes the door.

"You smell nice, by the way," Taylor says when she lays on top of him. "Reminds me of..."

Chris waits but she never finishes the sentence. Instead, she kisses him and they have the easiest, most comfortable sex of his life, like they've had sex millions of times before and knew what the other wanted and how to communicate with a touch. Afterward she lies on his chest and he gently runs two fingers up and down her back, following her spine, repeatedly carving the same path to memorize her shape. She nestles her face against him and exhales deeply, releasing the heaviness of years of hidden stress.

Taylor wraps an arm over him that clasps ensnares him with strength rivaling the world's strongest man. Suddenly, her body grows heavier than a meteor crushing everyone beneath it, pinning him to the bed. Her other hand's fingers are intertwined with his, desperately searching for something to hold into to save herself from drowning. She buries her face into him and sighs out a heaviness that could fight gravity.

Chris doesn't know what to say to her desperation for

someone to save her, so he gently rubs her back up and down with his fingertips and leans his head over to nuzzle his face into her hair. After remaining so distant all night, Taylor's complete release of her need to be saved startles him. Her sudden vulnerability makes him feel something for her.

"That is my favorite thing," Taylor says with barely enough strength in her voice to be heard.

"What?" he asks.

"My back rubbed exactly like you're doing it."

There are few people he feels comfortable touching without an immediate need to wash his hands or shower, especially after sex. He only wants to pull Taylor closer and never leave the bed. Chris closes his eyes and doesn't stop rubbing her back until he falls asleep.

The morning is much shorter than last night's three hour conversation. Chris wakes second, which he only knows because Taylor shifts non-stop in the morning, almost as if to wake him. His first instinct is to kiss her after last night. She doesn't wait long after he wakes to speak.

"Morning."

"Hi, morning."

He kisses her, and she returns it, though briefly.

"I probably have awful morning breath," she says.

"No, you don't."

He kisses her again but she keeps it brief. Even shorter is the amount of time she waits before climbing out of bed to shower. When she returns, she dresses immediately.

"Do you want breakfast or coffee?" Chris asks.

"Are those two different things?"

"Of course they are."

Taylor puzzles that for a moment, then continues getting dressed.

"No, thanks though."

Chris gets dressed with her so she doesn't feel out of place. She finishes surprisingly quick and then makes his bed, putting the pillows exactly where they were the previous night before they had the best sex of Chris's life.

"You don't have to make my bed," Chris says quietly, gently touching her arm.

Taylor hurries to finish the bed and doesn't let his arm stop her. When she's done, they head into the living room. Keith looks up from the couch, then stretches so his legs hang off the edge. When he notices Taylor heading toward the door, he climbs off the couch and joins her. Chris opens the door for Keith to head outside, then closes it as Taylor puts on her shoes.

"Thanks for having me over last night," Taylor says.

"Of course. You can come back anytime you want. Well I have a surgery in two weeks, so I'll be laid up for a while from... doing anything. But after that, I'm down to chill again."

When her shoes are tied, she stands up as erect and stoic as last night before the beer and her beauty shines despite wearing day-old work clothes. Her hand twitches to open the door but her tense body displays her obligatory feelings, so she kisses Chris once again quickly, holding it slightly longer than the previous ones. He feels her struggle to pull away, as if she doesn't actually want to leave. When her lips leave his, she looks him directly in the eyes. There are so many emotions creating a thunderstorm in her eyes that Chris doesn't know what to say.

"Sounds good. See ya later," Taylor says, as quietly as a whisper.

"Drive home safely."

When she walks out the door, Keith trots back in. He gives Chris an expectant look, but Chris can't close the door until he hears a car on the building's side start up and pull away. That goodbye was the most difficult part of that entire encounter.

3

TURN DOWN THE ACE

Mondays are meant to catch-up on a weekend's-worth of ignored emails from people and businesses who insist that bankers work 24/7 because bankers obviously don't have lives. Most emails and voicemails are polite, though a few are tinged with the need for immediate satisfaction or are follow-ups to emails or voicemails from Friday after the Bank closed, as if two days over the weekend is too long to wait for a response.

The revolving door on the Bank of Burlington's first floor spins endlessly when the Bank is open to let a never-ending stream of customers in to complain, deposit, withdrawal, and deal with any number of issues, which often includes expecting the Bank to resolve all their life problems. The tellers on the first floor deal with the majority of the customers, though a few customers manage to acquire permission to take one of the guarded elevators upstairs to various specialty departments, their requests requiring an extra touch that a teller is unable to provide.

Glass windows adorn the outside of the Bank, broken by thin beams on the building's corners and where each ceiling meets the floor above. It reflects sun across all of Burlington, an architectural side effect that the residents complain about but nothing can be done about. Inside, the pure white walls brighten the offices and cubicles like mirrors reflecting the sun. Chris reads through weekend emails, organizing them slowly with an untouched coffee sitting in a short mug in front of him. The carpet throughout the Bank muffles the sound of heels and heavy shoes from alerting him of anyone approaching. He wishes the carpet would absorb the sound of his co-workers typing and talking around him, too, but instead the cubicle farm drowns in conversations that are better left for Monday afternoon than morning, or better yet Tuesday morning.

"We've been here almost an hour and you're still sifting through emails, and judging by the blinking light on your phone, you haven't even started with the voicemails," Devon says from the doorway to his cubicle.

Chris had set up his L-shaped desk to run along one wall with the other arm creating a barricade between him and anyone who visits him. His monitors sit against the fabric cubicle walls and his back often brushes against the adjacent wall, where pictures of Keith hang. There aren't many, but there are enough to display his dog-obsession and de-sterilize the space. He wishes he had a window office.

"You've also got a meeting in an hour on the fourth floor."

Chris swivels toward the cubicle's entrance. Devon leans against it with her usual coffee mug, which has undoubtedly been refilled. Chris envies women's ability to wear light-weight dresses, especially on mornings like today when the heatwave still boils Burlington despite it being mid-September. He wears a polo but the pants are what killed him on his walk in.

"What do you mean?" Chris asks.

Devon sips her tea. "Have you not gotten to that email yet?

The woman I introduced you to on the yacht, Marissa, wants to meet with you."

"What for?"

Devon raises her cup toward Chris's computer. "Look for the email and accept her meeting so she knows you're actually coming. Then good luck. Accept it this time."

She walks away as Chris tries to ask more, leaving his questions hanging. Chris looks up, as if he can see through the third floor's ceiling. The CEO and Board reserved the fourth floor for their offices and meeting rooms, preferring the middle of the building: not too high to be in danger in case something happens, but not so low that they are only a floor above the tellers and public.

Chris had visited the fourth floor only when he was hired. Various board members attended random events and were sometimes seen coming and going from the building, though nobody ever approached them. Traditional dichotomies of who's who were difficult barriers to deconstruct, especially in a company where most of the employees were under 40. Pleasing the board is a puzzle nobody has been able to piece together.

"Why can't she just ever tell me straight up what's happening?" Chris mutters to himself.

He finds the email indicating his meeting and accepts it, annoyed Devon knew of it before he did. Too anxious to read properly for the next hour, he forfeits the rest of his emails and listens to the voicemails; most are trash but he notes the important ones. Mindless work bores him.

With 30 minutes until his meeting he decides to walk the floor and relax near the kitchenette that overlooks downtown. Windows stretch from floor to ceiling in the kitchenette, a feature of every space along the outside of the building on every floor. In addition to being the most contemporary building in Burlington, it also provides plenty of natural light, which the

CEO thought would create a more productive atmosphere than having employees trapped beneath fluorescent lights. It doesn't work so well for the hundreds stuck in the middle of the building in a cubicle farm.

Kelly sits in one of the large chairs facing the windows, an empty coffee on the side table next to her and a laptop opened to charts on her lap. Wireless headphones cut her off from kitchenette sounds, which is empty except for Chris; it's too late for anyone to not already have a coffee. She's newer to the company - maybe two years - making him feel like the grandfather of the staff having been there for 7 years. The looming 30th birthday in a year bites at the back of his mind but he ignores it; he won't get old. Despite her newness to banking, Kelly works harder than most of their coworkers.

He sits in another chair facing the windows, realizing for the first time that the kitchenette lights are off. He wonders if they are always off or if they are just off today. Kelly pulls her headphones out.

"I don't usually have company," she says with a smile.

"Don't let me stop you from working," Chris says. "I just needed somewhere relaxing to go for a few minutes. You can pretend that I'm not there."

Kelly sets the laptop on the side table, pushing her empty cup to the edge.

"You're fine. I've been staring at this spreadsheet since I came in this morning and I need a break."

"What are you working on?"

Kelly waves a hand nonchalantly toward the laptop, exasperated. "It's two new business accounts from a month ago. Whoever onboarded them mixed them up with another and I need to separate the two. Unfortunately, the onboarding wasn't done properly and the accounts are a mess."

"It was probably Jacob," Chris groans. "There is a reason he was let go. I can take a look at it quickly if you want, before I head upstairs."

Kelly gladly hands him the laptop.

"What's happening in a few minutes?" she asks.

"Some meeting upstairs," Chris says, getting lost in the spreadsheet.

The data falls into categories like a building made of legos that Chris constructs as needed. Glancing briefly at each of the business's names, he recognizes them from shopping at them but also from when the papers moved briefly over this desk. He was the one who recommended firing Jacob because of his inability to do something as simple as manage the onboarding of two minor clients. How was nobody assigned to correct this until now?

"What a mess," he says.

"Yeah, that's what I think every time I see a new column of data or see account numbers that shouldn't be there."

"It looks like at least the accounts were separated properly by the Bank's numbering system. Look for 10125 and 10145 accounts versus 10152 and 10451 accounts. That should be a good starting spot and the rest should fall into place once you get a handle on that."

Kelly takes the laptop back in shock.

"How'd you do that so fast?"

"Knack for numbers," Chris says. "I studied business and stats in college. The Bank's numbering system can take a while to grasp fully, but once you use it enough, things like this get way easier to see."

"You looked at that for 10 seconds and solved what I haven't in three days," Kelly says. "How are you not one of the directors?"

Being a director means responsibility he doesn't want because it means he's getting old. Chris shrugs and stares out

the full-windowed wall. Though it's as hot as yesterday, it's overcast. He also used to work at this window when he first started.
Things changed the longer he stayed in the same position.

"Enjoy the window. Something about it always helps me
think clearly when data like that becomes too much."

He stands and leaves, ignoring Kelly's thanks. With little less
than a half hour before the meeting, he decides to head to
Austin's office on the top floor. Despite more people visiting HR
than any other department, the director of HR insisted on being
on the top floor because firstly, nobody else wanted the space,
and secondly, she loved the view of Burlington from that high
up. Austin's second-in-command position couldn't sway her
otherwise.

Pictures clutter the walls on the top floor and quiet music
playing from every cubicle fills the space with a carnival-like
aura. Desk lamps in every cubicle replace the fluorescent overhead lights while the offices around the perimeter are lit only by
the floor-to-ceiling windows, their dusty lamps forgotten in
corners. Chris's step lightens as he walks around the cubicle
farm to Austin's outer office, which is opposite the elevators and
nearest the kitchenette. Austin somehow remains fit despite that
proximity to food and coffee, though visiting the gym on a more
regular basis than most people countered his food intake.

Chris plops into the chair opposite his best friend, who
greets him but finishes a document before closing it and
swiveling around. The large window behind Austin makes it
difficult to see more than his frame on too-bright days, but
today's overcast doesn't obstruct his outline.

"What are you doing up here?" Austin says.

"I need a distraction," Chris says.

Two pictures of Austin and Kyle sit on the desk, one of them
dressed in suits and the other of a hiking trip. Harris, Chris, and
Lydia are in pictures on the bookshelf, their pictures depicting

various groupings of the four friends skiing, vacationing on the West Coast, hanging out during college, and any other activity from hiking to sports to bars.

"And what exactly do you need a distraction from?"

"Just life." Chris throws his feet on Austin's desk as he leans back in the chair. "How's settling into your house?"

"Everything is in its place," Austin says with relief dripping from his voice. "That back deck overlooking the lake is my favorite part. I can't wait for Euchre tonight. It's been too long."

"Kyle better not permanently replace me as your Euchre partner."

Austin laughs and pulls a deck of cards from the drawer of his desk, which he opens and shuffles by bridging the cards repeatedly as they talk.

"Of course you're still my Euchre partner," Austin says. "Listen, I love Kyle, but I don't mess around with Euchre."

"Good, because I am *not* partnering with Lydia and I sure as hell am not going to be Harris's partner," Chris says.

"Harris will probably be too busy like always, chasing some one night stand," Austin says, his voice full of irritation.

"Maybe he's onto something," Chris says.

Austin tilts his head slightly. "Maybe he's not."

"You and Kyle are amazing together, but isn't it all a little permanent? I mean, I would love to have the support of someone like you do Kyle, but we're still in our 20s, and we don't have much time left in them. What happens when our 20s are over?"

"We continue with exactly what we were doing in life the day before when we were 29," Austin says. "Is that you talking right now, or is that Harris?"

Chris's eyes pass over the pictures behind Austin's desk again and the memories of college spent with Austin and Harris wash over him like a steaming thick sludge. Living with them was simpler; taxes weren't a concern, there wasn't pressure to settle down, and secret meetings weren't randomly added to his calendar. He recalls the bookshelf picture of the four of them at the top of a ski mountain. Harris was nervous but wanted to ride down the slope because a girl had promised to be waiting for him. As soon as the flash went off, Lydia pushed him forward and he slid, the other three laughing and pushing off to follow Harris down. Why can't life be only fun?

Austin waits patiently and Chris knows he'll wait as long as it takes him to answer. Best friends know how to give you time.

"I don't know," Chris says. "This isn't exactly the distraction I was hoping for."

Austin shrugs. "Harris's office is downstairs. That would've been a better distraction if you just wanted to joke your way through the morning."

"You can be quite harsh sometimes."

"Sometimes there isn't a difference between being harsh and being honest," Austin says. "I love you, dude. Don't put your life on pause while you live out a fantasy that is driving Harris down the path he's chosen."

Chris stares at the cards Austin is still bridge-shuffling.

"Deal a hand for rummy," Chris says. "I have a few minutes left to spare."

After a quick loss that Chris still isn't sure how it happened, he fist bumps Austin and heads to his meeting.

On the fourth floor he stands in the short hallway containing the stairs and bathrooms. Ten feet from him the hallway turns and opens into a reception area that spiderwebs into short hallways containing offices of the Bank's top people as well as conference rooms. Marissa waits somewhere behind the doors.

Chris checks his phone. Three notifications clog his home screen: two are reminders of events he doesn't care about but feels obligated to attend with the rest of the single, young people clinging to the last of their 20s, like leaving that decade means their bodies will wither and their only option will be a nursing home. Harris encourages them with his constant enforcement of the importance of attending every party before the warranty of their 20s expires. Chris swipes both away but hovers on the last message. An ex fling texted him, asking what he was up to this weekend. He starts typing a response but Marissa walks out of the bathroom before he finishes.

"Ah, Chris! I'm happy to see you again. Shall we head to the conference room?"

Chris deletes the text, then shoves his phone back in his pocket.

"Yes!" he answers louder than he meant too.

Marissa chuckles and walks up the hallway, speaking as if Chris is right next to her. He scurries to catch up to her, then doubles back a step so he isn't on equal footing with her. Decorum with the Bank's top people is in Austin's wheelhouse, not his.

"Nearly seven years with the Bank and one of the most talented we have," she says.

The receptionist smiles with a practiced fake smile as they pass. The art does nothing to eradicate how sterile the area is.

"Yes, I've been working on business accounts the entire time. I like what I do."

"We all do, or we wouldn't be involved with the Bank," Marissa holds the door open.

"I'm not sure why a board member wants to meet one-on-one with me," Chris says as he sits down.

Marissa laughs - something Chris notes she does too often - and sits two chairs away from him. The conference room's table sits seven on each side with a chair on each end. A projector hangs from the ceiling near the full window wall on the opposite side of the table from Chris and Marissa. Whoever chose the poor decorations in the hallway didn't bother to fake an attempt at decor in the conference room.

"I'm probably only a board member because my deceased husband was an initial investor in the Bank and built it. Were I not married to him, I would be a nobody to the CEO and the other board members. Luckily, my position grants me the ability to foster potential. I choose to have a more active role within the Bank than most."

Chris tries relaxing in the swivel chair, though he has never been able to get comfortable in these chairs. Faking being comfortable is a skill he lacks. To appease Marissa and prevent her from whatever she is going to reprimand him for, he gives it his all to look comfortable, which in turn makes him appear more uncomfortable.

"It's alright," Marissa says warmly, "I also dislike these chairs. You can stand if you want." Without pausing for Chris to respond, she continues, "I also have the ability to sway the board to vote on promotions. We need to create a new division because of an expanding client base. We need people to work specifically on large-scale international business projects. There are few who are qualified to oversee a venture like this. Your team consists of 17 people and will be located on the sixth floor. You'll have an outside office and you'll be able to order the specific furniture you want, though you'll also be traveling around the world to meet with businesses, so don't buy too-expensive furniture."

Chris rolls away from the table but grabs the edge with sweaty palms, which halts Marissa's monologue. Chris stares at the floor and breathes deeply, though he hides it from Marissa except for the heavy rise and fall of his body.

"If you'd rather order more expensive furniture, I guess that's fine," Marissa says. "I'll talk to the board and make sure that your budget will be large enough for whatever you need."

"Wait," Chris says.

He pauses and feels Marissa's eyes on him, not in an angry or irritated way, but patiently waiting for him to look back at her and say something. The two message threads he swiped away earlier return to his mind, their spontaneity something stripped away with this promotion. Harris pushed him to join both those groups and pushed him each time they got together to leave Keith at home and go out. His 20s are the time to enjoy his friends, not waste them being the Bank's dog and traveling the world at the Bank's leisure.

"I'm sorry, I just need a moment to think about this," Chris says.

Marissa smiles contentedly. "What is there to think about? You're well qualified, have shown the longevity to the Bank we like to see, and are highly recommended by your supervisors. The answer is obviously yes."

Chris sits straight but doesn't pull himself toward the table. Instead, he stands and the swivel chair rolls a few inches backward.

"I appreciate the offer, but I decline the promotion," he says.

Disappointment replaces Marissa's smile. She shifts in her chair to switch which leg overlaps the other. She plays with a pen in her hand, pushing one end on the table and running her fingers the length of it before flipping it around and repeating the process.

"This is quite an opportunity, especially for someone as young as you. This scale of a promotion won't come up again. I looked into your past with the Bank and you've already declined two similar offers. People here see your potential. You should accept their generosity."

Chris nods but has nothing to say. Marissa exhales in defeat.

"I do not like pushing people into positions they do not want. You were recommended by many as the top candidate."

"Thank you," Chris says with an eye on the door.

Marissa stands and walks him out but stops at the door to face Chris.

"It's your business why you don't want this position," she says. "Don't let inconsequential things stop you from reaching your potential. I've watched too many young people let life pass them by. What is it worth, the reason you're not taking the position?"

"What is the position worth?" Chris responds.

Marissa opens the door and Chris thanks her again before leaving. Rather than returning to his office, he climbs the stairs to the roof, where a small patio with a few tables sits, far away from the edge but still allowing for a full view of Burlington. Once in the fresh air, he finally exhales and then swallows gulps of the muggy, hot air. He leans on the railing and strangles any remaining life out of it.

Burlington from this height is a sight few get to see. The buildings spike randomly around the city like dandelions polluting a brick and green field. From his position, Chris can see directly down Church Street and all the vendors and restaurants on the brick, pedestrian-only street. During winter the street is lit up with lights weaved back and forth while the snow coats the rooftops white but leaves the red brick street alone. A mile to the east, Lake Champlain usually glistens when the sun is out, but on windless, cloudy days like today, it reflects the sky, creating two gray masses that sandwich the green mountains on the lake's opposite shore. The sight is one rarely appreciated by many of the people working in the Bank, but Chris appreciates it every day.

How dare Marissa look into his past. Whether he was offered promotions and whether he turned them down is his business, not some random board member's business. There has to be an invasion of privacy law he can throw at her. And how dare she ask him what his life is worth. She should think about what the job is not worth. His life is more important than the obligations that would come with that promotion.

Chris pulls out his phone and replies to two threads started by Harris diving into their jokes and confirming he will join them in whatever endeavor they plan. You only live through your 20s once. And he's going to extend that for as long as possible.

~

COWORKERS FILE out of the Bank of Burlington in streams ready to disappear into their Monday nights, their day of enslavement over. The endless line wiggles past Chris's office. All afternoon he switched between walking the building and sitting at his desk, not able to do either for more than 10 minutes without being driven crazy. He ended up returning to the roof and spent the past two hours there. No one came up, leaving him to stare at the beauty of Burlington in peace, and leaving him drenched in sweat when he finally left the muggy air.

Two coworkers stop in his office on their way out and attempt conversation but Chris has spreadsheets up and knows how to appear so entranced by them that everyone leaves him alone. When you are the best and in *that* trance, people understand to leave you alone. His office's position away from the elevators helps prevent people from pestering him.

"That's the third one," Devon says from his cubicle's entrance, apparently not understanding what Chris's trance means.

Chris types away, trained to not react when someone enters his cubicle or says something to him. People always leave when he's unresponsive if he doesn't offer a twitch in reaction to their presence. Well, usually, but Devon is different.

"Why did you turn it down?" Devon asks.

Chris sighs and swivels toward her, the spreadsheet unchanged all day despite his fingers fake-dancing over the keys to mimic working. Devon stands firm in his doorway, her arms crossed and her phone tight in one hand. She's one of the only people in the Bank that can stare him down with equal strength that he uses on others. She often wins against him.

"It's not the right time," Chris finally says.

"The right time doesn't wait for us to be ready," Devon says. "Either you take it when it's presented or you miss the 'right chance' forever."

"Then you take the job and make the decision to turn it down easy for me."

"I did."

Chris starts, unsure how to respond. His physical response would have made anyone else smirk for shocking him into breaking form his stoic presence, but Devon is too strong to gloat. She holds her hand close and waits, not needing sunglasses to hide her eyes. She wouldn't want them hidden as she stares down Chris, though he wishes he wore sunglasses so she couldn't see him as easily.

"Congratulations," Chris says with all the sincerity he can muster as he struggles to recover from declining a promotion thrust on him that morning, only to find out Devon accepted it. "When do you transition to the new position?"

"The board will approve it this week," Devon says. She shifts but her gaze pins Chris down like stakes. "We'll be moving up to the 6th floor in a week."

"What do you mean 'we'?" Chris asks.

"I need a team. I'm obviously going to take the best."

"I refuse," Chris says. His hands grip the chair's armrest and his back tenses. "I declined the offer to lead that team and I'll decline-"

"You don't have a choice," Devon cuts him off. "I need a team. You're the best at statistical analyses for accounts as large as what we'll be dealing with. Be ready to move next Monday when you come into work."

She steps away to leave but hesitates with half her face hidden.

"You can't keep avoiding life forever. Grow up."

"I refuse," Chris shouts. He's not sure what he refuses.

"We'll see about that."

She leaves before Chris can respond again. His phone buzzes as she disappears, though he ignores it like usual, slipping it into his pocket as he leaves.

~

"I SWEAR you love Keith more than any of us," Austin says as he pours the rest of the wine into the four glasses around his dining room table.

The glasses are placed strategically around two bowls of chips and pretzels and four smaller containers of dips, which are adjacent to a plate of brownies Lydia brought because 'that's what Mom always taught me.'

Austin sits at the table with Chris and Lydia, catching up on their days, while Harris sits opposite them with a beer and texting whatever girl he currently has caught in his bad-boy act. In the adjacent living room - which is connected by a large open floor plan - Kyle lies on the floor with Keith, who wags his tail and licks all over Kyle's face.

"Who's the best boy?" Kyle says like he's talking to a baby. He pets Keith's entire body.

In response, Keith crouches on his front paws and licks

Kyle's face more until the mask of wetness reflects in the dining room light. Keith tumbles to his side and lays on his back while Kyle rubs his stomach.

"I swear he likes that dog more than me," Austin says as he sips his third glass of wine.

"Listen, I can't get a dog in my apartment and you won't get one, so when Chris brings Keith over, let me love him," Kyle says.

"Oh, let him love Keith," Chris says. "I can't give Keith enough attention with work and whatnot. Plus Keith hates me."

Lydia picks up the Euchre deck and shuffles it.

"Well, with him being obsessed with Keith, we have exactly 4 for a round of Euchre." Lydia deals five cards out to each person and picks up her hand, flipping over an ace of spades in the center.

"Why do I have to play?" Harris says. "I need to leave soon."

"Shut the fuck up and pick up your hand," Lydia says. "We've already lost twice to these two and I need to redeem myself."

"Bold of you to assume you could ever beat us," Austin says. "Pass."

"Shut up and play," Lydia says. "Besides, Harris, whatever girl you're going to chase tonight can wait."

"I don't *chase* anyone," Harris says."They chase *me*."

"Yeah, yeah, and I'm not a borderline alcoholic. Just play," Lydia says. Her fourth wine glass is almost gone.

"We've never beat them in a best of 3 game," Kyle says from the floor with Keith lying on top of him. Kyle gently massages behind Keith's ears and the dog's eyes droop closed. "I don't know why you think today is going to be any different with Harris."

"Harris was here long before you. He and I used to stand a chance," Lydia says. "Just trust me that I can beat their asses."

"Go get them, babe!" Kyle shouts.

Lydia swivels in her chair. "You can shut up. You're not a part of this game."

"Gotta cheer for my boyfriend," Kyle says.

"Who invited him here?" Lydia says. "Turning down such a good card sucks." She flips over the ace. "Fucking cheerleaders..."

"Pass," Chris says.

Harris knocks on the table while still distracted by his phone.

"I did because he's better company than you, and pass," Austin says.

Lydia clinks her wine with Austin's. "Whatever gets your rocks off. God dammit why the fuck do we play stick the dealer? Hearts."

The hand of cards rotates through quickly and ends with Lydia throwing her last two cards on the table and finishing her wine before the next hand is dealt. Chris deals methodically compared to Lydia and takes time to consider his hand, while Lydia passes or calls a trump suit with barely a glance at her hand. Chris sips his wine before picking up the queen of diamonds.

"Your house is looking great, by the way, Austin," he says.

"The lights on the back porch were all me," Kyle calls from the other room. "Don't let him take credit for that."

"Kyle made me get enough lights to line a plane runway," Austin says. "I'm probably using half of the electricity in Burlington with all the lights he forced me to put up."

"And the lights are all *gorgeous*!" Kyle says.

"I think it looks great," Lydia says.

"You're drunk, don't encourage him," Austin says. "I don't have the capacity for any more lights in this house. It's like I'm under a spotlight when I'm sleeping so I just roll around in bed all night and can't fall asleep."

"Maybe it's your seventeen decorative pillows you insist on littering your bed with," Lydia says.

"There's no such thing as too many decorative pillows!" Austin says. "They add color and style and pull together my bedroom."

"God your gay is showing," Lydia says. "It's literally just you and Kyle in that bedroom. Who the fuck are you dressing it up for?"

Austin laughs. "Myself. Shut up. Also, your turn, and don't forget Chris called diamonds."

"Dammit, *why?*" Lydia throws her first card angrily on the table.

After another game of losing to Austin and Chris, Lydia throws her hands up and drunkenly zig-zags over to Kyle and Keith — still on the floor — and pets Keith's stomach while Kyle big spoons him. Keith's tail brushes the floor, his lips flopping back in a smile. Chris rolls his eyes.

"I'm out," Harris says. A slow night of two empty bottles sit in front of him.

"Where are you off to?" Austin asks.

"Meeting Bridget out at *Ralph's*," he says. "Tonight will be the night." He nudges Chris as he passes him.

"You should stay and chill with us," Austin says as Harris puts on his shoes in the living room.

"Nah, there are other places I need to be right now." He winks and waves to Lydia and Kyle before shutting the front door behind him.

"You can't reason with him," Chris says. "Nothing matters to him except women." He wishes he had gone with Harris, but it's too hot to go back outside.

"Somebody has to try. His family has abandoned him."

Austin picks up the empty dip dishes and Chris picks up the two bowls of chip crumbs and follows Austin to the kitchen. They set them in the sink and Chris grabs the 4 empty wine glasses on the table. He sets them along the sink as Austin picks up the dish sponge.

"You've never been able to leave dishes overnight," Chris says. "You were a nightmare to live with."

"Well luckily nobody lives with me now for me to be a nightmare for." Austin says with a smirk as he scrubs the first dip dish.

"Kyle will move in soon enough."

Austin shrugs. "Things are going wonderfully with him, but we've already talked about this. Not yet. Besides, even when he moves in, I'll still do the dishes. Nobody can do them correctly."

"That sounds like the controlling Austin I know."

Austin glares briefly at Chris.

"I don't know. I love Kyle but that's a huge leap. I just bought the house and I'm still settling into it. I don't know if I can settle into living with someone at the same time I'm settling into doing this whole adult thing to the extreme. You know what I mean?"

Chris takes the dish from Austin and dries it.

"Yeah, but if anyone can do it, it's you. I may be the one being bullied into more responsibility at work, but you're the one who's put together and has life figured out. You're the successful one here."

"You could be too, if you'd accept a promotion," Austin says, handing Chris a second dish. "So what happened today? Your text was confusing."

Chris groans and stacks the two dishes. "Some board member set up a meeting to offer me a promotion out of nowhere. I've never met her before. I don't want more responsibility."

"Maybe she sees that you're ready," Austin says.

"Hell no, I don't want that, I'm not ready. I'm still young. I'm still figuring things out and I don't know if I'm even going to stay here. I don't want to be pushed into leadership roles. Let someone who wants it take it."

"You're more qualified than you think," Austin says. "Do you not want to move up?"

Chris vigorously scrubs the towel on the third dish Austin hands him.

"Just because you're ready for all of this doesn't mean I am," Chris says.

"I am comfortable with it," he says, "and I do want it."

"Well, you also have a house and a relationship and love and what do I have?"

"You also have people who love you and want to see you succeed, and you have success in a different way than I do. Nobody's success looks the same."

Austin runs the water over the first wine glass and hands it to Chris, who dries it in silence.

"How was your hookup after the party?" Austin asks, sensing the need to switch topics.

"It was fine," Chris says with a shrug. "It was a good hookup."

He wants to word vomit everything about the night: how she asked him everything about his job, how she noticed his effort with the body spray, how she didn't force sex immediately, how the sex was the best of his life, how desperately she clung to him like she needed him to save her. He knows Austin is only asking to avoid making Chris more frustrated about the job offer, so he keeps it all bottled to himself. Besides, it does no good to dwell on a one-night stand.

"Well that's that, then," Austin says.

"Were you expecting more?"

"You were so confident walking off the yacht that I assumed there'd be more to tell."

Chris shrugs and finishes drying the dishes without talking to Austin. He stares out the window looking at the neighbor's yard, which has solar lights lining the flower bed and a child's swing set behind the house, which Chris has seen the child use every time he's visited Austin. Coming from either direction down Austin's street are signs stating, "Children at play. Drive slowly." He much prefers the street view of downtown from his apartment.

Chris hangs the four wine glasses in the rack situated between two cabinets. Above them are wine bottles in a lattice display, which itself is decorated with plastic leaves to accentuate the wine theme of the kitchen. There are over a dozen bottles in the lattice, which are replaced at somewhat rapid rates. Austin always says you can never have too easy of access to wine.

Chris folds his arms and leans backward against the counter as Austin wipes them down and obsesses over the kitchen's cleanliness. The dim lights on the underside of the cabinets provide the only light besides two scented candles, which bathe the kitchen in a sweet fruity aroma mixed with mood lighting, all of which is complimented by the lap of waves on the shore a mere thirty yards behind Austin's house. Chris could see the appeal in the house, if he wanted to leave the fun of downtown and his 20s behind. Maybe this is Austin's way of preparing to turn 30 in a few months.

"Well, I'm glad your hookup went well and you weren't murdered." Ausitn says.

"Thanks, Dad,' Chris says with a laugh, "though Keith would never let that happen. Except for right now. I think Kyle and Lydia have him so occupied that someone could attack me and he'd stay where he is to get more belly rubs."

Austin laughs and turns to walk back into the living room with Chris.

Chris's phone vibrates; a text from Harris inviting him to *Ralph's*. He replies that he's too drunk to drive anywhere so Harris offers to pay for a taxi. Chris hesitates, wondering if he'd see someone he could hook up with out at the bar. Maybe he could spread his wings and enjoy a night out with Harris like he did back in college.

Lydia saunters into the kitchen doorway.

"Come on, I'm heading upstairs to bed. Austin confiscated our keys. He's leading a drunk and exhausted Kyle upstairs. I guess this means Austin is cooking breakfast for us in the morning!" She turns to follow them but stops. "You ok?" she asks with a gentleness in her voice reserved for sparse moments when Lydia's mask comes off.

Chris closes the message from Harris and walks toward the stairs.

"Yeah, just tired and drunk. Definitely ready for bed."

He follows Lydia upstairs and enters one of the two guest bedrooms, regretting not accepting Harri's offer. His phone vibrates again but he doesn't read it. Bed calls for him louder.

4

TUGGING

Austin opens the car door for Chris but he sits there for a second, staring at the steps gatekeeping his apartment. Chris presses the thick white cloth covering his incision, the pain from the gallbladder surgery minor beneath the last batch of pain medicine. Though the ride home was painless, the thought of climbing steps sends shivers through him, the horror stories other people told about climbing steps after a gallbladder surgery ringing in his ears.

Slowly, he lifts and shifts one leg out of the vehicle, letting it drag along the floor until it drops to the ground, then repeats the process for the other. Little bursts of irritation ripple from the incision but nothing unbearable. He's not sure if the lowered pain is due to the numbing medicine working or if people exaggerated how painful gallbladder surgeries were. Austin would say the latter; Chris would probably agree.

"How do you feel about the stairs?" Austin asks outside the passenger door, ready to catch Chris if he falls once standing. "You can still come over to my place for a day or two until you're able to do stairs."

"I feel much better than I thought I would," Chris says. "I think I can do the stairs."

Austin glances dubiously over his shoulder, eyeing the enclosed stairs. He holds a hand out for Chris to grab onto. Once Chris has a firm grasp, Austin pulls and does most of the work to lift Chris to a standing position, who wobbles but grabs the car door with his other hand to steady himself.

"Not *that* much pain," he says. "Yeah, I'll be able to do the stairs."

"If you're sure," Austin says.

He extends an arm like a bachelor about to escort a date. Chris shakes his head in laughter but takes his friend's arm. Their progress is slow to the stairs as Chris inches forward, afraid of the pain that large steps might bring. His pain pills are working remarkably well, which he's thankful for. He's not afraid of pain or of stretching his incision to the point of tearing it open, but he wants to avoid pain if possible. He doesn't want to have to deal with it. Pain is for old people, not people in their 20s.

"Will you hurry up? I don't have all day to wait for your slow ass," Austin says sarcastically.

"Well, you shouldn't have volunteered to help me. Imagine I'm some guy you're taking on a date that's just really slow."

"If he was this slow, I would leave the date."

"How does Kyle put up with you?"

"I make a lot of money."

Chris's burst of laughter turns to crying as each laugh stretches the incision and shoots pain through him. He glares at Austin's grinning face.

"You're an asshole."

"Something about that must be endearing for you all to have stayed with me so long."

"I stay with you because you have money."

Austin laughs as they reach the base of the steps.

"Get a move on, asshole."

Chris glances up the stairs, then grips the railing for dear life. He pulls himself up using the railing and slowly lifts one leg, but no pain comes from it. He tries the other; also painless. Confident in the pain medication, he methodically climbs the steps with his hand always grasped around the railing. At the top, he lets out the breath he's held since the bottom, and with it all the fear of pain that didn't come on his climb up the stairs. Feeling like he could run a marathon, he wonders why people complain after this surgery.

"Wow, you did really well with that," Austin says.

"I'm telling you, these meds are really strong." He wobbles as he speaks.

Chris unlocks his apartment door and Keith merely glances across the living room from the couch, too unconcerned with Chris to waste any more energy. When Austin appears in the doorway, Keith's head picks up and he bounds off the couch. Austin squats and catches Keith's head over his shoulder, the dog's wagging tail whacking Chris's leg. He steps aside and watches Austin fall on the floor with Keith, rubbing his stomach.

"You know I pay for everything for you," Chris says to his dog. "You could show some excitement when I get home."

Keith rolls his eyes at Chris as he licks Austin's face.

"Oh, leave him alone," Austin says. "He just wants some love and you can't give that to him in that state."

"I should put him outside for the night."

Keith rolls his eyes again at Chris and appears to smile as his lips droop back on his face.

"If you change your mind about staying here, Keith is also welcome at the house for as long as you need."

"I appreciate it but I had to listen to you and your college boyfriends when we lived together. I really don't need to hear that as an adult when I can be somewhere else."

Austin laughs and shakes his head.

"Whatever you want to do. If you change your mind, just give me a call."

Chris struggles through the apartment to his couch, where he's already prepared a pillow and a blanket. He resembles a ballerina as he stands on one leg and lifts another, then puts a hand behind him on the armrest and lowers himself like a stiff corpse onto the couch.

"You look like an idiot," Austin says.

"Leave me alone," Chris says. "I don't want to irritate it and be in pain all day."

Ausitn doesn't say anything more but pats Keith's head. Austin is a good best friend to have.

"Thanks for the ride."

"Of course," Austin says. "I'll text you in an hour to see how you are."

"Thanks, Mom."

"Don't patronize me or I'll come stay the night here with Kyle so we can look after you and you can listen to us all night long."

"God I hate you. Goodbye."

"Talk to you soon, dude."

Once the door is shut, Chris and Keith look at each other. Keith climbs onto the chair - for once leaving Chris alone on the couch - which Chris takes as a sign of peace between them, for the time being.

"Thank you," Chris says.

Keith rolls his eyes and shifts on the chair. Chris does the same on the couch, pulling the oversized blanket over himself.

∽

CHRIS STARES around his apartment and out of the darkening window. Keith is still snoring on the chair. Anesthesia lingers in his system, pulling him back to sleep without him realizing. He stretches out his legs but the couch impedes a full stretch, though extending his toes releases an ache he didn't realize he had and also tugs at his incision. With no pain, he would've forgotten the dried, deep red-dyed cloth was there if he hadn't felt the tape pull against him. He pushes the oversized blanket off himself so it bunches at one end of the couch. He places a hand over his incision and uses his other arm to push himself up, avoiding using his core to pull himself up at any cost. Despite his effort, his incision tugs and a small pain stops him from moving. Once sitting up straight, he hunches over to not strain his incision at all, and he breathes out deeply as a head-rush lessens. He's wearing only a shirt and boxers because it's the loosest clothing he has without going naked. The kitchen clock shows it's almost 9pm.

Keith watches from the chair, which has been his perch since Chris arrived home after the surgery. Chris looks at Keith's blank stare as he takes a deep breath and holds it in to minimize the pain from standing. He wobbles less than he did yesterday, though he still uses a chair to steady himself. Once standing, he stares around his apartment as a method to delay having to move. Slouched like the Hunchback to avoid aggravating his incision, he takes a breath.

"If you need to go out, it's now or you have to hold it for another few hours," he says to Keith.

Dragging himself off the chair one foot at a time, Keith starts for the door half a minute after Chris but bullets past Chris's snail pace. Keith waits patiently at the door, staring at Chris as he crawls closer. When Chris finally opens the door, Keith stares at him for a moment.

"I've got to go to the bathroom, too," Chris says. "You have until I'm done."

Keith walks out of the door without any hurry. Chris breathes in the warm September air flavored with a drop in temperature and falling leaves. He leaves the door open as he takes his time shuffling to the bathroom, not caring if he loses some of his air conditioning to the open door. Walking doesn't hurt, but when he steps too heavily or stumbles and catches himself, the incision reminds him it's there. Walking slowly avoids the pain so for once takes his time doing everything.

After using the bathroom he grabs a bag of pretzels from his kitchen and curses himself for forgetting his water glass on the coffee table but resigns himself to using what little is left sparingly. His phone dings twice. He lifts his wrist but his smartwatch is in his bedroom. With the pretzels in one hand, he stares around his kitchen, wondering what else he will need for the next 5 hours while lying on the couch. He considers making coffee but that'll only keep him up and all he wants to do is sleep, so he fights the urge and leaves the kitchen with only pretzels.

Keith is back inside and on the chair, his head over the armrest.

"You couldn't help me and close the door?" Chris says.

Keith looks at Chris with the attitude of a middle schooler being asked to put on a jacket to go outside during winter. Chris carries the pretzels to the door and closes it, turning the lock with plans for a long nap. After setting the bag on his coffee table, he uses the chair back to lower himself onto the couch, wearing out his arms while avoiding straining his core. As he lays down, he pulls the blanket up and yawns, adjusting his pillow and putting a hand beneath it to sleep when he remembers his phone dinged.

Cursing Austin's over-caring spirit, he reaches for his phone, but starts when he sees that Taylor texted him. It's been two weeks but she remembered the surgery. He texts her back.

TAYLOR: How did the surgery go?
   Taylor: Do you need anything?
   Chris: Surgery went great! I have almost no pain.
   Taylor: Do you need anything?
   Chris: I think I'm all set. But I appreciate you asking.
   Taylor: Do you mind if I come over to make sure you're ok?
   Chris: I can't do anything like last time.
   Taylor: I don't want to have sex. I just want to make sure you're ok.

CHRIS REREADS THE TEXT STRING, not sure what he expected but also not sure he remembers how to read correctly. He doesn't know how to respond to Taylor. He assumed that when a waitress gives you her number and comes over to your apartment for sex, that she's not someone you see twice. Though, she did sit on the couch with him for over two hours before she even made a move, before she made anything about the visit sexual. And she asked about *everything* in his life. Maybe she is the type of waitress that gives you her number and you see twice.

He responds that she can come over but stresses that he can't have sex because of his surgery. She assures him, again, that it's fine and she just wants to make sure he's ok. He tells her the door will be unlocked. Then he looks at the door he just locked and sighs. If she hadn't asked everything last time that he needed someone to, he would've told her another night.

"Son of a bitch," he says.

Keith lets out a puff of air and repositions his head to better watch Chris struggle up and to the door and back, a grin beneath his droopy lips.

A half hour later a car grumbles into the driveway followed by Taylor slowly opening the door. Chris is half asleep but smiles when she's inside. Keith's tail beats against the chair back in rhythmic thuds until Taylor goes to pet him, rubbing his stomach, which turns him into a mesh of dog that melds further with the chair than he previously had. When Keith is satiated, she turns to Chris, who tries to haul himself up on one arm.

"No, stay," Taylor says.

She sets her phone on the coffee table and sits on the opposite end of the couch, carefully sitting around Chris's legs. He tries shifting them for her but she insists that he doesn't move.

"Thanks for coming," Chris says, "but you really didn't have to. I feel bad making you come here for nothing."

"I wanted to make sure you were ok," Taylor says. "Let me see the incision."

"Oh, you don't want to see it," Chris says. "It's red and looks like shit from being sewed up. It looks disgusting."

"I was in nursing school before I became a waitress," Taylor says.

"You were?"

"Yeah, I went for a year," Taylor says as if it were no big deal.

Chris lifts his shirt and is thankful he put on shorts when he got up to unlock the door. He lowers his shorts and boxers slightly to expose the incision, which Taylor examines.

"Did you not want to pursue nursing anymore?" Chris asks.

"Oh I still do," Taylor says. "There's just some...things that are preventing that from happening."

"Like what?"

Taylor doesn't touch the cut or stitches but she does stare at it for longer than Chris is comfortable with. She also doesn't answer his question, which makes him equally irritated. He stares at the wall to avoid seeing her hair or eyes or hands or infinity necklace or anything else that he couldn't stop staring at when she came over this weekend, but damn is it difficult to not look at her.

"It looks like it's healing well," she finally says.

She lowers his shirt and moves his hands but gently places his shorts waistband just above the incision. Chris rotates to his back and pulls the blanket up a little, half from the chill of his AC and half from exposing a disgusting incision to someone he only had a one night stand with. Careful to not rock Chris, Taylor shifts on the opposite end of the couch and covers her toes with the blanket, then slowly lifts Chris's feet onto her lap so he can stretch a little.

"How have you been feeling?" Taylor asks.

"I can't pull myself into a sitting position easily but I really don't have a lot of pain. The pills are really working. I'm worried about how much pain I'll have once they're gone."

Taylor nods and places her feet on the coffee table, Chris's oversized blanket easily keeping her toes covered.

"I'm surprised you came over," Chris says.

"I wanted to make sure you were ok," Taylor repeats.

"I thought seeing you a couple of weeks ago would be the only time I'd see you," Chris says.

"I can leave."

"No, no, don't get me wrong," Chris says, suddenly worried more about her leaving than the potential pain from the incision. "I'm happy you're here. I'm just surprised. I didn't think a hookup would text me randomly and come to check on me after surgery when we can't have sex."

Taylor shrugs and stares around the apartment. It isn't bare but it lacks the trinkets and homey touches that Austin's house has, though it's far superior to the barren-walled, nearly-empty box Harris rents. Keith's unused dog bed and a few bones and toys scattered around are the most abundant things in the apartment. Generic box-store canvas art decorates two walls and a handful of pictures sit on the small catch-all table near the door. Other than that, the two bookshelves and the barren TV stand with old DVDs on its shelves isn't much to look at.

"No plans tonight?" Chris asks.

"Nope." She gets up and goes to the kitchen. "Do you want anything to drink?"

Chris looks at his half-empty glass of water on the coffee table. "Sure, can you refill this? Thanks."

Taylor grabs his glass and fumbles through his kitchen cupboards for a glass of her own, and then struggles with the fridge settings to dispense ice cubes.

"How was your week so far?" Chris asks.

"It's been fine. Work has been work. Life."

"What does 'life' mean?" Chris asks.

"Just a lot happening," Taylor says.

Chris waits for an elaboration but of course there is none; that is Taylor's endearing but aggravating traits. He craves to have Taylor open up and tell him what she's holding back but he refrains from poking her. Taylor brings back two glasses of ice water and sits a little closer to Chris, again pulling his legs slowly onto her lap. Chris grimaces as his legs move.

"Are you ok?" Taylor asks urgently. The genuine worry across her face is endearing.

"Yeah, yeah," Chris says. "Just the incision."

"I'm sorry," Taylor says with the most emotion Chris has heard from her. "Does it still hurt?"

"No, it was only momentary when my legs moved."

Dribbles of water run onto Taylor's and get stuck in the crevices between them. She stretches the overly large blanket over her legs and down to her feet, wrapping them under the blanket.

"I need my feet covered," Taylor says.

Chris smiles at the vulnerability, even if it is insignificant. "You're fine."

"What are you doing while recovering?" Taylor asks to deflect the attention off her need to cover her feet.

"Just watching TV, playing on my phone. There's not much I can do. I have to give up fall kickball. This is an awful time to get surgery."

"Anytime is an awful time to get surgery," Taylor says.

Chris laughs, uncertain why she so easily makes him smile.

"You're right, it is. But taking away your last opportunity to go outside before it gets cold and snowy sucks."

"How long are you down for?"

"I can go for short walks after two or three weeks, but kickball with everyone or anything more than a walk? I'm out until the middle of winter, for all the good that timeline does me."

Taylor shrugs and sips her water. Her fingers clutch the glass like she wishes it were something that would get her tipsy but she doesn't ask for anything and doesn't complain. Her fingernail taps the glass quietly and the corner of her lip trembles.

"What are you doing about work?" Taylor asks.

"I'm off this week and am half in the office next week. I get paid medical leave."

Taylor nods and sips her water, his explanation more than satisfactory for her. Her toes wiggle beneath the blanket so subtly that Chris barely notices. He doesn't turn to look at them in fear that Taylor would stop if he did. Instead he shifts slightly on the couch but doesn't move his legs off her lap and she doesn't move them off. He smiles while she stares around the apartment more.

"Where was that picture taken that hangs on your fridge?" she asks.

"I have a picture on my fridge? Oh, the one of us in front of that castle?" Chris laughs thinking about the trip but instantly cringes when laughing stretches the stitches.

"Are you ok?"

Taylor raises a hand toward him, as if her touch would erase the pain and make the surgery go away, and he thinks it might. Her eyes appear watery and her eyebrows are raised in shock. Her body is tense, ready to move at whatever directions Chris gives.

"I'm fine," Chris says through a deeper breath than he intended. "Laughing just hurts."

"Then I won't make you laugh."

Taylor's face is stern and flat, as emotionless as the nuns that used to smack Chris's hand when he broke any of the thousand unwritten rules they expected him to know in Sunday school. Her seriousness at a shot of pain that disappears as quickly as it comes from something as trivial as a gallbladder surgery makes Chris laugh again and sends another jolt of pain through him.

"You're not helping," he says, breathing deeply to cut off the laughter.

Taylor shakes her head. She looks for a coaster on the coffee table but sees none.

"Just set it right on the table," Chris says. "It's an old table from college. I don't care if it gets ruined."

Taylor dubiously sets the glass down and shifts on the couch, pulling her legs under her so his feet slithers off her lap. Then she pushes herself up the couch toward him.

"Lay on your side," she says.

"I can't cuddle you tonight. I can't hold you because you'll press against the cut."

"I'll be big spoon," she says.

Chris stares at his stitched incision beneath the blanket.

"Just turn on your side, I won't hurt you."

Chris throws an arm over the side of the couch to grab the

cushion and pull himself to his side. The movement hurts him but the pain subsides when he's on his side. He inches near the edge of the couch while Taylor settles behind him. She pulls the blanket up beneath their arms as far as it will go while keeping her feet covered. He's thankful the couch is deeper as she wraps an arm over him and her hand finds his like a nesting doll settling into its home. He wraps tightly around her hand and pulls it as close to him as he can. Her head rests on the pillow behind him but her nose nestles into his back and her forehead rests against his lower neck.

Air conditioning caresses their bare arms while the sound of Keith's deep sleeping snores fill the apartment with sound. Chris warms immediately with Taylor's body wrapped with his, her legs weaving between his until he can't tell whose legs are whose and the bends in her body form to his like a nail fitting perfectly into a hole, despite her being two inches shorter than him. Stargazing in a field with your best friend, a comforting embrace from a parent when you're hurt, a moment of safety when everything feels too much; Taylor holding him is all of that and more.

She has no reason to be. Chris met her just 2 weeks ago and had one hookup with her, though a hookup preceded by hours of talking about everything that matters to him and her actually listening to him. He has no reason to feel as comfortable with her as he does with his family or Austin or any of his close friends, but the moment she walked through his door his body relaxed and his barbed fences rusted away. He has no reason to have fallen for her harder than he did his last ex after ten months of dating her. He has no reason to feel so clean with her, but his normal urgency to wash his hands when someone touches him is gone while she holds him.

"Am I hurting you?" she asks.

Chris shakes his head but realizes from her position she can't tell what he's doing.

"No, you're perfect."

He shifts on the couch and nothing hurts. He pulls her arms tighter to him and she worms tighter against his back and her legs weave more with his legs until he's not certain where his legs end and hers begin. He feels a drop of liquid on his neck, near her head. He's getting warm under the blanket with her but isn't sweating. He squeezes her hand and she releases a deep breath that reverberates over his body like a ripple in a pond that leaves behind a peaceful surface.

"How's the community garden wrapping up?" Taylor asks after a long silence in which Chris thought she fell asleep and nearly did himself.

"You remembered?" he says.

"Yeah," Taylor says as if it were preposterous for her not to.

When she doesn't say anything else, Chris takes it as his cue to speak.

"It's going amazing. I obviously won't be able to do anything with it for a week or two, but at this point we're just picking everything and giving it away to people. There's a give-and-take fridge effort in town and we donate a lot of the produce to that. Hopefully it's going to people who actually need it. But after we're done picking everything, we'll start cleaning out the beds and prepping them for winter so they're ready in the Spring."

"How many people are helping you?"

"We have a team of a dozen, maybe a little more. The volunteers keep flooding in compared to last year. I don't know why so many people took an interest in the garden this year, but I hope they come back next year. It's been so much easier with all the extra hands."

"Sounds like a really great project."

"Yeah, it's really grown and I'm proud of it. When we started it we didn't think the City would help fund part of it. I think part of giving us money is the Council's effort to seem like they care. I'm not complaining, but-"

"Politics is politics," Taylor finishes for him.

"Exactly."

"Politics is exhausting. How are the plans for the trip you're taking in a month?"

Chris smiles and rubs Taylor's hand with his thumb. He wishes he could see her, but being little spoon means he stares at the turned-off TV. She really does remember everything he says. He'd turn around and kiss her if he could without bringing on pain.

"I think the plans are ready. I meant to check with Austin about the reservations but he's usually pretty good at that stuff. He's the planner of our group," he pauses, "and the successful one."

"What do you mean?"

Chris sighs. Will Taylor actually listen to his complaints?

"He's the assistant director of HR at the Bank and bought a house and has a steady relationship and blah blah blah. The rest of our friend group are still single and living in apartments and at mediocre levels in our jobs. Though I don't think Harris wants to do anything more if it doesn't involve a woman."

"What do you want?"

"What do you mean?"

"Do you want everything Austin has?"

Chris is entranced in the black TV screen. He can faintly see a reflection of him and Taylor on the couch, though their shapes lack all definition. He images her lying behind him and how beautiful she looks every time his incision tugs at him and his face betrays a brief shock of pain. A dull yellow orb reflects in the blank TV from next to Keith's deformed reflection. He wishes he could see things more clearly.

"You ask really difficult questions."

Taylor pauses. "I like the cologne you're wearing."

Chris sighs. "One day I want it, maybe. I guess I want some of the things that he has. But I'm happy where I am right now." He doesn't say anything more.

In the morning Taylor showers briefly and rushes out as soon as the sun is up. His apartment feels less like home when the door closes and Keith stares at him from the chair with nobody behind him under the blanket. He doesn't feel dirty when she leaves like the other women that have left.

5

A DATE

A week after she came over to check on Chris after his surgery, he texted her and she didn't respond, so he texted again the next day and she didn't respond. One day, he grew brave and sent two messages in the same day. Everything was ignored. Then, at nearly midnight one Saturday night weeks later, she texted him and came over for the night. The night proceeded exactly like their first night: one of the best conversions Chris has ever had and then they had the most comfortable and easy sex Chris has ever had. They fell asleep holding each other, their bodies molding together as if one was made to fit against the other like a key into a locked door.

Another three weeks later Chris finally convinced Taylor to go out for a date with him rather than hide inside his apartment every time they saw each other. Chris wanted to go to a nice restaurant on Church Street but Taylor insisted on going to a small pub just off Church Street. He would settle for wherever she wanted to go.

The side streets are not paid as much attention as the main strip. Individual stores and restaurant owners decorate themselves rather than the Church Street Merchants Association.

Cheaper side street taxes balanced out the business owners needing to put in a little extra work around holidays, which most owners are fine with since they can decorate without having to worry about Church Street Merchants Association standards.

Chris likes the boutique he lives above. Their decorations are unique compared to the main strip's. The glass windows are framed by twinkling fairy lights that change to a different color every night and the door's small round window is covered by a wreath. The home products and clothing in the two display cases along the front are donned in lights that also change colors nightly and complement whatever color the fairy lights are that night. Waves of magic emanate from the displays whenever Chris walks by them, and little children often stop their parents at night walking past the lights to gape at their magic.

Approaching the pub, Taylor slows and looks over her shoulder up the street, where the orange and yellow October leaves obscure the lights from Church Street and block some of the sound of laughs and music from slithering down to where they are. Regardless, she hurries her pace ever so slightly. Chris draws in a deep breath of the crisp and chilly Vermont air, half the reason he fell in love with living in Burlington.

"I've never gotten used to the cold autumns here," Taylor says. "Why does Burlington have to be so cold?"

"You didn't exactly choose a southern city to live in," he says, wondering if that's where she is from.

Empty crumb-filled plates sit forgotten between their drinks as servers rush past their tiny patio table, rushing outside with steaming dinners and returning barren plates to the kitchen. A single tree stretches over the enclosed restaurant patio, some lights strung between the branches. Chris had heard of *Mona's* before but never ate here because it's on a side street, and

Church Street is just more exciting. He expected to come here when he was old, not 29.

Autumn back in New York City was beautiful in Central Park and in the decorations shops filled their windows with to commemorate the season as they ramped into the holiday season. Sandwiched between blacktop and cement, the City was always warmer this time of year than Chris liked. Enjoying the neighborhoods and boroughs with his friends as teenagers highlighted his memories but wrapped autumn in a ball of warmth that never felt right when October shifted to November and he expected to need a scarf and a jacket heavier than a light blanket.

Burlington's autumnal charm displays itself on every street and in the forests and mountains surrounding the city, and particularly along Church Street. In September the mountains and trees turn the mono-green landscape into an aurora rivaling the Northern Lights, while during winter, Church Street turns into a North Pole imposter that many mistake for the North Pole itself, with ice sculptures, lights strung back-and-forth over the cobblestone street, and Christmas trees and snowmen stretching the entire length of the street. Though the mountains were covered in barren trees, the snow contrasts with the brown and creates a beautiful web of brown over white covering every mountain, and small ice blocks float in Lake Champlain while its shores freeze and sparkle on sunny winter days. During autumn the apple cider made on farms five minutes outside the city are irreplaceable. Living in this bliss holds him here stronger than New York City could pull back.

"Have you ever been to this restaurant?" Chris asks. "It's cute. I should explore these little side places more often."

"Once or twice," Taylor says.

"It was delicious, though I'm tired now. That steak was a lot."

Taylor nods. Her second beer is nearly empty. Her fingers

rest on its neck delicately, though with a pinch they could end the bottle. Taylor fixes the uneaten food onto her plate, then stacks his plate under hers, and precisely sets the silverware on the stack. She does this every time she leaves his apartment: makes the bed, fixes his pillows just so, starts to do the dishes they used the night before until he tells her he'll do them later, makes everything perfect. He appreciates her attentiveness to contributing and making things how they should be, but he wishes she would accept that she doesn't have to do anything except be there with him.

"Did we save room for dessert?" the server asks as they clear the empty plates away.

Chris bends slightly away from the server as they reach for the plates to avoid being touched, thoughts of the countless dirty plates the server has carried throughout the night at the forefront of Chris's mind. Chris shifts his and Taylor's beers so the server has an easier time reaching all the plates, and doesn't feel the need to wash his hands after touching her beer.

"No, but I'll have another beer," Chris says. "Do you want one?"

"If we're walking back to your place," Taylor says.

The server nods and leaves, but returns a minute later with fresh beers. Chris takes a large sip, the coldness refreshing after devouring so much steak. Taylor matches his drinking enthusiasm, finishing the last dribbles of her own beer and starting the new one. Her infinity necklace catches the lights above in rare moments, the thin edges of the circles barely enough to catch any light, but it somehow manages.

Taylor doesn't look at him to start conversation nor does she offer conversation, though her eyes dart around the patio expectantly. A nervous state darkened her eyes and posture their entire date but she holds her shoulders back as if nothing bothered her. Chris admires her ability to continue despite something bothering her, the nonchalance she carries with everything when he could ruminate on it.

"How is Keith?" Taylor asks. "God, I wish you had given that dog a normal dog name."

Chris chokes on the beer he's swallowing as he laughs. "Keith is good. Lazy like always. I brought him to the garden when we closed last week."

"You closed the garden already? Isn't it a little early?"

"Maybe it's a little early in October to be closing it up but the weather's been so cold the past few weeks that there's no point in keeping it open another week or two. We'd rather save some of the money for next year than waste it on keeping it open this year."

"Are you going to stay on the board for it next year?"

"I don't know, probably," Chris says.

He leans back in his chair, his entire body relaxing despite his brain racing with what staying on the garden board would mean: long hours after his normal job and managing dozens of people. These are adult things, not something for a young person in their 20s to do, but he's seen the impact the community garden has had on Burlington too often to abandon it.

Without uttering a word, Taylor's stare demands him to expand. Without the usual guilt of feeling like an irritation when telling Taylor anything, Chris enjoys another mouthful of beer and smiles. Why can't everyone listen as well as Taylor?

"There's so much responsibility that comes with it. I don't know if it's something I want to keep taking on. It feels like it's taking away time from other things in my life, like if I'm not working on the garden then wasting my time doing other things. I don't know, like, I know that's not the case but it feels like it, you know?"

Taylor nods but doesn't contribute anything verbally to the conversation.

"What if I could be out doing things with friends instead of at the garden or spending more time with Keith instead of at the garden or enjoying a bar rather than being at the garden until dark some nights? Sometimes I wonder if I'm missing out on other things in my 20s by being at the garden so much during summer. I could get it all back if I gave up the garden and not miss out on anything in my 20s. We're only young once."

"So why stay?"

"It's...complicated."

"Life shouldn't be complicated. But it always is."

Silence settles for a moment as Taylor drifts off to another space, her fingers unconsciously twisting the infinity necklace in her hands, the first time Chris has seen her acknowledge its existence. He doesn't want to disrupt the rare moment of her mind wandering. From above, the hanging lights illuminate the center of her face but her cheeks are hidden in her hair's shadow. In the light, her face's usual stern features are softened and for the first time Chris sees the uncertainty on her face that he feels in her grasp every night they spend together. It doesn't last long; Taylor's eyes move back to him, the light reflecting on her face dimming and her sternness returning with the rigidity of a mountain against the elements.

"How is work? Is that woman still bothering you?" she asks, ignoring the momentary lull she let settle between them.

Chris nods. "She's persistent. I don't get why she doesn't understand what no means. It's like she thinks she can wear me down into taking a promotion if she asks me enough. I just want to be left alone to do my job and live my life. Why do people think others want to be forced into things? All we want is to be left alone to enjoy our 20s and hold onto the few months of being young we have left."

"Do you feel you can do that now?"

"Of course, that's why I don't want to give it up," Chris says. "I can go out with friends or take a vacation or take a day off without caring about work or taking it home with me. If I become a supervisor and the Bank dumps all this responsibility on me, I'll have to worry about it all constantly and be bothered by people constantly. I don't want that from work. I want to be young. All that shit's for old people."

Taylor nods encouragement.

"Devon wanted that promotion and she got it. She should be happy and stop bothering me. Sometimes it makes me want to leave the Bank altogether."

"Would that make you happy?"

"Not being bothered about a promotion every week by Devon would make me happy," Chris says.

"So leave the Bank."

"I don't know where I'd go. Despite Devon being a pain in my ass, the Bank pays well and the benefits are great. I don't hate my job, I just hate some of the people I work with."

Taylor nods.

"Thank you for asking about these things," Chris says, "and for listening. It means a lot. Sometimes it feels like everyone else is so busy with their own lives that they don't have the capacity to ask about these things. I don't always feel like I have someone to talk to about some of these things."

Taylor nods.

"Should we head back to my place?"

She nods again so Chris pays the bill - despite Taylor trying to give him cash for it - and they leave. Taylor wraps her arms across her torso in the chilly air while Chris struts comfortably, the three beers warming him against the cold.

"We're only a few blocks from my place," Chris says. "Sorry about the cold. I didn't think to bring a jacket that I could give you."

"It's fine," Taylor says.

"Have you ever walked the streets here?"

Taylor shakes her head.

"Keith and I walk them when he's not being lazy."

"He's not lazy, he's just a tired dog," Taylor says.

Chris laughs at her attempt at sarcasm, the first time she's tried to be funny with him. He wishes she'd try that more.

"There are two streets we avoid because people keep their dogs outside all day and they bark at Keith and he barks back and it turns into a back and forth between him and I as I try to get him to keep walking. It's great to see the energy from him but I wish he'd use that to walk and not antagonize other dogs."

"There are so many houses on these streets," Taylor says.

"It's an older part of the city," Chris says. "Turn left here."

Taylor walks next to him, never taking a step too big that would put her even an inch in front of Chris, though she holds herself taller than him as they walk. He's not sure if it's the alcohol doing that to him or if her presence is more dominating than his.

"Some friends and I are going out next week for someone's birthday," Chris says shyly. "Would you like to come out with us?"

"We'll see," Taylor says without missing a beat. "It's a busy week for me."

"Ok, just let me know. We're going to a bar on Church Street."

Her hand sways next to his as they walk the last stretch to his apartment, the shop he lives above now in their view up the street. Hay Bales line the street, the only decoration the Merchant's Association provided for the autumn holidays. Local vendors on either side of the street made their own scarecrows for a Merchant's Association contest and the orange and purple lights, as well as the Halloween decorations, were all bought by the shops along the street. Despite the lack of support from the

Merchant's Association, the street did well decorating for Halloween.

He glances at her hand again. His hand is inches away, their fingers so close to touching if he just reached out. They could wrap around each other and he could be there for her to grip tightly on their walk back home so she could feel like she isn't drowning. He doesn't have to be there for her just while they're cuddling in bed; he could be there for her at all times, if only she'd let him hold her hand. He reaches out his fingers but she moves a few inches away with her next stride. He considers shifting his stride closer again but he isn't sure how many rejections he can take before a void between them sprouts.

Their walk is quiet the last few buildings. Neither offer conversation, one because he isn't sure what to say that would impress her enough to engage in a conversation, and one because her eyes are busy darting around the street. A single car passes them the entire walk home, though one is enough to bring fear to Taylor. Chris shifts so he is between her and the street.

Opening his apartment door, Keith gradually crawls from his couch spot to welcome Taylor home, who accepts his warm welcome. Chris glares at Keith and he glares back.

"I'm not sure I can stay long tonight," Taylor says. "It's already late and I have a busy day tomorrow."

"You can always stay as long as you like," Chris says. "I'd love it if you could spend the night but I understand if you can't."

"Probably not tonight," Taylor says matter-of-fact.

She walks back to the couch and Keith follows her like she's his owner and not Chris. Defeated by both the prospect of spending a night with Taylor and by Keith, Chris grabs two waters from the kitchen and sets one down on the coffee table as he takes up the chair. Taylor rearranges the blanket over her toes before downing half the water.

"I'll probably leave in a little bit," she says, her attention drifting like she is speaking to the room as a whole and not to the only other person in it.

"What's going on tomorrow?" Chris asks. His stomach knots immediately after asking.

"Stuff," Taylor says.

Chris taps his glass while Taylor stares around the apartment and pets Keith behind one ear. They sit in silence for the next 10 minutes; Chris's mind swirling with what to say to make her stay so she understands how desperately he needs her after not hearing from her for two weeks. Taylor is unperturbed by the silence, seeming to enjoy it as she admires various aspects of Chris's apartment.

"Can I shower?" she asks suddenly.

Chris stumbles but nods. Two minutes later Taylor emerges from the bathroom, her hair seemingly dry despite Chris not having a hair dryer. Rather than say anything to Chris, she makes for the door, her shoulders pulled back and her expression placid, as if a business meeting has just ended and staying any longer would be an intrusion.

"Heading out?" Chris asks, jumping from the chair to join her at the door as she slips on her shoes.

"Yes, I can't stay longer tonight, I'm sorry."

"It's fine," he lies, "you're welcome anytime."

"Mmhmm," Taylor says.

She speaks in the same disconnected yet firm way she's spoken since their first date two months ago. Her eyes are as dispassionate as any eyes could be, yet she holds her gaze on Chris for a long time before making a motion to leave. More bubbles beneath her surface but she suppresses it. He wants to ask what it is.

"Alright, I have to go," she says.

"I can walk with you downstairs."

"It's alright," she says.

More of an obligation than a desire to, she leans in to kiss him goodbye. Not letting an opportunity of her initiating something pass, Chris leans in and kisses her back, putting a hand on her back, though being careful not to be pushy and scare her away.

"I'll talk to you later," Taylor says. "You smell good."

She leaves before he can say anything in return and she doesn't look back as she scurries down the steps. Taylor captivates his attention until her car grumbles from the driveway.

6

FILL THE VOID

Groans from decades-old nails being pulled from what they've held together for over 50 years consumes the kitchen like they're on a scratchy record amplified by wall-sized speakers. Chris comes back into the kitchen after tossing remnants of a torn out cupboard into the large dumpster Austin rented. Despite the snow and cold Vermont air blowing in the open windows, all three of them are in shirts and sweating. The counter is already removed, leaving the cupboards as skeletal shells. Torn drywall and dusty paint patterns cover the walls like artwork hurried through.

Austin leans against a crowbar jammed between the back of a set of cupboards and the wall while Kyle grabs the front of the cupboards and pulls. Nails groan like they're scraping on a chalkboard but the cupboard barely moves. Chris grabs the second crowbar and jams it a little down from Austin's, then leans into it. The effort is barely enough to separate the cupboard and walls another inch. With a renewed effort by Austin, the nails release their grasp on the wall and all three men collectively pant and collapse on the cupboard's frame.

"God damn who the hell built these?" Kyle pants. "I didn't think it'd be this much effort to tear out."

"Just be thankful these aren't stripped screws we're trying to yank out of the wall," Austin says. "Now *that* is hell. I hated tearing things out for construction jobs back in college. So many old houses had so much ass-backwards construction."

"I didn't know you used to work in construction," Kyle says. "Well that's hot. Still have any of the gear you wore?"

"Yes, we used to work in construction and no, you are not talking about this with me here," Chris says.

With Austin snickering, they easily pull the set of two cupboards forward as the last two nails holding it hit the floor. With nothing connecting it to the house, Chris knocks apart the loosened wood to carry the pieces outside.

He wishes his smart watch was still on his wrist or that his phone was in close enough proximity to check every time he walks in or out of the house. He removed his smart watch so it wasn't damaged in demolition and Austin had moved all of it - including their phones - into the living room. Chris hates him for it but he is less distracted with them out of reach. His wrist isn't used to the cold air freezing it or the scrapes from the wood rather than the silicon watch band. He thought some of the groans from nails was his phone vibrating, but he resists going to check it for fear of being scolded by Austin.

All that is left to tear out are a row of cupboards next to the sink, which they chose to tackle last because of the pipes. Neither of them picked up plumbing knowledge while working construction and Austin's dad advised them to be careful around the sink in case they knocked the pipes while removing the cupboards. Given how strong the other cupboards held onto the walls, they predict the ones around the sink will take as much effort and be more difficult to remove. They shut off the water in preparation.

Inside, Kyle leans against Austin, breathing hard but admiring their work. Austin's hand is wrapped around Kyle and holds him, dirtying Kyle's old tshirt. They see Chris re-enter but they enjoy the break a few seconds longer. Austin turns his head as Chris enters but doesn't shift away from Kyle. Chris stares at the two of them, wondering what being so open with affection in front of another felt like to have with someone.

"I'm not paying you two to sit around, let's go," Chris says.

"This is *my* house," Austin says.

"You're not paying us anything," Kyle says, then to Austin, says, "speaking of payment, you're also not paying me anything to help with this."

"I always buy dinner when we go out," Austin says.

"*Almost* always," Kyle says. "I guess living here rent-free will be payment for me helping you."

"Are you two moving in together?" Chris asks.

"Not right now," Austin says.

"But soon," Kyle adds quickly, breaking apart from Austin with a nudge.

Chris is jealous of the playfulness.

"But not right now," Austin says.

He watches Kyle grab the crowbar and prepare to tear out the next set of cupboards, getting distracted in the same way Chris does when he's with Taylor and gets lost in watching her. Small movements are distracting: the way she always holds a beer with her left hand, the shrug that follows any serious conversation right before she takes a sip of beer. Austin must see the same in Kyle: the way he always touches Austin's arm when he passes, always lying his head on Austin's shoulder when they're sitting together. Chris wakes himself from the trance as Austin kisses Kyle quickly on the cheek and grabs the front of the cupboards to pull. Chris joins them to help yank to the cupboard free.

He breaks it apart again and carries it outside while Austin and Kyle start the next cupboard. Chris tosses the broken cupboard into the dumpster, the clatter resounding in the echo chamber of the still winter air that sends the sound up the street and back to Chris. All of Austin's neighbors have their Christmas lights on and decorations line the street like Church Street, lit up as a guiding path for anyone looking for a little Christmas cheer to follow. Santas, snowmen, and reindeer weave between bushes and trees, and lights of rainbow, red, green, blue, and white give shape to bushes beneath piles of snow, creating dully glowing mounds.

Two foot tall thick snow drifts in front of Austin's driveway indicate the plow's recent trip up Austin's street, so Chris won't be able to leave without shoveling first. A light layer of snow that the plows never seem to be able to move coat the street. Snow blisters lazily across Austin's front yard as the north's tumbleweeds. Early-December is the beginning of snowy times and the bitter air drying Chris's lips makes sure to announce its arrival. The cold breaks through his layer of sweat enough to make a quick shiver run across him but it doesn't last. He reaches for his wrist and remembers he isn't wearing his watch. He groans and goes back inside, where the next cupboard sits waiting for him to take outside.

"You OK?" Austin asks when Chris wanders inside half dazed.

Kyle attempts to pry the last cupboard from the wall by himself but can't make it budge, though the wood splinters with each tug of the crowbar against it.

"Yeah, fine," Chris says with his usual cheery tone that Austin pretends he doesn't see through.

"He's cute, isn't he?" Austin says, looking at Kyle. "Remember when we thought we could do stuff like that by ourselves?"

The two lean against the barren wall, Austin with a smirk

that Chris hasn't seen him use with a guy since college. They watch Kyle put his full weight behind the crowbar as the tendons in his neck grow as he strains against the decades-old nails, making a hole in the wall where the crowbar pushes against while the cupboard doesn't move at all.

"I remember struggling with everything when we were new," Chris says.

"It's nice to not be the new guy, isn't it?" Austin says.

Chris rolls his eyes. "We're not talking about work today. Let's help him before he pulls something."

"You're probably right," Austins says, but he doesn't move immediately.

"Come on."

"He's just...everything," Austin says. "He gives it his all, even if he's doing it wrong. He always tries his damndest to make me happy. And he looks so cute doing it. He's..."

Austin loses words and Chris wants to check his pulse because he never loses words. Austin blinks rapidly and coughs once. Chris doesn't say anything.

Chris grabs the second crowbar and Austin grabs the front of the cupboards. With a few desperate tugs, they pry the last cupboard free from the wall. Austin's clumsy hands drop it on the floor, denting the linoleum and twisting the frame of the cupboard. A nail bounces across the floor, puttering into the wall. Austin sighs.

They slowly move the cupboard around the pipes, the cupboard heavier with the metal sink in it. Chris and Kyle break down the cupboard and pull apart the sink from the wood. They carry everything outside while Austin sweeps the dust and nails and sets up fans to blow the dust out of the windows. Kyle tosses the small pieces of wood into the dumpster while Chris launches a flat board over the dumpster's side. He collapses onto the porch steps while Kyle leans against the porch railings. Cold whips around them but both appreciate it. They're not sure if there is more sweat or dust on their skin.

"Thanks for helping," he says. "Austin's been pretty stressed about this kitchen "

"It's no big deal," Chris says. "He's helped me paint enough walls and build enough things for my apartment that I owe him a few new kitchens."

Kyle laughs once and then falls silent. Dust-flecked sweat covers his face and mirrors the sweat on Chris's own.

"How are you and Austin doing?" Chris asks.

Kyle starts worriedly. "We're doing great. Did he say something?"

A moment of worry crosses his face, which makes Chris smile. The past two months all he's been able to think about is Taylor: what she's doing at work, what she's doing not at work, why she only responds to his messages late at night on weekends when normal people have gone to bed, how each late weekend night she comes over she talks to him about him, how their bodies fit perfectly together while sleeping like she is the lock and he is the key, how she always grasps his hand like he's the only one who can save her from drowning; she fills a piece of the void in him in a way that he can't explain.

"No no no," Chris says, "I was just asking. Austin says everything is fine."

Tension vacates Kyle like a tsunami and the chilly air warms for a second as it escapes his body. Chris's laugh sends a new shock of worry onto Kyle's face.

"Everything is fine, I promise," he says. "I'm laughing because you are so worried and I love that you feel that deeply about my best friend. I haven't seen that before for him. Besides, Austin isn't the kind to have an issue and not tell you about it."

"I know but you're his best friend," Kyle says. "I assume he'll confide in you if there are problems. Damn, don't ask that again without prompting me first that everything is fine."

Chris laughs again.

"It makes me happy to see you so worried," Chris says. "You really do love him."

Kyle unconsciously stands a bit taller. "Of course I do. How could you not love Austin?"

Chris nods.

"After the assholes his last two relationships turned out to be, seeing how much you love him makes me happy for him."

"Thanks. I've had...quite a few more relationships than Austin. It's obvious that all of them were the issue, not me at all."

"Of course."

They laugh together out loud like they're two friends at a comedy. The ease with which Kyle made him laugh matches the ease at which Austin, Lydia, and Harris can make him laugh. That is a first with Kyle.

"But yeah, something about Austin changed my thinking and I was suddenly ready for only him. I don't know what clicked. One night we were chatting on the couch after I ranted for an hour about everything in life and laid all of my shit out on him, which I felt awful doing. He just leaned forward and kissed me and said that we'd get through it all together. I expected him to run away after I vented so much, not show me kindness like that. It's not every day you find someone like him. I don't know. He just is *it*. Like he fills this void that I don't know how to explain. It's difficult to explain."

Chris shakes his head as he stares at a snowman decoration across the street, a quarter buried by snow across the street with its black-mittened hand coated in a light layer of white. In an hour, the sun would be set and the street would turn into a lighted runway with the decorations reflecting off the glittering snow. He wishes he had a distraction from thinking about what it was like to have Taylor fill the void but not want to date him, to say she cares but not understand how much he needs more from her than that. Seeing someone every other weekend and showing them love like nobody else has only makes her fill that void more. When she leaves and doesn't text him, he somehow barely manages to swallow the loneliness. She's made him care. Too much.

"Everything you said about Austin is spot on," Chris says. "That's how he was when we were roommates in college, too. His exes never appreciated that part of him. I'm glad you do."

He reaches for his smartwatch but grabs only his wrist. He wonders if Taylor messaged him but he knows there won't be a slew of messages waiting to greet him; there never is. It's the weekend but it's not late enough, not dark enough for Taylor to message him. She'll ask how he is and he'll say come over. She'll say she has stuff to do, he'll say come over anyway. She'll push against coming, he'll insist. She'll give in. Chris will fall for her a little more.

"Thanks," Kyle says as he picks at the dirt and cobwebs that cling to his hands from the cupboards, a slight smile crossing his face.

"He'll ask you to move in soon," Chris says, which makes Kyle perk up. "He's ready. He's just incredibly cautious, to a fault."

Kyle's smile lights up the street brighter than if all the lights were on at once. Chris stands to go inside, though the cold winter air still barely has an impact on him.

"Thanks," Kyle says again as Chris reaches for the door handle.

Chris waves a hand over his shoulder and goes inside, though he quickly wishes he had stayed outside talking to Kyle. Austin has a spade in his hands and is leaning on it to peel up the linoleum floor while the crowbar is stuck under another part of the floor, peeling that up as well. Kyle stands awestruck behind Chris when he sees the corner of the floor Austin has already successfully torn up and the old yet still strong exposed floorboards.

"What the hell is this?" Kyle says. "Us tearing up the floor was not part of the plan."

"Plans change!" Austin says and he pulls up more of the floor, walking across the kitchen while he peels up linoleum like a bandaid. "I'll save a little doing this myself."

Kyle stutters and Chris puts a hand on his shoulder, pulling him back slightly to step forward himself.

"What do you need help with?"

"We need to pull up the sub flooring next and this needs to go in the dumpster," Austin says.

"The seam binders going into the living room also need to come up before you rip too much of the floor out," Chris says. "Kyle, carry the stuff outside."

Chris squeezes Kyle's shoulder as Kyle looks helplessly at the job Austin has already started. He looks ready to cry but Chris tells him to breathe as he starts pulling up the seam binders. Kyle moves slowly through the kitchen to the pile of floor pieces ready to go outside.

With the crowbar in use, Chris grabs a hammer from the floor.

"How are you and Taylor?" Austin asks without stopping his linoleum peeling.

"We're fine," Chris lies.

"Have you seen her recently?"

"Yeah, every weekend," Chris says. "We'll probably see each other tonight." Lying to his best friend came easier than expected, but the guilt came twice as heavy as he expected.

Austin rips the last of the floor up but leaves it crumpled for Kyle to drag outside.

"Uh huh. And when do I get to meet her?"

"It's not the right time," Chris says.

"Seems like it's never the right time."

"I don't know what you mean by that." Chris twirls the hammer in his hands and watches it to avoid looking at Austin.

"It's been months of late Saturday night hookups with her," Austin says. "I don't want to see you get hurt."

"She likes me and I like her," Chris says. "There's nothing to get hurt about. We're essentially dating."

"Are you, though?"

Austin watches dubiously as Chris rounds the kitchen wall. He doesn't say anything else because he's a good best friend who knows how to push but not push too much. He notices Chris grab his wrist where his watch usually sits.

Chris faces the living room and the tiny strip bridging the kitchen floor with the living room hardwood floor. Austin has no idea what he's talking about. Taylor fills the void but Chris can't say where that void is or why it needs to be filled, just that Taylor fills it.

As he kneels, his eyes sweep across the living room and pass over a few picture frames Austin has hanging on the walls and sitting on end tables. Some of the pictures are faded and grainy, taken on an old phone camera a decade ago during college, depicting Harris, Austin, and Chris in a dorm or graduating or one scandalous photo of them at a party. Mixed with these are pictures of Austin and Kyle dressed in suits at a party, at the top of a mountain in ski gear, standing at the top of a waterfall (Chris remembers taking that one, and neither of them had jumped), and a final picture of Austin and Kyle on Church Street during a Pride Festival.

He admires the photos for a second, wondering when they went up and how distracted he must have been that he hadn't seen them sooner. He kneels down and starts removing the seam binding.

~

IT'S after 11 at night when the door to Chris's apartment opens. The text conversation could have been copy and pasted from the previous Saturday night:

TAYLOR: How are you?
    Chris: I'm fine. Long day at Austin's. You should come over.
    Taylor: I have the cat to worry about.
    Chris: Put food in the bowl, refill the water, and come over.
    Taylor: I have to be here in the morning.
    Chris: Leave here early enough. Come spend the night.
    Taylor: I can come for one drink.
    Chris: One drink, deal.

HE COULD WRITE the texts like a book he's memorized. He could also predict the night better than any fortune teller ever could. It's never just one drink; it's always a long conversation about life and jobs and dreams that roll into a second and sometimes a third drink, then spending the night. Chris knows when she plans to spend the night because she always pulls around the back of the building rather than park on the street. He never tells her that he knows what she'll do; instead he lets her tell him she's decided to stay after drinking too much or that she's feeling particularly lonely. She'd never understand how lonely he feels when she doesn't message him back. That's a difficult feeling to convey when she only messages him past 10pm on Saturdays and ignores him every other day of the week.

When Chris sends the last text lying about only one drink, he looks around his apartment to wait. Keith lays on the couch, no longer granting Chris the peace of having it to himself. Chris gives Keith credit for doing such while Chris was recovering, but as soon as Chris was back to his normal self, Keith resumed his place on the couch, stretching out so Chris had to use the chair and prop his feet on the coffee table.

His apartment is already clean, a task he's taken to completing Saturday morning in anticipation of Taylor coming over, as she does every Saturday night. Well, most Saturdays. Sometimes Taylor waits two or three weeks before texting Chris back at all, but he tries every weekend. Every Saturday morning, he makes sure there are a half dozen beers in his fridge. Then he washes the bed and uses his mother's training to tuck the sheets in tightly and lay the comforter so an equal amount hangs over each side. He sets the pillows vertically and arranges the throw pillows just so, a magazine picture that would make Austin proud. He sterilizes the bathroom and by lunchtime has nothing else to do.

He usually takes Keith for a walk, runs to the supermarket, plays around aimlessly on the internet, sometimes goes to Austin, and after dinner he takes a short drive around Burlington, wondering which house is Taylor's and hoping the time would be 11pm when he gets home. At every vibration of his smartwatch he jumps, even though it is never late enough for Taylor to text him back.

When a car grumbles in the driveway around 11pm through the snow around the back of the building, and then cold air blows in as his door opens, he smiles and forgets about the agonizing wait for her. He jumps off the couch and hugs her as she takes off her coat.

"Hey, thanks for coming over," he says, same as always.

"Thanks for having me over," she says, same as always.

Predictability defines their visits, eliminating room for anything to change, so visit after visit has the same beats, the same words, the same progression of the night. Taylor asks about the same things every night, which nobody else asks about: why he is or isn't ready to move, what his dreams are, how much he misses his family, how much he loves the people here that are his family now; simple things that nobody but Taylor think to ask about. Then she'll ask to cuddle in his bed: they'll strip, fit together like a key in a locked door, have effortless sex, and then he'll stay holding her the whole night and wake up with his arms still around her and her hand clutching his arm to save her from sinking. He won't ask why she's drowning and she won't ask him to admit that he's fallen in love with her. He won't ever feel like he has to shower after being with her. Then he'll fall in love with her more.

He releases her from his hug, which he holds slightly longer than he would with anyone else, and she walks to his couch while he grabs two beers from the fridge, not needing to ask Taylor if she wants one because he knows she does. He opens both and sets hers on a coaster on the coffee table as she nestles onto the couch under the overly large blanket. Keith welcomes her to the couch by shifting so she has room to sit and Chris glares angrily at him but Keith smiles in return. Chris lifts part of the blanket that falls to the floor onto the couch and helps tuck her feet under it because she can't get comfortable unless her feet are covered. When he's near her, she doesn't brush his arm like Kyle does Austin. He doesn't let his disappointment show.

"How have you been?" he asks as he settles into the chair with a sip of his beer. That always helps hide the disappointment.

Chris predicts every movement as Taylor shrugs and sips her

beer. He prepares for the short, vague response. He prepares to be sucked into her mysteriousness.

"Life's been life," she says.

Chris doesn't wait for more, because he knows she won't say any more unless he asks precise questions.

"You smell good," she adds.

Chris smirks with a blush. After her last compliment on his cologne, he bought a few extra cans so he could always spray it when she's coming over.

"How's work been going?" he asks. "Did you think any more about going to nursing school?"

Taylor laugh-grunts.

"It's just not the right time."

"When is the right time?"

"Not now."

Chris taps his beer bottle.

"How's work? Is there much work on the lake during the winter?"

"If the lake freezes over too much the boat becomes stationary and we open it up to be a full restaurant. Work never slows down."

"Job security," Chris offers.

"Sure."

Taylor swigs a portion of her beer that takes her past the few sips Chris has taken.

"Do you enjoy your job?"

"I do," Taylor says. "Guests suck sometimes."

"Would you love nursing more?"

Taylor drinks her beer. Tonight's goes down faster than normal.

"You ask a lot of questions."

"Sorry about that," Chris says. "I'm just curious."

Taylor shrugs again. She has nothing else to add to the conversation.

"How is your job?" she asks.

"It's going great," he says.

Then he's off. A simple refocus onto Chris's life and he's diving into work issues and the unhappiness that blossoms a little more each day he has to work for Devon's team, the new tasks he's given and increased responsibility despite the lateral move to her team. He continually praises his coworkers and degrades his own work as a mask to hide how talented he is so people leave him alone. Devon takes none of his bullshit and he hates her for that. Her face is rigid whenever she speaks to him, her preparation to deal with his attitude. Chris loses each encounter with her, though he still refuses to let her win so easily. Devon then disappears and he does all the extra work he's assigned.

He predicted Taylor's immediate change in conversation from herself to him. It occurs every time she comes over, the same predictable storyline: small talk for two minutes, then she asks about his life and pushes him to divulge small details so he keeps talking and she doesn't have to; avoiding talking about your life helps to avoid confronting the things in it that you're unhappy with. After the first few nights, he recognized her pattern and now doesn't wait for her detail-specific prompts. He saves her from having to ask, removing the embarrassment from her of finding any reason to not talk about herself. Her evasiness intrigues him and makes him fall for her more, though he can't explain why. The mystery wrangles him as tightly as the few things he does know about her.

Taylor watches his soliloquy in silence. She doesn't interrupt or give a head nod to say 'I'm listening' or even offer a 'How dare she' or a 'That sucks.' She sits as a statue, motionless except to finish her beer, which she slows down on. Her eyes never leave him while his lands everywhere except her. Each glaze of his eyes passing over her pulls him deeper down the infatuation spiral while she remains at the surface, watching him fall without offering a hand.

"Why do you not want a promotion?" she asks.

Austin asked him that every time he declined a promotion over the past two years. He never lied to Austin: promotions and advancement are for adults, for people out of their 20s, for aging people who have let go of their youth and are ready to no longer have fun. Austin always asks how much everything Chris is so desperately holding onto is worth. Chris's response is always more than Austin can understand. Austin never accepts that as a response.

Responding to Taylor is different than Austin. She has never scolded him or told him his choice is wrong or used accusatory language that he's the problem. She always calmly asks why and then sips her beer. There is no aggression behind her question, not a hint of judgment or belittlement. He knows Austin doesn't intend to sound like all of those things tied in a bomb he drops on Chris every time he asks a question, but when they're at work, Austin unconsciously takes on that persona, more like a concerned father fixated only on money and power than a best friend sincerely asking about Chris's happiness. Taylor fills that void instead. His eyes pass over her infinity necklace.

So Chris tells her the truth, when he can't bring himself to tell his best friend.

"What if I lose everything I have in my life now and I can't get it back? What if once I get the promotion, the pay bump, the power, the title, everything, what if I get arrogant or start wanting more? I don't want to stop being able to play cards with everyone at Austin's and I don't want to move into some rich house and start acting better than everyone. I don't want to lose my life here, the family I've made from Church Street friends. I don't want to lose the ability to fuck off if I want to or leave for a weekend and not care. I don't want to have to worry about work at night. I don't want to be forced to grow up."

He searches the walls for words but everything clumps together in a tight, tiny circle.

"Why are you afraid of all that?" Taylor asks.

"I don't know," Chris says.

His head falls against the back of the chair, his eyes landing on the smoke detector on the ceiling. Warmth covers his body though his apartment is chilly. His body aches to climb onto the couch and cuddle with Taylor, because feeling like she's his key to his locked door while holding her makes grappling with why he can tell her everything but Austin only half truths less guilt-ridden.

When he looks at the couch, Taylor doesn't move. She doesn't break her gaze off him, though her beer is empty and her finger taps the bottle quietly. He waits for her to ask him to join her on the couch, to shift forward and lay down to indicate that he can join. Instead, she raises a hand and scratches Keith's ear. The dog lets out a large sigh that makes all the emotions raging in Chris's throat scream.

"I think you'd do wonderful in an admin role," Taylor says.

Chris sits a little straighter.

"Really?"

Taylor nods, shrugs, sips her beer. Chris watches each move-ment and hopes for something more but she settles into the couch and Keith digs his head further into her lap and the blanket draped over her, which covers her feet. Chris fumes at his dog's luck. Chris wonders if he should get her another beer but he doesn't want to disrupt their conversation in fear of her leaving before he's had time to hold her and feel how tightly she holds him back to save herself from drowning.

"You live across town, right?" Chris asks.

Taylor nods in the slightest way that if Chris hadn't been staring directly at her he wouldn't have noticed.

"Can I come over to your place sometime?"

Taylors immediate vigorous head shake creates an earthquake. She stops quickly but the earth still vibrates with the ferocity of her 'no.' Tension fills the air for the first time since meeting her, freezing Chris. His next words linger like a boulder about to crush an unsuspecting traveler below.

"Wher is-"

"Let's go lay down," Taylor interrupts.

Chris doesn't protest. He follows her into the bedroom and they crawl in their underwear into bed. Taylor doesn't make any sexual move, nor does she say anything else. She rolls onto her side and Chris pulls himself tight against her back, one arm under the pillows and the other wrapped over her. Taylor grabs his outstretched arm beneath the pillows with one hand and simultaneously finds her other hand in his arm wrapped over her. No space exists between them as she adjusts and pulls him closer, wiggling and shifting in the right ways to make herself as small as possible while still pressing against every part of him. She squirms for a few minutes, as if something isn't right where she is until finally she stops moving with an exhale that carries a lifetime of secrets. Their legs are tightly wound so that Chris isn't sure which legs are his, where his chest starts and Taylor's back begins, where his neck is and how her head is still her own, or who is holding whose hand tightest. Sometimes both people need to be rescued from drowning.

She still tries pulling him closer, as if no matter how hard she tries, she never feels that he is close enough. She doesn't hurt him, but she holds on as if every man she's reached for has been covered in slippery oil and hasn't bothered to holding her back, as if every man she's reached for has let her sink further until the ocean's weight crushes her and any chance of rescue from drowning vanishes. The tightness of her embrace reveals how her heart has been shattered by every man that's held it. Her death grip on his hand reveals that she won't recover from even one more shattering. Being the savior she needs in times like these are why he falls for her so hard. How can you not fall in love with someone who needs you and trusts you so deeply, even if they don't say it?

Chris kisses the back of her neck and digs his face deep into the back of it. A faint scent of peach lingers like dead petals refusing to fall. Some nights they don't have sex, don't think of the other in a sexual way; some nights they both just need someone to hold them so they don't drown. In the morning, he'll rub her back gently so she can exhale the weight she carries but tells no one about. Sometimes the void is too infinite.

7

HOLIDAY PARTY BLUES

The Bank's holiday party rivals the Bank's summer bash's extravagance. Hosted at the Rennigan just south of Burlington, the ballroom is decorated with lighted garland streaming from the vaulted ceiling to pillars perched between windows that lead to a patio overlooking Lake Champlain. Dozens of tables draped in red and green tablecloths sit beneath mounds of desserts, appetizers, and empty alcohol glasses, some stained with lipstick and others stained with half-melted ice cubes. Servers in black and white and Santa hats joke with the Bank employees as they clear empty plates and glasses.

Chris chases Harris through the crowd as the latter pinballs between female coworkers faster than Chris can follow. Part of Chris's slowness is his phone in his hand, which hasn't lit up since Harris called him an hour ago when they met up at the party. Most of the single women are too young for Harris, but men like Harris don't care. Chris shakes his head and declines one woman's advancement after Harris leaves her. Chris stops at one of the bars for his one beer of the evening before chasing Harris the rest of the way through the crowd, losing him once but finding him quickly because of a woman's fake laugh echoing above his coworker's heads.

The packed room is a reminder of the hundreds of people the Bank employs. Chris doubts any of the higher ups are here; some things are for show, not for the bosses to galavant with the lower employees. Many people are already a few drinks in or half asleep in a food coma, smothered by the endless plates the servers carry: scents of chocolate followed by steamed mushrooms followed by shrimp douse Chris as he chases Harris rebounding between women.

"What is the point of this?" Chris asks.

"Before we're tied down in marriage, we have to have our fun," Harris says. "A 20s buffet, if you will. There are plenty of single women here that would love to go home with you. You're quite the talk of the office." He nudged Chris so hard it winds him.

"Harris, I'm-"

"Whatever her name is, sure, whatever, but have you met... Carol?" He forces his way between two groups of people and emerges at the side of a young clerk from the first floor working her way through college. "You are beauty incarnate in that dress."

Chris doesn't follow Harris through the crowd. He takes his beer to the nearest high table and leans on it, sipping enough of it to need another shortly but he won't repeat a mistake. The party started an hour ago and is at peak capacity. With the patio doors closed to keep out the chilly December air, the crowd pushes together and makes navigating the space a challenge. Chris shudders at the thoughts of all the germs that were scraped onto his people as he struggled through the crowd.

Chris's table is against one of the glass patio doors, which are locked tight and draped in white sheers concealing twinkling fairy lights to mimic glistening falling snow. He sets his phone on the table in front of him, close enough to his hand so he can stretch out his pinky from his beer and reach the device. A red tablecloth drapes onto the floor like a floor length gown twisting around Chris's feet.

"I think this is the most I've ever seen you get dressed up," Kelly says

Chris jumps, tearing his eyes away from the black phone screen.

"You never wear a bow tie, unless you're hiding it beneath the sweaters and polos you constantly wear," she says.

"I'm, uh, we're all wearing them," he mumbles. "I mean, the others, Austin-"

"I'm not judging you," Kelly says with the kindest smile Chris has seen all night.

She sets her own beer on the small table and leans on it, positioning herself so neither of their backs are to the party. Her pantsuit clings to her and elevates her demeanor to a CEO. She emanates power like a generator does electricity. Chris stares in awe at how naturally she holds the illusion, though he suspects that one day it won't be an illusion. Few at the Bank impress him as much as she has, and if he's noticing, others are, too.

"Did you not come with anyone?" Chris asks, hopeful to not be the only single at the party.

"My boyfriend is around somewhere," Kelly says. "He saw a friend and ran off to say hello. I saw you and decided to escape a long conversation with friends of his that I don't know and don't want to know."

Chris forces a chuckle to coat his disappointment and sips his beer.

"Who are you waiting for?" Kelly asks.

"What?"

"Who are you supposed to match with that bow tie?"

"Oh," Chris says. He checks his phone. "Austin and Harris

are supposed to wear them, though Harris came dressed like he's going to a dance club. I haven't seen Austin yet."

"Ah, I know who Harris is," Kelly groans.

"I'm sorry," Chris says.

"You mean us women don't love when a full-of-himself man tries groping us and asking for a threeway?" Kelly says.

"He's pretty unbearable sometimes."

"All of the time," Kelly corrects. "I don't know Austin, though."

"I'm sure you'll know him soon enough," Chris says. "He makes friends with everyone. He's aiming for the 4th floor one day."

"Ah, so I definitely want to get on his good side," Kelly says with a smirk. "I'm sure you could be there one day, too, if you wanted to."

"Maybe," Chris says. "What is that worth?"

The two stare around the crowded room, though Kelly peaks at Chris periodically, waiting for him to say something. Chris continually glances down at his phone even though it hasn't made one sound or lit up since arriving. He also reaches for his watch despite it mirroring his phone.

Chris searches the crowd for a distraction, but the faces blur together. Paying attention to anything except for his phone is impossible when nobody here can ask about the right thing or capture him with their eyes or hold him like he's the only thing saving them from drowning. How could she go so many weeks without even a 'hello' when for him a minute without a message is a black hole that tears him apart? The void between their last goodbye and when she'll say hello feels infinite when life moves forward without her caring. The crowd's chatter is so loud that the gentle but quiet drum beat of whatever song is playing is non-existent, but the crowd can't drown out the constant phone ding he hears but is never from his phone.

"You two look depressing standing here and not talking to each other," Devon says.

A wine glass is nestled in her fingers, the contents dangerously close to slopping over the side. Kelly instantly stands a little straighter and the grip on her beer tightens. Chris notices her eyes dart from their classless drinks and to the fancy glass in Devon's hand. He shakes his head and swigs his beer.

"How long have you two been here?" Devon asks. "Lucas and I just arrived from the pre-party."

"How was that?" Chris asks as two beads of wine escape the glass and streak Devon's hand.

"Oh, you know..." Devon says.

Had Chris taken the promotion he was offered, he would have gone to pre-parties and Devon would be at the corner table at this party. Regret lightly tickles his arm but he shakes it off easily like pollen from a dandelion.

"You'll have to let us know if this party is any better," Chris says. "We haven't found much enjoyment from it."

"Well not stuck in a corner you won't," Devon says. "Where's your boyfriend, Kelly? I thought he was coming with you."

"He's talking to friends," Kelly says with a nonchalant hand wave.

"I didn't know he had such an investment in friends here," Devon says. "Did he used to work for us?"

"No, he's just a social butterfly."

"What about that girlfriend of yours you keep alluding to, Chris?" Devon asks.

Chris stutters and looks to Kelly for support, though she looks confused at the mention of Chris being in a relationship. He checks his phone as a distraction and in case he missed it dinging while Devon was talking, but there are no notifications.

"She's home visiting family," Chris lies.

Making excuses for Taylor is his primary language at this point.

"You didn't go with her?" Devon asks.

There's no malice in her voice but it impales Chris with spikes that threaten to break his resolve to not show how upset he is at Taylor for not responding to him for the past few weeks. Devon rarely asks about his personal life, though when she does she peels it back board by board until the life she is prying into is a pile of broken boards. He suspects she'll eventually turn this conversation into offering him a promotion *again*, which he'll not-so-politely turn down again. He wishes he could drink more than one beer, but he can't do that again at a work party.

"I had other stuff here to take care of," Chris says. "Plus I'll be making a trip home to New York City so I don't have the extra time nor money to make both trips."

"Well you know, if-"

"I'm Kelly," Kelly interrupts Devon to introduce herself to Devon's husband, who found their table.

"Nice to meet you," he says. "Lucas. Devon's told me a lot about both of you."

As Devon leans on the table for support from her empty wine glass, a server notes that she needs a refill. Chris had met Lucas before, but in Devon's shadow, he rarely speaks. Devon stares sadly at her near empty wine glass, unimpeded by Kelly's interruption but also forgetting what they were just talking about.

Chris and Devon used to race drink the other when they first joined the bank, determined to beat the other in quantity of empty glasses. Their tolerance to stay on their stools is infamous at one particular bar on Church Street that they both now avoid out of respect for their friend who owns it. Their drinking rivalry ended when Chris made that mistake two years ago at the holiday party. Everything has been so different between them since the company decided they should be promoted. Why did companies have to ruin peoples' lives? Why do businesses take away people's youth?

"Oh, Kelly's just wonderful," Devon says. "Best promotion I ever made. Our national growth has been fabulous since she started."

"I had good mentors," Kelly says, glancing at Chris.

Whatever else is said is lost on Chris. Someone in the crowd catches his attention, a woman with hair matching Taylor's and a necklace that briefly catches the light. His eyes follow her as she approaches but when she's in full view he sees that she lacks the same air of nonchalant confidence Taylor holds and lacks Taylor's cold eyes that are desperate for someone to love her. He checks his phone again.

"What a group we have at this table," Austin's voice booms from the crowd as the sea of suits and dresses splits to let him and Kyle through. "Lucas, how's life going?"

"Hey Austin, great suit," Lucas says.

Austin raises his arms and does a quick spin to show off his dark blue suit and brown shoes. His yellow bow tie matches Chris's and Kyle's, which contrasts with his black suit. Austin shines in the blue suit brighter than anyone else at the party. Kyle is thankful to blend into the background as Austin absorbs all the attention.

"You two look great," Chris says as Kyle takes a spot between him and Devon at the too-crowded tiny table. "I'm surprised you two aren't in matching blue suits."

Kyle rolls his eyes in a playful way. "You know how Austin is about making a statement at a party. We all know I'd overshadow him if I were in blue with him."

"But of course. We can't hurt Austin's ego now, can we?" Chris says with a laugh that Kyle matches.

Austin finishes his flaunting and joins the table that has no room for him to join. Kelly squeezes tightly next to Chris, pressing against his side. The suit makes Austin's already broad shoulders even wider. With everyone bumping the table, Chris keeps checking his watch, expecting it to have vibrated but there is no message waiting for him.

"Alright everyone, time for a shot," Austin says, waving over a waiter.

"Oh no, I don't think-" Kelly starts, but Chris interrupts her.

"Once Austin gets his mind hooked on an idea, it's hard to get him to change it. And when he says, 'everyone' he literally means *everyone*. He's not about to let you escape this."

Kelly looks awkward but nods, though only Chris sees it. Austin begins a speech after placing the seven-shot order. He relays an inspiring speech about how badass they are and how they all deserve more than just a shot but that is all the Bank is going to buy for them. At the end of his speech, the server returns with the shots, setting them down in front of everyone, though he struggles to get his arm between them. When the server sets down the last shot and leaves, Harris pops up in his place.

"I heard there were shots."

"Where the hell did you come from?" Kyle blurts, unaccustomed to Harris's ability to disappear for hours and reappear at your side halfway across a city when he was needed or when something he wanted was involved. Austin continues the toast as if Harris had been there the entire time.

"There are shots, so I'm here," Harris says quietly as Austin gives a final toast.

"So with less than two weeks until the new year and the past 12 months of working our asses off, here's a toast to a new year full of everything we want and a break from the endless russian roulette of capitalism. Cheers!"

They all raise their shots and throw them back as one,

though Kelly hesitates ever so slightly. They all slam their empty glasses on the table as Devon steps back to throw her head back.

"Why the hell is the alcohol so smooth tonight?"

A server brings her a full glass of wine. Devon waves goodbye to the group and steps away with Lucas, but suddenly hops back to the group and pulls Chris aside.

"I'm not sure why you're still resisting this promotion," she says while Chris groans. "No no no, don't do that." Her alcohol-coated breath matches Harris's. "You are the only one I trust with this international position. I need you to take it. Listen." She hands him her glass of wine and cups his face in her hands. "I get to build my own team. Kelly accepted the promotion and now I want you on my team, so be on my team. Got it? Promise me."

"I'm not against your team," Chris says. He shakes her hands off his face and hands back the wine.

"Not being against it isn't the same as being on my team." Devon laughs and shakes the liquid in her glass a little too much. "Embrace it. This is growing up."

She hobbles off with Lucas supporting her, though she veers away from him and into another group, sloshing wine onto them as Lucas chases her.

"She's quite something," Kelly says when Chris returns to the table.

Everyone is in conversation except him and Kelly, so he turns to her, wondering where her boyfriend is.

"You and her have known each other for quite some time, haven't you?" Kelly asks.

"Yeah, she went to school with us," Chris says. "She and Austin were always in competition while Harris and I trailed behind them."

"I assume Austin won their race to success?"

"What makes you think that?"

"Look at how successful he is, and so young," Kelly says. "HR Director, a house. He's doing the thing."

"There are other indicators of success than a big job and a house."

"Oh I know, but within the company, he seems to have really taken off. Devon has too, but only recently."

Chris lets the conversation die with a mouthful of beer. He is proud of Austin but he doesn't care for others to compare Austin to him. His parents did that enough.

"How long have you been dating Taylor?" Kelly asks.

Chris starts again. "Well it's been...a few months."

"How come you haven't mentioned her before today?"

"I just...haven't...thought about it," Chris stumbles. He isn't sure if Devon's question or the endless swirl of thoughts about Taylor fog his mind more. "It's been almost 5 months."

"Does she work at the Bank?"

"No, she works elsewhere."

Embodying Taylor's short answers and dodgy personality while lying for her is surprisingly easy.

Kelly shifts her beer between her hands.

"Will we get to meet her sometime soon? I like getting to know coworkers outside of work. It makes working with them easier when you know them as more than the Bank's robot."

"Possibly. We haven't really talked about it."

"It takes time, I know," Kelly says. "What's she like?"

"She's great at listening and knowing what to say," Chris says. "She can be a little closed off."

Kelly snickers. "Must be weird for a man to date someone who is closed off."

"It's definitely not the norm," he laughs.

"Your smile tells me you like that about her."

Chris spins his beer in his hands. "There's a lot I like about her."

Kelly shifts while considering what to say but her boyfriend appears from the crowd and interrupts the table to introduce himself. Kelly introduces everyone but her boyfriend breaks into a conversation over her. She quietly waits for him to finish.

Chris wonders how long Kelly and her boyfriend have been dating and why she is still with him. Their small encounters in the kitchenette at work displayed Kelly's intelligent beauty. Whoever this guy is sees none of that, though Chris has his own relationship issues to deal with before he obsesses over someone else's. He checks his watch again.

When his stories end, Kelly's boyfriend and Harris have become best friends for the night. They disappear into the crowd with Kelly following. She waves goodbye and Chris is confused about how he feels watching her leave. His beer is gone by the time she is.

Kyle knocks gently into Austin's side. "This is one of our songs."

"You say that every song is our song," Austin says, but Kyle wraps his arm with Austin's anyway and sways with the music.

Chris looks around the table, noticing they're the only three left.

"Where'd Harris go?"

"Who knows?" Austin says as if nothing mattered less. "I'm sure he'll pop up a few times before we leave, as he tends to do."

"Is there actual food here," Kyle says, "and not just a bunch of snacks? How are we supposed to get full with bite-sized everything?"

"I'm sure there's food somewhere," Austin says.

"Well I'm off to look for some," Kyle says as two men approach the table. "I'll grab you something, too." His hand slides down Austin's arm as he leaves.

"This isn't exactly the type of event you two usually attend," Chris says.

"We're looking for Harris and figured you might know where he is," one of them says.

"We never know where Harris is," Austin says. "Check all the bars."

"Did you both come alone?" the second asks.

Austin points in the direction Kyle went. "My boyfriend just walked away."

The two men ignore Austin and wait for Chris.

"You also didn't come with anyone?" Chris notes.

"Nah, Harris will hook us up with some girls," the first says. "As long as you two aren't going to take them first."

"We're both in relationships," Austin says.

"You got a girl?" the second says to Chris. He looks around. "Where is she?"

"I do, and *he* has a *boyfriend*." Chris stares at them with ferocity. "Harris isn't here, so you can move on. Your desperation reeks."

The second steps closer to Chris, though he is an inch shorter despite being bulkier. Chris towers over him with some extra height from his dress shoes. After a moment of staring down Chris, they both walk away.

"Those two are assholes," Chris says. "Why did we hang out with them in college?"

Austin shrugs, unphased. "We were probably similar to them in college. Harris rubbed off on all of us that way."

Chris shakes his head when a server scurries over with another beer.

"How do you not just yell at them when they ignore you? They're such assholes."

Austin shrugs again. "There comes a point where you become numb when enough people pretend that part of your life doesn't exist."

"Someone needs to knock their heads together. Like what the fuck?'

"People are bigoted assholes," Austin says. "If I got angry at every small exchange like that, I'd be exhausted by lunchtime."

"I'm sorry about that," Chris says. "It shouldn't be like that."

Austin pats his friend on the back. "I know, and thank you. But let's go find Lydia. I heard the cards are in one of the corners by the windows."

"What about Kyle?"

"He'll find his way. He has some weird way of always knowing how to find me. Sometimes I swear he implanted a tracker in me while I was sleeping."

A small round table large enough for eight to sit around is in the corner, with Lydia in one of the seats hoarding a respectable number of bills and coins. Chris notices that she's in the middle of those that have a lot and those that have nothing.

The table is clear of any empty glasses, and each time one drink is finished a server waiting in the shadows springs forward with an exact replacement. They discreetly collect their generous tips before hiding in the shadows again. Five people sit around a table as the current round finishes. When it does, a man stands up without a word, furiously grabs his drink so it spills slightly, and storms away. Lydia and Jeanne split the pot of money as someone else deals.

"What are you freaks doing here?" Lydia says without glancing back at Chris and Austin. "Your cologne could overpower a shithouse.'

"Great to see you, too, Lydia," Austin says. He pulls up two chairs, not daring to touch the empty four at the table. "How's the night going?"

"That fucker who just stormed away generously donated all of this to me, so pretty damn great," she says. "Did you two finally get bored of this circus?"

A new man takes one of the vacant chairs and throws some bills onto the table. Chris knows Lydia has her sights set on the $20s. Chris waves to Jeanne and Josiah, though neither waves back. Even waving to them is a gamble when there is money to be won. He is surprised Lydia said anything to them, though her position in the game is comfortable enough. He sits behind Lydia with Austin and a server brings them drinks, which only Austin accepts. Chris requests water.

Bidding begins when the last card is dealt. Chris and Austin sit in silence as the round occurs, watching each player ante or raise the others until the next card is flipped. Nobody looks at each other but each player knows every movement the others make. They eagerly watch what the others gamble and their hesitancy. Jeanne folds first and angrily throws her cards into the discard pile so they slide far across the table. Lydia remains emotionless. When the bid is raised after the next card, Lydia and the new player both fold.

"Fucking cards," she says, shoving what she bid farther away from her.

Kyle emerges from the crowd with two plates that contain food that none of the servers carry around. He hands one to Chris, who gladly accepts it.

"Who'd you have to sleep with to get this?" Austin jokes.

"One of my coworkers works here as a part-time gig on weekends. She gave me whatever I wanted."

Two of the poker players glare angrily at Kyle for speaking so loudly. He blushes and buries himself in the food.

"I don't like it here," he whispers to Austin.

"Just speak between rounds and don't talk to any of them directly while they're playing."

"So many rules," Kyle says. "I want to go dance when I'm done eating."

Austin nods and watches the next round. Kyle shoves food

into his mouth as the round carries on. Nobody watching the game finds it interesting, but being around this table prevents others from bothering you. The players each have pull within the Bank and their retribution scares away even their bosses.

The round extends longer than other rounds when the new player raises the bid with a $20. Chris pulls out his phone but it's still blank. He unlocks it and refreshes the messages app. Austin watches but Chris ignores him. He's used to Austin worrying, but nothing has ever actually been wrong.

"No Taylor tonight?" Lydia asks Chris when the round ends.

Another of the poker players leaves and two more sit down. Lydia takes note of each and smirks at the one.

"She's visiting home for the week," Chris says.

"Hopefully she's around for our Friendsmas," Lydia said. "I'd like to meet her."

Austin raises his eyebrows toward Chris, who waves off Lydia's comment as the next round begins and the table newbies ante up. The two new players are no match for Lydia, Jeanne, and the big billed man. Chris thinks his name is Chuck. He plays poker intermittently, but Lydia always likes it when he plays because he brings large bills. Lydia's eyes rarely grow so large, but with $20s and $50s sitting in front of Chuck, she can't help but drool a little. The round ends with Lydia pulling a small pile of bills toward her that doesn't change her actual winnings by much.

"Can we get up now?" Kyle asks.

Austin leans over to Chris. "We'll meet up with you later."

Kyle leads Austin through the crowd to nowhere in particular. Chris shifts his chair closer to Lydia so he's near her shoulder but remains quiet as the next round is silently dealt. Everyone within a 10 foot radius remains silent as well.

Years ago at the second work party where poker was played, someone drunkenly stumbled into the table, knocking the deck into the discard pile and ruining the hand. One of the men at the table stood up and threw his drunk coworker onto the floor, then Lydia and another poker player spilled their drinks on their coworker. Nobody has dared come near the poker table since.

"You always choose interesting places to hide," Lydia whispers during the round, though she doesn't take her eyes off the table.

Chris isn't sure the other players can hear her because he barely can. He hides out at the poker table enough to have perfected his whisper.

"This is my escape from everything."

"Hiding because everyone keeps asking you about Taylor," Lydia says, "or because Devon keeps asking you about accepting the promotion?"

Chris starts, "I don't appreciate-"

Lydia interrupts him. "Date her in secret, date her openly. Accept the promotion or don't. I don't give two fucks. But if you're going to hide from everyone because of everything, then you need to figure out what the hell in your life is worth sharing with people you love. Ha, take that you asshole, full house," she says loudly.

She throws her hand onto the table, scooping up the winnings into her unkempt pile. One of the players leaves the table.

"I love you, dude, but you gotta figure life out." She talks in a whisper even between hands, as do the other players.

"It's complicated."

"Bullshit always is," Lydia says, "but doing what makes you happy and being open with those who love you is what makes life bearable and worth it. Besides, Austin's worried about you, and I can only keep him at bay so long. Bring her around so he can meet her and then he'll leave me the hell alone about it."

"Don't you have a hand of poker to play?" Chris folds his arms.

"I can tell you to grow the fuck up and beat these assholes in poker at the same time," Lydia says.

"Shove it up your ass, Lydia," one of the fresh players says.

Lydia flips him off and raises the blinds. He folds.

The round takes a long time to finish. Chris checks his phone but there's still no message, so he sends Taylor a message asking what's up. He stands, sets a hand on Lydia's shoulder (to which she brushes him off and nods), and then heads through the crowd toward the door. He keeps his phone in hand the entire trip home, hoping it will buzz.

8

DROWNING FASTER

Christmas basks Church Street's cobblestone walkway in the glow of string lights strung back and forth between buildings. The lights reflect off the ice sculptures and complement the dozens of Christmas trees decorated with lights and ornaments from various merchants along the street. With snow coating the outdoor seating areas of all the restaurants along Church Street, the insides of each restaurant are packed tightly to leave little room for the servers to maneuver. In recent years, a speaker system was installed to play music the entire length of the street, filling the air with jingling bells and string arrangements.

Approaching midnight, the last patrons of the restaurants leave and many bar-goers head home as Chris is dropped off by his taxi a few blocks from his apartment. He enjoys walking down Church Street, surrounded by Christmas. The joy it brought heightened his elation from Taylor's response on his ride back home.

TAYLOR: I'll be over in a half hour.

Chris: How about I come over to your place tonight?

SHE DIDN'T RESPOND for a few minutes, though three bubbles repeatedly appeared to indicate her typing and erasing a response. Chris waited outside the Rennigan for 20 minutes as the bubbles came and went like bursts of warmth on a cold night that leaves you chillier than before they encompassed you. Not responding to her bubbles took all the restraint in him.

TAYLOR: I don't know if that's a good idea.

Chris: I don't have to stay long. I can just come over for a little bit.

Taylor: I don't know.

Chris: If you want me to leave after five minutes, I'll leave. I won't stay longer than you want me to.

Taylor: My house is on the other side of Burlington.

Chris: I don't mind the drive. You've made it before.

Taylor: It's already so late. Are you sure you're ok to drive?

Chris: Of course. I'm happy to drive to you any time.

Taylor: It's cold. Do you want to go outside when it's so cold?

Chris: I'm already outside. I'm leaving a work party.

Taylor: You can't spend the night. I have something in the morning.

Chris: That's fine. Can I come over?

TAYLOR LET the conversation hang without a response for another five minutes. Chris watched for the bubbles but the message thread was stagnant. When they finally appeared, they sent her address.

The chill disappears as exhilaration flows through his body

like piping hot coffee after a day of snowboarding that froze your face from the rush of wind against it. He contains his excitement by squeezing his hands in his pockets.

Driving through Taylor's quaint neighborhood a half hour later isn't where he thought she'd live. Small communities of newer housing make up the area east of Burlington, packing all of Burlington's housing expansion over the past two decades into these neighborhoods, with the Bank spurring most of that expansion. Chris rarely drives through the streets crowded with families and toys and lawns trimmed flush with sidewalks. He prefers to stay in the city or else drive directly into the mountains to ski and hike, avoiding suburbia entirely. Certain aspects of life were not for him yet. Only old people lived in suburbia.

He's thankful for his GPS as he navigates the unknown streets. He swears he's passed the same two story house three times. "Santa Stop Here" signs and flashing lights line the gutters of most houses, yet the GPS keeps him moving deeper into the very adult neighborhood. He turns down the radio and can suddenly see better, though the snow reflecting his lights back at him is enough to land a plane by. His heat is off because his excitement generates enough warmth, though his steering wheel is as frigid as he is when Taylor scurries from his apartment in the mornings. He squeezes the wheel tighter, willing it to never leave his hand.

"Your destination is 300 feet on your left," the robotic GPS says.

He steps on the brake too hard, jerking himself forward as his car's speed drops instantly. He cracks his window to let the winter air cool him down. Five months of only knowing Taylor on his couch, in his bed, and in the dark is about to end. It is a destination with walls he finally broke through. He's full of apprehension that knots his tongue as he approaches Taylor's impenetrable defense.

His GPS announces his arrival. He pulls into the driveway of a two story house with a large front porch that hosts a Christmas tree with a roof lined with large lights that look as if they hang there all year long. Shrubs lining the porch and the cement walkway to the stairs resemble bowling balls, perfectly rounded despite being cut months ago, and the stone beds surrounding the shrubs are visible at the base of the bushes, where the Christmas lights start and twirl upward, melting the snow around and on the bushes.

He cuts his car's engine and the headlights die, leaving Taylor's house in the glow of the Christmas lights. Only 1 light inside is visible from the driveway, in the farthest window from him. He breathes heavily in the dark as the lights inside his vehicle dim. He taps his phone against his hand, wondering if he should just go knock on the door or call Taylor or turn around and leave. Her protectiveness of her home for so long makes unbuckling and going inside a mountain to climb.

A second light flickers to life behind another window. Chris snaps from his trance and opens his door but his seatbelt jerks him back into the car. He falls back into the driver's seat and fumbles to unbuckle, then slams his car door hard and jumps at his own strength. He tucks his phone into his pocket, takes a deep breath, stomps up to the door, slips on ice he doesn't see, and struggles to stabilize himself but manages to not fall. He calms himself and tiptoes across the wooden porch. Taylor opens the door as he raises a fist to knock.

"Hi!" he shouts.

Taylor waves and barely whispers a 'hi' back, then moves aside for Chris to step inside. Her eyes dart at her neighbor's quiet, still houses. It's past 10pm but her neighbors could be watching.

Chris stares as he removes his shoes. The entryway white walls are bare. He hangs his coat in the closet and follows Taylor into the living room. The walls are as bland and white as the entryway, except for two pictures. A painting above the couch is some cheap canvas abstract of trees, most likely from some home goods store. A second hangs from the opposite wall above a bookshelf. As if it were possible to be more uninteresting than the first, this one depicts nothing but a mass of swirling colors, likely 'art' some small town hippie created and sold at a farmer's market. The rest of the room - and the house - is bland and white and black. He peers into the kitchen but Taylor turns off the hallway light, leaving the small lamp from the living room as the sole light, which doesn't reach far enough to illuminate the kitchen. Taylor settles sideways on the couch, a craft beer can on the end table. She pulls the blanket over her lap - making sure her toes are covered. Chris helps cover her toes with the blanket as he sits on the opposite end of the couch. He looks at the blanket but she doesn't make a movement to let him join her under it, so he pops up the footrest. He grabs a craft beer on the other end table that he assumes is for him.

"Thanks," he says.

She nods and sips her own. He examines the label but doesn't recognize the brand or flavor. Taylor silently watches him. Though she is quiet and keeps a lot to herself, she is always observant, though she never judges or questions. He wishes that sometimes she would.

"How was your day?"

"I cleaned and then did errands," Taylor says. "Last night was a late night at work."

"You overwork yourself sometimes," Chris says.

"I'd be bored if I only worked one job," Taylor says.

Chris gestures around the house. "Your place is gorgeous. How long have you been here?"

Taylor hesitates. "A few years."

Chris looks around but sees no pictures on the end tables

showing her friends, no pictures hanging on the wall showing her personality, no display of her life anywhere in the house. When he looks back at her, her eyes are on him, full of weariness from working 60 hour weeks, her pupils vacant from having so few people she can talk to. Water gathers at the edges of her eyes as she looks at him. That tenderness is his favorite part about her.

"You look tired." Taylor says distantly.

He sighs. "It's been a long day. The party was long."

"Sounds tiring. How'd it go?"

"It was more socialization than I wanted. I would have been happy with doing a boring Secret Santa and not having my night taken by the party. And I'm sore from helping my best friend remodel his house this week."

Why is saying random things so easy around her?

Taylor sips her beer but says nothing. Her toes bob beneath the blanket. It slips off one foot, so Chris reaches to pull it back over her. He thinks she smiles at that but her face is stoic when he focuses on her.

"Sometimes I miss college and working construction and being able to leave work without responsibilities. It's only seven years later but the Bank's made it feel like 20. Do you ever miss being in college?"

Taylor shrugs.

"Not a good experience?"

"College wasn't my strongest moment," Taylor says.

"It's not everyone's thing," Chris says. "My siblings hated it. Things were always simpler back then. If only we could stay 21 forever. No people forcing jobs on you, no drowning in bills and needing to work to survive. Fuck life sucks sometimes."

Taylor chuckles in agreement and raises her eyebrows for a moment.

"Sometimes I wonder if this is all worth it," Chris says.

"Should we keep overworking ourselves and should we keep paying these high living costs and should we keep going on all these dates and spending money on restaurants for overpriced beers?"

Taylor shrugs.

"I'm just frustrated at the whole...at everything! I mean, I was so free in college to do all kinds of things. We could stay up late if we wanted and we could spend our money on being happy rather than surviving and we could not go home and not feel guilty about it. Sometimes I...sorry, I'm rambling."

Taylor shakes her head, the water in her eyes reflecting in the strand of lights circling her Christmas tree, one of the few inside decorations other than some smaller trees scattered around the TV. Chris waits for her to speak but she says nothing, but he doesn't need her to. Nobody else would let him ramble about hating adult life, about wanting to return to a simpler time in life. Everyone else expects so much of him, demands him to do more than he wants. Taylor only asks if it's what he really wants.

"It sounds like you're tired from more than just construction and the party," Taylor says.

Chris shrugs and realizes he's tearing up, so he yawns and stretches on the couch. Taylor's feet are so close but her blanket is armor. He loves the way she has to have her feet covered but hates that he can't get under it with her until she's ready. Instead he stretches farther on the foot rest.

"Life is just a lot sometimes," he says.

Taylor stares in silence but raises her eyebrows in agreement. He notices every one of her little gestures, knows what an eyebrow raise or a shrug means. How could he not notice the way her cheek twitches when she's trying to hide a smile, the way she looks away and becomes distant whenever they talk about her, or when she opens her eyes wide and rubs them because she can't break eye contact with him otherwise?

"Sometimes I close my curtains and just sit in my dark apartment," Chris says.

"Why's that?"

"Something about the isolation. Shutting the world out. Sometimes it's nice to feel disconnected from the world, to feel the responsibility lifted, even just for a little bit. Things feel... normal...peaceful. I don't have to think about work or promises I made or piles of obligations. I can just...be me. And breathe."

His thumb rubs the edge of the beer can. Taylor focuses on him while he focuses on the Christmas tree lights. The can doesn't feel cold, doesn't have any weight to it. He's alone for a few seconds, nestled into the couch and breathing deeply, the darkness of the room his blanket. He smiles at his thoughts without fear of being judged or caught in imagining what he wishes were real. He doesn't have to vocalize the embarrassing mountain of promises he would make to Taylor if she dated him rather than keeping him as her secret. For a few seconds, he has what he loves.

"Sorry," he says, tearing now though he holds back the sobs. "Just kind of got lost.'

Taylor shakes her head in an 'it's fine' way and rotates her beer in her hands. She can nurse one all night, waiting to take the last sip until she's ready for bed. She's never drunk around him. He appreciates that.

"I get what you mean," Taylor says. "Escaping is nice."

Chris nods, his crying reduced to a light mist. Taylor's feet wriggle under the blanket and inch closer to him, though the armor isn't removed. Eventually she always lets him cuddle with her, though it's always on her terms. He's fine with that. She doesn't reveal her feelings by talking, but she lays everything bare by letting him cuddle her under her armor. When he's behind her and her hand reaches for him to save her from drowning, he knows that she needs him as much as he needs her.

Their sole date at *Mona's* is firm in his mind though the edges start the blur as it's buried beneath their nights together. Most of their time together is spent on his couch, usually after 10pm, talking about whatever came up until past when the bars would close, when she'd finally ask to cuddle and lead him to the bedroom. Half the time the night ended in sex, but half the time it ended with them wrapped in each other, nearly naked but neither wanting sex, just wanting to feel the other next to them, to feel that someone loved them enough to hold them. Chris waited for that moment every night as he wrapped his arms around Taylor in bed and felt like their bodies meld, like there was no other lock for him to be the key to. He told her that once, but he's not sure if she understood how perfect he felt holding her: the way her hand wrapped around his arm, the gentle movement of her body backwards farther into his betraying how much he saves her, too.

"I haven't seen you in, what, three or four weeks? What's been happening?" Chris asks. He despises the long void between when they say goodbye and hello, but the desperation in her grip at night must mean she loves him.

"Oh, the idiots and bureaucratic bullshit of things," Taylor says.

"Sounds like you've had as rough a time as I have," Chris says.

"You could say that, but different."

"You're never very clear when you tell me about things. Did you know that?" Chris says mockingly.

Taylor's cheeks flutter more than she probably would have liked, but Chris sees it all.

"I'm not sure what to complain about. Three of my idiot

coworkers got fired for stealing so now the rest of us are working nearly 60 hour weeks. The guests treat us like doormats. The neighbors' kids throw snowballs and run through the street pulling each other on sleds, careless of us driving."

"You live in a more family-oriented place than I thought you would."

"Do I not seem like the mother type?" Taylor says as she swigs a large portion of her beer.

Chris gives the laugh she seeks and raises his beer to her. "You seem like an amazing person to me. Regardless of what else you are."

Taylor's cheek twitches again but she doesn't react otherwise. Chris doesn't need another reaction.

"I can't control people around me. I just wish they weren't so stupid."

"If people around us weren't stupid, then what would there be for us to clean up after?"

Taylor inches her feet closer to Chris again. Her toes beneath the armor presses against his side.

"How's that gambling friend of yours?" Taylor asks.

Chris guffaws. "I actually think she'd prefer that name to her actual name. Lydia's great. I think she's trying to set something up for Valentine's Day next month to distract from her being single."

"She seems like quite a character. Is she still vulgar?"

"Yeah. I don't think anyone will ever tame that out of her. She had a boyfriend that she loved quite a bit, and he tried, but she's unbreakable. It's quite something. Even with her boss around, when it comes to gambling, she has the mouth of a sailor. She actually always has the mouth of a sailor."

Taylor snickers and Chris watches every movement, capturing her rare display of happiness so he can remember it when he doesn't see her for another month. She rarely responds, no matter how many times he tells her he wants to see her.

"I never really come out to this side of Burlington. I usually stay in the city or go north to the mountains. You do have a very nice house, by the way. I am slightly jealous."

"Benefit of family leaving you shit," Taylor says quickly, a tinge of fear in her eyes.

"Well we should hang out here more often. My apartment is just so...apartment-like."

"I prefer your apartment," Taylor says. "I love seeing Keith. And being somewhere other than home is nice. I'm still not over that you gave your dog a man's name."

"Ok, but know that I'm always ok with coming here, too, if it's easier on you."

Taylor nods. "Come here."

Chris perks up and shifts on the couch. Taylor never asks him to hold her or asks to cuddle. She always tells him to 'shift around' or 'come here.' When she's ready to cuddle, she bites her lower lip so it pulls in the side slightly. The move would be invisible to anyone not paying as close attention as Chris. He saw her lip quiver a few seconds ago and knew the ask was near.

"Let's go to the bedroom. I'm getting tired," she says.

Chris nods. So much for him not spending the night. Taylor downs the last bit of her beer and sets the empty can on the end table. She turns off the lamp, then leads Chris to the stairs. Passing the kitchen, Chris peers in and sees the outline of the counter and cupboards from the overhead light above the oven. Two decorated and tiny lit Christmas trees are on the counters, which are otherwise bare. The fridge has nothing on it. Had Taylor not been right in front of him, he would have assumed nobody lived here.

Upstairs mirrors downstairs. The hallways walls are bare and white and the two spare bedrooms are nearly as bland and black and white: one contains a desk with a laptop and a few bookshelves, while the other's door is closed. He uses the bathroom before they climb into bed. She nods and turns on the bedside lamp while Chris closes the bathroom door. A gray hand towel hangs next to the sink and a single shower towel hangs on the bar beneath the window. There aren't any decorations and he assumes the cupboards would be bare if he opened them.

Taylor is already under the comforter, her bra strap all that shows with her arms over the blanket. Chris strips as he takes in the room: a single picture is on the wall, one of her from what he assumes is her college years, and on the dresser is a small box to hold jewelry. The closet doors are closed and in the corner are two laundry baskets with lids.

He isn't repulsed by the thought of germs when crawling into her bed like he is with other women: sometimes women present a vibe of having let their sheets go a day too long without washing them, and if not, he's nervous to touch their feet or legs in case they haven't showered, even if he knows they're perfectly clean people. He can't stop himself from seeing everyone as germ-infested. When he looks at Taylor, he sees nothing but pure clean. A breath of relief rushes out as his germ anxiety disappears. He could hold her all night and not feel the need to shower. He knows Taylor will shower as soon as they're apart.

As he pulls the comforter over himself, Taylor slides backward until she presses against him. Chris throws an arm over her and her hand instantly wraps around his wrist so tightly her emotions drown him. She wriggles against his body until his larger frame fully protects her. He buries his face into the back of her head and takes in her minty-fragranced hair. She's frail as he holds her, like one move could shatter what she desperately is trying to keep together. He stretches an arm out beneath both of their heads under the pillow, and she stretches out her arm to hold his hand. Her fingers slide into place as easily as water forming to a container.

"Thank you for coming," she whispers, a slight crack in her voice.

He kisses her neck and settles behind her. No sex tonight. Tonight, she just needs saving. Being enough for her is all he needs.

"I'd come hold you any night you needed me to."

He thinks her body shudders from a sob but then she is still. He tenses his arm and pulls it closer to his chest, in turn tightening his embrace of her. She lets it all happen, and tightens her own grasp of his wrist. How do you tell someone you love them when you know it would just make them drown faster?

9

KITCHEN FLOOR NIGHTS

P eople don't break from the hundredth ten-ton mess being tossed carelessly onto their back; people break when someone throws a toothpick onto a mountain of items that should have broken them but somehow didn't manage to. People are truly broken when the weight of that toothpick stops them from standing.

Chris rubs his neck and considers Austin's advice to get a standing desk but quickly disregards it. He'd have to ask upper management, and he is in no mood to ask them for anything. He shifts his chair lower and raises his head higher but he still looks down at his monitors, his head hanging.

HR got involved when Devon tried forcing Chris onto her team. After two days of meetings and uncertainty, HR sided with Chris and let him stay in his position. In retaliation, Devon took a handful of their department with her to the 6th floor, leaving Chris to pick up their abandoned work as the Bank determined how many to replace. Debating that question has taken the Bank since they moved 5 months ago and showed little promise of being answered. Papers and folders shuffle between stacks of plastic trays and forms are pushed from space to space like going through twenty levels of approval made them any more important. He loathes having to remember which tray means what and which stack belongs to which company and which trays management thinks are most important. Bureaucracy has run rampant in the mess left behind when Devon demolished Chris's perfect work life. He tried labeling the trays but papers were shuffled so quickly and the forms he needed became so numerous that switching out Post-It's every day became cumbersome.

Devon brags in passing that her new department has digitized a third of the forms; Chris would never admit to her that that makes him regret turning down working for her, slightly. Then he's reminded to not regret it when he leaves at 4:30 every day and Devon is still in her office. Getting drunk on freedom every night and leaving work at work drowns the regret.

"We're not telling Austin that he's right about the desk, are we?" Harris asks.

He twists noodles onto a fork from a Chinese takeout box. His tie is forgotten in the bottom of his closet and too many of the top buttons of his shirt are undone where it's uncertain if he's supposed to be at work or crashing a wedding. Chris knows Harris's preference.

"Not until I can get one without asking management," Chris says.

Harris picked lunch up for both of them, but Chris's remains lukewarm and untouched on the desk between them. He'd reheat it later if he got hungry, though hunger rarely came at work anymore as the stack of clients he has to onboard grows taller than his cubicle wall. Management sees nothing wrong with adding more to that stack, his new supervisor reinforcing with a finger gun and a wink that Chris is the best in the department.

"We're going out tonight," Harris says with half a mouth full of noodles, "to that Irish place on the other side of town. I forgot the name."

"*O'Hanney's*," Chris says. "I haven't been to an Irish pub in far too long."

Taylor's neighborhood is a few blocks from there. He could always call her for a ride after and pretend that he drank too much, though like usual she probably won't answer. The chance of seeing her is all the more reason to go. He checks his phone; no notifications.

"I swear, Austin better have some drinks and loosen up tonight," Harris says. "Kyle is turning him into a 'one beer and I'm good' drinker and I won't accept that. Damn could he drink back in college."

"We could all drink more back in college," Chris says.

"Yeah, but Austin could keep up with me. *That* was a feat."

Chris nods in agreement and leans back in his chair, debating on eating the takeout before diving into four hours of work until he can go see Taylor - he means go to *O'Hanney's*. His stomach hasn't grumbled at work for months but he forces himself to eat. His one beer rule only applies to work functions, so maybe he will get drunk tonight. He'll be able to claim he needs to stumble home and instead call Taylor. Who cares about a hangover at work the next day? You only live through your 20s once.

"Is your girl coming out tonight?" Harris asks. "Are you two still fucking?"

"Come on, man, a little quieter," Chris says. "We're at *work*."

"Yeah yeah whatever. So are you?"

"We're still *dating*, yes."

Harris hogs more noodles into his mouth. If Chris hadn't lived with him through a year of college, he would have vomited at the pig of a man eating like he is starved from years of fasting.

He learned to ignore it long ago, as roommates do. Damn, it was so long ago.

"We are dating," Chris repeats.

"Sure, whatever you say. So she is coming? My fuck bud isn't coming for drinks. Last time I drank one too many and Harris did not satisfy her fully that night. I'll have to make sure I'm at least mildly coherent when we leave. She's all, 'Do you have to drink so much' and I'm like 'let a man drink, dammit'. You know, if I could fuck dudes I would because they'd complain less." He shivers and shoves his fork back into his takeout container like a fisherman does a spear in the sea. "I don't know how Austin does it."

"Well he likes dudes, that's how," Chris says.

"Like how could you want to fuck a dude over a woman? Anyway, is your bitch coming? I still haven't seen her and I gotta judge if she's got a body worth keeping or not."

He slurps a noddle tendril into his mouth, a droplet of sauce splashing onto Chris's desk, dangerously closer to a pile of papers. They're all clients that management said didn't need to be added to their system immediately but that Chris, 'Shouldn't take too long to process, either.' Chris stares at the drop of sauce on his desk and at Harris's ignorance.

"I've got to get back to work," Chris says.

Harris lifts his head, a noodle hanging from his mouth.

"What do you mean? We get a half hour for lunch."

"Yeah, I've got a lot to do, so get out," Chris says with more emphasis on the end than intended but his neck aches and his computer has beeped seven times in the 15 minutes. Chris's irritation has beeped far more times than that. He wishes his phone would beep once.

"Someone's balls are squeezed today, damn," Harris says. "I'll see you tonight at *O'Hanney's*."

He drops his fork into the takeout container, then grabs Chris's and leaves the office.

Chris sighs when Harris's footsteps disappear beneath the beeping, typing, and phone calls drowning the cubicles. He reaches for a tissue from the box hidden behind two stacks of folders, then slowly wipes up the sauce droplet. It's as big as a small droplet of water though carries the Chinese cuisine odor that never smells good unless he's actually eating it. He stares at the tissue and the small brown-red dot in its center, which crawls outward like a spiderweb. Stretching away from it are small spider legs of sauce, a brown-red snowflake on a white tissue. He crumples the tissue and tosses it in his trash.

His watch vibrates as his phone dings and he tilts his wrist immediately, ready for disappointment while lying to himself that he won't be. That second of excitement, of adrenaline falsifying his relationship with Taylor before demolishing him, has become his hourly drug whenever his phone dings. Some days he sends a message to someone just so that his phone will ding and he can pretend that it's Taylor until he sees another name on his smart watch. Each disappointment is accompanied by a longing for the process to repeat, because maybe, just maybe, it will be Taylor's name and maybe, just maybe, it'll mean that she wants to see him. Or maybe it'll mean that she cares about him, too. Who's going to save him from drowning?

"Go eat lunch," his new supervisor says from his cubicle door, two new folders in his hand.

Chris sits straight in his chair and grinds his teeth to stop himself from revealing the pain in his neck that sitting up straight brings.

"I'm fine," Chris says. "I'll get back to these."

"Chris-"

"I'm fine," Chris repeats.

He refused to let his tiredness or neck pain or serious need for a vacation show around management. They can't see him break. He's not ready to grow up yet.

His new supervisor sets the two folders on top of the others and hesitates before walking away. Chris counts to 10 after his new supervisor leaves in case he comes back. When he doesn't, Chris slumps in his chair and wishes the stacks were higher to hide him completely. He stares at the new piles on his desk. His watch vibrating electrifies him but it's a promotional email. He leans forward on his desk, sending a tinge of pain down his body.

~

A SHORT MAN expertly strums a guitar and taps his foot to fill O'Hanney's with a few dozen patrons chanting along drunkenly to an Irish pub song he wails out. As he switches songs, the entire pub sings along, filling the small establishment with a chant that sounds like 40 voices singing different things but everyone knows every word. Their sing-along grows louder than any club. While the crowd doesn't dance, it claps and stomps, exerting more energy than a room full of teenage club-goers.

As the song ends, a table of five raise their beers and clang them together, waving at the singer, who raises a grateful hand and takes a well earned swig from his own beer. Harris is the last at the table to stop drinking and slams his empty mug on the table. A waitress he knows too well nods as he raises his pointer finger in the air.

Kyle and Lydia point at someone across the bar. Lydia gives a disgusted look but continually peeks at the man, who repeatedly looks back at her, though neither would admit that they've looked at each other a dozen times in the past 5 minutes. Nor would either walk to the other to say anything, leaving their quiet glances their only exchange, despite Kyle's encouragement.

Austin's three-beer buzz keeps him warm as a late-January storm blusters across Burlington. A winter storm is nothing more than a challenge to a group of drunk 20-somethings; though to late-20-somethings, a winter storm is more of an obstacle. Throughout the night, they peek out the window more often than they used to, judging if they should leave yet and if the few inches are too much already. The answer is always one more beer, mostly at Harris's encouragement.

"You're looking more energetic than earlier," Harris says proudly as Chris finishes his third beer.

"Life doesn't suck as much once you leave work," Chris says, "and a few beers helps!"

Harris high fives him, though Chris's hand tingles afterward and he doesn't feel like he should stand too quickly but standing too quickly doesn't matter to someone in their 20s. After all, they're not old.

"Isn't that more than normal?" Austin asks as the waitress brings Harris's new beer. "Especially for the middle of the week."

"It's fine,' Chris says loudly.

Drinking more than one when he's not at a work party means a work mistake can't happen again. He thinks his watch vibrates but his hand is still tingling from Harris's too-hard high five. He checks his watch anyway because he can never be too certain that he didn't miss a message from Taylor. The empty notifications tray tells him to stop thinking about Taylor and have another beer, but how do you stop thinking about someone when they finally let you in after 6 months?

"Should I just assume you're not coming to work tomorrow?" Austin asks, only slightly condescending, though Chris blames the alcohol for dressing his question in such an ugly tone.

"I'll be in, I have too much to do, and it's only three beers," Chris says. "They think I can do the work of a hundred people and they're not replacing those people Devon took. Like what the fuck? Hey, you're a higher up in HR. Why aren't they hiring more people?"

"It's all incredibly complicated," Austin says quietly. "You're good at so much more than what you think you are."

Chris doesn't look over at him because that would mean he agrees. Not that he doesn't want Austin to be correct, but that means management is also correct, and he can't let them be correct. Instead, he spins his third mug of beer on the table as the waitress smacks Harris's hand away from her ass.

"Y'all need anything else?" she asks.

"We're good, thanks Caity," Austin says.

She smiles at Austin and leaves the table as Austin smacks Harris for reaching his hand toward Caity again.

"Why do you have to be a buzzkill?" Harris says angrily.

"Why do you have to be a predator?" Austin snaps back.

Harris laughs loudly though it is drowned beneath the singer's guitar and stomping and the crowd singing along to another traditional Irish pub song.

"You're fucking funny," Harris says, "and a buzz kill. Alright, time for shots!"

"Not me," Austin says. "I've had enough for tonight. I think most of us have."

"Bah," Harris says, "let everyone have some fun. Just because you have a stick up your ass doesn't mean the rest of us can't enjoy ourselves."

Kyle and Lydia don't hear any of the conversation as Kyle nudges her to talk to the guy she continues to check out. She nudges him back and finishes her whiskey over ice. A second is immediately placed next to her empty glass. She at most nurses two drinks when going out.

"Do you have every server everywhere waiting to serve you?" Austin says. "We're not even gambling tonight!"

"When you tip well, you're well taken care of," Lydia says, starting her second whiskey on the rocks.

She turns to Kyle and whispers with him more about the man at the bar, who trades seats with his friend so he can stare in her direction without turning around. Lydia fixes her sweater and boobs. It's a crew sweater, though she places her necklace so the pendant rests on her boobs.

"Shots!" Harris says.

He waves his friends away aggressively when nobody responds. He joins those at the bar and announces shots. A few of the patrons at the stools cheer and clap him on the back, while another three approach the bar when they notice Harris at it. Some pub reputations preceded their owners.

"How long is he going to be a regular at bars before he grows the hell up?" Austin says.

"You sound bitter," Chris says.

Austin leans back in his chair while Chris leans forward on the table and holds his head up. He doesn't remember the last time he drank three beers in two hours; Austin did well at monitoring him. The bar tilting back and forth reminds him why he hasn't. Austin stares longingly at Kyle with a smile that crack's Chris's shell, allowing his jealousy to show. Chris wonders if Taylor would ever stare at him that way. He knows the answer.

"I'm not bitter. I'm just tired of having to stop drunken idiots from touching people they shouldn't and being called a buzz kill for doing it," Austin says. "I swear, if you ever end up like him, I will make your life even more of a hell at work."

Chris twists his mug between his fingers and ignores Austin. How could he not understand how much Chris needs the release tonight of getting too drunk? Hell, even Austin complains at work occasionally; doesn't he need the release, too? He debates joining the 9 people surrounding Harris at the bar, all of whom hold shots and sing along to the end of the Irish song. When the song ends, they all raise their shots into the air - some too quickly so some of their alcohol splashes out - and then down their shots and call for another round. Harris cheers for another round the loudest. As each shot glass is slammed upside down on the bar and two of the participants keel over to catch their breath, Chris reconsiders joining them.

He brings up Taylor's text thread on his phone. The last messages cover the right side of his screen like blue bricks stacked on top of each other, disappearing without a break at the top of his phone. He rereads the messages as if he doesn't have each memorized. He scrolls up farther than he would admit before a message on the left breaks his stack.

"Speaking of people who are drunken idiots," Austin says.

Chris lowers his phone quickly and presses the screen against his leg under the table.

"Are you really going to pretend you weren't just scrolling through old messages and considering messaging her?" Austin asks.

"You could find some business of your own to mind," Chris says. The beers provide a bravery and insubordination he never has.

"I could, but I also won't let my best friend chase after someone who hasn't shown him the same commitment he's shown her. Hasn't shown him any commitment, really."

Chris sets his phone on the table but keeps a hand on it. "It's just not that easy."

"I've been there plenty of times," Austin says. "Gay men are not the easiest to get to commit to you. But I also learned my worth after the first few fucked me over. I just want you to learn yours."

"I know my worth," Chris says. "It's just a complicated situation."

"'Complicated' is a word to veil the reality of things we don't want to admit," Austin says. "If you knew your worth, you'd act like it. I just don't want to watch my best friend waste months of his life grasping for life in empty promises."

Chris removes his hand from the phone. "I need another drink."

"But do you?"

"Listen, just let me drink tonight. Everything is so-"

"So what?" Austin interrupts. "Hard? Fucked up? Sad? Lonely? What do you think drinking more is going to do other than make you think about her more and check your phone more like it isn't already your life support? You've already drank more than you have in years. Drinking more is not going to make her text you and isn't going to make her love you."

"Fuck you," Chris says.

He watches people swarm Harris like locusts at the cost of shot after shot. Even in college, Harris was what crowds gathered around, not Austin nor Chris. Two women he's certain Harris doesn't know approach him and touch him, one from each side. He immediately orders drinks and the two women flame his ego further. One grabs Harris's hand.

For the first time since college, Chris is jealous of Harris. He's jealous at the ease of which he forgets about work as if it's a piece of paper he can shred each night and tape together each morning. He's jealous of how easily Harris transitions from woman to woman without a thought of the one he left. Most of all, he's jealous of how women actually want to talk to him, even if it's just for free drinks and meaningless sex. He wonders what it's worth to them or to Harris, the endless nights of flirting and sex, the waking in the morning with someone you haven't felt a connection to since one rolled off the other the night before.

The beers' toll wears on Chris as Kyle and Lydia's loud whispers break through the pub's commotion like survivors emerging from a wreckage. The singer downs a shot and chats with a handful of people that are as regular at the pub as Harris is. Chris leans his head back against the wall and stares at the abundance of irish regalia hanging from the ceiling: various flags of sport teams, the Irish flag, random objects from the Island, and an upside down chair someone thought would be funny to nail to the ceiling two decades ago that nobody bothered to take down because it is hilarious. His head spins as the full effects of the beers demolish him and any resolve he has left.

Austin's voice brings him back, though he's not sure how much time has passed. Harris is back at their table with a strange woman; so much for his fuck buddy coming over later. Kyle's head leans on Austin's shoulder and Austin points lazily at various people around the bar, his other hand wrapped in Kyle's. Chris notices the vacant expression in Kyle's eyes and recognizes his polite nods as Austin explains who each is. Kyle's eyes watch Lydia at the bar talking to the man she made eye contact with all night. Chris looks down at his phone to avoid everyone else.

"I'm calling an Uber," Chris says.

"Yeah, we're ready to head out, too," Austin says, stopping mid-explanation to Kyle but Kyle doesn't mind.

Halfway through ordering an Uber, Chris checks for a missed message, just in case, but there are no unread messages. He taps his phone's screen hard - a mixture of disappointment and drunkenness - and announces that an Uber is two minutes away.

"Can we hop in with you?" Austin asks.

Chris nods but doesn't feel much like talking because of the alcohol and his anger at Austin's comment. His empty phone fuels his anger, an endless supply of oil continuously dumped on an old burning building.

"We're going to hang here," Harris says without caring who listened.

While the woman next to him struggles to hold herself upright, Harris has mastered that drunken skill. Austin doesn't say anything as he and Kyle leave the table but Chris pats his friend hard on the shoulder.

Austin stops at the bar while Chris and Kyle head outside to wait for the Uber. Snow isn't falling at the rapid pace the meteorologists threatened, but a solid coating covers everything. The pub's location in a residential location means plowing the street is secondary to making sure the heart of Burlington is well plowed. Two other establishments form a small triangle with O'Hanney's, and both are as busy as the pub. Chris notices the snow in the street and hopes whatever vehicle picks them up has snow tires.

"Isn't Austin just wonderful?" Kyle says cheerfully, bouncing slightly and swaying as snow quickly dots his hat.

"Just a peach," Chris says.

"Yeah, he's a peach," Kyle says warmly.

Alcohol wafts from Kyle's breath a few feet away, though Chris might be smelling the alcohol on his own breath.

"I just want to go home and snuggle into him and go to sleep," Kyle says. "He's so warm and it's so cold outside. Stupid snow."

He kicks the few inches of fresh snow playfully, though his aim is horrible while drunk and instead a few flakes from the top layer spray into the air. He giggles and his foot comes down hard. His gloved hands are in his coat pocket as he sways.

"Burlington is such a pretty place," he says. "I love the snow."

"It's a nice city," Chris says.

"I want to go home and snuggle with Austin," Kyle repeats.

"You've already said that."

"Oh. Well it's true."

Kyle's grin encompasses his entire face. Chris watches one of the restaurants across the street. The windows are small compared to the large picture windows of O'Hanney's that fully displays the singer and bar crawlers inside and the warmth from the Irish ale. Both parking lots are full and cars line the street with the ancient technique of parallel parking.

"I wish Austin would come out here," Kyle says. "I'm cold."

"He'll be here soon," Chris says.

He's thankful the alcohol fights away the cold. Chris widens his stance so he doesn't fall as the cascading snow dots his vision and the world tilts. He guesses it's been over an hour since his last drink but downing three so quickly after such a long period of avoiding more than one doesn't let the inebriation leave.

Car headlights pull his attention to the parking lot entrance and his phone beeps, but he doesn't look down. Beyond the parking lot entrance and across the street stands Taylor with a scarf wrapped around her neck and tucked into her coat, her hair sparkled with snow. She's waiting next to one of the parallel parked cars with her arms folded over her chest and clouds of visible air puffing from her mouth. She waves to someone Chris can't see.

Instinctively, Chris steps forward to join her, his heart beating so fiercely the world pulses around him. He slips in the parking lot but catches himself on the SUV that pulls up next to him. The driver rolls down the window.

"Are you Chris?" she asks.

"What?" he says.

"I'm the Uber for Chris," she says.

"I'm um, Chris?"

He doesn't look at the Uber driver. A man approaches Taylor. She unwraps her arms from each other and wraps them around him as he gives her a kiss, which she returns by falling into him, not a second of hesitation in her movements. One of his hands is on her neck, holding her near him. She pulls away from him laughing jovially and slaps him playfully on the arm, nodding toward the car. He opens her door and holds her hand as she gets in, then closes her door and carefully moves to the driver's side. He gets out a snow brush and works on the windshield, waving like a child to Taylor inside the car while he clears her window. He wears a jacket similar to hers, though he doesn't wear a scarf or gloves. He holds his shoulders back and wears dressy boots and his jeans fit him like a second skin. Though Chris can't make out any specific facial features, in his drunken state Chris thinks his head looks more perfect than normal, like it is rounder than an average head should be. Why did Taylor kiss this man? He doesn't know how she needs someone to hold her to save her from drowning. He doesn't know how to hold her properly.

Chris grabs the open window of the Uber to stay upright. His legs lose their strength but not because of the icy parking lot. A headache wallops him in an instant, which blurs his vision further. He feels his stomach churning and prepares to throw up but all he can do is cough. That man doesn't know how to hold Taylor right.

The alcohol must be playing tricks on him. He watches the man get back in the car, though it doesn't move for a minute. The street lights are spotlights illuminating the parked cars to make sure Chris sees everything about the navy blue Ford Explorer, which is a terrible choice of vehicle for Taylor to be in. She must be as drunk as he is, that's why she kissed that man and got into a car with him. She would never be with someone who doesn't know how to hold her. Their bodies can't fit together like a lock that's found its key.

Chris pulls out his phone but leaves one hand on the door to stay stabilized. He checks his messages but there are none. Immediately he pulls up Taylor's number and sends a message, adding to his stack of blue sent messages. He watches the text string, waiting to see dots showing Taylor typing. He anticipates the dots though the text messages remain stagnant. He sends another in 20 seconds in case she didn't receive the first, since that can happen, though he's never heard of it happening. Then he sends a third. No dots appear.

"You ok?" Austin says, appearing behind him.

Chris jumps and Austin catches him before he falls to the ground. His hand tightens around his phone, holding it for life. He pulls it close to his face to check for a reply but there's still nothing.

"This is why you shouldn't have so much to drink," Austin says. "We're not 20 anymore. I don't know how Harris bounces back but fuck if we can. Is this our Uber?"

"Are you Chris?" the driver asks.

Austin points. "He is. Come on, let's go."

"I'm so glad you're outside now," Kyle says next to Austin with one of his hands wrapped around Austin's arm. "I was getting cold without you here."

"Hell, I hate going out with all of you," Austin says. "I turn into Daddy Austin."

He helps Kyle into the back seat, who jokingly calls him Daddy Austin the entire ride home, then reaches for Chris but he's staring across the street as a blue Ford Explorer pulls out of a parking spot and drives off. Chris lifts his phone to his face in disbelief, the light too much for his eyes as snow melts on his face and runs down his cheeks in rivers.

"Ok, we're getting in the Uber now," Austin says, lowering Chris's hands and leading him to the Uber. "You get the front seat."

"Let's all go," Lydia says, storming out of the bar.

She climbs into the back, squishing Kyle between her and Austin.

"What happened to that hot man at the bar?" Kyle asks, innocently swaying.

"He thought he could just grab my boob so I pushed him off the stool, called him a pervert, and left. Fuck if a man is going to grab me as he pleases again. Drive."

The Uber driver nods with shared experience in her eyes. "Good for you."

The Uber pulls out of the parking lot in the opposite direction the blue Ford Explorer went. Chris whips his head around to check if he can see the Explorer on the road behind them, but he whacks his face on the now rolled up window.

"Sorry about that," Austin says. "We'll tip you good."

"You're fine, it happens all the time," the driver says. "Long night?"

Austin sighs. "It's going to be for these two."

The driver nods, with another shared experience in her eyes.

Chris spins the other way in his seat, looking over the center console through the back window, though Austin blocks his way with Kyle half asleep, leaning on Austin's shoulder. Lydia glares out the window.

"What are you looking for?" Austin asks.

"I'm uh..."

Austin waits but Chris says nothing. He swivels back to facing forward and unlocks his phone, checking the messages he sent to Taylor. There is still no reply nor dots indicating she's typing. Chris closes the app and reopens it in case it malfunctioned but there are no new messages when the app reloads. He checks his other apps to make sure they're working before going back to messages. He checks the settings but everything is activated.

He stares out the window as the Uber driver takes her time on the snowy roads. He's afraid if he grips his phone any tighter it'll break but he doesn't let up. He curses his inability to drive and his decision to drink tonight and Harris for encouraging him to drink so much. Was it worth it if he's unable to go talk to Taylor in person?

"What an awful night to go out," the driver says.

"The snow isn't as bad as the meteorologist predicted," Austin says.

"Snow's no bother to drive in," the driver says. "I'm from Burlington. I meant because it's a Tuesday."

Austin laughs for all four of them, though the last thing Chris wants is to laugh.

"Sometimes you need to let loose a little mid-week," he says.

The driver nods as if she understands this.

Memories of Taylor cross Chris's mind the rest of the way home like a film real on an endless loop: covering her feet at night, rubbing up and down her back with just his fingertips, pulling her closer the few nights she actually came over and feeling her loneliness in the way she held him. That man was a hallucination from the snow and Taylor wasn't really there tonight. When they get back to his apartment, he'll go inside and there will be a message from Taylor saying she was home all night. She'll ask him to come over because she needs him as much as he needs her.

Austin waves goodbye as Chris walks along the building to his apartment door. When he opens the door, Keith runs at him and his weight nearly knocks Chris over but he sobered up enough on the drive home. He reaches a hand down and pets Keith, then holds the door open for Keith to run down the steps. Chris follows him. He checks his phone now that he's home, excited to see the message from Taylor and the explanation that alcohol and snow are a bad combination, but his phone has no new messages. Keith bounds up the stairs with all the energy of a 20 year old while Chris begrudgingly follows with the energy of an almost 30 year old who realizes that he's no longer 20.

Chris drags his feet to his kitchen and leans on the counter as Keith wags his tail at Chris's side, a toy in his mouth; a rare sign of Keith's return to being an energy-filled dog. Chris swipes up repeatedly from Taylor's messages, waiting for a new message to appear with each swipe. He's not sure how many failed attempts it takes before his phone sends him a message telling him she doesn't love him, but he'll keep trying until that happens.

Or until a wail escapes him and his body loses all of its control and he collapses on his kitchen floor, sobbing like he hasn't since his grandmother died 4 years before. Keith immediately paws gently at Chris's legs, but Chris doesn't stop crying. Keith lays down and nudges his head under Chris's arm until one of Chris's relents and wraps one around the gentle bear of a dog. Chris pulls Keith closer and Keith turns his head to lick Chris's face. Quietly, Keith whimpers in unison with Chris's sobs, staring at his owner in confusion but matches each of Chris's blubbers with a sad exhale of his own.

Chris and Keith stay on the floor all night. Chris continues to swipe up on the messages, waiting for Taylor to tell him that she wasn't with another man. That man doesn't know how to hold her properly. Keith licks Chris's arm and nestles closer to him, which Chris desperately accepts. When Chris finally passes out 10 minutes later from exhaustion, his phone slips out of his hand. Keith stares at it until the lights go out. Then Keith nods and rests his head next to Chris's and falls asleep. It is the first night they've slept on the kitchen floor together since Keith was a puppy.

10

IT'S COMPLICATED

Wednesday spirals from the moment Chris wakes. He doesn't remember letting Keith outside in the morning or showering or walking to work or the bitter cold wind pushing him backward in spite of his effort to move forward. He forgets to stop for a coffee and resorts to the bland generic blend in the Bank's break area. He forgets what time his first meeting is and which pocket he keeps his ID in to swipe into the Bank. All that crosses his mind in the morning is how that man from last night doesn't know how to hold Taylor to save her from drowning.

His office is foreign: the stacks of trays overflowing with paper are mysterious mountains that he doesn't dare climb and his dual monitors are vacant eyes that reflect a fragmented man. He sits but doesn't turn on his computer or remove his coat or pay attention to the few people passing his office, their worlds spinning as if a fissure hadn't broken the world last night. He has never envied offices with doors as much as he does at this moment.

Chris pulls out his phone and opens his messages to Taylor. His blue stack from last night consumes the screen. He repeats his refresh methods from last night and this morning: close the app and reopen it, restart his phone, check that other apps are working, turn on and off the reception. Method after method collapses like dominoes leading nowhere. He sends a text to Austin to check that his app is working and is disappointed when Austin's reply confirms it is.

"Hey, are you coming to the meeting?" Chuck asks from the office entrance.

Chris jolts and focuses on his coworker filling the cubicle doorway. Despite being one of the biggest gamblers in poker, Chuck is one of Chris's most soft-spoken coworkers. Chris looks at his turned-off computer and the unreadable hieroglyphic writing on the sticky notes around his monitor.

"The meeting at 9 with Walter?" Chuck clarifies, as if this helps resolve Chris's confusion. "You ok?"

Chris turns on his computer but instead checks the empty notification tray of his phone.

"Yeah, meeting." Chris says. "Yeah, I'll meet you there. Tell Walter I'll be a little late."

Chuck inhales deeply but reconsiders saying anything and leaves. Chris waits until his coworker's footsteps are gone before setting his hands on his desk. They both shake enough to rattle the pen lying on his desk. His breathing grows jagged and he struggles to hold himself upright in his chair.

He grips the edge of his desk to stop himself from drowning as tightly as Taylor always clutched his arm when he held her. He isn't sure if it ever saved her from drowning. Now, he feels the water fill his lungs no matter how white his fingers grow clutching the desk. He plants his legs apart and pushes his feet into the floor, though his knees don't regain any strength. He closes his eyes and hopes nobody walks by his office and peers in to see the usual solid man inside cracking like a fragile egg.

The office is quiet. The monotonous thunder of keyboards

typing and mice clicking is replaced by the silent hum of the heat blowing through the vents and Chris's shaking hands rattling his pen. Even the patter of shoes on the carpeted hallway morphs to puffs like cold breaths in frigid air. Cold like the night he saw that man kiss Taylor. He doesn't know how to hold her properly.

Chris pulls himself to a standing position but the drowning makes the effort equivalent to an ant trying to stop a roof collapsing on it. The quiet is replaced by sharp intakes of breath through sobs that resemble a bad smoker's cough. His entire body shakes and his legs give way so he nearly slips from his chair, like a paralysis dart removed all his motor skills. Chris checks his phone but there is still no message from Taylor. He notices the meeting started a few minutes ago. He sends a text to Chuck that he's sick and needs to go home. He bolts from the office, beating the world record for fastest man alive.

In the stairwell he tries hiding his face as he passes Devon. She cradles a tablet like a baby in one arm and a wireless earpiece is in one of her ears.

"Hang on, hang on, I'll call you right back." She hangs up before they give an answer. "Where are you off to in such a hurry?"

Chris slows down but doesn't stop descending.

"I'm not feeling well so I'm taking the day off."

"The day just started! I have some things I wondered if you'd look at."

"I'm not on your team!" Chris shouts up the stairwell, more than an entire floor beneath where Devon leans over the railing. He speeds up again.

"You can still help co-workers out," Devon yells back as Chris's footsteps grow distant. "It's called being a good co-worker and an adult!"

Chris doesn't register whatever else she says. He runs faster as that last word chases him down the stairs. No matter how quickly he moves, how many steps he skips, how many turns he makes in the stairwell, the word pursues him even quicker and trips him twice. He barely catches himself before continuing, the weight of that word pushing on his back while the discovery of Taylor's man last night pushes on his chest, squeezing the air from his lungs so that he's bent over and panting, leaning against the wall when he reaches the base of the stairwell. He doesn't have the energy to push the door open and walk home but he forces himself to collapse against it and drags himself home through the mountains of snow and heartbreak.

Keith's head tilts to the side when Chris stumbles in. Keith looks at the clock, then at Chris, then at his sprawl on the couch with a blanket piled for him to rest his head on, then back at Chris. Slowly Keith lays his head back on the blanket but keeps his eyes on Chris. Only when Chris struggles to take off his shoes and immediately goes to the bedroom does Keith take his eyes off him, but within seconds Keith groans and drags himself off the couch and into Chris's room.

Keith puts his front paws on the bed to balance himself in a standing position as he inspects his owner and inquires as to why he disturbed Keith's rest. His owner is curled into a pathetic pile on the bed, his phone in his hand and his fingers continuously swiping to refresh the messages. Streaks where tears dried in the bitter cold mar his face and fresh ones create new paths. Keith rolls his eyes and climbs onto the bed to lay next to Chris.

"Don't look at me like that," Chris says.

Keith sighs.

"Don't give me that, either," Chris manages to say before breaking again.

He tries ignoring Keith watching him as he re-scrolls through the same stack of blue messages but Keith's gaze is too loud.

"What do you want me to say?"

Keith moves his paw so the tip of it holds down Chris's arm. Without being able to raise his arm to look at his phone, Chris drops his phone on to his bed, though his fingers twitch without holding anything. Keith moves his paw into Chris's palm.

"Why?" Chris asks with a voice as weak as someone on their deathbed.

Other than his body jostling from uncontrolled bursts of sadness, Chris stays motionless on the bed with Keith until after lunch, when Keith takes advantage of having his owner home in the middle of the day. He sniffs at Chris's sleeping face with his nose, waking him up and tickling him with his wet snout, making Chris crack a smile and his body shake from something other than sadness.

Chris rolls over and stares at the ceiling. His apartment is bathed in light. He's warm despite his apartment heat set low and his poorly isolated windows welcoming in the chilly late-January air. The lower part of his blinds are doused in shadow from the piled up snow on the windowsill. He opens and closes his hand multiple times, thrilled with the feeling of nothing in his hand. Keith jumps off the bed and Chris's memories hit him at once. He doesn't cry but his limbs turn to cement and depressed chains strap him down. Keith stares at him from the bedroom door, his tail wagging and his ears perked.

"I'm coming," Chris says.

When the weight of six months of lies burdens you and the fatigue of loving enough for two people holds you down, moving is an easier said than done statement. He tries pulling himself up, but the chains wrapped around his abdomen won't let him leave the bed. The comforter and soft mattress claw at him and restrain him. Chris inhales deeply, the dried tears on his face cracking like dried paint. In an effort that hurts more than when he broke a bone as a child or when his grandparents died, he pulls himself to a sitting position, though he fights the force dragging him back to the bed. Keith approaches him and lays his head on Chris's leg. Chris pats him and Keith licks Chris's hand, then turns toward the door. Chris looks at the door but his stomach somersaults nausea like a rollercoaster. With what remaining strength he can muster, he stands but wobbles, and is saved by Keith pushing back against his legs to balance him. Together they walk toward the door at the pace of a funeral march. Keith is all that holds him up.

When Keith comes back in, he settles on the couch but leaves enough room for Chris to join him. Taking the rare opportunity of his dog letting him join him, Chris begins a walk toward the couch but his fingers long to grasp something that's not there. Chris looks down and adrenaline runs through him as he realizes his phone isn't there and his watch is no longer around his wrist. He desperately runs back to his bedroom, the emotional weight relieved for the few steps it takes to reach his bedroom and phone. He wakes his phone and checks the messages.

A simple message from Taylor states that they need to talk and that she'll be over around 10 tonight. All the weight burdening Chris disappears and he bounds back into the living room without the chains tying him down. Keith watches in disappointment and rolls his eyes when Chris tells him about the message. Keith still doesn't reclaim full ownership of the couch and doesn't move when Chris finally sits down.

As soon as Chris is on the couch, his body loses its strength. Though the chains don't return, fatigue commands him from a night on the kitchen floor that reminds him he's no longer 20. The fatigue even fends off hunger and eases the pain in his neck from sleeping on the kitchen floor. He keeps his phone clutched in his hand. Though he responded to Taylor and said he was excited to see her tonight, she didn't respond.

~

HE DOESN'T WAKE until well into the night. Keith shifts multiple times throughout the day and nibbles on his food between naps, always returning to the couch and keeping some part of himself touching Chris. The blanket he used as a pillow earlier is now open and spread across Chris. Sparse dog hairs cover the blanket and couch. Chris would have grabbed a lint roller to clean the couch when he got home but depression removed his desire to complete his normal routine. Keith noticed but cleaning is not part of their roommate contract.

Chris stretches on the couch and feels his body release tension for the first time all day. Keith moves toward the door again. Chris groans and finds it eerily easy to stand and let Keith out. Parts of his body feel heavy - particularly his chest - but he can move about his apartment without the same restraints as earlier. He woke fully aware of what happened today and last night. The strongest thought he has is that Taylor is coming over tonight.

When Keith is back inside, Chris starts dinner for them both, though he doesn't have the motivation to make more than eggs and toast, mainly because they're easy to make and easy to clean up, though he'll leave the dishes in the sink all night. He checks his messages and his chest grows lighter each time he sees Taylor confirming she'll be over at 10. He checks the time every five minutes, angry at the slow crawl toward their meeting.

He throws a mindless movie on and sits back down, though Keith doesn't seem pleased to continue sharing the couch with someone. He doesn't protest, however, which Chris sees as a sign of growth for his dog. Maybe there is still hope for him.

A few minutes before Taylor is supposed to arrive, Chris suddenly jolts up. The dishes are still in the sink and his bed isn't fixed to look nice after he spent the morning sleeping on the covers and he hasn't cleaned the bathroom or checked that there are beers in the fridge or sprayed on the cologne Taylor likes. In a frenzy, he tornadoes around his apartment until the messy parts are tidied, the dirty parts are cleaned, and the beers are confirmed to be in the fridge. Keith watches the routine occur in less than 5 minutes, though he refuses to get up and help. Chris goes to the bathroom to spray himself with the cologne Taylor likes, the extra cans he bought so he'd never run out of her favorite scent still under his sink.

Chris's phone dings as he finishes the last chore. He rushes to his couch - none of the earlier weight remains - and grabs for his phone like not holding it would stop his heart. He replies to Taylor's message that she's on her way. Then he waits.

Waiting for paint to dry would pass quicker than waiting for the door to open and Taylor to burst through and throw her arms wide open and tell Chris that he's the only man in her life and then profess how much she cares about him. His fingers tingle and his leg bounces as his stomach flutters, all melding into him being unable to remain on the couch while he waits. He grabs a glass of water for himself, sets it on the coffee table, then thinks that he better grab one for Taylor, so he goes back to the kitchen, then thinks Taylor probably won't want water, just beer, so he dumps out the water and puts the glass in the drying rack, then second guesses whether Taylor would want only beer.

He checks his phone repeatedly but there are no new messages from Taylor. He grabs the TV remote but she'll be here soon so starting a show would be a waste. Instead he flips through socials on his phone though he just stares at the pictures and doesn't actually read anything, though even those are a blur of color with no definition. His eyes secretly peek toward the door with every finger swipe, though he remains discreet because Keith wouldn't approve. He already rolled his eyes at Chris more than usual today. Keith sighs without opening his eyes, but he shifts and pushes Chris against the couch arm, leaving his owner little space to sit. Chris contorts so Keith would have all the space he needs.

Chris hears a vehicle pull up alongside his building, though it doesn't pull all the way to the back like usual. Heaviness returns to Chris's chest when the vehicle turns off and his phone dings with an "I'm here" text. He texts back that the door is unlocked. He barely manages to fend off the urge to bolt downstairs and open Taylor's car door and wrap his arms around her. His toes dance and he sets his phone down and picks up his water glass, his fingers tapping it incessantly. His throat is sandpaper dry and a weight presses on his stomach, worrying him he'll vomit.

Taylor's steps on the stairs outside are thunderous drum beats announcing a war. This does nothing to diminish the growing weight in his stomach and chest and only brings back the chains that tie him down. He grows lightheaded when the thunderclaps are outside his door and the handle turns. Keith looks up. Chris's vision grows blotty until Taylor enters.

When the door closes he focuses and says hi in return to her greeting. He stands and walks toward her once her coat is off and her boots are tucked against the wall. He wraps her in an embrace that she returns fully and without a moment's hesitation. Her speedy hug releases the apprehension he held since she texted him hours earlier. She moves to release the embrace but he holds it for a second longer. He's always afraid that every embrace with her will be the last, that every time she walks out his door, he'll never see her again. That's a void he doesn't want to experience.

"How are you?" he asks.

She feels so safe to hold; he doesn't crave to wash his hands after. He gets two beers from the kitchen, which she thanks him for as she takes his seat on the couch. Keith gladly shifts for her and turns around so his head is next to her. His tail whacks the couch like applause.

"I'm well," she says with a larger swig of her beer than her normal paced sips. Chris doesn't like that. "You smell nice."

"Thanks. How was your week?" Chris asks as he checks that her feet are completely covered by her blanket armor before sitting in the chair.

He never knows how to dive into asking her what he wants; how do you ask someone if they even remotely like you when they're the first thing you think about in the morning but you're the one thing they never consider until you bother them? How do you let someone know everything you feel when everything will scare them away forever?

"It was quite a week," Taylor says, "and it's only Wednesday. I'm glad it's February. Closer to this snow melting."

"Yeah, it's nice seeing you during the week," Chris says, half afraid that would make her leave.

Taylor shrugs in that way that shows her entire interest and disinterest in one movement. Chris wants to join her on the couch and hold her but he remains in his chair, like always, while Keith gets all the attention from her. Damn dog.

"What's been going on since Christmas? It's been almost a month since I've seen you."

He knows she doesn't care about when she saw him last. Some people are priorities, some people are casual encounters. Chris knows which he is, but that doesn't mean she isn't the other to him. Taylor's head falls against the couch's back, which cradles her like Chris wishes he could. She stares at the ceiling with the beer in her hand.

"This place sometimes," she says. "*Burlington.*"

Chris relates: the job, the loneliness, the growing up. It all seems exacerbated in Burlington. Is it this place, or is every place going to feel the same as here? Would he escape adulthood if he ran to Colorado to live with the rest of the young people running from life to escape in a paradise of other young people? Would staying home in NYC provide enough opportunities to live in Manhattan and party with the other young people even when he turned 30? Would any place save him from growing up?

"There's just something about this place," Taylor continues without being prompted. Chris's butterfly stomach soars. "The people here sometimes. They are just such trash. There are so many other places to live that would be better."

"Why do you stay?" Chris asks quietly, shrinking so Taylor doesn't feel like he's there but instead is hearing a disembodied voice. The more space he can offer her, the better.

Taylor sips her beer, again a little more than usual. "It's complicated."

"Life is always complicated," Chris says.

Taylor shrugs, her shoulders moving up and down effortlessly like shrugging is her first nature and being any other way is foreign to her. Chris holds his breath to prevent the butterflies in his stomach from going lower.

"There are better jobs elsewhere, too," she says. "Just everything. Why do you stay here? You could do amazing if you moved to New York City or one of the big tech hubs in the south."

"Why don't you move?" Chris offers.

Taylor starts and the beer slips between her fingers as they lose their strength for the millisecond it takes Chris to speak. Her usual stoic expression is betrayed by a bite of her lip and a tick of her toe beneath the blanket. Chirs notices each as if they were outlined by blinking lights while highlighted on a billboard in Times Square. His eyes flicker to her neck but the usual infinity necklace is buried beneath a crew neck sweater.

"So why do you stay here?" she repeats. "There are literally thousands of places you could go across the country."

Chris's hope fails that she'd actually talk about herself. She's a master of pivoting away.

"It's complicated," he says in no mockery of her.

He refuses to admit out loud that it's partly been because of her these past 6 months. She shrugs to acknowledge how complicated life is, then she stares at him and waits.

"As much as people may suck, there's also a charm to Burlington. At least more of a charm than home has for me."

"And you don't think you'd find that elsewhere?" she asks.

Chris shrugs, again not to mock her. His shrug feels unnatural, like he's stealing Tayor's copyrighted body movement. He drinks quite a bit of his own beer.

"My best friends are here."

"You can make best friends anywhere."

Chris nods, unable to refute that.

"I don't know sometimes," he says. "I guess this is now home and I just don't know what to do next. I don't know where I'm supposed to go or who I'm supposed to be with or what job I'm supposed to have. I don't have a plan for what's next. The plan before the Bank was to get a job at the Bank. Once I got there, the plan was done and I just kind of...kept going...and just yeah. I'm...I'm just lost."

Taylor takes more of her beer. She shrugs. Chris sees her eyes flicker toward him mid-shrug. She doesn't reply.

"It's, um, I..." he stutters.

Taylor's eyes settle on him, two spotlights waiting for what he's wanted to say since she walked in.

"Who...who was that guy?"

Taylor nearly finishes her beer, which Chris doesn't like. She always nurses a beer all night. He checks that her toes are still covered.

"That was my husband," Taylor says passively.

She twirls her beer and doesn't look at Chris, though all of her attention waits for his reaction. Husband? She must be joking with him to see how angry he'd get to prove his feelings for her. He considers rising from the chair and throwing his beer into the kitchen, shattering the glass into the million pieces she turned him into with that admission. He wants to storm across the room and scream at the wall but he's afraid of falling into the void that opened wide when Taylor confessed.

Husband?

With four words, Taylor rips his throat out and uses it as a noose to hang the previous six months of Chris falling in love with her. He recalls how she was never on her phone when with him but never rushed to answer it if it dinged, how vaguely and with such uncertainty she described timeframes she was able to come over, how she showered before leaving each morning, how she always needed to rush home in the morning to feed her dog and how he doesn't remember seeing a dog when he went to her house. This must be a joke.

"Oh," he manages with a voice crack.

Husband.

It can't really be her husband. She's spent so many nights with him, holding on to prevent her from drowning, craning into him until no space existed between them, an effort to use him to protect herself, kissing him at night with the desperate love of a thousand relationships exchanged with each kiss. She couldn't have done all that for any reason other than she loved him like he does her. He never felt he needed to say it out loud because she showed it in return; always displayed that she needed him as much as he needed her.

Husband.

"Oh," he says through a constricted throat. He isn't sure she hears him.

Six months of his life are gone. Six months of falling in love with someone who didn't care at all, six months of the highest elation of his life encouraged by her every word, action, and level of caring. Taylor's spotlight eyes illuminate 6 months of emotion being erased until the last wisps of it dissipate like a puddle on a too-sunny day.

"How long...have you been married?" he asks.

"Three years," she says casually, as if this is another conversation between two business partners in a coffee shop talking about their donation to sponsoring local teams.

No amount of beer wets his dry mouth enough to speak without scratching his throat and no amount of deep breaths can quell his lightheadedness. No amount of glue or tape can repair the shattered pieces that Taylor ground into dust. He tries collecting the sandy remnants of his emotions but he can't grasp them before they filter through his fingers. He tries to speak but the words turn to a grumble in his throat.

Taylor doesn't respond. She has no more reason to prompt him, nothing else to contribute freely without being asked, and Chris doesn't know what to ask. There isn't much to ask: she is married to someone else, Chris is a nighttime affair, Taylor doesn't care about him at all. Neither needs to ask for clarification on their situation; both just need to accept it, and Taylor already has. Being the second to accept a shitty situation you didn't know you were in makes it impossible to accept yourself in the shitty situation.

"Do you want a second beer?" Chris asks quickly before the sadness interrupts him.

Taylor shakes her head. She stands herself - uncovering her toes - and walks to the kitchen and gets a glass of water. She returns and Chris instinctively wants to help cover her toes but she manages to do that herself. The past playfulness where she used to let him cover her toes when she was perfectly capable is now gone and replaced by an independence from Chris that he disdains. Her allowing him to do those small things hallmarked her feelings for him and highlighted her need for him. Doing them alone, she doesn't need him. She just needs her husband. Husband.

"It's getting late," Chris says, though it's barely past midnight. They used to stay up talking until 3a.m. How much would be the same after this? Does he want anything to be the same?

He should kick her out of his apartment. She lied to him for 6 months and used him like a whore. He wouldn't be kept a secret in her life when she is the centerpiece of his thoughts. He deserves better than to be buried with her other secrets and resurrected only when drowning becomes too much for her. He isn't going to be someone's hidden toy.

How is he going to admit to everyone in his life that his relationship with Taylor isn't a relationship at all? Austin would say he told him so, while Lydia would tell him that Taylor is a piece of trash and offer him a drink. Harris would tell him to keep sleeping with her - Harris has slept with enough married women. Chris is now the other person, the ruiner of a relationship, the other person. He can run from growing up and escape taking on responsibility, but now he's the centerpiece of a very adult mess.

No, this is Taylor's relationship. None of this is his fault. Taylor knowingly acted on everything, continued everything, kept her husband and Chris in the dark. This mess is on Taylor. Chris is an innocent participant. He would never have partaken in the mess if he had known. So why does he want Taylor to still sleep over? Why does he still feel the need to wrap around her as they fall asleep and save her from drowning? Why does he feel she's drowning even more after admitting this? Why is he letting her let him drown?

"It's turned into more of a roommate situation," Taylor says.

Chris starts and realizes he's been silent for far longer than he thought. Taylor is looking at him without judgment or anger. Instead her eyes hold regret. He swallows a lump that hurts the entire way down.

"Why are you still with him, then?" Chris asks weakly. He can barely muster the words.

Taylor shrugs and for once, the movement doesn't pull Chris in.

"You just get to a point, and how do you change it?"

"You just tell them you're done."

Taylor raises her eyebrows and shrugs, and the attractiveness returns. She pets Keith slowly.

"It's complicated."

Chris nods slowly, with tears ready to stream from him. It's a roommate situation. She doesn't want to be married to that man. He's fine to continue seeing her. Maybe he can show her what a partner is supposed to be like, what someone who loves her is really like. Then she'll divorce her husband that she doesn't love anyway and will realize she should date Chris and then they'll actually be together and he can stop making excuses to his friends. They'll never have to know.

No, she dragged him along as the other person for 6 months. He needs to not let her stay the night, not let her continue to make him the other person. Whether she loves her husband or not is not his business. At this stage, his only business is to kick her out and not text her as soon as her car pulls away, not text her in the morning telling her how sorry he is that he kicked her out. She's the one who should apologize.

"Are you ready for bed?" Chris asks instead.

It's complicated.

Husband.

Taylor nods, with tears ready to stream from her, but she's an unbreakable dam.

They go to Chris's bedroom, strip, and climb into bed. Keith stretches out on the couch, grateful the impediment left.

Taylor wraps her fingers up in Chris's before he has the chance to securely wrap an arm around her. He slithers another arm under the pillow beneath her head and her other hand finds his, intertwining their fingers. She moves as closely into him as she even has, before he has the opportunity to pull her close. He feels a wet drop hit his arm. He feels her body shake once. He doesn't have anything to say before he falls asleep holding the person that fits him like a key into a lock.

This is how you hold Taylor properly.

Husband.

It's complicated.

11

ONE PERSON ALWAYS LOVES MORE

C hris's typing adds to the endless rhythm of his coworkers'. He mistypes repeatedly as his new title of 'Taylor's Side Whore' weighs like a war criminal's title. Rather than add to the ant farm making progress that none of them actually see, Chris leans back in his chair and wishes his cubicle had a proper door. His screens are lit up, one with a spreadsheet and the other with PDFs to sign and send off to the next stop in the ant farm chain. His lack of accomplishments over the past hour would betray that he's been at work for that long.

He arrived later than usual, marching in with the other ants rather than a half hour before them. The last time he arrived with everyone else was his first month, before he knew he could arrive earlier in complete silence before the club springs alive with typing, phones, conversations, and dull thuds of shoes on carpet. Maybe his late arrival is why he hasn't done any actual work this morning; his usual stack that would have been two or three clients shorter is now one taller.

Maybe Taylor's visit last night distracts him from working, though that doesn't explain the past month of lackluster work.

She'd been over twice in that time - the most frequent her visits had ever been. Wearing the red letter A that depicts him as Taylor's side piece sticks with him daily even if he doesn't see her. It's a shameful badge that he can't bring himself to tear off, a title he can't bring himself to delete, a sea of memories and feelings and comfort that nobody else has filled. How do you rip off the red letter when you're afraid that you'll never find this feeling in someone else? How do you tear it off when you're almost 30 and haven't found this feeling in someone else?

"Can you check this at some point today?" Chuck sets a folder on Chris's desk.

Chris nods and waves to his coworker, who leaves before any further conversation starts. A month ago, people would sit and visit to avoid work and to beg Chris to find the small details they couldn't. Now, most of his coworkers leave folders or notes on his desk and run off before Chris can respond. With Taylor taking up his thoughts and his newly defined role as her whore constantly nagging him, he cares little for them to stay for a visit.

He adds the folder to his stack. He detests the mountain of paper displaying his lack of progress to everyone who walks by his office. He'd rather it be in queues on his computer, a secret so nobody can see his shortcomings. Then at least he could keep some of his pride, or as much pride as you can keep when you have secrets and are someone's whore. How much pride did he maintain after Taylor made clear what he is to her last month?

He stands - itself a miracle when most times thoughts of Taylor makes his knees give way beneath his weakness for staying with her but also the weakness he knows he'd feel if he told her he's done being her whore - and grabs his coffee mug. He didn't get coffee on his way to work because the other ants beat him to the coffee shops along Church St., stretching the lines too long. With his slow pace, he wouldn't have had the time to stop for coffee, anyway.

The aisles between and around cubicles are empty except for the lone straggler like Chris seeking a morning motivator before they can dive fully into work. Everyone else is already deep into long conversations on the phone with clients Chris hasn't cared about in weeks or working through their own mountains of paperwork or waiting for meetings. Chris purposefully navigates the maze of cubicles to avoid walking by his supervisor's office. One thing he appreciates about paper files is that his supervisor can't see what he has or hasn't completed without stopping by his office, which his supervisor has done less and less recently.

Taylor is probably at home, washing the clothes she wore to his place last night and explaining her lie of a night to her husband so he won't know she is having an affair. Texting her would be a pointless practice since she never responded to him during the day or in the days after seeing him; whores aren't a pre-dusk person you text. Regardless, he pulls out his phone and opens the text thread with her. He's used to seeing his stack of blue messages with no response. What else should a whore expect? One person always loves the other more, one person never cares: the void between those two people is always present, even when they're together.

He types out a message. It doesn't matter what it says: how was work? how's the weather? what are you up to today? do you love me like I love you? Whatever the message says, he'll stare at it for a few minutes and think about how to reword it, if a different verb or tense or syntax or message entirely is better to send. He'll rewrite it because unless it is perfect, Taylor won't respond. He's sent so many messages that weren't perfect that Taylor didn't respond to. He always says the wrong thing or sounds like an idiot or the message just isn't right. He sometimes spends an hour thinking about what to write and another hour workshopping his message. Then, he'll delete it.

Whores shouldn't text more than once a week. He always breaks that.

Empty Keurig pouches litter the empty break area's counter, scattered like forgotten bullet casings that served their purpose. Chris grumbles and throws them away, then refills the Keurig because the assholes before him couldn't be bothered to refill what they use. He pulls out his phone again while waiting for the grumbling machine to heat up the water.

"Isn't it the worst when people don't refill that?" Kelly says from the chairs near the windows.

Chris starts. "Sorry, I didn't see you there."

"You're fine, I'm pretty quiet," Kelly says.

She's in one of the more comfortable chairs meant for relaxing rather than the hard backed chairs meant for working, though she's typing away on her laptop.

"Why are you down here?" he asks, joining her in a plush chair.

Kelly laughs. "Territorial now?" she teases. "I like the view from this window better than the one upstairs. It feels a little more like part of the City here than it does looking down at everything from above."

"How are things going up there?" Chris asks.

"They're fine." Kelly shrugs - it's nothing like Taylor's. "We could definitely use someone to oversee the international clients full time." She side-eyes Chris, though he ignores it.

"I'm surprised you haven't found someone. There's plenty of other qualified people in the Bank."

"You know how stubborn Devon can be," Kelly says, "once she has her mind set on something, she'll work until her vision is met."

Chris jumps up to fill his coffee mug as the Keurig stops chugging along. He puts in a new Keurig packet and watches the coffee dribble into his mug. He shouldn't have asked about the 6th floor.

"How are you doing?" Kelly asks.

"I'm fine," Chris says. Damn, the Keurig dribbles slowly.

Kelly hesitates. "What have you been up to? How's Keith? That's still an odd name for a dog."

Chris smiles, as he always does when people say that, even if they've told him that a hundred times.

"Keith is fine. He's as lazy as always. I'm also uncertain if the butt imprint on my couch is from me or him."

Kelly laughs - it's nice to hear someone laugh when Taylor rarely does.

"Keith is wonderful. Does he like the snow?"

Chris brings his full coffee mug over to the lounge area and sits down again. Talking about Keith always eases him, even when he's on high alert in defense mode.

"When I let him outside to go to the bathroom he stares at me with more hate than any dog should be able to possess."

"Well he's a smart dog," Kelly says happily, half-closing her laptop. "I would also hate to have to pee outside."

"When you're as lazy as Keith is, I'm surprised he bothers to go outside to pee at all."

"My boyfriend's dog loves to go outside. He'll lay near the door to go play in the snow and when we take him for a walk, he insists on bringing a large chunk of snow or ice inside. It's a pain but he's so cute."

"He sounds like a more energetic dog than Keith. I think Keith is just too old to have that puppy energy anymore, even though he's only 6 years old."

"I thought he was younger," Kelly says. "Did you get him when he was a puppy?"

"I rescued him when he was two. And he's been my pain in the ass ever since."

"Well he's an adorable pain in the ass with a great dad," Kelly says.

"Thanks."

Chris relaxes in the comfortable lounge area chairs, his mug scalding his fingers so he sets it on the side table. Kelly's own coffee is empty, or at least it's cooled to the point no steam rises from her mug, so it might as well be empty. Kelly shifts the laptop screen further downward, not closing the laptop but making it obvious she intends to chat and not work. Chris allows the chair to encase his back and sides. He checks his watch when he thinks it vibrates but it is nothing.

"How's working with Devon's replacement going?" Kelly asks. "I can never remember his name."

"His name isn't important," Chris says quickly, then walks back his statement, "he does a great job. It's fine. He bothers me less than Devon did but he puts more on my desk than Devon ever did. It's like he expects me to be a robot that burns through a dozen clients an hour. Nobody can get through processing that and setting up the meetings and dealing with the bullshit."

"You used to barrel through work," Kelly says.

Chris picks up his mug by the handle, the coffee swooshing dangerously close to capsizing the mug. He doesn't respond to Kelly's statement because there's nothing to respond to. He doesn't need reminding that he's slowed down at work.

"You can join Devon's team and be the one who controls the workload," Kelly says.

"I don't want to work for Devon," Chris says coldly.

"Did something happen with her?"

"Nothing happened with her. I've worked for her before and she's fine but I just...I don't want to work for her."

Kelly angles the laptop screen upward again to type. Chris watches the coffee settle as Kelly's keyboard clicking replaces their conversation. He rarely has an edge in his voice and though he may be sorry, apologizing is beyond him in this state. He checks his watch but there are no messages. The vibrations are almost always in his head at this point, though medicine wouldn't make them stop. He thinks he knows what would make the false vibrations stop, but he's not able to do that.

"I've got to go back to my office," he says, though he remains seated.

"I'm not sure what's been eating you up inside the last month," Kelly says, "but you're better than whatever it is. And you're good enough to do my job, hell you're good enough to do Devon's job. I'd hate to watch you not capitalize on opportunities that you'd be amazing at because of something else in your life."

"Thanks," Chris says without emotion.

Kelly's keyboard clicks grow faint as Chris leaves the lounge area and the coffee's steam is almost wispy as it floats back to him and swirls around his body before dissipating. He doesn't return to his office. He doubts Harris is in his office, and if he is, then Harris is doing no work and would gladly accept a distraction from doing nothing.

As predicted, Harris is scrolling through his phone with his feet on his desk as pictures of local bars flip through a slideshow screensaver on his computer. Scuff marks on his desk where his shoes rubbed too hard against the surface blemish the desk. A smell of laziness hangs in the office as Chris sits. The piles of paperwork for Harris to work through are less than half the size of Chris's.

"Well I ll be damned, he does leave his office," Harris says. "What the hell are you doing up here? Ready to plan some bar trips this weekend?'

"No, nothing like that, just needed to get away from my desk for a little bit," Chris says. "How's your morning been?"

"It's been a fucking drag, man," Harris says. "My boss came

in first thing and demanded a meeting with me. Like fuck you, I don't function well enough before 10am to have a meeting about shit. So I follow him into his office - which smells like the dude sweats as he works - and I have to listen to him talk about our division's impact on the company and those doing well and those underperforming and blah blah. What a drag the morning turned into. How am I supposed to focus and have the energy to work after listening to that moron talk for half an hour? I came back here and have been relaxing since. I'd relax better if I knew we had a bar trip planned for the week."

"I can't go out this week," Chris says. "Besides, I can't keep up with you anymore."

"Nonsense," Harris says. "We just gotta train you back up. You used to keep up, and Austin, too, though you'd never know it with how much of a stick up his ass personality he is now. That's what a fucking relationship and house does to you, and that damn promotion. He's been leaving us behind like our time together in college means shit."

"He's just busier-"

"'Just busier' is bullshit," Harris says. "He's buying into all that adult shit. Sometimes I think the only place I can see him anymore is at work, and even then I have to trapeze my way up to his office on whatever floor he's been promoted to and talk to a receptionist - a receptionist! To see my best friend. What does a decade of friendship mean?"

"If you send him a text to let him know you're on your way, he's usually quite flexible."

"I shouldn't have to text my best friend to see him," Harris says. "That's the problem. People get these adult jobs and promotions and what happens? They leave everyone behind who doesn't keep up with an equal promotion. I never thought he was the kind to just leave us behind like that. That's why you and I gotta go to the bar this week. I'm not ready to leave behind fun and my 20s."

"I'm busy all week," Chris says, though his calendar is wide open. He checks his phone.

"Well make some time on the weekend," Harris says.

"I'll see about it." Chris regrets coming up to see Harris just to listen to him complain. "I've got to head back to my desk."

"And that devotion to work," Harris continues, "is a problem everywhere. Why are people so devoted to 'getting back to their desk'? It's like we're chained to our desks and we're reprimanded if we leave them. Why can't we just be trusted to do our work without this expectation that our desk is our second home for 8 hours a day? Fucking adults ruining everything."

"I'll see you later," Chris says, his coffee empty.

"Let me know about this weekend," Harris says. "We'll start at the pub downtown at the opposite end of where you live, and we'll work our way back. There's this new place that opened..."

Chris leaves him talking to his phone screen. Harris probably wouldn't notice Chris's absence for a few minutes as he rambles. Chris doesn't want to go back to his cubicle and the mountain of work. He checks his phone but there are still no messages. He debates visiting Austin but he and Lydia will be at dinner tonight. They told Harris a week ago but as usual, he half-listened and forgot their plans to have dinner at Austin's. Nobody cares to remind Harris of the plans.

He returns to his desk, thinking about the chain tying Chris and all of his coworkers to their desks. There was never one when he was in his early 20s, never an anchor restricting him, never a contract binding him. Eight hours of his day is accounted for by someone else in everything but his blood: his social security number, his livelihood, his money. When he sits, an invisible restraint wraps around his midsection, fixing him to his chair, and glue sticks his feet to the floor while a magnet attracts his fingers to his mouse and keyboard.

Taylor's text thread beckons as strongly as his keyboard's magnets. He scrolls through it, her gray bubbles intersecting his blue pillars every few scrolls like a speed bump he wishes he could collide into more frequently. His messages are always short, merely a 'hey' or a 'what's going on?' without much commitment in any single line. His commitment spreads across multiple messages like a paint stroke across the blank canvas of their text thread, desperate to be beautiful and continued by Taylor, but it never is.

He flips through the top folder on the stack. The client's name means little and he reads the numbers like they're the complicated password to a safe that only he understands. Arduously, he inputs information and sets up meetings with the client.

Kelly's offer to join Devon's team and be the one who assigns work floats through his mind. He could divide clients between people he oversees, organize the workflows, and solve large scale problems. He's been brought in as a consultant on various larger projects for the Bank multiple times, often on an informal basis by coworkers who can't figure out how the larger puzzles fits. He could do it full time. But at what cost to his personal life?

~

KEITH STRETCHES OUT on the area rug that also manages to fit Austin's coffee table. His back presses against a table leg while his neck stretches so his nose almost reaches another leg. When Kyle isn't on the ground to cuddle, Keith often lays under the coffee table.

Austin stands at the sink, his OCD driving him to clean all of the dishes before he relaxes in the living room with Lydia and

Chris and a glass of wine. Chris and Lydia sit on opposite ends of the couch, their legs pulled under them and their bodies positioned toward one another. Chris finished a first glass of wine during dinner and his second is half empty, while Lydia just began sipping her third. Chris isn't sure he'll finish his second.

"I can't believe Harris said that shit," Lydia says. "He's such a dumb fucker. I'm glad he forgot about tonight."

Chris shrugs but keeps his wine glass steady. Lydia always fills it too full, though she has no problem ensuring that it's all finished. Chris twists his wrist to check his watch but there are no new messages. He's tried to start hiding his impulses, often checking his phone as soon as his friends' eyes are diverted or hoping his watch face lights up when he takes a drink so his wrist is already in front of his eyes. Lydia dubiously glares at him each time. He misses Taylor's shrug.

"He's probably at some bar preying on some unsuspecting girl," Lydia says, swallowing a large portion of her wine. "He's such a scumbag. We should've parted ways back in college."

"Maybe we were more similar to him back in college, or maybe we were just idiots back then."

His wrist twitches.

"We may be here physically, but mentally some of us are elsewhere," Lydia says, watching Chris very obviously check his watch. "I have no energy for bars anymore. The loudness, the crowds, the young drunkards sloppily falling against you or dribbling beer on you or yelling when their favorite song comes on. What the fuck was ever attractive about going to a bar?"

"That's where the men were," Austin says from the doorway.

Each of his hands holds an empty wine bottle. Lydia always says there are two glasses of wine in a bottle; three when she's forced to share.

"That's just one more reason to avoid bars now," Lydia says quietly.

She stares into her wine, a daze crossing her eyes.

"I'll grab a third bottle," Austin says, noting her near empty glass. "Why bother using the coasters I bought? Let's just leave them in a stack and put your glasses directly on the coffee table. That's fine, that's totally fine," Austin mutters to himself as he carries the empties into the kitchen.

Lydia shifts the glass onto a coaster.

"Sometimes he can be an annoying Dad," Lydia said, "but he also gives us wine and cooks us food, so..."

Chris laughs. The wine helps.

"I'd rather sit here with my best friends and be able to talk to you about everything than have strangers listening to our conversations and random dudes hitting on me. This is just the next phase of life. Plus, I can snuggle up to Keith whenever I get too drunk."

The dog opens one eye but doesn't put forth the effort to lift his head to look at her. Chris taps his glass.

"You really think this is what we should do next?"

"What, sit at home and play cards or watch tv together rather than pay for overpriced alcohol in gross bars where men prey on us? Yes. Bars are for the young."

She pulls the throw blanket off the back of the couch and tosses it across her lap and feet, though the tiny blanket wouldn't have covered an infant. She masterfully maneuvers the blanket while not letting go of her glass or spilling a drop, and she even takes a sip while unfurling the blanket. Chris notices she doesn't care to cover her toes. He wants to do it for her like he does Taylor.

"How do Austin and Kyle cuddle on the couch without a proper blanket?" she complains. "Damn this is a ridiculous sized blanket. Like why do people even buy these? Just for decoration? What is he, an 80 year old woman?"

"Is there anything you miss that we used to do?" Chris asks.

Lydia finishes fighting the mini-blanket.

"I wouldn't say 'miss' in that I want to go back to that point in my life, but 'miss' the feeling of some things, sure."

"Like what?"

"Fuck I don't know. The ability to go away for an entire summer during college, or not having to pay bills, or not wake up with a hangover. But like, those had their moments and had their own drawbacks."

"What kind of drawbacks does freedom have?"

"Reliance on others, mostly. Sure, we could do tons of things when we had whole summers off or we could go out at night and not care the next morning, but we had no future, no goals to work toward. We were filling time because we didn't know what else to do. I don't mind some uncertainty, but I don't want to be a floundering child reliant on help from Mom and Dad as I'm working a job that doesn't pay shit. Now I can do whatever I want, I'm not reliant on someone else, and I have money. I still have freedom, just different freedom. This is the freedom I prefer."

"Freedom to spend all of your money gambling, you mean," Austin says, rejoining with a fresh bottle of wine, the cork already popped out.

"If that's what I want to do, I'm allowed to," Lydia says. "Part of the freedom is freedom from judgment, which I left with my parents, thank you very much."

Austin pets Keith's stomach before taking a spot on the other couch and stretching his legs the length of it. He cradles his wine glass, which is as empty as Chris's.

"Chris is asking about college," Lydia says.

"What a long time ago that was," Austin says. "Sometimes I forget that we're turning 30 this year."

"Don't remind me," Chris says.

"It won't be bad," Austin says. "It's just another year. Nothing's going to change."

"People are going to see us differently," Chris says.

"So let them," Lydia says. "We'll still be working, having dinner and drinks here, living where we live. It doesn't matter if our age starts a '2' or a '3.'"

Chris awes at her nonchalant attitude toward everything that accompanies adulthood, at both of their carelessness with leaving their youth behind. Austin already has one foot in the grave of 30, with a house and coasters and mini-blankets meant for decoration and not comfort. He wiggles in his seat as thoughts of 30 weigh over him like a too-large blanket he can't escape from under.

"Look at Keith," Austin says, "he's already well past 30 and he's still the cutest one of us all."

Keith opens an eye but is too lazy to lift his head to show he cares at all.

"If I was pampered all the time, I'd be fine with getting old, too," Chris says. "When he gets home he'll have a nice bath and get a treat. All that's missing is being carried in a palanquin."

Their laughter brings Chris back to college, sitting in their apartment with cheap posters of bands and movies decorating their walls, a shrine to their teenage obsessions that they couldn't leave. Enough empty beer cases to quench an army filled their apartment's corner and the kitchen was full of dirty dishes from the last two days while the cupboards were full of ramen and chips, a dinner of champions for college kids. Their couch was secondhand from whoever lived in the apartment before them; they bought a cover and agreed to never ask about what happened on the couch before them. On the counter were piles on unopened envelopes, agreed to be forgotten until payday each week.

Their laughs in Austin's living room are so light and the wine warms the room so the tiny blanket is more than enough for all three of them plus Keith to fit under. The coasters are a nice decorative touch and Austin's wall art is lit by the dim lamp and candles scattered around, which create a dream-like air that tires Chris as he drinks. Knowing there are soft beds upstairs if they get too drunk and need to sleep over, with fresh sheets and no history of a previous college owner, comforts him.

He wonders how long this can last. If he gives in to being an adult with his friends and accepting this as his life, at what age will he give up this life with them as they all transition into whatever the next phase is? Will they suddenly just be old and decrepit, forgotten by the rest of the world because they can't contribute anymore, or will they become the weird single adults at random events that comment on how happy everyone else looks while they themselves wonder what they did wrong when they were in their 20s or 30s? He declines a wine refill, to Lydia's dismay. Dinner was filling enough that he could drive home in an hour and be fine.

"Are we going to the St. Patty's parade downtown next month?" Austin asks. "Kyle wants to know if we're going or if he should make plans with his other friends."

"I enjoy parades," Lydia says.

Austin waits for Chris to respond, but he's silent as he flips through his phone.

"Alright then, I guess we're going. We might meet up with Kyle's friends, if that's ok with you two."

"Sure, I could always use more friends. Maybe they'll play poker."

"You can't just make everyone you meet gamble so you can take their money," Austin says.

Lydia shrugs and refills her glass with the fresh bottle Austin opened.

An hour later, Chris takes Keith out to pee and then bids his friends goodbye. Lydia drank her fourth glass before Austin capped the bottle of wine with the promise of finishing it tomorrow so it doesn't go bad.

Late-February sees as much snow as January, though the fresh snow is plowed and dumped on top of existing mountainous piles, some of which reach to the porch roofs to create mini-Everest's. Turns become dangerous as the banks lining the roads are impenetrable walls rivaling SUVs in height. Chris doesn't care as he pulls farther into intersections than he should and his stops turn from nearly-complete to not-even-close. The only time it becomes a real issue is when he drives in residential neighborhoods, which is only a nightly occurrence now. Tonight will be no exception as he leaves Austin's to take the long way home. Keith groans in the back seat.

Mud coats the bottom of the snow banks while the tops are padded down in areas where children built forts. Pathways created from sleds paint the snow banks' sides, leaving extra paths of snow in the road where the sleds dragged snow off the banks. As usually when driving after 11pm, Chris ignores all of the signs of families living in the area. Nobody can see into vehicles in the dark.

The long way home is second nature, a memory as solid as his memories of the streets of New York City he walked with his friends growing up. After the first two nights, the lefts and rights were memorized, embedded like how the mitochondria is the powerhouse of the cell or that $2 + 2 = 4$. Even in the dark, the houses are familiar and the trees' locations are etched in stone.

His heartbeat increases as his destination grows closer. His phone is forgotten in a center cup holder, though his eyes slip down to its black screen. His mouth dries and he drives perhaps a bit faster than he should through residential neighborhoods, but it's night during winter so nobody will be out. There is rarely anyone out at this late.

The final turn sends blood rushing to his head and a slight headache pounds at him. He's been past here dozens of times, though the rush never fails to excite him as he finally sees Taylor's house on the left out of the corner of his eye. He's afraid to turn and look at the house in case she's watching from the window, waiting for him to drive by to text him and call him out on being creepy. From his half-second glance at her house, he sees the Christmas tree is off the porch and most of the lights are off inside except for one that shines dimly behind the drawn curtains. The heartbreak comes when he sees the second vehicle in her driveway. He doesn't press the brake as he passes her house but he does let up on the gas slightly. He takes it all in and memorizes everything about it as his heart pounds his eardrums: the two vehicles, the empty porch, the plainness, Taylor's happiness without him.

He blames the wine for his tears as he drives home, but he knows they're his own fault. Once he's fully past her house he swivels and sees the side of it before it's hidden by her neighbor's house. His body is on fire and doesn't stop shaking until he's home. One person always loves more.

12

THE SMALLER MAN OF THE TWO

R are nights when Taylor sits opposite him on his couch are moments he treasures like a pirate does a chest full of the riches he's searched for his entire life. Chris sits in ecstasy on his couch for hours, listening to Taylor talk or shrug or casually nurse a beer. He checks her toes every half hour to make sure they're still under the blanket. Why is he here? She has a husband.

Their conversation crests the three hour mark just after 4 in the morning. Around midnight - after being asleep for an hour - his watch vibrated and he thought it was his mind being hopeful again. When he tapped his phone screen, a message from Taylor waited for him. He lifted his head quickly and felt his upper back strain from the sudden motion after being still. Damn being 29. Taylor asked if she could come over so Chris fought his tiredness into a closet to stay awake until Taylor arrived nearly 45 minutes later.

Taylor shakes her beer bottle, sloshing the pathetic sip that is left in it. Chris's anxiety heightens as he waits for her to say that she should go home, that she needs to be there for the cat he knows she doesn't have but won't call her on out, or that she's busy in the morning and needs to be home even though they both know there's nothing she needs to do. Other than say 'good morning' to her husband, that is. Chris prepares his usual speech to convince her to stay. Even if she doesn't need him in the morning because she has someone else, he needs her because he has no one.

"What time is it?" she asks, though she's in the perfect position to see the wall clock next to the door.

"Almost four," Chris says, checking his watch.

"Wow, I can't believe it's that late."

She stretches on the couch and her feet shift closer to Chris, though they don't invite him under the blanket. He craves to touch Taylor, to have his feet intertwined with hers, for her to approve of him showing her affection. They sit on opposite sides of the couch. She stretches and wiggles her legs between Chris and the couch back. Chris lifts part of the blanket to cover his lap. Small steps.

"I should probably get home soon," Taylor says. She doesn't finish the last half-sip of her beer.

"Did you figure out that bank stuff with your house?" Chris asks, digging through hours of conversation from weeks ago when he last saw her. "You were having trouble refinancing or something"

Taylor groans and rolls her eyes.

"There's no hope with banks sometimes. All I want is my house refinanced but without a paperback novel full of signatures they won't do anything, and not just my signature. I need... other signatures, too. And months of pay stubs. I swear doing anything in life is impractical when all of these institutions make it so difficult to even buy a pack of gum. What is it all even worth?"

Chris wonders the same thing. He doesn't mention how he's avoided the home-buying process for similar reasons, and to avoid growing up. Chris doesn't need to ask about the other required signatures. He'd prefer to forget that part of her life existed.

"So what are you going to do?"

She shrugs and he's pulled in. Small steps backward.

"I just keep giving them all the bullshit paperwork they want while I figure out how I'm going to get the signatures I need." She sighs loudly, as if to capture the attention of a dozen people; Chris is already enraptured. "It's all unfair. I do everything in life I'm supposed to and I keep up with my mortgage and I freaking serve people for a living and when there's something I want, I can't have it. Maybe I should just stop contributing to society like all the other losers and maybe then things will start going my way like it does theirs."

"You can't sit still," Chris says. "You told me once that you work so much because you don't like sitting around doing nothing. You'd be bored."

Taylor laughs in a mocking way. "Maybe. It's bullshit that life is set up this way."

"It sucks when you can't have things you want," Chris says solemnly.

"It really does," Taylor says, equally somber.

She finishes her beer with a chug that provides Chris the opportunity to look away and swallow the tears before they can form. He'd spent more than one night on the kitchen floor with Keith shedding tears for what Taylor could never be for him, draining himself of everything for what he loves but will never be able to show he loves. He isn't sure what Taylor would say if she saw him cry, if she thinks crying is a sign of weakness that would make her leave or if she would understand how much he cares, divorce her husband, and be with Chris. That second thought lingers.

Taylor will never leave him for Chris. There's a reason

they're still together through Taylor having an affair, a reason he loves her and she loves him. Chris wonders what that reason is if she's here with him tonight. Chris's feelings stem from the attention she shows when she's with him and the caring way she listens and remembers everything, all a contrast to the countless women that can't remember his name after 5 minutes. How afraid is he that if he stops pursuing Taylor that he'll never find someone who will care as much as Taylor does?

"I've thought about renting recently," Taylor says. "If it wasn't for the cat, I could. So many places don't allow pets. So I'm stuck in a house situation."

Excuses are easier than truth.

"Have you thought about giving up the cat if you want to move out of your house that badly? My place allows pets. Obviously," he adds.

"I don't want to give her up," Taylor says.

He knows that. He also doesn't want to give her up.

She fetches another beer from the kitchen. Chris takes the opportunity to go to the bathroom. He stares at the mirror and wonders what he can say to make her move out of her house and get her own place, what that would mean for the possibility of them dating. He doesn't know how he can continue to sit with Taylor without yelling at her to leave her husband, but he holds it in. He wants to prove to her that they could make it, that their relationship would be enough to make her not want to find another.

His sweaty hand slips from the bathroom counter and he catches himself in a breath he didn't realize he held. Walking back into the living room is simultaneously the most anxiety inducing and relieving moment of his life. Taylor is sprawled on the couch with the blanket over her lower half. She is closer to the front of the couch so that someone could fit behind her. She pats the back of the couch.

"Come here," she says.

Small steps. Chris obeys without hesitation, maneuvering behind her and wrapping one arm beneath the pillow and the other around Taylor's side. Immediately, her 'save me from drowning' grasp tightens around him and she pushes backward until he's pressed against the couch back and she is as close to him as physically possible. A light strawberry perfume floats to him as he breathes in the scent on her hair. His cologne fights back and consumes her.

"You smell good," she whispers. "I'll have to shower in the morning."

Chris holds in the sigh. All those wasted bottles of cologne under his counter.

He closes his eyes to imagine a world where this is the norm: Taylor with him every night, no trouble with banks or promotions, no stress from a marriage, no pressure to grow up, feeling every night like he found the lock his key belongs to. His life's stress would be taken away and he could hold her knowing that in the morning she wouldn't get up early to shower and leave as soon as possible. He wonders how it feels to never have to wash his hands after touching someone. He imagines his void feeling filled. For a moment, it's all real, all exactly as he wants. For a moment. Stretching it out does nothing but make him sad when he opens his eyes and is reminded that none of it is real.

He pulls Taylor a little closer and squeezes her fingers between his a little harder. She doesn't react so he squeezes more but she remains motionless. He loosens his firm grip but doesn't let her fingers go. He often falls asleep holding her and wakes in the same position, her still pressed against him, and his hand still holding hers. That is also a first for him; normally he spins away from whoever he's with.

"If you could move anywhere, where would you move?" Chris asks.

"What an odd question," Taylor says.

"That's not an answer."

"To a very specific town in Texas," she says.

"Does the town have a name?" Chris asks.

"It does," Taylor says.

Chris smirks at the return to the Taylor he knew when they first met. He misses that version of her more than he realized, or maybe he misses the Taylor from before he knew about her husband. Maybe he misses not feeling like a piece of shit.

"Why Texas?"

She lets silence hang before answering. "It's complicated."

"Everything is complicated," he says.

They barely whisper but their voices ricochet in the quiet apartment, with only Keith's loud snoring from the bedroom interrupting them. The air is still and their breathing is synchronized. Their heartbeats thump wildly but also at a near-death pace. Chris slowly sinks lower into the couch and into Taylor's world as the minutes tick past, an eerie calm he's never experienced. A dozen times he nearly drifts to sleep, but then Taylor speaks.

"Where would you move?"

"You never answered my last question," Chris says, "but I'd move to Boston."

"Why Boston?"

"I'll answer if you do." She doesn't respond, so he takes that as a yes, even though he knows it's a no. "I've visited there a few times and I just love the city. The layout, the history, the blend of old and new, the ocean. It's for a lot of the same reasons I love Burlington and wanted to stay here after college."

"I still don't understand why you like this city," Taylor says.

"There's just something about it. It's also a huge change from New York City. Maybe if I had lived somewhere else after leaving home I would like that place more. I don't know. Some places just feel like home."

Her grip tightens on his arm.

"Why do you want to move to No-Nameville, Texas?"

She sighs. "I guess for the same reasons you like Burlington. I moved there after I left my parents and I just had a feeling about it."

She falls silent and Chris sinks further into the mattress. He isn't sure he catches more than every other word that Taylor says. Maybe she doesn't say much more.

"I should probably go home," she says, as if she hadn't suggested this earlier. "The cat is there."

"I could always come to your place, so the cat isn't an issue with staying over," Chris says.

Taylor's eyes go wide and she shakes her head vigorously, as if Chris's suggestion were a disease she could fend off if she hated the idea enough and subdued it into the ground with a forceful enough head shake.

"I don't want you to go," he says quietly. "Please stay tonight."

Taylor's head nods slowly but she doesn't move. Chris climbs over her and off the couch. He holds out his hand to help you get up and he follows her to the bedroom. She walks sure footed but she's slow, the 4 a.m. time increasing the struggle to rise from the couch. Chris has never thought she looked more beautiful.

In the morning, she wakes before Chris, stirring him. She's in the bathroom before he registers what's happening and he hears the shower turn on. Another shower before she leaves and returns to her husband. Another instance of her washing herself clean of him. She nearly sprinted to the shower today.

Chris isn't sure why he wanted her to stay last night when she won't think of him beyond walking out his door. When it closes behind her, he might have to wait a month or two before he sees her again, before she'll even respond to his texts. Their thread will have a large blue block from him to her, and her last reply will be buried. Her husband is more important than him. He knows what will happen but all he thinks is what he'll text her later this week.

After the shower, she dresses in yesterday's clothes as he watches from the bed.

"Sorry about rushing out, but I have to get home to the cat," she says. "Thanks for the shower."

"My cologne is strong," Chris says. "I put some on last night before you came over."

"It smells great but I can't smell like it when I leave," Taylor says. "The cat doesn't like it."

The cat. She finishes dressing and Chris crawls from bed and throws on a shirt to walk her to the door. Keith watches from his dog bed, wishing they'd both be quiet so he could sleep.

"Thanks for coming over," he says.

"Thanks for having me."

"You're literally welcome here any time," he says. "I can give you a key if you want to come over when I'm at work and you need to get away from home."

He leans in and Taylor kisses him distantly back. When she pulls away, she rushes out of the door, leaving it for Chris to close. He holds the handle, struggling to swing the door closed while the cold air has no issue rushing into his apartment and icing him. He waits until hears Taylor's car start up and back slowly out of the driveway, in case she changes her mind and decides to stay with him all day. Unlikely. She has a husband waiting for her.

He turns after the door is closed and is greeted by the handful of empty beers from last night lined like statues on coasters. He plops onto the couch. Is he making a mistake? Is he a bad person? How do you stop loving someone in a heartbeat?

~

STACKS OF FOLDERS and papers piled on Chris's desk creates a barrier to protect him from anyone who looks into his office. Behind the wall, he could feign working while keeping his phone out and open to Taylor's text thread without anyone seeing and judging. He needed to keep the folder level from growing or his manager said he would have 'repercussions' but all he wants is to text Taylor, even if she won't respond. He's hopeful his lack of motivation would prevent another promotion conversation with Devon.

How can he focus on work when he wrestles with himself daily on whether he is a good person or a piece of shit? Two weeks have passed since Taylor last came to his apartment but the texts he sent since are an unanswered blue skyscraper in his phone. If he knew which he was, his mental space wouldn't be taken up with conflicting images of himself: Taylor's boyfriend or adulterer.

Winter started to ease the last week in Burlington, which means it snows a little less but the temperatures are still cold, though not as frigid as they were in February. He started standing outside when he let Keith out to pee and started taking Keith for walks again, which the lazy dog viewed as unnecessary. As dedicated to his 'man's best friend' role as any dog, Keith suffered through the walks and then disciplined Chris by sprawling larger than normal on the couch.

Chris's first cup of coffee wears off. He grabs his cup stained with a circle around the rim and begins the trek across the cubicle farm to the break area. His coworkers wave as he walks past and one tries to start a conversation but Chris is too tired to answer, so Chris waves and pretends not to hear them. As he cares less and less about work and his mind can't tear itself away from Taylor, he's mastered the ability to dismiss his coworkers politely, or perhaps he just stopped caring if ignoring them made them angry. It didn't matter to him which it was.

Halfway to the break room he hesitates. Kelly is most likely at this floor's break area to escape from her floor and to enjoy the view. He didn't disagree about the view, but he also wants non-confrontational coffee. He pivots and heads toward the stairwell. He hasn't seen Austin in a while. He texts him to let him know he's on the way and Austin replies that he's free.

Getting past Austin's secretary is simple, a far cry from the cage wrestling match Harris complained it was. When Chris approaches and waves, the secretary smiles warmly back with sincerity. She even greets him by name and tells him he could go into Austin's office but that he'd have to be quiet for a minute as Austin finishes up a conversation. To not intrude on whatever matter Austin is handling, Chris stays at the secretary's desk and chats with her. Their conversation is cut short when Austin throws open his door, his phone hung up.

Though the 4th floor has a wonderful view, few spots in Burlington beat the expanse that the roof provides. A close second is the 7th floor and Austin's view looking toward the mountains. Chris has learned to accept the adulthood his best friend's position and office demands: four chairs surrounding an unusable small meeting table, a wall of books that would never find a fingerprint on them, and the full wall of windows that lets too much light pour in. He shivers every time he walks into the office and feels his youth and freedom return when he leaves.

Austin works throughout the beginning of Chris's visit, mindlessly answering bland emails that don't distract from his conversation with Chris. Over the past three years, Chris has grown accustomed to his work visits with Austin as visits where his friend works. It never ends for the assistant director of HR. Would that be Chris's life if he accepted a promotion?

A small cutout in the bookshelves holds a keurig and various coffees and teas. Chris picks a dark roast and braces for the same wail as the machine on his floor, though Austin's is quiet, the hot plate inside making the reasonable amount of noise a keurig should make. Jealousy pricks Chris momentarily until he remembers the position Austin's office holds within the Bank and the lack of fun it means he can have in life. That isn't worth a quiet keurig.

"Thanks for rescuing me from all of the bullshit today," Austin says. "I had the next hour blocked off my calendar so people can't bother me."

He tosses his suit carelessly onto his desk before collapsing into one of the plush chairs with a thump so strong Chris swears the building shakes. Chris makes a second coffee for his best friend.

"What's going on that you're so exhausted?" Chris asks as the keurig quietly heats up water. "I thought you loved all of this." He waves his hand around the air.

"I do love my job," Austin says, "but sometimes we all need a break when it becomes a little overwhelming. Today is one of those days."

He accepts the coffee Chris hands him. Chris sits in another of the plush chairs, the table separating the two. Chris appreciates that Austin's office has a door and solid walls so people can't look into it like his own fish bowl cubicle. Austin takes advantage of this and throws his feet on the table without a care if they leave scuff marks.

"What's going on today?" Chris asks hesitantly.

"Angry employees, contract renewal season, benefit negotiation time," Austin says. "The list seems endless today."

"That's a lot of responsibility."

Austin's coffee sits on the armrest as he stretches, his shirt coming untucked in one spot and his pants rising to display his Mario and Luigi decorated socks. His tie is uncentered, the knot sitting to the right of the buttons. Chris has never seen his friend this disheveled at work. He briefly enjoys the lack of perfection.

"Take the rest of the day off," Chris says. "That's what I do when it's a long day or I just don't have the energy to be here."

"Nah, I just need a quick recharge." He closes his eyes and wiggles deeper into the chair.

"I couldn't handle it like you," Chris says. "Not being able to take time off when I want? Dealing with that list of shit? It sounds like hell."

"Aw, it's not that bad," Austin says. "It's no busier than what you do, just a different type of busy."

"It sounds like it's a lot worse."

"It's all perception. For example, my perception is that you could handle the promotion to Devon's team to lead her international team. Though from what I've heard, you're slacking."

"Wow, one-two punch right there," Chris says darkly.

"If I'm hearing about something, it's usually a big issue," Austin says calmly. He keeps his eyes closed and remains slack in the chair. "What's going on with you? It's not like you to have your supervisors reporting to me that you're not doing your job. You're consistently one of the top performers. Is this your way of rebelling so that Devon and co. leave you alone?"

Chris wishes there was a solid wall between him and Austin so they couldn't see each other. Conversations are easier when there isn't someone watching and judging you the entire time you're talking.

"Nah, there's just other stuff."

"You're not leaving my office until you tell me what's going on."

"I thought this was your break time?"

"It is, and you're my best friend," Austin says. "We never get a break from being best friends. So spill."

Chris shifts in the chair, unable to find a spot that doesn't gnaw at him like fire ants. He downs half his coffee in the hope that it would deter Austin's interest in what's happening or would end the visit so Chris could go back to his office and ignore confronting what he's avoided splendidly for weeks.

"Must be something bad," Austin says.

He doesn't press further but Chris knows the conversation isn't over. Austin prods like a million little needle pricks that don't stop until at least a dribble of blood seeps out. Chris's discomfort is accentuated by Austin's silence. Austin's pricks may be persistent, but minutes of silence pass between them as he lets their effect settle over their victim. Chris despises this ability of Austin.

"Relationships are complicated."

"I'm gay. We know nothing but complicated relationships. Why is yours complicated?"

Chris runs his fingernail along the cup while he spins it in his hand, tracing an invisible mark. Though he keeps his eyes focused on the cup, he knows Austin's head is turned toward him. How do you admit to your best friend that they were right about someone you like so much? How do you admit to anyone that you are the 'other woman?' Chris hasn't even admitted it fully to himself.

He could say nevermind and run from the room. His inability to tell Taylor he was done with her the night she admitted that she had a husband proved how cowardly he is, how little he respects himself. Nightly tug-of-wars between staying in love and doing what is right keeps him awake, rocking his mind and heart back and forth across his bed like a pinball machine where nobody wins. Countless nights are occupied with staring at her name and typing out thousands of deleted messages, wondering if he should drive by her house, just in case she might see him and text him. Just in case her husband's car is gone for good.

No length of time being friends with someone makes it easier to admit to them how atrocious of a human being you are. No amount of nights spent through college helping each other get over assholes or being there when one or the other's family member died or standing by each other through every job promotion and supporting the other as they climbed the work ladder, none of the bridges built between them through all of that made Chris certain that it would last when he admitted this to his best friend. He checks his watch to see if she texted him. Nothing.

Fear of what would happen when he admitted what he is to Austin rages like poison through his veins and freezes and burns his blood at the same time. It laughs at him for being too weak to do what is right. He swallows what little pride - if any - he still possesses.

"Things with Taylor took a turn."

"You're going to have to elaborate a little," Austin says.

Chris smacks dry lips in an attempt to wet them to speak.

"Do you remember a month or two ago at the Irish pub?"

"The night it snowed like crazy? Was she in the pub?"

"Not exactly." Chris wonders how many fingernail laps around his cardboard coffee cup it will take before he saws it in half and coffee leaks out the side. "She was across the street." Austin leaves the silence alone for as long as Chris needs it. Chris appreciates that. He doesn't deserve a best friend like Austin. "With her husband."

The air stills and the white noise from outside becomes quiet. Austin's eyes slowly peel open like a garage door.

"You're going to have to say that again."

Chris's lips have never been so dry.

"She was with - her husband."

Austin sits up, leaning his elbows on his knees. He grabs his coffee cup and drains most of it.

"Did you know?"

"Not at the time."

"When did you find out?"

"A week or two later. I messaged her asking who it was. When she finally responded and came over-"

"Well then it's no surprise it took her weeks to even answer you," Austin says.

"When she finally responded," Chris continues, "she explained that he's more of a roommate at this point. She wants to divorce him but some things are stopping her."

"Like what?" Austin's voice is even but the strength he uses when in business mode emanates from it.

"Things," Chris says.

Austin falls back in his chair and finishes the rest of the coffee.

"And you're no longer seeing her."

Chris grimaces at the statement and wishes it were a question.

"I am still seeing her."

Austin stands and paces around his office. He sets the empty coffee cup on his desk so quietly that Chris doesn't think he did anything. He waits for Austin to speak. There isn't anything more for Chris to say. After a minute of pacing, Austin resumes his seat.

"Why?"

Chris looks up from the fingernail-indent coffee cup. "Why what?"

"Why are you still with her? If she has a husband."

Chris doesn't know the answer. Or he does, but doesn't want to admit it.

"I don't know. I like her a lot. She says he doesn't mean anything to her."

"You believe her."

Chris is over Austin's statements that should be questions.

"Yes."

Austin taps some fingers together and stares at Chris. His brow isn't furrowed and he looks like he has everything to say but will say none of it. Chris knows to wait with Austin.

"I don't want to see you hurt," Austin finally says.

Chris tears up.

"I don't believe her," Austin says. "She's been playing you this entire time. She's been dragging you around while having someone at home that she actually loves. I don't like to see my best friend used like this, hurt like this. It's unfair to you and it makes me angry. And it makes me angry that she's cheating on her husband, and that you don't seem to care."

"It's her relationship with him, not mine," Chris says.

"And you think if she dated you that anything would be different, that she wouldn't cheat on you?"

Chris has no response. His best friend verbalizing what he's avoided thinking, hurts.

"I will always love you and you'll always be my best friend," Austin says. "I can't believe you'd continue with this, though. Please end it with her."

"You can't ask me to do that," Chris says quietly. He isn't biting back at Austin; he's begging. Hearing him say out loud what his conscience has said to him for the past two months is a nail through his head. Your best friend's ire is worse than anyone else's.

"I've watched this woman drag you around for over half a year," Austin says "Now we know why and it's horrible and you're still letting it happen. I'm sad for you. I want to see you happy because you deserve to be happy. You deserve to be with someone who will put you first and love you instead of making you a side piece. You deserve to have what you've always wanted and not fill the role of side whore. It hurts me to watch you get hurt repeatedly like this."

"It's not like that." Chris can't put anything behind his words except for patheticness. He can't make himself believe his words.

Austin leans forward.

"Please promise me that you'll tell her that it's over," Austin says. "You can write a text right now. I'll take off the rest of the day to cry with you or be here to bitch about her with you. We can go home and order food and hang out with Keith and move on from her. I'll help you get over her and move on. I'll even write the text for you."

"I..."

"I want to go over there and bitch her out and yell at her how she's ruining an amazing person and being an asshole." Austin raising his voice at Chris is a terrifying rarity. "I'm not going to let her continue to hurt my best friend. Fuck her. She can't do this to you and get away with it. I won't let you let her do this. I'm your best friend when you're at your highest and I'm your best friend when you need a kick in the ass to get your head on straight. So send her a fucking text and end this and then delete her number."

"I...I can't," Chris says.

His will to hold back his emotions fails as his cascading tears put Niagara Falls to shame. He sinks into the chair, enveloped like a child in a too-big-seat. His voice gives away completely when he tries to speak.

"And I can't let you keep getting hurt," Austin says. He moves to the chair directly next to Chris. "Let's send the text and end this."

Chris shakily pulls out his phone. He unlocks it and opens the text thread with Taylor, his blue wall of messages too tall for him to climb right now. He tries reaching his fingers across the keyboard but can't, tries formulating a word in his mind but can't string letters together. He looks up at Austin, whose face is also covered in tears but his eyes burn with rage and passion. Chris breaks even more and drops his phone.

Austin lets his best friend cry everything out. Neither is sure how long they're in those two chairs, Austin sitting up and crying with resolve while Chris flounders in a pile, always the smaller man of the two. Chris doesn't know how he's going to go on with the day, how he's going to focus at work, how he's going to walk home without the hope that he'll see Taylor again. He can't abandon his feelings in a single text.

He picks up his phone, his hand still shaky. He locks it and puts it back into his pocket. Austin says nothing but the fury in his eyes reddens. Chris stands, his legs finding strength they lacked a few seconds ago. He looks down at Austin.

"I can't," he says, his voice strong for only those two words.

He walks toward the door, expecting a hand on his shoulder to stop him or an angry follow-up from Austin. His walk isn't rushed. It's almost a crawl, giving Austin plenty of time to stop him and force him to send the text to Taylor.

"I'll make sure today isn't counted against your time off when you go home." Austin says evenly. "You don't need to talk to your supervisor. I'll take care of that."

Chris doesn't turn to look at his best friend. Best friends just know what you need. He doesn't deserve a best friend like Austin. He grabs the handle and leaves.

13

AUSTIN'S 30TH

Mid-March is a roll-the-dice time for birthdays: either the rare warm Spring day appears where everyone still needs to wear sweaters, or it's relentlessly cold and rainy. Austin's 30th is the later, forcing the planned party to move inside his house. With a finished basement spanning the length of his house and a roofed back patio for the two guests who can't stand being around others, his house is perfect for the planned attendees.

Decorations mar the usually pristine house and normally unblemished pictures and shelves, while platters of finger food, desserts, and various dips and dipping foods sticker the orderly kitchen. A few platters are already set around the house on folding tables and on the dining table, creating a catastrophe Austin would have shut down immediately had he been home while Lydia and Kyle were decorating. Chris did his duty of distraction by taking Austin out for a birthday drink at Austin's favorite bar. Austin's arrival home is met with a mix of joy at the group that gathered to celebrate with him and distress at the disarray of his house. A kiss from Kyle alleviates enough of Austin's horror for the party to continue.

Lydia waits for Austin to be swallowed by the guests before grabbing a tray of pigs in a blanket and carrying them to a table in Austin's overly-large office, where a folding table is set up with four people seated around it, waiting patiently for her to return to start the next round of poker.

"It's about time," Derrick says. "We were about to start a round and kick you out."

"I would have kicked you out from being our normal dealer," Lydia says.

"Who would you find that is as good of a dealer as I am?" Derrick says as he shuffles for the next round.

"There are others," Lydia says.

"Both of you shut up and let's just play," Jeanne says.

She reaches down and pets Keith, who sits with his head on her lap to guilt her into constant ear rubs. His tail flops lazily with every other rub.

"Why did Chris have to give him such an un-doglike name?" she says.

Chris watches Lydia disappear into the poker room with the tray of food. He sits on one of the couches next to Kelly, who holds her second beer. Her first had disappeared almost immediately upon arriving at the party. Lydia had been concerned with how quickly it disappeared but Kelly insisted it was fine.

"Good job with keeping him away for the day," she says when Chris is seated.

They're on the narrower of Austin's two couches, leaving just two cushions for them to sit on rather than the three of his other couch. Chris's leg being mere inches away from Kelly's makes him uncomfortable; they are work colleagues. He twists his head around to scan for her boyfriend but he's not in eyesight. He doesn't need a repeat of *that* Christmas party.

"It was easy. He loves that bar. Plus, he knew he'd be stressed if he were here when Kyle and Lydia were prepping everything.

It would've driven him insane and he would've ended up cooking and decorating for his own birthday."

"Sounds like Austin," Kelly says with a laugh. "Though I suppose having someone that gives so much care to everything is beneficial as the head of an HR department."

"No work talk tonight," Chris says with a sigh. "Let's just forget about work for the night."

"Rough week?"

Chris shrugs. "Austin turning 30, his responsibility at work increasing. I just want to not think about work, even though over half the people here are from work."

"Weren't you and Kyle in charge of the guest list?"

"Yeah yeah but still. I took care of the work friends and some college friends he's still in contact with while Kyle took care of their other friends. All the work people of course showed up because they love drinks, food, and Austin, and have nothing else going on Friday nights. Some of his other friends showed but it's very work heavy."

"Maybe we need new friends so we don't have to talk about work while not at work," Kelly says, "or maybe we need to start being more personable with people at work. Imagine if we shared more personal things at work and stopped just talking about clients and graphs and money? Maybe then we could have a conversation on Austin's couch with a beer that wasn't about those things."

"Non-work talk at work," Chris muses to himself. "It sounds peaceful."

"It sounds nearly impossible," Kelly says with a giggle. "Talking about life on the company's time. How dare employees even think of something like that."

"One more way work takes away the fun of life. Maybe we could all hold onto our youth a little longer if we were allowed to enjoy it more."

"Sounds like there's something more there."

Chris sighs. "No work talk tonight, right?"

Kelly eyes Chris but he stares elsewhere, his gaze vacant yet full of conflict. Instead, she says, "By the way, where is Keith? Damn, I wish you hadn't given him such a weird name."

Chris smiles and leans his head back on the couch's high back. "He's somewhere around here. Probably with whoever will pet him the most or give him the most food. That dog doesn't care about me at all."

"Well give him more food and pets and maybe he'd like you more than us," Kelly jokes.

"I don't think anything will get Keith to like me more than y'all."

Kelly stares around the room, her second beer empty. Austin stands in the dining room with a drink and the platter of pizza within an arm's reach, a group of friends surrounding him with their own drinks and food. Kyle weaves between people with fresh platters of food to keep people well fed. The kitchen's state doesn't improve as the night progresses and empty trays and dishes pile up, but that is an issue for Austin in the morning.

"So what have you been up to besides work?" Kelly asks. "I think someone said you're involved with the Community Garden and something else that I've forgotten."

She shifts on the couch with her legs under and and her body positioned toward Chris. Chris quickly glances around for Austin, hoping he will freak out that people had drinks on the furniture.

"Yeah, I help with the Garden," Chris says. He's thankful for the plate of pizza on the coffee table. The bar drink with Austin followed by nursing his current beer is a little much on an empty stomach. "I volunteer for Church Street projects. I live right there so keeping it all looking nice matters a lot to me."

"I didn't know you lived on Church Street."

"On one of the side streets, yeah. It's less than a minute walk to get onto Church Street."

"What's it like living downtown?"

Kelly stares with such interest Chris feels obligated to pull up a presentation, then share the notes afterward in an email. Other than Taylor, people rarely ask him about what he does, so he dives into the Church Street board, the projects they work on annually around the shopping district, and the food supply the Garden provides the community. Kelly listens to everything and asks clarifying questions at random moments. He forgets momentarily about Taylor and his breathing feels lighter for the first time since August.

"Sounds like that all does a lot for Burlington. You must be proud of it all."

"Yeah, I really enjoy it."

"How long have you been doing it? Seems like it'd be a time commitment."

"Since I moved in five years ago. It's not that much of a time commitment, especially when I enjoy it. That makes it feel like something I'd do anyway rather than something I donate dozens of hours of time to."

"Well I'm impressed at all you do for the community. Especially downtown. It's always so pretty and welcoming. It's one of the reasons I stay in Burlington. Do you think you'll run for the city board?"

"Oh I don't know. It's a lot, Tay-"

Chris stops himself and stares with horror at Kelly. With her third beer started, she doesn't recognize his almost slip-up. The comfort level he slipped into while talking to her is too reminiscent of Taylor: the persistent nature of her questioning, diving deeper into what Chris does, showing legitimate interest in his life. It mirrors his late night conversations with Taylor so closely that it's not Kelly but Taylor sitting on the couch with him, a beer in each of their hands, an infinity necklace around her neck, the desire to crawl into bed and cuddle with her, the prospect of saving her from drowning once again and being needed. Chris makes a note to text Taylor at some point, then grabs his watch with his free hand. Knowing he'll be ignored always feels better when he's a little drunk.

He finishes his beer despite not feeling full enough to be two beers deep. He sets it on a coaster - despite nobody else caring if empty bottles were put directly on the table, which would horrify Austin - and grabs another slice of pizza while searching for a reason to leave the couch and Kelly. His savior comes when Harris bursts through the door with a woman in tow whose uneven steps and constant need to hold a hand out to steady herself on a wall or chair or person displays how much she has already drank.

Harris bounds toward Chris, leaving the woman to fall.

"Sorry I'm late, but she just couldn't get enough of The Harris," he says, leaning on the couch back and pouring whiskey breath across Chris and Kelly.

"Austin is somewhere," Chris says, standing. "I'll help you find him."

"I'll talk to you later," Kelly half-asks, half-says.

Chris waves but doesn't reply. He refrains from tearing up while breaking away from Kelly and leading Harris through the house. Having her listen like Taylor listens, having her ask questions like Taylor asks questions: Chris can't get Taylor from his mind and the way only she can listen. Well, her, and now apparently Kelly.

When he passes from the living room into the open-floor plan dining room, Harris is gone. Chris looks around but Harris is near the back door, the woman he brought again in his clutch, with two of the people Chris wishes hadn't shown up standing with them.

Being drunk makes it easy to forget Harris but Kelly's attentiveness doesn't waver from his mind as he searches for someone
new to talk to. He passes through the living room and escapes
into Austin's office, where Lydia is reliably playing poker. Chris
sits against one of the bookcases with a sigh that makes all of the
poker players angrily look at him for disrupting the peace of
their game.

Grumbling and shifty glances erupt from the poker table
until finally one of them tells Chris that he can stay if he's quiet.
He nods at the warning he's received a few times before. He
pulls out his phone and opens Taylor's text thread. It isn't late
enough for her to respond, but he needs to send something after
the conversation with Kelly. A simple 'hey' satisfies his craving,
for now. Though he doesn't want to have a third beer at an event
with so many coworkers, and the second is already a treacherous
territory for him to venture into with so many coworkers
around, he might need the third.

After sending the text, he stares at the ceiling with his phone
held between his hands like he's holding the hilt of a sword. The
screen doesn't light up but his eyes never stop peaking toward it.
He didn't think it possible for someone else to mimic so
perfectly the feelings that Taylor gave him, to act and treat him
like Taylor does. The urges he felt in the few minutes on the
couch with Kelly reflected too closely how he feels about Taylor
every time she comes over. The incredibly rare times she comes
over.

No, it's not the same as Taylor. Noone is like her. Before
Taylor, date after date, he was disappointed by how bland the
women were, how unexciting they were, how they didn't care to
ask more than a surface level question and conversation
between them never deepened beyond the first question. Then
there was the issue of how the women who did turn into second
or third dates never returned his curiosity or persistence. After

years of failed dates and women who didn't care about what he wanted to talk about, finding Taylor checked off all the boxes nobody else could. So many failed dates convinced him that there would never be another that could repeat the feelings that Taylor was finally able to give him. Then that conversation with Kelly happened, all the way down to the way she sat on the couch with her toes hidden between the cushions.

"What is your problem?" Lydia says, sitting on the floor next to him.

He glances at the now half-empty poker table.

"Bathroom and drink break," Lydia says. "It sucks when there aren't waiters here to bring us fresh drinks. So that's why I'm in a bad mood. What's your excuse? Why are you sulking?"

"I'm not sulking."

"You're on the floor hiding where we play poker so nobody will come in here and find you," Lydia says. "I don't know what else you'd call it other than sulking."

Chris huffs and pulls his knees to his chest, wrapping his arms around them with his beer still in his hand. Lydia relaxes against the bookcase, the alcohol melting her body into rubber that slouches onto the floor.

"I don't know if the issue is that woman you keep pining after or if you're still pissed off at work or why you're so angry, but it's getting tiresome," Lydia says.

Chris sits up straight with a force that thumps like a distant echo against the bookcase.

"Oh, stop acting all offended that I'm telling you what nobody else is willing to, about how much of a bother you've become with this girl and you resisting work so much. It's made us constantly worry about you. Is he going to rage quit work and become homeless because he refuses to just accept the position he's ready for? Is he going to come to one of us having a break-down when this mysterious woman that none of us have met finally shuts him out from her life? It's not been easy being your friend for the past 8 months."

"Well thanks a lot," Chris says. "That doesn't make either of us sound like an asshole at all. I feel so much better. Sometimes you're awful."

"Compliments, compliments. Despite all this shit, we're all still here," she puts a hand on his arm, "and we always will be. That's what best friends do. We're family. No matter how many bad decisions we watch you make, we'll still be here for you. You're still a good person, even if it's sometimes difficult to love you as a friend. And even if you can't see it."

The poker players return, one carrying a drink for Lydia.

"I've got to go kick these idiot's asses to take their money," she says. "Mama lost too much last time we played."

She wraps an arm around Chris. "I love you. I just want you to be happy."

She lets him go and resumes her seat at the table as Derrick deals. Jeanne raises her drink to a teary-eyed Chris, though she doesn't keep her glass raised long when the round starts.

"There you are!" Harris booms from the door, pointing at the heap that is Chris on the floor. "Come on, we're reminiscing stories from college and you just have to tell that story-"

"You can either shut up or I'll knock you the fuck out so you shut up," Lydia says to Harris. "We're in the middle of business."

"A bitch as usual," Harris says. He laughs under the glare of the other poker players.

"She's not the only one who wants you to leave," Jeanne mutters.

Harris ignores them and lifts Chris by an arm. "Come on, you just have-"

"Will you shut up dude?" Josiah says. "You may not care what other people are doing but we'd appreciate some quiet."

"Why is everyone in this room so uptight?" Harris says.

He leads Chris out of the room, though not before annoyed mutters from the poker table reach them. The rest of the party is progressing as expected: the coworkers who are always tired from long weeks sit around the coffee table still nursing their first drink, Austin politely visits each guest, and a few small groups stand around the house, their conversations louder than necessary above the quiet music. Hanging from the walls, draped over windows, and cluttering every surface are reminders and decorations about turning 30. Each stands as a dark shadow Chris diverts his eyes from. He just wants to go back to the floor and talk to Lydia more. There's no reminders of his age there and she did make him feel better.

Harris drags him into the dining room, where half-empty trays cover the table. A handful of guys from their office stand around one end of the table, laughing with beers in their hands, their voices the loudest in the house. Austin sits around the coffee table with his other exhausted coworkers, though he irritatingly glances into the dining room. Chris wishes he could join Austin at the coffee table, but Harris's grip is tight and once he has his mind set on something, it's difficult to get him to think differently.

Chris lets himself be led to the guys in the dining room but busies himself with food before he can be forced to talk. Harris talks plenty for both of them, but points at him repeatedly throughout the story. He's heard it hundreds of times at dozens of parties; worn retellings of a frat party they went to their sophomore year that ended with a small explosion because of *other* dumb people and a cop call that used up all of the good will everyone at the party had garnered with the campus police. Harris's retelling has added in the two of them somehow being involved in starting the fire (even though they were out back when it started inside) and a fight with a cop that ended with Harris temporarily arrested but released when a cop friend of his let him go. Chris keeps shoving food down his throat as Harris's story derails more.

Across the room Chris watches the woman Harris arrived with. She's leaning on the doorframe of the back sliding doors, the stem of a wine glass gracefully gripped inside of her fingers. She's Harris's type: as tall as him, thin, long hair, a too-shirt shirt, and too much makeup. Chris is thankful he and Harris have never had the same interest in women because Harris would steal all of the women Chris liked; it happened often enough to other coworkers. Harris dove so deeply into his own story that he didn't notice Chris sidestep away and into the kitchen.

His only companions in the kitchen are the few remaining trays of food and Alexander, who is known for finishing all the food at a party. Austin and Alexander are at the top of their respective departments. As such, they work together nearly daily, though often it is one giving the other a headache, which is often followed by laughter from both of them. Chris never understood their relationship but he never needed to.

"Hey, I haven't seen you yet," Alexander says. "How have you been?"

"I've been fine. How's the food?"

"Delicious," Alexander says. "I don't know where you all got it from but good job."

"Kyle made all those decisions. I just paid for stuff and distracted Austin. What's new with you?"

"Oh, just life. Baby number 2 is on the way and we're going to start building a shed so we can park in the garage during winter. Who would've thought we could gather so much shit living in the house for only 5 years?"

"It seems so much longer. Is Alicia 3 now? Or 4?"

"She turned 3 a few months ago. Just as she's become inde-pendent enough for us to not have to watch her all the time, we get pregnant and are going to start the process all over again. But

I'm glad I'm getting it done when I'm still young. I can't imagine having a baby in my late 30s or 40s. I just won't have the energy I have now to chase around a toddler."

"You'd still be able to chase a baby around. You wouldn't be *that* old."

Alexander laughs with the understanding that only a father has. "There is so much more to babies than just chasing them around. I also don't want to be turning 60 when my kids graduate high school. Now that would make me feel old. I could be some of those kid's grandfather!"

Chris searches the trays for something to distract from the conversation or something he could eat so he doesn't have to respond, but nothing looks appetizing when there are 30s plastered around the kitchen like stars on a student's paper after they receive an A. Instead, he grabs a new beer from the fridge. Empties cover the counter. Austin would be furious if he came in the kitchen, but Kyle redirects him every time Austin starts in that direction.

"How's the downtown apartment?" Alexander asks.

Chris wishes people wouldn't ask about his apartment because it's always a precursor to a homebuying conversation or some other 'next step' conversation that people think he should take. When he's ready, he'll take the next steps. Why should other people decide when he should be ready?

"It's great," he says. He's learned the more he speaks fiercely about the apartment, regardless of how much he says or if he makes sense, people back away from the homebuying conversation.

"My wife is jealous. She never got to live downtown. We went from shitty college apartments to living together in the cheapest apartment we could find within a 10 minute drive to buying a house. She always wanted to experience what it's like living on the main strip of a city." He shrugs and takes a bite of pizza, which he talks through while chewing. "But she doesn't regret any of what we did. She loves our house and we saved money in the long term." He sighs. "Which we'll now have to stash away for our kids' college."

"Sounds like one expensive thing after another," Chris says. He checks his phone but there are no new messages.

"Yeah, but all worth it."

A commotion from the back door gives Chris an excuse to escape from Alexander. He passes through the dining room and sees Kyle holding Austin back to distract him from the clatter with a kiss. Kyle silently begs Chris to take care of whatever caused the clatter before Austin could escape the kiss and investigate himself.

On either side of the sliding glass doors are stands with plants potted in ceramic, color coded to match the curtains and walls. One of the pots is shattered on the ground and its stem is cracked. Chris grabs a broom and dustpan and cleans up the ceramic and dirt, then throws the plant out the back door over the patio's side as one of Austin's friends apologizes profusely with alcohol-scented breath.

"It's fine, we've all been here," Chris says. "I can't tell you how many plants I knocked over at parties when I was younger."

Now I'm the one cleaning up after others who do it, he thinks.

He pauses while sweeping. The drunk perpetrator asks if he needs help but Chris shakes his head. He checks his watch but there are still no new messages. When he looks up, all he sees are 30s: covering the walls, sticking out of plant's pots, shaped by the food on trays, and sewn into some shirts. He quickly resumes sweeping so the motion conceals his shaking hands. He doesn't remember where he put down his beer. He checks the dining room entrance but Austin isn't in sight so Kyle must have distracted him long enough to make a drunk Austin forget about the clash.

"What a bore," Harris says as he comes downstairs, a different woman than the one he brought following him. "What's going on here?"

His voice lacks any concern and is drowned by the music and chatter around the rest of the house. Chris ignores him as he finishes cleaning up the mess and returns the broom and dustpan to the basement hallway.

"What do you say we get out of here?" Harris says. "I just picked up this chick, Amber, I think is her name, and I have the one I brought. You can have one and we'll go to a bar for a little bit before taking them home."

"It's Austin's birthday party," Chris says. "I'm not going to leave."

"Oh, he doesn't even care who's here, just come out with us. Otherwise, I'll need to handle two women at once. Not that I can't."

Harris puffs his chest and brushes non-existent dirt off his shoulders. Chris rolls his eyes and walks away from him.

"Fine then, be a pussy." Harris turns and grabs the new girl, yanking her slightly from the conversation she started with one of his coworkers. "Let's go."

"We can leave in a little bit," Amber says. "I just met-"

"Yeah, I don't care who you just met," Harris says. "I'm ready to go."

"I didn't come here for you," Amber says. "I'm here to celebrate Austin's birthday."

"Harris, leave her alone if she doesn't want to go," another man says. "If she doesn't want to go, she doesn't want to go."

"Fucking women are all bitches," Harris says, searching the house for the woman he brought.

Chris rushes after him to prevent any fights from starting. Plenty of scuffles arose from Harris's attitude over the years, and Chris always stood behind him, watching but never interfering.

He often had to recount the story to Harris in the morning, which Harris demanded every detail of. On more than a few occasions, Chris left out the part of how someone else at the party intervened and threw Harris out, after which Chris would have to half-carry him home. Chris thought having to interfere in Harris's drunk rampages was in their past, making him detest having to babysit Harris as he storms around Austin's house. Chris shrugs as he rushes past Kyle and Austin, who is too distracted laughing with some of his non-work friends to notice Harris or Chris. Harris doesn't find the woman he brought in the kitchen so he storms back through the house and bursts into the poker room.

"I thought we told you stay the fuck out," Jeanne says from the table.

"I'm looking for someone, so shut up," Harris says.

Derrick moves to stand but Lydia pulls him back down. Harris quickly leaves the room, but the space drowns in the alcohol his breath left. Chris waves an apology as he chases Harris out. Lydia shakes her head but stands and follows them out.

"Let's go," she says as she slides the back door open.

Harris is standing next to it, searching the house for his date.

"She's this way," Lydia says.

"Why the hell is she outside?" Harris asks.

A few guests stare at the three as they go outside, though most of the guests know Harris enough to ignore the entire situation. Lydia closes the door once she's on the back patio with them. The rain stopped, but the clouds hang above Burlington and Lake Champlain.

"What the hell are you doing?" she yells, the door preventing her voice from reaching Austin.

"I'm looking for this bitch." Harris leans over the railing, searching the yard through the dark. "You saw her come out here?" He whacks the railing.

"No, you fucking idiot," Lydia says. "You need to calm down. This is Austin's birthday party. Stop fucking it up."

Harris spins toward Lydia. "Don't tell me what to do, you addict."

Lydia walks toward Harris, who squares her up, though his drunken state makes him wobbly in the wind, which easily whips across the lake and smacks the trio. He steadies himself on the railing as Lydia approaches him. He raises a hand toward her but she raises her foot faster and kicks his balls. Both his hands fly toward his groin and his legs give way, bringing him to a pile on the deck. Chris gasps from behind Lydia but doesn't say anything.

"Do not talk to women like that or like you were earlier," Lydia says. "You have 5 seconds to get the fuck out of Austin's yard before I call the cops."

"Crazy bitch, what the fuck is wrong with you?"

"Me? What is wrong with *you*? How you talk about women is no way to talk about anyone. We're not here just to be 'some bitch' for you to take advantage of. Now get the fuck away from here before I kick you again."

Harris pulls himself up using the railing but keeps one hand over his groin. "Not until I find her."

"She left," Lydia says, "an hour ago, while you were galavanting with another woman. How do you expect someone to wait around for you when you go off with someone else? Nobody is going to just sit around and wait forever for you while you're fucking someone else. So pull yourself up and get out of here. Now."

When Harris finally stands back up, he is miniscule beneath Lydia's wrath. Her shoulders are back and her fists are clenched, her leg buzzing for another kick, while Harris still reels from the first and the one-too-many beers unsteadying him.

"Fuck you," he spits at her.

"Fuck you," Lydia says back.

Harris looks at Chris for help but Chris backs away. Harris flips them both off, spits on the patio at Lydia, then stomps through the yard, squishing the entire way until the side of the house hides his steps on the muddy lawn.

Lydia reenters the house without saying anything to Chris, marches to the front door, and locks it. Then she returns to the poker room. Chris follows her inside but doesn't follow her back to poker. A few people watch Lydia in confusion as she marches through the house but everyone is too lost in their own conversations and laughter to worry about one angry person.

Chris isn't sure what to do, so he checks his watch but there are no new messages. He anticipates a message from Harris at some point, though he's not sure what he would say in response. Lydia's words echo to him the rest of the night.

Kelly has moved to one of the wingback chairs along the wall, the other filled by a coworker. They're talking about something but neither seems committed. Chris wonders where her boyfriend is but someone else calls him over to the couches. He joins a few people in sports talk as he helps them work their way through a platter of pigs in blankets. A 30 catches the corner of his eye.

14

VICES

Christmas and winter are distant memories for Church Street: the wreaths and trees are replaced by patio furniture and umbrellas, and the overhead red and green string lights are replaced with white ones. As Spring creeps its way into existence, Chris is happy the sun rises before 7 so his walk to work isn't in the dark. The downside of Spring is the line at his favorite coffee shop grows as people are willing to brave the slightly warmer late-April weather. He moans and pulls out his phone to order online. He is already cutting it close to making it to work on time and his boss is being a bitch again about his performance.

He saw Taylor last night after more than a month hiatus. The night progressed like every other: a late night text that woke him up, her car crawling into the driveway, a long conversation about his life updates that brought him to the verge of tears, the comfort of chatting with someone who listened to every word, the easiest sex of their lives, and the deepest sleep wrapped into each other with her hand clinging to his arm to save herself from drowning, Keith not caring about either of them. The morning progressed the same, too: she showered quickly to rid herself of his scent before he was aware of what was happening, then she ran out. Chris barely had time to get out of bed before the door closed behind Taylor, and his text afterward will remain unanswered for weeks.

His coffee waits in a spike field on the counter with a dozen others. After battling through the line to get to the pickup counter, he scans the barely visible receipts beneath each cup, the dim lighting inhibiting his reading.

"Shouldn't you be at the office already?" Devon says jokingly from behind him.

He jumps at her voice. "Oh, hi." He spots her name and hands her coffee to her.

"Thanks."

He feigns not finding his own coffee as Devon waits for him, his eyes having picked it out three times. He can't fake stupidity any longer and picks his coffee up, crunching the receipt into a ball. Why did she have to wait for him? He's not ready to suffer through work bullshit yet.

"I'm surprised you're not at the Bank yet," Chris says as they break out of the coffee shop's crowd with a freeing breath.

"I need my morning coffee," Devon says. "How have you been? I haven't seen you in a while, like you've been avoiding me."

Chris groans inside, holding in his fatigue after just two sentences with Devon. Conversations don't happen until he's at least halfway through his coffee, a tradition which Devon rudely ignores. Obligation to respond boils in his stomach.

"Life's been fine. It is what it is."

"Doesn't sound particularly optimistic," Devon says. "What's been going on?"

He imagines Taylor asking last night. To her, he expunged everything like a lie detector was strapped to him. She barely had to press as he divulged more than was necessary but nothing he said was sufficient, so he kept rambling. Taylor listened to him like each piece of new information revealed something she didn't know. It egged him on to explain more. He realized he rambled, but it was difficult to stop when Taylor shrugged in her way and watched him over her beer glass with eyes that told him to never stop talking because then she'd have to fill the silence, and she wasn't brave enough to.

"Life has been fine," Chris says. "There isn't much more to say about it."

"Usually people have something in their life that they're excited to share," Devon says. "Children, a house, a new car, a new TV. People have all kinds of things they're excited to share. Something exciting has to be going on in yours."

"Sometimes people's lives are just what they are," Chris says.

Devon sighs. "Well that's depressing. You do a good job of bringing down the mood sometimes."

"Thanks. That helps to hear."

"Sorry, didn't mean for that to come across like it did. I'm sure there's something positive in your life, even if you don't want to share it."

They walk in silence a block. Their tension encases them in a portable bubble that rolls along Church Street with Chris and Devon as the epicenter. Chris searches for openings to tie his shoe so Devon has to walk the rest of the way by herself or a reason to turn around and run back to his apartment, but nothing sounds legitimate enough to separate from her. He inhales deeply crossing one of the perpendicular streets.

"What's been going on at work recently?" Devon breaks the silence and Chris's patience.

He audibly groans, forgetting to keep his reactions buried. Devon luckily just laughs at him, which makes him want to groan again and leave her even more. The Bank is less than two blocks away: freedom from Devon is so close.

"I don't know what you mean," Chris says. He doesn't convince himself of that.

"You're one of, if not *the* best, we have at the Bank for reviewing and tracking accounts and working with clients," Devon says. "The past few months have seen decreased productivity from you and a general slacking that I've never seen in you."

"No disrespect, but isn't information like that meant for my supervisor, not for someone else at the Bank?"

"It is meant for your supervisor, or for anyone above them."

"Of which you're neither...?"

He slows slightly to let Devon enter the Bank's sliding doors first. "Let's take a trip upstairs," she says.

"I have to get to work," Chris says. "I'm already a little late."

"Your supervisor is fine with it," Devon says. "Come on. You haven't visited my office since I got my promotion. You should also see our floor."

She walks toward the elevators with the expectation he follows. The tellers aren't even in yet, though other Bank employees trickle in like mosquitoes slowly marching toward a bug zapper. He hesitates briefly but knows Devon will just come down to his office if he doesn't follow her. He preferred their confrontation to be behind the closed doors of her office than in the open cubicle he's cordoned to, so he follows.

With her office door closed, Devon makes a fresh cup of coffee in a keurig that is as silent as Austin's, her coffee shoppe cup emptied before she set foot in the Bank. She offers Chris a second cup, which he accepts because he'll need the energy to escape whatever corner Devon is going to use this meeting to push him into.

"So explain what's been going on with work," Devon says with a newfound strength and dictatorship that was missing during their walk to the Bank.

"I've been distracted with personal stuff," Chris says.

"Mmhmm. Care to elaborate at all?"

Sitting behind her desk, a new air of authority drips in Devon's every word. The nameplate on her desk presents her like she's about to deliver the speech of the century. Chris despises how authoritarian she looks and how much like a peasant he feels beneath her gaze. A ping of jealousy smacks him as he momentarily sees himself as the one who should be in her spot, looking down on her.

"Not really."

"That's fine," Devon says. "I'm here to talk about it if you need to or if there's something the Bank can do to help you." She pauses and he leans forward unconsciously. "I have other things to talk to you about. Namely, your new job that starts today."

Chris nearly spills his coffee as he jolts to attention like a soldier seeing their commander walk into their barracks. He spills coffee on his hand and nearly drops the coffee cup as he sets it on her desk to wave his wet, hot fingers in the air.

"Excuse you?"

"I think I was pretty clear," Devon says. She slides a piece of paper across her desk. "As of this morning, you are the Director of International Clients. We've had the position open since I was hired 8 months ago. Kelly is the Director of Domestic Clients and you'll be her international counterpart. You'll be-"

"Director of what - I think not - how is that even possible - I refuse," Chris rambles, his burned finger forgotten.

"You don't much have a choice in the matter," Devon says, though there's no satisfaction in her voice. "The board has been pushing me to fill this position for months. I've been putting it off to wait for you to be ready to fill the position. To be blunt, there isn't someone else I trust to be as successful as I know you will be. I don't want some idiot to work as my second in command. The board said either force you into the position or hire someone else. So I chose the option that I thought would be the better option."

"You can't force me into this promotion," Chris says. "I refuse. I'm not taking this job. I won't be forced into being old."

Devon grimaces.

"Both of our hands are tied in this situation. The board said that either you take this promotion or they'll fire you."

"They can't do that!"

Chris springs from the chair and knocks her desk, the contents of his coffee cup rocking despite the desk's large, immovable size. Devon casually picks up her cup and swallows a mouthful of coffee.

"It's out of both of our hands," Devon says calmly. "Sit down so we can talk."

Chris storms away from her desk. Her office isn't as large as Austin's, but there's still a separate section where a tiny round table is surrounded by 4 chairs. He walks to the table and back to Devon's desk. She watches him go back and forth half a dozen times without saying anything. She doesn't touch her computer or answer her phone the two times it rings; she simply keeps drinking her coffee. When the cup is empty, she makes another.

He could decline the promotion and find a job elsewhere. There are plenty of banks in Burlington that would hire him, even if he had to start as a teller. Hell, his savings could get him through a year of rent if he keeps his spending down. He could even buy a house if he wanted to but he'd never waste his money on something like that. Houses are so permanent, such a commitment. People in their 20s shouldn't be tied down to one place. Freedom is the hallmark of youth.

Turning down the job is career suicide. Years of devoting 8 hours every day to the Bank's clients, the Bank's goals, the Bank's success, would be wasted if he turned down the promotion. He couldn't throw away all that he's done and be bullied out by a board of old people. First they gave Devon his job and now they're forcing him into a promotion. One way or another, they insist on controlling his life. Youth's drawback: older people thinking they own you.

Chris leans on the back of a chair opposite Devon, who has resumed her seat as steam pours from her fresh coffee. His own has stopped steaming, though he still picks it up and downs it; cold coffee is still coffee. He slams the empty cup on her desk; small splatters jump out and mar her desk. He drums his fingers on the chair back while glaring at her. He thought people were done making decisions about his life when he left his parent's.

"How could you let them do this?" he asks bitterly.

"I tried to fight them, but I only have so much power," Devon says. Her stoicism under the lasers of Chris's anger only ignites him further.

"SO FIGHT HARDER!" he yells, wondering how thick her office door is.

He looks down at the chair back straining beneath his fingers turning whiter as he strangles life from the chair. He releases the chair and steps away, waiting for Devon to say something beneath his gaze. He doesn't know what he wants her to say, but her lack of emotion over the situation infuriates him more.

His life is over. He'll have to give Keith up for adoption (nobody will take him because Keith is an awful name for a dog) and he'll have to spend his savings on a house and start buying decor that's minimalist and pointless but will make his contemporaries ooh and aah when they visit. He'll purchase overpriced paperweights that nobody will know what they actually are and he'll start wearing a Rolex and stocking a minifridge full of fancy wine that nobody can afford but everyone expects their hosts to always have on hand. He'll throw away all his non-plain clothing and swap out all of his sneakers for dress shoes, his jeans for slacks. Finally, he'll start color-coding his calendar and laughing every time he has to check it to schedule plans with friends like their hang outs will be business meetings to be squeezed in between watching cricket and clockwork bathroom trips. He already knows which aisle to buy adult diapers in.

"I would have preferred that you voluntarily joined my team," Devon says.

"Well, now what choice do I have?" he yells.

Devon sets her mug down, her nerves expertly veiled with strength perfected over years of standing up to angry men. Maintaining a steady voice is a mostly-accomplished skill.

"I don't want to force anyone onto a team," Devon says, a slight crack in her voice's smoothness. "My hands are tied."

"Well, do your job better and fix this. Don't ruin my life."

"This was supposed to be your team," Devon shrieks back. She stands to rival him, leaning on her desk to steady herself. "You were supposed to lead this team and elevate this division of the company to the next level. Instead, you ran like a scared child and threw away a future! It's about time you grow up and accept that you can't run from responsibility forever. At some point you're going to have to face the fact that you're an adult and start behaving like one rather than a pre-teen throwing a temper tantrum because people expect something of you. So grow the fuck up and accept some responsibility for once in your life and let's move forward and stop this childness."

Chris retracts from the desk. Devon's voice extinguishes his anger and fills all the vacant space in the room like darkness does when the last light goes out. Devon's coffee is forgotten on her desk, though the liquid quivers beneath Devon's words. He slumps into one of the chairs. As if her outburst hadn't occurred, Devon sits and folds her hands around her cup, the mug cooled.

The waiting game begins. Devon expects a response from Chris, but with his anger fleeing beneath her outburst, he has no emotions left to say anything. Without another option, he hangs his head. Quitting isn't an option. He'd rather jump off a bridge to avoid his only path forward. Holding in the last of his pride, he sighs.

"I don't want to fight with you," she says, breaking the silence he is unable to.

"Well, you're doing a pretty shitty job at that if this is how this promotion is going to start," he snaps back.

"You may not think so, but I really did fight to not push this on you, and as your supervisor I will continue to fight in your corner. But I need you to accept that I can't win every fight. There are people with bigger fists than me."

He wishes there were more coffee in his cup. He grabs the cup for something to occupy him. There aren't other distractions in the office to keep him from talking but his stubbornness is always available. Until Devon was given her promotion, their relationship was great: they rose in the same department in the Bank, they sifted through similar friend groups, they went on vacations with the same friends. Their competition through college was friendly, more like two stars at the top of their class fueling each other rather than wishing the other would burn out and fall from the sky.

When the Bank offered him the promotion, his first thought was that Devon would be an equally solid choice for the position, a choice he wished the Bank had made first. The reality of her actually being in the role hadn't changed his opinion of her ability to succeed in the role. His anger started when the first proposition for him to join her team was offered. He turned down one job in that department, and he'd turn down another. He is comfortable in his job and department, and disrupting his life isn't an adventure he wants to explore.

He stares across the desk at Devon. She stares back, though the sharpness in her eyes is gone. There isn't a contract between them for him to sign or a stack of HR paperwork or even a twitch of her lip as her impatience grows. There's just a piece of paper that tells him what his life will become. Her self control squashes his urge to speak without giving him the first opportunity. He wonders if he could have learned how to do that, too, if he had accepted the promotion months ago.

"Tell me what to do," he says. His voice is as flat as he can make it without being rude.

Devon's shoulders rise and fall barely enough to perceive. Had she not been so still for the past few minutes waiting for Chris to speak, he wouldn't have noticed. He wonders if her response is from relief or exhaustion.

∽

THE TWO MINUTES he spent filling a box with his few measly items is embarrassing as Devon watches from the cubicle's entrance. She doesn't ask him to hurry; when he walks toward the cubicle's entrance, she leads him upstairs to the sixth floor, a death walk leaving behind comfort and years of his life. And his youth.

The box weighs nothing as he trudges up the stairs behind Devon. With nothing for either of them to say, their journey is silent. Devon leaves him a turn behind in the stairwell, her quick steps winding upward while his slow thumps echo forgotten behind her. The steps and walls blend together in a mesh of cement gray. With nothing for his eyes to focus on, everything blurs into other people making choices for him, his free will strangled by the Bank. He wants to run to Taylor to be near someone that won't try to tell him what to do, but adulterers don't get what they want.

Is he an adulterer? When he started to fall for Taylor, he wasn't aware of her marriage. She hid it from him and strung him along, lied to him for 6 months as if only what she wanted mattered, as if whatever future he envisioned with her didn't matter. She made him fall in love with her. This situation is her fault, not his.

But he continued it after he found out. He did the right thing by texting her that night to talk about it. He hoped the conversation would change something, that Taylor would recognize that her husband is wrong for her and that she should be with Chris. Many days, he still hopes that she will divorce her husband and say yes to a date with Chris. He should let her go. She lied to him for so long about her entire life and acted without consideration for him, his feelings, or what she was doing to him. He has no reason to still want her or love her, but some people are the only lock your key fits into. Some people show you that you matter, and a gift like that isn't easily forgotten. How do you say goodbye to that forever?

Devon shuts his new office door behind him, the snap cracking like a bone breaking. She said nothing before she left, but she hesitates so briefly before she shuts the door that he isn't sure she hesitates at all. He holds the box and stares around the office long after she's gone. Besides a cobweb-decorated desk and a round table with two chairs around it along one of the dark blue walls, the office is empty. He wonders how long it will be before he joins the ranks of oldies with a silent keurig in his office.

The wall of windows catches his attention more than the emptiness of the office. Burlington sits beneath his view, which extends to the closest ski mountain. Though it's swathed in brown, as the buds haven't yet formed, the mountain is a superior view to the felt walls he worked in for years. It took him a few minutes before he realized that the windows provided enough light to not need even a small lamp.

Lines in the rug show where the cleaner recently went over

it, another courtesy of his new position that nobody would have even thought to offer to him in his cubicle. In spite of the view and the emptiness of the spacious office, he can't hold himself up beneath the weight of what it all means. He's glad his moving box contains nothing breakable as he drops it and collapses to the floor in sobs. He grieves for the parts of his life that are gone and for the things that are now a part of his life that he hoped to avoid for years. His youth is gone.

When he has no energy to continue crying over the change, he pulls himself up and cleans off the cobwebs before removing the box's contents. There are no walls near his desk to hang the pictures on, so he piles them and sets them in the top drawer of the desk. A few desk trinkets lay on their sides in the box like forgotten remnants of a past. He looks around the desk but placing them anywhere on it seems childish, so he leaves them in the box. With nothing else to empty, he sets the box on the floor and sits at the desk. His desk.

It doesn't announce itself with the same grandeur that Devon's desk does. The drawers stick slightly at first and he has to fix two of them before they slide. There are some leftover pens in one and a stack of sticky notes in another. He leaves the drawer contents alone. He logs onto his computer and plays with the settings to mirror his setup downstairs. His wireless mouse and keyboard are strange in his hands, the drag of the chords across the desk from downstairs a sound he wishes he still heard.

As he types in his password, the clicks aren't shadowed by the monotonous typing of the few dozen cubicles around him. His breathing isn't hidden by the talking of a dozen people on phones. The shuffle of dress shoes along the carpet are gone. Instead, his typing echoes around the empty office and every adjustment in his chair squeaks as loudly as a cough in a silent auditorium. His movements are thunder that shake the building.

A gentle knock on his door is a drum beat at a club that won't leave his head. He too eagerly jumps and bolts to the door as if he'd miss an important package if he didn't answer it immediately. He opens the door and it nearly swings into the wall. Lighter than he expected, he starts a list of things in his head he'll have to be mindful of in the new space.

"Hi," Kelly says as cheerfully as possible, though the uncertainty in her greeting betrays the happiness it should contain.

"Hey," Chris says.

She waits a few seconds before saying, "Can I come in?"

He realizes he now has an office with a door he'll actually need to invite people through. Not having an open space for people to come and go as they please will be a difficult adjustment.

"Of course."

Kelly stands awkwardly in the middle of the empty office, staring around it until her eyes land on the view outside the windows. Chris isn't sure if proper etiquette is to leave the door open or closed, so he shuts it until there is a thin crack between it and the frame. He joins Kelly in the middle of the room and stares outside as well.

"Same dull view as my office," she says. "Our old floor is so much better. How are you doing?"

"I'm here," Chris says plainly.

Kelly nods. They stand there for a few minutes, just staring out of the window, two prisoners longingly hoping that they could break out and experience freedom.

"Have you given any thought as to how you're going to decorate?" Kelly asks.

"Decorate what? It's an office."

"That doesn't mean it needs to be boring and plain," she

says. "You can get furniture in whatever color you want and you can order wall paintings or canvases or really whatever you want to hang. I brought some stuff from my old office. Personalize your office a little."

"I could," he says with a sigh.

Kelly breaks from the window and explores the sparse furniture. She sits at the little table along the wall.

"You need a chair opposite your desk, at least. The rest doesn't matter much, but sometimes you'll want to be talking to clients or coworkers from behind your desk rather than this little table."

"I don't want to become too comfortable here," Chris says.

Kelly folds her arms and legs and settles back in the chair a little more. Chris sits at the small table with her, though walking to it is a struggle.

"I'm sorry you're in this situation when you don't want to be," Kelly says.

"Is anyone really sorry about this? Austin didn't even hint that this was coming. Devon seemed to not care that I so strongly said no." He rubs his face, pulling at his skin. "Nobody seems to have even cared that I wasn't asked about this."

"Sometimes the board doesn't care what we want," Kelly says.

"Just another board in charge that doesn't listen to their employees," Chris says. "It's this bullshit that I wanted to avoid."

"You can't avoid dealing with these situations forever. Sooner or later, you were going to have to face it."

"But maybe I wouldn't," Chris says desperately. "Maybe I could've stayed in my previous position forever and retired from there. I wouldn't have to worry about a new job or being pushed around by the board or risk losing any part of my life. I would've been happy staying there forever."

"I'm not sure you would have," Kelly says.

"You don't know much about me."

"I know enough from when you've helped that you're talented at this. I know that the monotony of that position for 30 more years would have bored you. It's meant to be an entry-level position just above a teller. There's no challenge to it."

"Maybe I liked not having a challenge."

Kelly bounces the foot of her top leg.

"Do you think you can do the job?"

"Of course I can do this job," Chris says. "It's just a more advanced version of my previous job. With supervision."

A soft knock at the door interrupts them. Austin's head appears through the crack. When he sees Kelly and Chris, he opens the door to pop his entire upper body through it. Kelly stands but Chris doesn't follow suit.

"My office is the next one over," Kelly says. "Feel free to stop by whenever you want. You can get some ideas for decorating."

"Thanks," Chris says with a bite.

Kelly says hi to Austin as she leaves. Austin fully closes the door and sits across from Chris with a large exhale to prepare himself.

"Surprise," Austin says with a shrug.

"A warning would have been nice," Chris says. "Really anything. What's the point of my best friend being at the top of HR if I can't even get a heads up about something like this?"

"I wasn't allowed to say anything until Devon told you," Austin says. "My hands are often tied. There's not much I'm legally allowed to say."

"I would have yelled at you but I wouldn't have told anyone. All I wanted was a little heads up that my entire life is going to change."

"Oh stop being so dramatic," Austin says. "Your life isn't going to change except for where you spend eight hours a day in this building."

"What about work trips I'll be forced to go on or if I have to stay late or if there are late night parties I'm obligated to attend? What about if I can't finish reports and someone yells at me to finish them or get fired? What about if my staff can't do their jobs and it reflects on me and I get fired and then my life is disrupted because of things I can't control? What about-"

"Dude, pump the brakes," Austin says loudly. "You need to take a breath and just get settled before you start worrying about anything. You're not going to have to worry about any of that. It's going to be fine."

"You don't know that," Chris says a bit louder than he means to be. He appreciates that Austin shut the door. "Next I'll be buying a house and have to schedule a time to see friends and have work on my mind 24/7 as I hope that everything that needs to get done gets done."

Austin laughs and pulls a granola bar out of his pocket. The wrapper crinkles loudly as he tears it apart and pulls it down. Everything echoes in this damn empty office. He bites it and talks as he chews. Chris finds it disgusting but appreciates Austin's attempt to be as disgustingly casual as possible.

"The reason Devon wanted you so badly for this position and that I also recommended you is because we know you'll be able to get this part of the Bank up and running. We also fought to not extend your hours. Supervisors usually have an extra hour a day they're expected to work but we kept your schedule the same as your previous job. We're trying out a new policy and you're the guinea pig. If it goes well with you, all supervisors will shift to your schedule."

"Great, so on top of being forced into responsibility I don't want, you're also messing with my position and trying new things. Why don't you just start deciding what I wear for the day and when I can eat and take a shit."

Austin sighs and leans his elbows on his knees. He clasps his hands and stares at Chris.

"This was the best we could do. Our hands were tied."

"Now you sound like Devon," Chris shouts. "Me being forced into whatever the Bank wants me to do without my considera-tion isn't your best. Your best would have been to prevent this entire situation from occurring."

Austin takes another deep breath. Chris is envious of his best friend's control. When one inconvenience arises or one person raises their voice, Chris loses his control and matches the energy. Sometimes he wants a fight, wants Austin to shout back to validate Chris's own raised voice. Sometimes Chris needs the anger thrown back to quell his own.

Chris springs from the chair and paces around his room, his long strides easily carrying him most of the distance across his office. He curses the lack of items in his office, the lack of things to fidget or large furniture to move around to exhaust his energy. He wants to leave to go to the lounge on the fourth floor and stare out the window but he can't leave Austin.

Moments like this make him miss his family. When he and his siblings got into fights, they would throw insults and aggres-sion back at him with as much force as he delivered it. When he and his parents got into fights, they could argue for hours, wearing down everyone within earshot. After they stormed off to their respective rooms, they'd emerge hours later with no hard feelings and no apologies, but the fight would never be talked about again. Chris wishes Austin would do this, but that isn't the type of person Austin is. He appreciates Austin for that.

"If this position wasn't filled, the board was going to recon-sider how this department works and whether it's worth the investment to continue it if we couldn't find an acceptable and accomplished person to fill the role," Austin says quietly. "Devon and I fought the board to wait but they were insistent that a

position of this level shouldn't be left open for so long. The
conversation has been happening for a month and Devon and I
had almost daily meetings with the board to try to delay this
because we knew it wasn't what you wanted. I'm sorry this
happened. Making your position a guinea pig position for
working hours was the most I could do to make the transition
easier. I did everything I could. Devn did, too. We are both sorry
you were forced into this."

Chris drops into his desk chair. The space between him and
Austin is enough that Austin can't see Chris's watering eyes;
Chris likes the privacy of a closed door. Both can hear the
others' ragged breathing in the quiet the office offers. Fighting
can occur in the silence between two people.

"I need to go back to work," Austin says. "Let me know if you
need anything."

When he stands, Chris says, "I'm sorry."

"I know. As am I."

Austin closes the door behind him. Chris spins slowly in his
chair, taking in the enormity of the office compared to his cubicle. Austin's words ping around his mind but he pushes them
out. He doesn't expect to get any work done today. His emotions
are pinballing all over the spectrum and he has no motivation to
get everything set up or dig into whatever Devon's going to
assign him. He groans and lays his head on his desk.

His phone is in his eyesight, forgotten about since he first
stepped into the office. He picks it up and opens the messaging
app. His fingers hover above the keys. After how many messages
will he no longer be able to say that Taylor is the one who used
him? What magical number of messages will make him a fully
complying adulterer ruining someone else's marriage? When
can he no longer forgive himself? Can he forgive himself now?

There are worse vices.

15

MOVING FORWARD

Winters remnants cling to Burlington in brown streaks and puddles along the roads, birthed from multiple late-April snows that melt the next day. Church Street is a stained victim with empty flower pots and patios often forgotten about in the rain and melted snow. As Chris walks to his usual coffee shop, he sidesteps around a group of beggars and avoids eye contact with two coffee carts selling questionable smelling coffee. He lifts up his jacket's collar to add a small barrier to the back of his neck against the morning's chilly wind, but little has helped to cut out the cold since his promotion almost a month ago.

Arriving at least a half hour early to work is his new norm, an unwritten obligation to arrive before his staff that he loathes, not because they're bad workers, but because the responsibility for them was forced on him. Initially, waking up earlier was a battle he lost when he muted his alarm and ignored its repeated screams. After a week of being ashamed to walk in when some of his employees were already at their desks, peering out at him like he betrayed them, he forced himself out of bed and to the Bank earlier. Other than not being a morning person, the line at the coffee shop a half hour earlier is always a few people longer, but he refuses to give up coffee shop coffee. He'll hold onto parts of his old life if it kills him.

Walking into the Bank when almost nobody else is working is a phenomenon he isn't sure he'll ever be comfortable with. Motion lights flicker on when Chris walks into the building, like unwelcoming will-o-wisps lingering in a cemetery, waiting for new residents. Hallways he once strutted through he now scurries along to escape the loneliness of being at the Bank this early. If he slows down, he's convinced the Bank's emptiness will capture him.

Hiding in his office with a cup of coffee is his new morning ritual. He misses his previous ritual of bullshitting with a coworker or two for an hour while going through two cups of coffee. The acquiescence of a door with his promotion is a benefit he won't admit out loud that he enjoys; it's outweighed by the expectation to arrive earlier than everyone else. When he watches Kelly roll in an hour later and Devon shortly after her, he wonders how long the obligation in him will last, and how long it lasted in them.

At the end of the day, he stays until the last person he supervises leaves; they always dawdle until 5pm rather than leave with the others at 4:30. People in other departments linger longer, though he doesn't have to wait for them. The only lights remaining on are the one or two cubicles where the dawdling employees sit, lighthouses announcing a disruption to Chris's schedule. When they finally leave, all the other motion sensor lights in the Bank are off. Arriving and leaving in darkness is not his idea of an enjoyable start and end to the day.

Devon pops in at least twice every day, but Chris finds an excuse to shut his door and lock her out, often remembering a meeting on another floor or excusing himself to call a client. She had full access to his calendar, though she never says anything about his fake meetings. He knows eventually he'll have to be in a room alone with her and listen to whatever she says, though he'll delay that until avoiding her is no longer an option. He won't give her the satisfaction of again getting him where she wants him, even if Austin claims they had no choice. There is always a choice.

A date planned tonight with Taylor is the motivation to not rage through the day and burn the Bank down. Last weekend she came over at 1 a.m. and like clockwork they each drank a beer, talked for a few hours, and went to bed fitting together like a key in a lock. He wasn't sure who needed who more that night. The following morning, he finally garnered enough bravery.

"I have a question," he said as he laid behind her with an arm over her and a few beams of morning sunlight breaking through the slits in his blinds.

"Mmhmm," she responded without moving.

"How is, uh, how are things going at home?" he asked.

"They're happening."

Two words that shared everything.

"So, it's, uh, it's been a while, that you've been coming over here," he said. "With nothing really happening at home, and, you know, I was-"

Continuing was impossible. Would she say yes or would she leave and never speak to him again? Would his texts be forever unread and would she block his number? He'd played with how to word this question for so long, struggled with what time to bring it up, if he should bring it up. The risk of her leaving accompanied his ask, no matter how perfectly he prepared. Now felt less right than any other time, but everytime she was over might be their last time together. Either he finally grew the courage to ask or he would keep wondering what could have been.

"What?" she said patiently.

"It's just, given how things are...for you," this would be easier if she would finally divorce her husband, "and we seem to get along well. So I just thought that we could go out to eat sometime. Rather than always meeting here," he added quickly.

He hoped she didn't notice how sweaty his hand wrapped around hers was and that the sweat rivers on his forehead didn't run down to her. The comforter was a blazing sun covering him and the mattress pushed back into him like a brick wall covered in spikes. He immediately regretted asking her.

"Sure," she said with the same detachedness she held all night.

He impulsively squeezed her hand and pulled her closer. Hiding his excitement was impossible but Taylor didn't seem to mind. For once, he didn't worry about not seeing her again.

Five days later he's sitting in his office with his door closed and an empty second cup of coffee, his new quiet keurig in the corner shining green, ready to pour another cup. His stack of unanswered blue messages to Taylor over the past week glare back at him.

CHRIS (SUNDAY MORNING): Does Thursday work for our date?

Chris (Sunday night): Where do you want to go for our date?

Chris (Monday afternoon): Hey =) are we still on for our date?

Chris (Tuesday night): I'm still thinking Thursday night?

Chris (Thursday morning): Should I plan for six-ish?

HE STARES at the text he sent this morning and swipes up so the blue stack bounces. He hopes that each swipe up would reveal some hidden response but he's met consistently with disappointment. He types out a hundred other messages that vary from long to short, accusatory to apologetic, inquiring to demanding. None are sufficient; a thousand desperate messages deleted like they never existed. He tries rewriting a sentence on one and replacing a word on another, but each adjustment is as inadequate as what they replaced.

He tosses the phone so it flops twice on his desk before settling next to the mouse. Both monitors have long been in screensaver mode, though his phone knocks the mouse, waking them so their bright blue screens glow at Chris as another reminder of his forgotten blue texts. He shifts files around his screen and types in numbers as if any of them could be a distraction strong enough to forget about the ignored date. She still has time to respond. He repeats to himself that there's still time for her to respond.

The rest of his day is consumed with fumbling around on his computer and two meetings that could have just been emails. He's grateful for them anyway because they're more distractions. The longest distraction of the day comes when Austin lets himself into Chris's office with barely a knock but two Chinese takeout boxes. He sets one down on Chris's desk with a pair of chopsticks.

"Did you check with the secretaries to make sure my calendar was open?" Chris says without reaching for the food.

"Just shut up and say thank you," Austin says as he plops in one of the two chairs Chris ordered for opposite his desk. "Fuck, are you ever going to stop being so passive aggressive about this promotion? And again: I had *no* control over it."

Chris grunts but accepts the takeout box and pulls apart the chopsticks with a snap. His favorite noodles and fried chicken waft from the box.

"Is there-"

Austin tosses a wrapped sticky bun across the desk.

"Of course I didn't forget to get sticky buns. I may be 30 now, but that doesn't mean I've forgotten how to order Chinese food properly."

"Well, you are older than me," Chris says, letting a smile crack for the first time with Austin since the promotion, "and I can't let you forget it."

"You're barely six months younger than I am," Austin says through a mouthful of rice.

"Younger is still younger," Chris says. "I'll always be the more attractive one."

"Debatable," Austin says. "Keith will always be more attractive than you."

Chris laughs, the memory of what that feels like with his best friend returning after a month of not letting Austin see him happy at work. He lets out 30 days of laughter that Austin matches. The source of their laughs may have started with the joke but quickly becomes the two of them laughing at nothing. In seconds, their laughter fills the office and Chris can't help but feel the pressure from his job fade as the anger he's held for the past month dissipates.

"How is Keith?"

"As lazy as always," Chirs says as he digs into his Chinese food. "Yesterday was the first non-rainy day in a week, so I figured we'd go for a walk. Instead, when he was done going to the bathroom, he climbed back up the steps and went straight back to the couch. I swear that dog is just a lazy human."

"He's the cutest lazy human I've ever seen."

"Yeah, everyone thinks he's so cute but nobody has to take care of him."

"And yet you'd be bored without him," Austin says.

"I never said I dislike him, just that he's annoying. It's like a child that can never express explicitly what they want."

Austin jabs at some pieces of rice that aren't sticking together well and succumbs to scooping them up.

"It's campfire season now that it's getting warmer," he says. "My first summer having fires on the lake. My house has room for everyone to have a place to sleep if we drink too much. No more floor sleeping! And with Kyle there permanently soon, I'll have someone to help me clean up the next morning every time."

Chris slows down chewing.

"Permanently? Did he move in with you?"

"Not yet, but we're going out to dinner tonight and I'm going to ask him if he wants to move in with me."

Chris falls back in his chair but doesn't stop slurping up the noodles. He didn't realize how much he missed takeout lunch dates with his best friend.

"That's quite the large step," Chris says.

"He won't be on the mortgage or anything, not yet. Not until we're married."

Noodles drop from the chopsticks halfway to Chris's mouth.

"Married? When did you ask him?"

"Not yet," Austin says with a smirk. "I've been thinking about it a lot recently but I haven't been able to talk to you about it because of...everything." He swirls his chopsticks in the air. "But yeah, I'm thinking of proposing. I have the ring picked out and I think I know when I want to ask him."

Chris blinks rapidly and tries to find something to say but shock twists his tongue until he eventually screams out a congratulations.

"Thanks " Austin says with a smile as innocent as when Chris first met him in college and Austin was just a nervous freshman in a new place with no friends and no idea what he was doing with his life. Austin's life may have changed, but Chris feels like he's still in that place some days.

"Do you think Kyle knows you're going to ask him? Are you going to ask him about both at the same time?"

"He has no clue. I love him but he is truly oblivious most of the time. He's the easiest person to throw a surprise birthday party for. I've never had to try hard to hide things I plan for him because he never notices things. I swear men are so dumb."

Austin laughs and all of the tension between them vanishes.

"Do you need any help? When are you going to do it? Are we going to be there?"

"So many questions," Austin says jollily. "I'll ask him when it's just us. He loves crowds and people but more intimate things like that he prefers to be in private. Plus I don't want something like that being super public. At most I'd have you and Lydia over."

Chris raises an eyebrow. "No Harris?"

"I haven't seen him since he ran out on my birthday and left that poor woman there alone. I don't really have a desire to be around him. That was sort of the last straw for me. And now if he confronts me, I have a legitimate point in time I can point to as the last straw. It's been a long time coming."

"I can't believe you're writing off Harris," Chris says. "He's been with us since college."

Austin shrugs. "Some people aren't meant to be in your life forever. Harris is one of those people. I'm sad because of the last decade with him but he's just no longer the type of person I want to have as a friend."

"Don't you think you're being a little harsh? He's one of our best friends."

"You're my best friend, not Harris. I've had people leave my life for far less than the shit Harris has pulled and said." He pauses. "I've lost so many people that losing one more almost doesn't even register."

Chris swirls the last few noodles in his takeout box.

"I just can't imagine cutting someone out of my life that I have so much history with."

"It's never an easy thing to do," Austin says. "It hurts every time but it hurts more to keep pretending like I'm ok with how he treats people and how he talks. I'm tired of acting like we're still in college. You can still hang out with him, but he won't be invited to my house anymore."

"This conversation sure took a turn downwards," Chris says solemnly.

"Difficult things always come at inopportune times. Nobody's ever prepared for what they're going to have to do. You have to make a choice about how you're going to handle difficult choices. I'm choosing to remove toxic people from my life so I can be happy."

Chris finishes his takeout and tosses the empty box in the trash. They sit in silence while Austin slurps up the rest of his, their thoughts on what capacity they each want Harris to be in their lives. Chris struggles to care much as thoughts of his date with Taylor tonight consume his mind. She hasn't texted 'yes' but she also hasn't texted 'no'. He clings to that sliver of hope stronger than the cloud of 'no' creating lightning streaks above his head.

"I've got to head back upstairs," Austin says. "Meeting in ten. I'm sorry to have brought up the situation with Harris."

Chris shakes his head. "It's fine. I'm excited for you and Kyle. I can't wait to hear the story of how you do it."

"Thanks." Austin lingers with his hands on the back of the chair for a moment. "Do you want to come with me to pick up the ring? I need someone else to approve it."

"Sure, dude, just let me know when."

Austin smiles and starts toward the door. "And Euchre this weekend."

"Yeah. We'll kick ass."

～

STARING at the clock makes it tick slower, as if it senses Chris's apprehension. He left the cologne Taylor likes in his closet so she doesn't have to shower before going home and his knuckles are nearly white as he squeezes his phone tight enough to crush it. Keith stares from the couch with his 'over it' eyes. His head lays on his paws as he waits for Chris to leave so he can sleep in peace.

Since leaving work an hour ago, he's added more bricks to the blue skyscraper of messages to Taylor. All of his messages are unanswered but it isn't yet the time for their date. There is still a chance, and if the clock keeps crawling forward, she has more time to respond. If the clock can freeze forever, their date will never pass and he won't have to face that she won't respond. If time can just freeze, he doesn't have to move forward to meet the inevitable stand-up from Taylor.

The minute hand finishes its final crawling ticks to the 12 as the hour hand points straight down. Chris checks his phone and swipes up in Taylor's text thread but no message breaks up his blue tower. He restarts his phone, then does the same to his watch. When both are powered back on, he refreshes the thread repeatedly, then checks the internet for a breakdown in communication apps. He sends Taylor another text saying that it's 6 and he's ready to meet for their date.

Gravity becomes a burden that drags him to the floor and against the bookcase that his TV rests atop. The next hour passes in a flash of his living room tilting and his seemingly broken phone sending him all types of notifications except one from Taylor. He looks to Keith for an answer but his dog is asleep, or at least pretending to be asleep. The hour passes like a movie rewinding the last 9 months, replaying everything Taylor said and everything she made him feel. They all pass out of him through tears that have fallen too frequently because of her.

Two hours later, Lydia answers Chris's text with the devotion of a Knight of the Round Table. She walks into his apartment just after 8 with a box of Krispy Kreme donuts and a six pack of beer. Keith leaps up when Lydia walks in and she's forced to set everything down to assuage his excitement. She observes Chris as she scratches Keith's ears: Chris's legs are splayed out in front of him like a murder victim's lifeless corpse and his phone is just out of reach of his fingers. He doesn't look up as she enters or when Keith bounds off the couch.

"Maybe I should've brought a second box of donuts," she says.

She sets the donuts on the floor before plopping next to Chris and pulls two beers from the six pack. She twists off their tops with her jacket and hands one to Chris as Keith resumes his seat on the couch. When Chris doesn't take a beer, she sets the open drink nearby, their legs touching. She takes a long swig of hers before opening the donuts.

"Other than King Keith demanding you get off his couch, why are we down here?"

Chris shrugs and grabs the beer bottle but doesn't drink from it. Lydia is halfway through her donut before she speaks again.

"I'm not there to just talk to myself. I could just do that at home while watching serial killer documentaries. So you're going to have to say something eventually."

"I don't know what to say."

"Is this about Taylor?"

Chris drinks some of his beer.

"I'm not here to tell you how to communicate with me. You better eat a donut."

"You don't have to feel obligated to feed me."

"That's not what I mean. If you don't eat a donut now, I'm going to rip through the box and there won't be any for you."

Chris dubiously takes a donut and sets one on his leg.

"So what happened?" Lydia asks.

How does he explain the last 9 months so that she'll understand? Lydia is a brick wall that doesn't take shit from men. She wouldn't have been strung along by someone for 9 months. She wouldn't let him hear the end of being the other man to a married woman.

"We...were supposed to go on a date tonight," he manages.

"What happened that I'm here instead of her? I'm beautiful but I'm not going to fuck you."

He sighs and finally realizes how uncomfortable the bookshelf is to lean against. Keith's snores help to fill the long gaps it takes Chris to respond. Nobody seems to care that Chris's responses are choppy, like a child who knows some words but is still learning how to say others. Alcohol doesn't hinder his speech; he knows exactly what he is going to say, exactly how to explain the situation. Admitting to Lydia that he knowingly helped a married woman cheat for months is what stutters his speech. How do you forgive someone for doing that to another person?

"She...didn't respond."

Finding the words to explain himself is searching for a friend in hide-and-seek who has already quit and gone home. Lydia doesn't pressure him and none of her responses are harsh or biting. Her first beer empties before she speaks again while Chris's is barely touched.

"When did she respond last?"

Could he show her the unresponded to mountain of blue texts he sent Taylor? Lydia's response would be to tell him to stop being a bitch and delete Taylor's number. He didn't care to listen to Lydia be her usual self and write off relationships, but between her and Austin, she is less likely to judge. She knows Chris and Taylor were a thing - whatever that thing was - but knows little of the details. When did Chris become the person who hid these things from his best friends? When did he lose himself in chasing Taylor?

"When we hung out last?"

"For fucks sake," Lydia says desperately, downing half of her second beer. "When was that?"

Chris takes a bite of the donut.

"Little over a month ago." He hopes his words are muddled in the mouthful of donut.

"Uh-huh. Why so long ago?"

"We, uh, we usually only hang out that often. Sometimes longer."

"Why's that?'

"I'm not sure. It's when she messages me back."

Lydia notices Chris finished the first donut so she takes another one from the box and sets it on his leg. She did buy a dozen, after all. She's a good friend.

"How do you feel about it?"

"I'm pissed," Chris says louder than he intended. "Sorry."

"Be fucking pissed if you're pissed," Lydia says. "Feelings aren't something you should ever be sorry about."

Chris crushes part of the donut between his fingers.

"She'll sometimes not respond to me for weeks or months at a time. I'll sometimes spam her two or three messages in a row, thinking that multiple dings will get her to respond, but she never does. I just send message after message with no response. When she finally does respond, it's usually near midnight and she comes over and we talk about everything until we're ready to sleep. She always pretends she has to go home and I pretend like I don't know she's going to stay, so I convince her to and then we go cuddle as we fall asleep and it's literally the safest, most comfortable time I've ever had with anyone. It's so weird how well we fit together in bed and how I feel like I can tell her everything, things I feel awkward telling Austin about. It's just not fair.

We're so good together. We are perfect for each other. Why did she have to lie to me for so long? Why does she have to be married?"

He abruptly stops when he realizes tears are accompanying his rant. Lydia is unphased but her second beer is empty. Their six-pack isn't going to last long.

"How do you feel about being her whore?" Lydia asks.

"That's a rude way to put it."

The truth isn't something he likes to hear others say out loud.

"Don't be mad when someone calls a spade a spade," Lydia says. "Answer my question."

Keith rolls onto his back, his legs in the air and his paws bent.

"I don't like it," he says quietly. Speaking about it out loud feels like standing under a hot shower after being caked in mud in a thunderstorm. "She had said for so long that her husband was more like a roommate and that she didn't love him anymore. I thought that maybe I could finally ask her on a proper date and we could go out and I could show her what a real relationship is like. I never thought she'd actually say yes, but the dumb side of my brain thought, maybe." He pauses. The next part he doesn't want to admit. "I knew she wouldn't follow through with a date." There's no controlling the tears.

"It's hard breaking through to someone when they stay in a relationship simply because it's too difficult to leave."

They eat another donut each, after which a belch escapes Chris. Lydia slows downing beers, though her third is as empty as Chris's first.

"It's just not fair," Chris says. He hasn't stopped crying since he started 20 minutes ago. "I've tried so hard. She's said how comfortable she is with me and how calm she is with me. She's said everything you say to someone you want to date. She doesn't even love him! Why won't she go on a date with me? What's wrong with me? Why can't someone love me?"

"There's nothing wrong with you," Lydia says. "Sometimes it's just not meant to happen."

"But everything with her is perfect," Chris pleads. "*Everything*." His voice cracks while whispering.

"Obviously it's not," Lydia says, "or we wouldn't be here eating donuts on the floor."

Chris reaches for his empty first beer and is immediately handed a second by Lydia. She'll polish off the last one sitting in the six-pack when she finishes the last donut in the box.

"It's easy for you to say that when you haven't experienced this, when you're not in it," Chris says. "If you knew what Taylor made me feel, what the moments were like we spent together, maybe then you'd understand the position I'm in."

"Loving someone who has done nothing to deserve your love and has done everything for you to leave, but you just can't?" She rolls a sleeve of her hoodie to her shoulder, revealing a faint scar that blemishes her from behind her neck to halfway down to her elbow. "This is what happened the last time I loved someone who didn't deserve it but gave me all the warning signs that I should run."

"Oh my god, Lydia, I didn't know-"

"None of you did. It happened two years after we graduated." She opens her fourth beer, emptying the six-pack. "He was just like Taylor: said all the right things, made me feel the right things, touched me right. Storybook perfect. He rattled my bones, his love was so powerful. But thunder doesn't always rattle your bones in a good way: the nights he spoke to me like I was a hooker he could pimp out, the mornings he'd verbally degrade me until I cried. The night this happened.

"He swore afterward that he never meant to hurt me, but don't they all swear that afterward? If they didn't mean it, it wouldn't have happened for them to apologize for in the first place. We were discussing moving in together and went to visit a condo. On the way home, we stopped for dinner and to discuss the condo, which ended with a disagreement. Then we got back to his place and he drank a few beers. He yelled about the condo, so I raised my voice to match his. They never like that. Next thing I knew, it felt like a truck plowed into me and I was on the floor with blood pooled around me. I couldn't move. The door shut."

Her tears streak as thick as Chris's, though her voice doesn't crack and she doesn't fumble for words. She stares straight forward with fury and an unwavering tongue, a woman who has conquered the fear, or at least conquered it enough to not let it rattle her bones anymore.

"I don't remember how I got to the hospital. He showed up eventually. I let him explain to the doctor what happened, some lie about my falling while making dinner and a knife fell beneath me. My own clumsiness. I wasn't going to let someone make me the victim. I couldn't stand to be his toy anymore. I was tired of being muffled for his happiness. I stopped him and told my story. The doctor had him leave and called in a cop and it turned into a 7 month investigation that ended with an order of protection. That day in the hospital, I decided I was done letting anyone else tell my story or drag me along or decide what was going to happen in *my* life."

"Lydia, I'm so sorry. We never knew."

"Because I didn't want you to. At the time, I wasn't sure how to tell other people and I was embarrassed. I hid everything, even from my family. A man physically attacked me and I ended up in the hospital with a lifelong scare because of it. How could I face anyone and tell them? How could I tell anyone that I fell in love with someone that made me look so dumb, that literally broke my body as well as my will? How could I tell anyone how weak I was to fall in love with someone like that?

"Eventually, I found the courage to tell one person, and three years later finally told my family. And now I'm telling you because I don't want to see you dragged around and used like I was. I don't want to watch you be in love with someone who will hurt you like he hurt me. You may not see it and she's not physically hitting you, but she is emotionally abusing you. Nobody deserves this treatment. She's an asshole. There's someone out there who will message you back and won't blow you off on dates. There's someone out there that won't make you eat a dozen donuts on the floor with me."

Chris wants to say something to console Lydia but nothing seems adequate after years of her keeping it a secret. She stares at him with conviction reserved for when she's winning a poker hand and wants to trick others into gambling more. He shrinks beneath her gaze. She is equally terrifying and inspiring him. How can he ever be as strong as she is?

"I always wondered what happened that changed you," Chris says. "You were always so quiet in college."

"I learned how to stand up for myself. Guys are turned off when I throw back at them whatever they throw at me, but I don't care. If they can't handle being called a bitch, they shouldn't call me a bitch first. I've met a few guys who don't say that stuff but they tend to be complete pushovers that can't hold a conversation. I don't know where the happy medium is. Guys seem to be one extreme or the other. I can't find anyone that's in the middle. Sometimes I'm terrified that I'll be alone forever unless I settle for a guy that's one way or the other."

"What stops you from settling, if you're nervous? What keeps you moving forward when you might have something if you just settle?"

"Knowing that I'm worth being loved by someone good. Knowing that we *all* are worth being loved by someone."

"Am I still worth that, after what I've done?" Chris begs.

"We are not our mistakes," Lydia says. "We are who we choose to be tomorrow."

Her tears don't stop but neither does her steady voice. Chris marvels at her strength. He rubs his thumb along the beer bottle, wiping the bead of sweat that runs down it. Beneath the quiet of his apartment and the sternness of Lydia's gaze, there isn't more for him to say. He doesn't know how to move past his situation, though he isn't sure he wants to. What waits for him if he moves forward without trying for Taylor? A life of searching for someone who will make him feel what she so easily pulls out of him? The task is daunting, though so is pursuing someone who doesn't care.

Blocking one number would help him move forward, an action that takes a second but erases 9 months, like they didn't happen. Such a simple thing. Such a difficult thing.

He pulls his phone to his side and unlocks it. Taylor's text thread is already open, his embarrassing pile of blue messages shining proudly for Lydia. For the first time, he doesn't try to hide the messages or conceal the situation. He lets it hang before Lydia like an opened journal full of secrets he thought would stay hidden forever. He expects judgment but that's not what Lydia offers. Instead, she takes his hand in hers and says nothing. She is the best friend he could ask for.

They don't move from the floor or speak for the next hour. In her free hand, Lydia maintains a firm grip on her fourth beer, which she sips from gradually to make it last, while in Chris's free hand is his phone, which he gradually picks up and puts down to check that no new messages have come in. Their hands grow sweaty but neither of them lets go.

"I don't know if I can stop," Chris says quietly. His voice isn't as steady as Lydia's.

"It's not easy," Lydia says in an equally quiet tone. "If it were easy, you would have stopped after the first time she hurt you. But you are not alone. And you *can* stop. You don't have to do it right now. But you can't keep this up forever."

There isn't more for them to say, though they don't let go of each other's hand until Lydia stands to go to the bathroom and let Keith out. Back inside, she marches to Chris's kitchen to make food, the four beers taking their toll on her ability to walk and stand. Chris watches from his spot on the ground, his own urge to piss irritating. Having not eaten dinner and rarely drinking more than one beer once a month on nights when Taylor decided to make an appearance, he also stumbles to the bathroom and then joins Lydia in the kitchen. She has plates of pasta and sauce. He sits at the counter and she slides the plate of pasta toward him with a fork. She gets her own plate and sits next to him.

Chris grabs for his phone but it's back in his spot on the floor. His hands feel weird without being able to grab it immediately. He breathes a sigh that is more relieving than sad. Lydia's phone is also on the floor by the bookshelf. He enjoys sitting at the counter without worrying about his phone or feeling like he has something to hide or something to explain. Pasta has never tasted so good.

16

WHO DOESN'T LOVE YOU

Two months have passed since Austin's birthday but hauntings of the number 30 pop up around Chris at every turn, like red flags warning him of what awaits him in July. He tries escaping them, but the number knows his moves and readjusts itself so he'll run into it regardless of the effort he puts in to avoiding it. Social media is the largest offender, as all of his friends seem to post about 30 creeping up on 90s babies.

Harris drones about his escapades, his bar adventures that are the same night after night. The names always change and the pickup line is always fresh, but the plot never differs. After not having seen Taylor in more weeks than he remembers, and no longer wanting to be a part of Harris's escapades, he doesn't care to listen to any of the stories.

He spends an hour each day over lunch in Austin's office. Harris doesn't come by Austin's office anymore but stops by Chris's daily, often two or three times daily, though the extra walk upstairs deters him some days. Chris doesn't mind; he'd rather spend the lunch with Austin and hearing about Kyle's reaction to being proposed to or the latest project the two of them tackled on Austin's house, which has transitioned to outdoor projects as the weather warmed up. May isn't hot, but the soft wet earth makes ideal conditions for digging and landscaping.

"I used to hate presenting with you in college," Austin says over a small pizza, half of which is history. "You were always so lazy. Now we're doing it together professionally."

Chris finishes his third slice while relaxing in one of Austin's chairs, his belt a tad tight as he debates starting slice number 4.

"I thought you would always be too far ahead of me to present together again," Chris says. "Head of HR is a title far above what I'll ever achieve."

"Don't doubt yourself," Austin says as he starts on slice number 3.

Though they couldn't eat as fast they could back in college (and Kyle often reminds Austin that a dad bod starts when you hit 30, a reminder that Chris ignores because he refuses to turn 30 anytime soon), the two still tackle the challenge with the confidence of their 20 year old selves.

"Did you finish the presentation?" Chris asks.

"Of course I did," Austin says. "We may not be able to eat as much as we did in college but my work ethic hasn't changed. And neither has your lack of contribution."

"Hey, I know you'll do a better job than I ever could, so why take that away from you? Plus I gave you the numbers. You made them look pretty."

"That's not as helpful as you think," Austin says. He sets half of the slice down and exhales deeply.

"Oh come on, you can't start a slice and not finish it. We aren't quitters."

"If my body would let me finish the slice, I would."

They stare out of the wall of windows at the Spring mountainside and landscape of Burlington, the buds a harbinger of warmer weather. Chris would miss snowboarding and the white mountain faces glistening back at him from his office window, but he would gladly welcome being able to walk home down Church Street without shivering and without a coat. He checks his phone but there are no new messages. Austin sighs, and though his eyes aren't on Chris, he knows why Austin sighs.

"We're not all as lucky as you," Chris says in response. "Let us have the little happiness we have."

"It's not about being as lucky as I am," Austin says, "it's about knowing your worth."

"I know my worth."

"If you did, we wouldn't be having this conversation right now." Austin stretches and has to retuck his shirt into his pants. He's stopped wearing a tie as of late, though he'd have on a full suit when they presented in an hour. "When did she message you last?"

She hasn't communicated with him since she bailed on their date. More messages from him have gone unanswered, his blue skyscraper higher than the tallest building in the world. Each new message is a hope that ends in disappointment. Chris can't admit that Austin is right. He's wrestled with this since his breakdown with Lydia 3 weeks ago.

He's sat on his floor multiple times with the delete button hovering just beneath his finger, a red button that dares him to press it, but he never can. Memories can't be erased with the press of a button, but 10 months of communication with Taylor can be erased with a button. Deleting her number would end so much frustration and sadness in his life, but it would simultaneously end the source of bliss. Removing one at the cost of the other isn't worth it. Though, his mind does drift more often to deleting her number than it ever has.

"Why do you always ask me that? Does it really matter that much?"

"When I watch you put yourself through that, yes, it matters quite a bit," Austin says. "If you knew your worth, you wouldn't wait weeks or months for her to message you and then run to her when she does. You're worth far more than waiting for someone who doesn't care about you."

"Harris wouldn't judge me like this," Chris says, knowing he crossed the line. Chris considers his plans to meet Harris out for drinks tonight.

His best friend stiffens. "If you want to make yourself feel better by comparing how he and I react, fine, but think about which friend you'd rather have. We're no longer in our 20s able to go out every night and party with a bunch of single women and go on thousands of dates. You'll be 30 in a few months, too."

"Thanks for reminding me," Chris sighs.

"Just reminding you as often as you compare me to Harris."

Chris folds his arms and asks to see their presentation. Austin pulls it up on a tablet and tosses it into Chris's lap. They sit in silence as Chris pretends to review the slides while silently fuming over Austins comment.

A callback to the countless presentations Austin created for the two of them back in college, the slides Chris scrolls through for the board is even more pristine: succinct information, cleaner colors, and a more minimal approach that highlights only the parts that matter for asking for more money to expand their department. Devon would be in attendance as well, though only as an observer and to clarify questions above Chris's pay, though she told him she has little doubt there will be anything the board can throw at Chris that he won't be able to answer. She often reminds him since his promotion that his expertise in data is the reason she insisted on forcing the promotion on him. He refused to let Devon know how much he appreciates it now that he's in the position.

Most days he starts with a quick emptying of the emails that poured in overnight. Despite his elevated position, he refuses to check his email after leaving work. He won't let work take over his life or his personal time. After the quick email dump, his secretary waves as he passes and walks downstairs to the break area that Kelly can always be counted on to be in. He sits and chats with her as a debrief about their respective areas, then heads back to his office; that is the highlight of his day. He closes his door, gladly taking advantage of that benefit of his promotion; another thing he appreciates that he won't admit to Devon. To decompress, he stares out his wall of windows at the Vermont beauty while drinking his coffee. Then his day's hard work begins as he trudges through the admin tasks he put off from the previous day. At some point, he expects a visit from Devon. He's no longer cold toward her, but he still doesn't look forward to her visits. He's still not happy being forced into the position, but it's not as bad as he expected it to be.

"Satisfied?" Austin asks.

Chris nods and hands the tablet back to him. He stares at Austin's half slice still in the box and at what would be his fourth slice, abandoned and never to be touched. Chris keeps his phone in his pocket the rest of his time with Austin, which causes more stress on him than if he had checked it. Confirming there is nothing relaxes him more than wondering if there is nothing.

A half hour later, the board members leave the conference room in duos and trios. Devon stays seated near the back along the wall; the chairs around the table were reserved for the board members. Next to her is Austin's secretary with a tablet full of notes, mainly on the reactions she witnessed during the presentation so Austin knew who he'd have to win over later.

Austin plays a character with the few board members who dawdle after the presentation. Instead of continuing to talk about the funding increase, he asks about their families and pets and other personal items that Chris knows nothing about. Austin's personality may be tiresome, but having that on Chris's side is helpful, and it takes away the need for Chris to feign interest in any of their lives.

Marissa corners Chris in the round conference room. Since his promotion, he's dodged into stairwells and found reason to miss meetings she would attend. Chris's life grew tumultuous after her initial offer last summer, and he isn't sure he's ready to face the reason for his upended life. Hiding from her is his only hope he has of not having more of his life thrown out of the normal youthfulness he strives for.

"Great presentation," she says with an empty mug in her hands, the sides and bottom of it stained with coffee. "I'm very impressed with the job you're doing. I think it is very likely you'll receive increased funding for the positions."

"Thank you," Chris says. He tries pivoting but Marissa blocks his way even when he turns, as if she could disappear and reappear directly in front of him.

"How has the new position been going?" she asks.

Chris refuses to tell her the small pieces of the job he appreciates - the office door, the windows, the functional and quiet keurig - and throws around the negative parts in his mind to paint in the darkest way possible the 'gift' of the forced promotion. Nothing comes to mind other than menial complaints that mirrors his previous position: minor miscommunications and outdated computer systems. Instead, he pivots the conversation.

"The job is fine but Austin did most of the heavy lifting for our presentation. He's stellar at his job and can explain any questions you have better than I can."

"Yes, he's quite exemplary at his job," Marissa says. "How's your work with the community garden going?"

Chris is startled at how Marissa easily shifts the conversation to something entirely non-work related. He expected this to be an interrogation of his new position.

"We've started to plan for the summer and organize who is responsible for which plots."

"Do you still have open plots? I'd like to join the garden and take care of one of the plots. We can't have a garden at our current residence."

"You want to work in the garden?" Chris hopes his surprise doesn't translate as disrespect. He may hate the board for forcing the promotion on him, but he doesn't want to make enemies.

Marissa laughs the exchange off in the most genuine way he's heard anyone laugh at the Bank. Her careless laugh eases the tension Chris brewed when she cornered him.

"Sure, we still have multiple plots," Chris says. "There's an application you'll have to complete so our garden board can officially assign you to a plot and send you our information packet about allowable vegetables and a list of your responsibilities."

Marissa bounces on her feet and smiles broadly to Chris.

"Of course! I'll look for the application on the garden's website and get it done today. I'm glad we could make this partnership work. I've been looking for more ways to get involved in Burlington on a grassroots level and this is perfect. It's a great way to get my hands dirty." She smirks at her pun. "Good job again on the presentation. We're meeting tomorrow to discuss the proposals."

She winks at him before spinning to free him. He sighs relief and checks his watch. No message from Taylor and still too early to leave work. He silently thanks Marissa for his office door and disappears behind it until he can leave.

~

RALPH'S is the diviest bar Harris could find. Dim lighting, paired with the cheapest drinks in town, attracts a crowd that densely packs the bar so everyone's shoulders collide. Harris often accidentally 'collides' with a woman and then buys her a drink, a move that works on people despite half of the bar's female patrons having been subjected to Harris's pitiful move. Being a regular and good friends with the owner means he always gets a spot at the bar, even if it is full, a benefit Chris is thankful for; he hates tables.

"So many ladies to choose from tonight," Harris says when he starts his second beer, though he's repeated the phrase three times since they arrived. "You could have one, too."

"I'm alright," Chris says. "I just want a drink or two and then to go home. It's been a long day. It's been a long week."

He is disgusted with himself for admitting that work was long: between preparing all week for the board presentation, firing someone for poor performance, taking on all of that person's clients while they find a replacement, and starting a new initiative with Kelly's team, he's wiped out. He understands why Austin has been fulfilled with one night out a month rather than multiple nights out a week, and he understands why Austin and Lydia welcome a night at home having dinner as opposed to visiting Harris's dive bars. He hates admitting it but he's half-ready for that life, too.

No, that would mean he's getting older. He's not 30 yet, and he's not going to lose his youthful freedom to this job. He would take back what he just said if he could and drink until he blacked out with Harris. If that's what holding onto his youth means, he'd cling to it like a hospital drip in his arm keeping him alive.

"Fuck, these drinks are cheap," Harris says, though his attention is everywhere in the bar except on Chris. "I can buy three women drinks for the price it would cost me to buy one at those fancy downtown bars. Fuck them. Yo, what about that one?"

Harris slaps Chris's upper arm playfully and points toward one of the walls, where a woman sits alone, though a half-empty glass with a coaster across the top is across from her.

"Looks like she's not alone," Chris says.

"Of course she isn't, she's too pretty for that," Harris says quickly, nearly cutting Chris off. "But while her friend is in the bathroom, I can sneak my way in there. Fuck, here she comes. Too slow. I'll get the next one."

"How was your week?" Chris asks, though the sentence sounds unstructured and wobbly.

"There's another one, oh two!"

Harris points to the next table over from the first woman. Chris squints through the dim bar, trying to make out any features on the women other than their long hair and round breasts. He can't see their face or discern the colors of what they're wearing.

"How can you even see anything?"

"Listen, they're not ugly, and that's all that matters," Harris says. "Besides, the lights will be out when we go home so we won't see them much anyway, not that we need to, right?" He laughs and nudges Chris hard with his elbow, the two beers and his lack of caring making his nudge too strong.

"I, well," Chris starts, but isn't sure how to finish the sentence, so he pulls out his phone to check the messages.

"Not this shit again," Harris says. He grabs Chris's phone and puts it on the bar face down. "Listen, there are plenty of other women in this place that will actually give you the time of day. Hell, they'll go home with you tonight! No waiting, no checking your phone. Then tomorrow night you can come back and get another one. What more could you want from life?"

Chris barely hears Harris's monologue. He stares at his

phone beneath Harris's palm and wonders if he missed a message from Taylor before the phone was ripped from his hand or if, in the few seconds since it was ripped from his hand, Taylor had texted him. He turns around his wrist and checks his watch, but there are no new messages.

"God damn when did you become such a bore to go out with?" Harris says exasperated. "I remember when you used to be fun. Now you're just obsessed with whatever the hell is going on with that girl."

"You can do what you want, and I'll do what I want," Chris says.

"Do you even get to do what you want?" Harris says and drinks a large portion of his beer. "Like damn, at least I can get laid when I want to You can't even get a text back."

Chris raises his head to stare at Harris. With Taylor, he has a consistent person to look forward to talking to (when she messages him) while Harris has a new woman every night, most of whose names he doesn't remember. With Taylor, he has something consistent to look forward to, while Harris never has something for more than a night. Chris is tired of listening to Harris. His situation is fine and Harris knows nothing about it. In response, Chris grabs his phone and focuses his attention on his beer.

"What is even going on with her?" Harris says, looking at Chris. "What's so special about her?"

"There's so much," Chris says, though what it is and how he feels because of it escapes him. "There's so much..."

"Mmhmm," Harris says dubiously. "Sure sounds like it. What's the issue, then? She's not good at taking dick? She wants a family? She's married?" Chris damns Harris's ability to see the slightest muscle twitch, which Chris uncontrollably makes with his ear when Harris mentions marriage. "Well, ain't that a bitch," Harris says. "Is it even worth it to have to share someone you love with someone else? I mean, I share women with each other all the time, but a married bitch, why bother?"

Chris tightens his fingers around the beer bottle, making him nervous it'll shatter.

"Listen, bud, I've been there before. Well, not in love or anything, but I was involved with a married woman, a few times. They just want someone to listen to them when their husbands won't and some quick good dick and then they're back to their husbands. They're never going to love you, and you'll always be chasing them while they always choose someone else. I learned that with the first married woman that wanted The Harris. Fuck her. Pick up a chick here."

"They're not all like that," Chris says.

Harris laughs, though in the tightly packed bar with enough commotion to warrant a sound warning like at a concert, his laugh disappears.

"Sure they're not. That's why you're here with me without a message from her." Harris finishes his second beer. "I don't think it's worth it to fall for someone who doesn't love you. That's why The Harris never lets himself get attached. These women aren't worth letting yourself get hurt."

"Maybe if you cared a little, you'd find someone who is worth loving. Just because you haven't found that doesn't mean the rest of us can't."

"God, you sound just like that faggot Austin," Harris says.

Chris slams his fist on the bar counter, rattling the glasses and coins on it. The patrons nearest him stop their conversation to look at him, and the bartender takes a step toward the duo, though Harris raises a hand to calm down the bartender. Nobody's eyes leave Chris.

"Don't call him a faggot, and don't try to minimize what I'm feeling with Taylor," Chris says.

"This is why I'm glad Austin has stopped coming out," Harris says. "It's always a lecture. I just want to have some fun before I'm old and my dick can't get hard. That woman is ruining you and ruining my chance of having a fun night out picking up chicks with you. Fuck her."

Chris stands abruptly, prompting another approach by the bartender. He pulls out his wallet and throws $10 on the counter.

"Fuck you," he says to Harris through tears. "It *is* worth it to love someone. One day, it'll be worth it."

"Fuck you, dude, get the fuck outta here," Harris says.

"And these women aren't here for you to talk about like they're pieces of trash for you to fuck and throw away. They're people. Treat them like it for once, you asshole."

Harris laughs and flips Chirs off as he walks through the bar. "Go home and cry your heart out that your little slut doesn't love you," Harris calls after him, though he's again drowned out by the overly loud bar crowd.

Chris bumps into everyone he passes and hits the back of two chairs not from drunkenness but from the patrons packed like sardines. Two people take offense but the rest are regulars and have learned to not care if they're bumped into. He trips over a purse forgotten on the floor, grabbing the back of a chair to save himself. The table's occupants glare at him, but quickly return to their conversation, though their side-eyes follow him out of the bar.

There are no empty spaces in the parking lot behind Ralph's. Damp air hangs around after an earlier rain, though now the sky is clear, the moon lighting the parking lot where the broken streetlights should have. Chris's one beer has no effect on him, though Harris's aggressive words don't leave him. He pulls out his phone but there are no messages. There are never messages.

He walks through the parking lot and down two blocks to Church Street, which he crosses over quickly, and takes an alley to walk the back way the last three blocks home. Crossing Church Street, he straightens his jacket's collar to partially hide the lower half of his face, which by this point is a cemetery for tears. There are never any messages from the one person he loves that loves someone else.

It's not late but it's also past the point anyone would be out who isn't already at a bar. The back streets are quiet except for the occasional car. Every other streetlight is hidden behind empty tree branches, creating a spider web of shadows on the sidewalk. His phone hasn't vibrated once with a new message. Fuck Harris.

"Someone who loves someone else," echoes.

He turns up his street. Looking up, the opposite end of his street ends in a dazzle of lights from Church Street and he sees the undecorated sides of all the buildings facing away from Church Street. Everything is dark beneath the moon's dim glow except for the dazzle of Church Street, which looks less colorful and welcoming than normal.

He trudges up the slight incline to his apartment but stops at the first building. Out front is a navy blue Ford Explorer. The beer in him lurches up his throat and he stumbles as flashes remind him of the night he saw Taylor and her husband getting into his navy blue Ford Explorer. Everything suddenly moves: the incline tilts sideways and the navy blue Ford Explorer crashes into him and he blacks out but his feet keep running until a cold night breeze whacks him from between two buildings, snapping his eyesight back and realigning the street. The navy blue Ford Explorer is unmoved, he's unhurt, and Church Street is still a light at the end of his street. He heaves deep breaths that don't calm his pulse.

His building is four away, though it seems much farther as he power walks back home, glad that nobody else on his street is outside. Hurrying to his apartment is less embarrassing when nobody watches. The lights lining his windows beckon him home, the only other source of light on his street outside of two flickering street lights.

Keith watches in confusion, though his lack of a physical response other than an annoyed eye roll shows his level of concern as Chris slams the apartment door behind him and collapses against it on the ground, his breaths heavy. Sweat coats his forehead and his arms shake.

"Fall for someone who doesn't love you," plays through his mind.

His hand shakes as he pulls his phone from his pocket, the phone as heavy as all the weights in the gym compacted into one small device. Lifting it to eye level proves impossible, so he sets his hand on his lap and opens Taylor's text thread. There is no hiding the emotions painting his face. He struggles to reread his endless messages to Taylor through tears and his shaking hand, as if he doesn't have them all memorized.

He taps on Taylor's name and pulls up the info. Diverting his eyes from her number is impossible. He scrolls to the bottom of her information. In red, "Delete Contact" waits for him, as it has countless nights. Pushing it is simultaneously stabbing himself and also releasing Taylor's stranglehold on him so he can breathe for the first time in months. His thumb hovers over it, unable to drop on the button to erase Taylor from his phone and life.

A paw appears on Chris's arm. He looks up and Keith is a foot from his face, his droopy eyes staring into Chris's, his paw supportive on Chris's arm. Chris sets his empty hand on Keith's paw and takes a deep breath, then presses "Delete Contact." Taylor's name is replaced with a string of 10 numbers that could be anyone's number. His whole body shakes. Keith sits next to Chris, their bodies pressed together.

Chris goes back to the list of text threads, a string of 10

numbers at the top. He swipes left and a red trash can icon appears. Keith's paw presses down on Chris's arm. Chris squeezes Keith's paw lightly. He breathes raggedly through his mouth and droplets of water splatter on the phone screen and on the floor. Chris is thankful he's already collapsed on the floor because he wouldn't be able to hold himself up. He's barely able to lift a finger to swipe on his phone.

How do you act on a moment that will make hundreds of moments over the last 10 months mean nothing, like whispers that disappear into a dark night? Months of wrapping into someone who knew him better than his best friends, of tossing every bit of his hope into the same basket that always catches fire, of finally finding someone who he never feels dirty with, will be erased with a tap. When did people become something we could easily remove from our lives, a string of actions we can bury without anyone knowing it ever existed? How can love mean so little?

He breathes out a breath so long he wasn't aware he could hold that much air in him. Keith's paw is everything on his arm. He presses the red trash can. In a second, 10 months of memories with Taylor are gone forever. He marvels that love can be deleted so easily without any remnants of it except for foggy memories that will never be real again, that will wisp away into nothing.

He texts Austin, "Please come over" and waits for his best friend to arrive.

17

DAY ONE

Blackout curtains trap Chris in a black box with no hope of light breaking through. He rolls across his bed and pulls a pillow beneath his head, gripping it for life but not knowing why. His fingers act on their own, twisting the rough, worn fabric of the pillowcases between them. Watery morning eyes blur the digital clock on his dresser. His alarm didn't go off, so it must be the weekend, meaning he can sleep in.

A drip from the coffee pot manages to pierce his black box. He perks his head up, wondering who slept over last night. He has no memory of anyone in bed with him last night and he didn't feel anyone get out of bed this morning. Keith would make noise if he needed to go out but he couldn't turn on the coffee pot. Chris rubs his eyes and the digital clock morphs into 9:30. He shoots upward and jumps out of bed, sending his phone flying off his comforter to the floor. Fumbling to untangle a foot from the blankets, he grabs his phone and checks the messages. No thread from Taylor is there. His legs give way and he chokes down bile. He throws his phone onto his bed, not caring if it hits the wall and shatters.

Austin opens the door in sweatpants and a sweater - his all-day lazy outfit - with a cup of coffee in each hand. Without asking questions, he sits on the floor next to Chris and hands over a coffee cup. Memories of last night flood down Chris's face but he eagerly sips the coffee, burning his lips, the steam doing nothing to dissuade him from downing more of the hot coffee.

Austin's legs are pulled near his body, giving his arms a resting place to dangle his coffee cup between. The two men sit close enough that part of Austin's foot is under Chris's leg and their thighs press against each other. Chris sets his coffee cup down and lays his head on Austin's shoulder to cry while Austin slowly sips his coffee, his free hand on Chris's leg. Chris puts his non-coffee hand on Austin's and squeezes. He doesn't like being on this side of things.

"At least it's the weekend," Chris says.

"It's Friday," Austin says softly.

Chris's eyes shoot awake but his body has no energy to do more.

"We should be at work," he says quickly.

"We should both be right here," Austin says.

A level tone replaces his usual bounciness. As Chris exhales, his body vibrates, quaking the coffee in their cups. He closes his eyes but no amount of will or physical force can stop the tears, no amount of wishing and praying to a God he long ago stopped believing in would change what he did last night. Two of Austin's fingers find their way into Chris's palm. He squeezes Austin's fingers.

"What happened last night? I remember texting you...but nothing after that. I feel so sad."

His voice quakes in a whisper.

"You were on the floor when I got here. Your phone was thrown across the room and you looked like you had cried for a month straight. Keith was lying in front of you and you were wrapped around him. He looked relieved when I walked in."

"Of course he did," Chris says with a laugh that is a half-cry.

"I wasn't sure what happened at first but you said her name and I checked your phone. I'm proud of you."

Chris's sobs increase to violent shakes against Austin, though his best friend remains rigid. Light from the open bedroom door sets a dim haze over the room. He squeezes Austin's fingers, though they don't fit between Chris's likes Taylor's did.

"I hate this," Chris says.

"I know," Austin says.

"Why is it like this?"

Austin sighs deeply from experience. "It's awful, and it's not easy. Life sucks sometimes, and the pain from deleting her number is probably some of the worst you've ever felt. It feels like you no longer have a reason to look at your phone or get out of bed, that there's never going to be a replacement that can say things the way she said them or fall asleep wrapped up with you fitting the same against you as she did. There's a lot of lonely nights ahead and they hit like a train when you're tied down and can't fight back and all your breath is permanently knocked out of you." Austin reaches his other hand across his body to place it on Chris's arm. "I'll be here until you can breathe on your own again. Day one is the hardest."

For the next 20 minutes, Chris devolves into more blubbering but Austin stays on the floor with him against the bed the entire time, waiting for Chris to calm down. He sips his coffee so it doesn't grow cold but Chris's has lost all of its steam, the mug cooling as he cries. Slowly, Chris's sobs grow spaced out until they are sniffles. He wants to check his phone in case she messaged him, but it's too far away and he knows she will never message him again. He twists his arm to check his watch but it's dead. Old habits are hard to break.

Austin eventually stands, reaching a hand down to pull Chris up with.

"I'll make some breakfast."

"I'm not hungry."

"I am, and you're going to eat some of it."

Chris sullenly looks up at Austin offering his hand. He grabs it and allows himself to be pulled up. Austin goes to the kitchen, leaving Chris for a moment alone in his room. He doesn't like the hollowness of his room, the space that should be filled by Taylor that never will be again. Chris stares at his phone, a forgotten piece of trash on his floor. He's unable to pick it up because he knows what he wants won't be there, but he also craves to check for a message. Old habits. A headache attacks him and heat rushes through his body like adrenaline. The clatter of Austin in the kitchen quiets as Chris's pulse is the only sound as his phone dares him to pick it up just so it could disappoint him. If he hadn't cried for the past half hour, he would have started again.

Sizzling eggs and slightly burnt toast wafts to him as he walks in only boxers and a shirt to his counter, his bed head angled like miniature pyramids from the rough night of sleep. Plopping onto one of the chairs, Austin slides a glass of juice across the counter along with a warm cup of coffee.

"Two or three eggs?" Austin asks.

He spreads butter on the slightly charred toast as he cracks three eggs into a buttered pan.

"Don't we have to get to work?" Chris says.

"I've put in for both of us to be off today," Austin says. "Being the assistant director of HR has its benefits. I rummaged through your freezer but you don't have any bacon. What kind of monster doesn't have bacon?"

"Aren't you a vegetarian now?"

Austin laughs and flips the eggs.

"Hell no. Kyle suggested we try that shit a few months ago and I said hell no. I'm not giving up bacon."

Chris rubs his face and leans his torso on the island counter. His phone is still on his floor a room away, and it doesn't leave his mind despite how desperately he wants it to. His watch is dead on his wrist, mimicking how empty he feels. His phone nags like a memory whose edges are blurred, and the more he focuses on it, the blurrier the edges grow until the entire image is blurry. His fingers drum the counter, wishing they were wrapped around his phone in case she texted him. Without it there, the void between their last goodbye and their next hello widens.

Keith vacated his couch spot when Austin started cooking, taking up his second favorite spot: next to the stove. Austin doesn't allow a drop of food to reach him, but he reaches down to pet Keith repeatedly, generating a tail wag from the dog before he realizes that he's not getting food, at which point his ears droop. The look Keith gives Austin is one to start a war over.

"How many bad dreams did you have last night?" Austin asks as he finishes cooking Chris's eggs and toast and slides the plate to him.

"Too many," Chris says. He stares at the food, his head resting on his arm.

"The nightmares after ending something like that are the worst. It's non-stop night sweats and nightmares and waking up checking your phone and wondering if your phone is charged and wondering if they're as uncomfortable as you." Austin begins two eggs and toast for himself, though he turns down the toaster setting.

"You sound like you went through it."

Chris picks up a fork to gently poke the eggs, testing how long they'll last until they break and the yolk runs out.

"*Everybody* has been through it, Chris. I was there enough in my 20s to have the sad feelings ingrained in me all too well. It fucking sucks."

"But you seem so happy now, and you have Kyle."

"I had to go through a lot of shitty guys and a lot of nights crying and wondering what was wrong with me until I finally found Kyle. Then I realized that all of the guys that hurt me are just moments that I could grow past. It took a lot of effort, and falling in love with Kyle helped. I do believe time and love are healers, but fuck are they slow healers."

One of the yolks slowly drains from its container. Chris picks up a piece of toast - cut diagonally, just like he likes; Austin is a good best friend like that - and swirls one of the ends in the yolk.

"It doesn't feel like I'm going to find that."

"It never feels like we'll find it the day after we decide to end something. But just because something seems hopeless doesn't mean it won't one day happen. Sometimes, we need to drown in our tears before we're able to move forward."

"I'm so tired," Chris whispers.

"I know." Austin slides his eggs onto a plate as he butters his toast. He pours another cup of coffee, draining the pot. "Making it past the first day is the hardest and feels like pushing water up a cliff. Then, you wake up on day two and the cliff isn't as steep and you can grab a bit of the water. Eventually, you're throwing the water down the hill and turning around, not caring what happens."

"But how am I supposed to make it through today?" His bread is soggy from rubbing it in the yolk so long. "It seems impossible."

"It always does. That's why I'm here today. One day, you make it through the day without crying and you'll realize that isn't impossible anymore." Austin sits next to Chris with his own breakfast and coffee. "You'll wonder why you thought it was impossible in the first place. You'll wonder why you thought a lot was impossible in the first place."

"I wish I could be that optimistic."

"You're not supposed to be optimistic when you're sad and hurting." Austin takes a bite of egg. Chris wonders how his best friend stays so thin but his two sports leagues and Kyle's healthy cooking keeps him fit. "Right now, you're supposed to want to just cry and hate life and do something desperate like driving to her house. That's also why I'm here. To stop you from doing something stupid and drastic. Like driving to her house."

"I hate you sometimes," Chris says, though a slight smile creeps onto his face.

They eat in silence, Austin too engrossed in breakfast to be bothered to speak. Chris appreciates the moment of not having to talk or listen, the moment of being able to be lost with his thoughts while knowing that Austin will stop him from acting on any. He doesn't deserve a best friend like Austin, though he's not sure many people deserve how amazing their best friends are to them.

Driving to Taylor's house crossed his mind multiple times since deleting her number. A barrier to prevent that from happening is exactly what he needed. He knows driving there would accomplish nothing but he can't let the idea go, can't get false situations out of his head: Taylor running out to meet him, apologizing for lying to him, divorcing her husband, admitting that Chris is the better man for her. He runs through thousands of scenarios but he knows they're all as unlikely as Tayor actually messaging him. He's exhausted from crying, though every thought is a new catalyst for more tears.

There are any number of things she could be doing right now as he sits at the counter trying to eat eggs he doesn't want: she could be driving to work or sitting eating breakfast with her husband or she could still be in bed with her husband being held the wrong way. That thought refills his supply of tears. He isn't sure if tears or the yolk made the now-cold toast soggy.

"The thoughts are the worst," Austin says without looking at Chirs. "Wondering what they're doing is the worst." He finishes his breakfast and replaces his plate with the newspaper crossword.

Austin forces him to eat all the eggs and toast or incur Austin's fury. Chris shovels everything down and pushes a mostly clean plate away. Keith relocates next to his chair, giving him a deeper look of disappointment than he gave Austin for not feeding him at the stove. Chris pulls the lukewarm coffee toward him and cradles it between his hands. He isn't thirsty but the warmth calms him.

If Taylor had spent the night, she would have showered and already be gone. Now Chris can wear all that cologne he bought that Taylor loves that he could never wear around her. Every morning, she'd roll out of bed and immediately shower for barely a minute to rinse off any scent of him or his apartment. When she returned from the bathroom - fully dressed - she'd say goodbye and he'd crawl from bed to walk her to the door. She barely gave him a kiss as she left, and rarely a hug; better to minimize how much of his scent could get on her when she returned home to her husband. He stocked up so much extra cologne after that first night she told him how much she loved the scent. Now, they are soldiers left for dead in the back of a cupboard.

"I need to shower," Chris says.

Austin doesn't say anything as he concentrates on the crossword, his second coffee over half gone. Chris leaves his plate on the counter, knowing Austin would clean everything by the time Chris emerges from the shower. He really doesn't deserve a best friend like Austin.

Inside his room, he freezes at his dresser. His phone lies on the ground, a shiny item teasing him to pick it up. Everything else in his room disappears as the gleam from his phone brightens. He knows if he flips it over, the screen won't light up and there won't be any notifications from her. There's no more pretending she'll text him and no more comfort in knowing he can text her; he removed that himself. He wishes last night had never happened, that he'd never been driven to delete Taylor's number. He wishes he could have continued believing that something would come of it. That is easier than knowing it's over.

Last night's events rush back at him. He realizes that he can't take back what he did. The exact sequence of events is fuzzy: he recalls being at the bar with Harris and something happening and him telling Harris he's done with him. Which then led to him deleting Taylor's number. He wonders if there will be a message from Harris on his phone, an apology for last night, but just as Taylor isn't the type to initiate contact, Harris isn't the type to apologize.

Being done with Harris doesn't bring any of the tumultuous feelings that accompanied deleting Taylor's number. He no longer has to listen to Harris's escapades and feel inadequate because he's stuck on one person while Harris whores around. He never again has to listen to Harris objectify his female coworkers or be forced out to a bar he doesn't want to go to. Though that doesn't lift his spirits, his shoulders don't sag quite as low.

Another moment passes with his eyes on his phone. His head pulses and his mouth dries before he grabs fresh clothes from his dresser. When he emerges 20 minutes later, Austin sits on the couch under a blanket with Keith's head across his lap and a fresh coffee. On the TV is some British drama. Chris gets coffee for himself and sits in the chair. Keith doesn't bother glancing in his direction as Austin's fingers work their way deep behind his ear.

Austin's toes aren't covered by the blanket. Chris's instinct is to pull the blanket over Austin's toes but he strangles the chair's arm instead. Taylor always needed to have her toes covered, not Austin. He's afraid the ceramic mug will break in his hands so he sets it on the coffee table. His leg bounces as he resists covering his friend's toes.

"This show is ridiculous," Austin says with a laugh. "They're so passive aggressive and rude. I wish I were like them. They just deliver those lines so brilliantly. What do you think it would be like if our lives were a sitcom? I hope I'd be the funny one."

"Of course you would be," Chris says. "You are the gay one, after all."

Austin laughs. "True, true, nobody can top my funniness."

Chris pulls his legs onto the chair, tight to his chest. He doesn't follow what's happening in the show, nor does he care. Steam fades from his mug as the show progresses. Austin makes comments about the character's outfits and laughs at their dry quips back and forth. Keith makes moves halfway through the third episode to go outside, so Chris lets him out and walks down the stairs to stand in the comfortable noon air and escape his apartment.

It's in the mid-50s after an overnight rain that cooled Burlington; the randomness of May's weather is like it is picked out of a hat. Car doors slamming shut from the front of the shop resound to Chris as Keith explores the backyard. Patrons meander up the sidewalk without a care of what happened to Chris last night, their lives moving forward despite Chris's life having ended. Watching everyone live while he drowns worsens his sadness and lets it ensnare him in a net that tightens the more he struggles. He wants to scream at them to suffer with him, make them see what he lost last night by deleting Taylor's number, but nobody would care. He wipes tears away as Keith pads back to him after leaving a pile at the furthest point in the backyard.

"Really?" Chris says.

Keith nods before climbing the stairs and settling back on Austin's lap. Chris picks up after Keith because he's not ready to leave the fresh air yet. He should be colder with only shorts and a sweater on, but emotions are sometimes lava in a volcano, bubbling and ready to burst.

Before climbing the stairs, he leans against the back of the building and stares at the street, wondering if she would drive by, wondering if he should leave and go to her house to explain how stupid he is for deleting her number, explain how sorry he is. Would she say anything or would her husband be at home and kick his ass? If she is home alone and he knocks on the door, would she answer or would she ignore him like the stack of blue messages on their now-deleted text thread? Nine month's worth of emotions deleted in a second with a swipe. He cries at how easily moments with someone can be erased, at how flimsy memories can be in someone, and how foundational they can be to someone else.

Another episode starts and ends before Chris is pulled from his trance. His eyes were on the television but his mind visited the cruise ship at last year's work party, sitting on the couch with Taylor under the blanket and making sure her feet were covered, curling up with her in bed after a 4 hour conversation ending at 3a.m., and not having sex because their moment didn't need it to be perfect. His mind escapes to the shrug she always gave, her stoic face as she asked about his passions that nobody else asked about. His mind drifts to thoughts of never finding someone who understands what to ask and when to ask it in the way that Taylor did. His mind drifts to them walking to the bedroom, both of them putting their empty beers in the kitchen sink, Taylor brushing against him accidentally, her arms wrapping around his waist and his arms around her shoulders, her face disappearing into his chest as her tears came, her embrace desperate to find happiness. He'll never feel that from her again.

He looks at the wall clock when his stomach grumbles; it's almost 5. Austin has been up and down, sometimes returning with a sandwich or a bag of pretzels, sometimes returning with a glass of water or fresh coffee for Chris even though he hasn't drank any since he managed a cup at breakfast. Keith remains on the couch with Austin. At one point, Keith lays in the other direction, his head on the couch arm facing Chris. He huffs loudly and closes his eyes to sleep when Chris reaches his hand out.

Austin's phone rings.

"Hey, how was your day? Nah, go out and have fun. Tell the guys I said hi. Yeah. Sometime after 8 or 9. Love you, too. See yeah."

Chris's body creaks like an old ship sent out to sea that has seen one too many voyages.

"How's Kyle?"

"He's good. He's going out to dinner with some friends. I'll probably pick him up on my way home if he stays out for drinks."

"How's living with him been? It's been a few months, right?"

Chris's voice is weak, though he projects it just enough so Austin doesn't have to turn down the TV. Regardless, Austin notches it down two or three, just to be safe.

"Better than expected. You remember what it was like living with me. Kyle is managing quite well."

"So he's learned to pull a mop after himself and spray air freshener and disinfectant at everything he touches?"

"Ha ha, very funny. That was just what I did because you were my roommate."

Austin's laugh blends with Chris's, though the latter's is as quiet as a whisper.

"Living with your fiancé. It sounds so weird to say."

"It's so weird to be doing."

Chris starts.

"You think it's weird? You never think any of the things you do is weird. Buying a house, getting the biggest promotion to HR manager you could get, doing all of the adult things the rest of us haven't done. You've never said it's weird."

"Just because I do them doesn't mean that I don't think they're weird," Austin says. "Accepting a promotion that would change how everyone at the Bank sees me was nerve-wrecking. It felt weird as hell a year ago to sign away my life for a mortgage. It felt awkward as fuck asking Kyle to marry me. It was weird to say goodbye to Harris after so long. But everything I've done has made me happy. So I do it even if it feels weird."

Keith's eye peeks open at Chris. He picks up the coffee, the last tendril of steam melding with the air. He swirls the dark brown liquid gently in the cup, entranced by the circular motion.

"You do a great job of putting on a facade when you're doing all of that amazing stuff."

Austin guffaws. "Amazing is subjective. Millions of people a year ask others to marry them. Plenty of people run HR departments. Though, I must say, not all of them look as dapper as I do."

"Dapper, fuck, are we 80 or 30?"

Austin laughs and manages to pull an equally loud sound from Chris.

"Well, you're not 30 yet. What do you want to do for your 30th?"

"Crawl into a hole and die," Chris says.

"Aw, it's not bad being 30. You get the day done and over with and realize you're exactly the same, except you're one year closer to an AARP card. You just have to get day one over with and everything is fine. Come on, what do you want to do? We can have a cookout, go on vacation somewhere, stay in and watch movies and drink and eat food?"

"I don't know, I'll think of something. But right now, I don't want to do any of the above for my birthday. I want to crawl in a hole and die."

"Eh, we'll figure something out. Anyway, what am I cooking for dinner tonight? Some broccoli chicken cheese casserole?"

Chris grabs the chair arms. "With the bread crumbs on top?"

"What other way is there to cook that?"

Chris salivates. "Damn, am I going to have to sleep with you after this? Kyle might get jealous."

"Best friends before hoes," Austin says, "until we're actually married. Then you're going to have some very stiff competition."

He laughs at his own joke and navigates to the kitchen, exploring the cupboards with knowledge of where Chris keeps everything. He pulls together the ingredients and begins chopping fresh broccoli and slicing the chicken. Keith's ears perk up longingly and both of his eyes open and light up with the knife slapping the cutting board. He remains on the couch but is poised to jump at the sound of food falling.

"Thanks," Chris says, unsure if it will reach Austin.

"What else are best friends for?" Austin says. "Though, if Kyle divorces me one day, we are burning that fucker's new house to the ground and slashing all of his tires."

"Yeah, not crazy at all," Chris says.

Austin sips some water through a straw as he chops food. "Calculated."

His rhythmic chopping is perfect, like everything he does in life. Chris awes at how easily his best friend moves through the kitchen, how it seems as flawless as the rest of him. Chris reminds himself of Austin cooking most nights during college, how comfortable he became in the kitchen in a few months. Austin doesn't say anything as he chops food; he just prepares what he said he would.

"I'm sorry I didn't listen to you," Chris says, "or Lydia. I'm sorry I've been a pain in the ass the last few months."

"Life happens," Austin says, though he doesn't look up.

"I didn't know she was married when we first met. I guess I thought something weird was happening, or maybe I chalked it up to she just wanted a fuck buddy, some easy way to explain why she rarely texted me back and even more rarely saw me. I didn't want to admit it wasn't real when she made me so happy."

"It was real," Austins says softly. "Just because she put you through all of this and just because it didn't work out, doesn't mean that what you felt wasn't real. What you still feel."

Chris is crying again and happy that Austin is in the kitchen.

"I found out she was married that night at O'Hanney's. I saw her kiss her husband across the street. I didn't know what to say or do or how to tell anyone. Everything froze and I couldn't think, couldn't speak. I fell in love with her before that. Seeing her love someone else and not care about me, I didn't know how to say anything about it. I didn't know how to tell you. I'm so sorry I did this."

He breaks down in the chair and pulls his legs closer to himself. Keith raises his head concerningly, though he looks to Austin to comfort Chris so he doesn't have to.

"She was so perfect. She asked about things nobody else did, and at night when we were falling asleep together, I felt her pull me closer like she needed something that only I could give her. I just, I didn't know what to do when I found out. I couldn't let her go. I loved her."

"It's ok," Austin says with the same soft tone, his chopping slowing but not stopping. "When Kyle and I first started dating, the first night he spent the night, we were lying there falling asleep and he snaked his fingers into mine and pulled me closer than anyone ever has and I felt him tremble. In those trembles, I felt all of the sadness from the guys in his past that have hurt and abandoned him. I probably fell in love with Kyle that night. We fall in love with people when they open up to us in those moments when they aren't aware of how deeply they're trusting us, how deeply they're opening up to us." He looks up from chopping, at the wall. "I'm not mad at you for what happened. I don't blame you for not knowing how to leave. I'm not sure I could have left if I loved someone. I was sad during all of this because I knew you should be with someone who loves you the way you loved Taylor. Seeing you not have that love in return made me sad for you. I was never mad at you. I just wanted you to be happy. So don't apologize. You never have to apologize to me. You're my best friend, dude. I'm always here for you."

Chris's sweater sleeve is soaked with the tears he consistently wipes away. As Austin talks, Keith stops checking on Chris.

"Do you need help preparing dinner?" Chris asks, unsure how to follow up Austin's statement.

"And have you ruin it? I remember your cooking from college. You just keep your ass in that chair."

Chris laughs through the tears and Austin does the same. Chris really doesn't deserve a best friend like that.

~

FOUR HOURS LATER, the two stand at the door as Keith walks past them, his outside business done. He crawls onto the couch, ignoring both of them for not sharing their dinner, though he'll get all the leftovers if Chris can't finish the casserole in a few days. The TV is off and the apartment is well aired out after Austin opened the windows, the breeze carrying all the scent of

Chris's cologne from the previous night out of the apartment and off his bedsheets. Taylor would actually lay in it now and not need to shower after. She would never be in his bed again. He grips the door tightly as Austin finishes tying his shoes.

"Feel free to text me if you need me to come back over," Austin says. "Tomorrow's the weekend, so I have all the free time in the world."

"I'm sure Kyle wouldn't be happy if you abandoned him all weekend to mope with me in my apartment," Chris says.

"Eh, you're all alike. Satisfy him in 5 minutes and then he'll be good till the next day. I swear men are so easy."

"Well thanks for that bit of encouragement," Chris says.

"Hey, I had to make you a whole casserole to satisfy you. *And* put breadcrumbs on top."

They laugh and Chris's shoulders are now only weighed down by tiredness.

"Thanks. I needed today."

Austin steps forward and embraces Chris fully, who hugs him back like a missing brother reappearing after 8 years away. They stay wrapped in each for half a minute, Chris gripping Austin to stop himself from drowning as tightly as Taylor always held him. Chris isn't sure how Taylor let go of him every day because he found it impossible to let go of Austin. What if he drowns? He definitely will, though he hopes it's not too deep.

"Come by tomorrow, ok?" Austin says. "Kyle and I will cook - I will cook - dinner again. Now that it's warmer, you can help us decide on some furniture for the back patio."

Chris nods and Austin releases him. They back away from each other and say goodbye, then Chris watches him walk down the stairs. With each step, Chris's mind backtracks further into his phone that he had forgotten all day, to the stack of blue messages he wishes he could see again but never will, to the hope that there is a message from her, even though he knows there is none. When Austin's car pulls out of the driveway Chris locks the door and rushes to his room and grabs his phone. There are a few notifications, mostly missed emails and a text from Lydia, though there is no message from Taylor.

Despite that, his legs don't buckle. They grow weak and he wonders if he still has legs, but they hold him upright. His spine doesn't crumble beneath the disappointment and his shoulders don't sag as low as they did earlier, though they lose some of the pep that Austin massaged back into them with coffee and broccoli chicken cheese casseroles. That was a difficult day one, but he survived. His best friend made sure of that.

Chris crawls into his bed and sets his phone on the nightstand. The patter of slow paws is followed by Keith in the doorway. He sees Chris on the bed in the dark, Chris's body slowly shaking with the last sobs he has for the day. Keith looks back at the kitchen floor, then back at Chris and wags his tail once. He crawls into bed with him and lays in front of him so Chris can put an arm over him. They graduated from the kitchen floor.

Sometimes Chris doesn't deserve a dog like Keith.

And sometimes Keith doesn't deserve such an awful name for a dog.

18

NOTE NUMBER...

Keith's head rests on Lydia's lap. His eyes are closed but Lydia's are glued to the TV as a serial killer documentary closes with a debrief of the situation. This morning, she claimed that weekends are the perfect time to watch serial murder documentaries; had it been Tuesday, she would have claimed weekdays are the best time to watch serial murderer documentaries. Chris thought no day was the best day to watch serial killer documentaries, but the glint in Lydia's eyes scared him.

Remnants of Lydia's attempt to cook dinner overflows from the sink. Her lack of cooking skills required most of the dishes Chris has. He knows the dishes will sit there until tomorrow when he gains the motivation to wash them. He wishes Austin were here because he'd have them clean a few minutes after Lydia loaded the sink with them.

His back aches from sitting in the chair all afternoon while Lydia plays episode after episode. He pulled out his phone after the first episode to play a game while Lydia stayed engrossed in the mass market murder shows. She didn't mind his lack of interest and he didn't mind her being there; it helped to distract from checking his phone messages and hoping that Taylor would text him.

Two weeks passed and he didn't think about her any less, though he did check his phone less. Weekdays are easy because work is too busy for him to think about anything else. On days it's less busy, he stays an extra hour or two so he won't have to be home alone as long. Staying extra at work; he never thought that would happen. Weekends are worse unless both days and nights are filled with plans. The thoughts creep in with too much free time. Last weekend, Austin kept him company. He can't expect Lydia and Austin to constantly fulfill his desperation for a distraction, but he'll gladly accept their distraction until they stop.

Despite the distraction of work all week and friends all weekend, Taylor still clings to his mind like a parasite. The first few days after deleting her number he still jumped at any buzz of his phone, still checked it even in complete silence. Chris jumps at everyone else's ringing phone like a child after candy. He can never hide the disappointment when it's never Taylor calling. Best friends know everything.

He hoped every day that Taylor would text him and that she would divorce her husband. When that hope went unfulfilled every night, it pushed him off an edge to remind him that he's alone and that Taylor doesn't care about him. Each night, his hope faded as quickly as it came, though he returned to it the next day.

"You need to watch this part," Lydia says. Chris looks up from his phone. "This is where they show all the puncture wounds on the body."

Chris looks back down.

"If you've already watched this episode, why are we watching it again?"

"Because you can learn something new every time you watch an episode, even if it's the seventh time."

"Don't you want to watch something different? Something a little less deadly and a little more happy?"

Lydia laughs but doesn't answer. Keith doesn't budge during their conversation, though he opens an eye to glare at Chris for disturbing his sleep. The TV is background noise that helps him sleep; Chris talking is a jarring nails-on-chalkboard screech that wakes Keith up.

Chris delves into social media on his phone while Lydia becomes deeper engrossed in the show. He scrolls through post after post, reading a few, admiring the pictures on another, and reacting to others, though he doesn't remember what was in the posts. It's all just a distraction from Taylor, and he hopes that Taylor will be in one of his friend's posts, even though none of his friends know Taylor. Hope is dangerous.

A knock at the door perks Keith's head up, though he doesn't move from the couch. He sniffs, then lays his head back down as Chris yells to come in. Kyle walks through the door with a bag that resounds with the clinking of bottles.

"Well aren't we a solemn group today?" he says.

"Where's Austin?" Lydia asks.

"Well that's no way to greet me," Kyle teases. "I brought wine, after all."

"Fuck Austin, pour me some," Lydia says. She checks her watch. "It's almost four o'clock. That's a fine time to start drinking on the weekend."

"It's just past three," Chris says.

"Yeah, so it's closer to four than it was a minute ago. That's close enough."

Kyle returns from the kitchen with three wine glasses and fills them, though Chris doesn't drink any most of the night. Kyle curls on the couch with Lydia, though doing so gets him a glare from Keith. Once Kyle is settled on his end of the couch, Keith does his second least favorite thing (his first being giving up the spot to Chris) and curls up on the center cushion. His glare travels back and forth from Chris to Kyle every few minutes, and when he tries sleeping, he makes sure he snores as loudly as possible.

"What an awful way to move a body," Lydia says about the serial killer episode number whatever they were on.

"And how else would you move it?" Kyle challenges. "Not all of us have ridiculous upper body strength or someone to help us."

"Never have someone help you or you'll have to move that body by yourself," Lydia says, "but also don't wrap your arms around theirs. It's too awkward to move and takes longer. So many killers have been caught on these shows because of that. Tarps are easier. They slide on the ground well."

"That's how I'd have to move Austin," Kyle says.

Chris looks up from his phone, thoughts of Taylor momentarily forgotten. "Excuse me?"

"Oh please, every girl has planned out how to murder their boyfriend at some point in their relationship," Lydia says. "It's what we do."

"What the fuck is wrong with you people?"

"You just don't understand," Kyle says.

"Well if Austin ever turns up missing, I know exactly who to blame it on."

Kyle leans forward on the couch slightly, but it's enough to catch Chris's attention. "Is that so?"

Lydia leans forward to match Kyle's blank stare at Chris. He stares back at the two of them, then pulls back when Keith's head raises and his glare matches Lydia and Kyle's, though his eyes are the fiercest of the trio.

"Now look at this dumbass," Lydia says and throws her hand

at the TV. "Amateur, trying to clean like that. Where are the effective chemicals?"

"Not everyone can be good at murder or there wouldn't be all these shows for us to learn from," Kyle says.

Chris returns to scrolling through social media, his attention only a fraction on his two friends sitting on his couch. Keith's attention is still on him, his head still raised and his eyes as piercing as they have ever been. Chris shakes his head and Keith lowers his head, his eyes still on Chris.

Social media repeats itself after a half hour, his network not posting quickly enough to keep him distracted. He opens the note app on his phone and starts typing, tilting the screen away from his friends so they can't see what he's doing despite neither of them watching him. There isn't a place that feels right to start, so he just starts.

TAYLOR,

I'm sorry I deleted your number and can't text you anymore. I regretted it the moment I deleted it. I'm confused because it feels like you made it quite clear how you feel by not responding to me, and only responding when you needed me to distract you from the life you don't want to be living. How is that fair to me?

HE HIGHLIGHTS ALL the text and deletes it, erasing it forever like his texts with Taylor. It is one of a hundred letters he's started but always reached a point in where the words feel like something Lydia and Kyle would sit on the couch and criticize if they were on a TV show. Either he uses a word too vague or he turns accusatory or it becomes too much like pleading and begging, which would be embarrassing and not make Taylor want to text him. None of his messages last more than 5 minutes on his phone, wisps that evaporate into air without leaving a trace except for the weight in chest.

Hundreds of phrases cross his mind daily. He can't text her, so he writes messages instead, extending it into paragraphs of word vomit too putrid to send to her. Each one is worse than the last, meandering through the labyrinth of everything swirling in his mind like a typhoon. He cries with each note he types because he knows they'll never be more than wasted moments. He cries because he thinks each message holds the key to her lock that will bring them back together, and deleting each tears a piece of his body until there's nothing left to break. Each deleted message widens the void since their last goodbye.

Do love letters actually work? Has anyone received a love letter and actually ran out of their house and to the airport, or is that entirely Hollywood? How many would he have to send before Taylor understood? What sappy words or memories did he have to string together like a romantic poet for her to message him? Would any words ever change her mind, or is Taylor molded to being unhappy regardless of the possibility of happiness with someone else?

Sometimes writing everything he wants to say - even if he deletes it - relieves enough pain to be able to sleep when he otherwise rolls around crying, wishing he could drive to her house and tell her everything he wrote. Even if he decides to send a message, how could he give it to her? Sending it to her house means the possibility of her husband intercepting it. Going to her work would be stalking. Sitting outside her house and waiting to see her husband leave and then sliding it under her door would be creepy. Even if he finishes a letter he finds mildly acceptable, he can never get it to her.

Being powerless compounds his situation and makes writing the hundreds of deleted notes impossible. He can't write anything adequate, he can't get her the notes, he can't tell anyone this is happening, he can't get through a day without a dozen breakdowns, can't get through an hour without his heart sinking. As he looks up from the hole he's fallen into; the exit above seems as distant and tiny as a star. How long will it be until it putters out?

What happens if the letter moves her hand to cut the non-existent string between them? Losing her forever because of his own letter is worse than losing her forever because of someone else. Hours of sitting on his couch until 4am and talking about everything except how he actually feels slaps him with each letter. If he just said one thing, let one emotion slip to her, would he have to write these meaningless letters, or would she have told him that she loves him, too? How much would she have listened to until his words were what drove her away? How do you continue when you're the reason for everything?

Lydia's announcement that dinner is ready jolts Chris from his writing. The new note is one of his longer attempts. He blinks away the tiredness and tears and sits opposite them at his counter, the drawers of the island stopping his knees from going under it. They both brought their wine glasses to the counter and refilled them, though Chris's is still full.

Dinner mimics the afternoon: Kyle and Lydia talk more loudly than is necessary, and every time Chris glances at Keith, he glares back before turning his attention to Lydia. The casserole steams and more wine is shared. Chris's glass is still mostly untouched, but he does sip it, if only to appease Kyle for bringing a bottle.

"How's the wedding planning going?" Lydia asks.

"Really well," Kyle says happily. "We think we have a venue and they'll even cater, which is great so we don't have to search for a caterer. The inside has some awkward pillars we're going to have to figure out."

"How many did you two decide to invite?"

"Somewhere around 150. It's much larger than I wanted but his family is large and our friend group is just as big." He scoops himself some casserole. "It's still so far away. Sometimes I don't feel like working on it because it's so far."

"The next year will fly by. It always does. Then you'll be complaining that you didn't have enough time to plan."

"I hope so. It's such a weird feeling, being engaged. I don't know. The finality of it, the reassurance of it. It's such a huge step. Doing it with Austin helps."

"Oh he'll make sure everything is perfect and he'll put enough work into your marriage for the both of you."

She scoops Chris some casserole when he doesn't reach for the spoon, then glazes over him briefly, but he notices her eyes hover. He quickly picks up his fork and takes a bite, then blows air out of his mouth because the food is too hot.

"Have some wine, it's good for your heart," Lydia says. She turns back to Kyle. "I'm so happy for you and Austin. You two are so cute."

Kyle blushes and for once doesn't make a point to tap his ring on the glass or lay his hand on the counter.

"Thanks. I'm obviously excited about it but at the same time I don't know how to feel about it. I mean, I know how to feel about it, I'm excited, obviously. But like, how did I get lucky enough for this? Sometimes it feels like it isn't real because it's hard to believe this could happen to me. The person I was when Austin and I met..."

Lydia nods like she's reliving a similar feeling from some unshared memory.

"Sometimes love finds us in ways we never expected but that doesn't mean we're less deserving. Often it means that we're more deserving of that love because of what we've been through."

Her solemnity deepens as she speaks. She perks up and pats

a tearing Kyle on the shoulder while sadly watching Chris pull out his phone.

He knows she's watching him but he doesn't care. Looking down means it's more difficult for them to see his tears and it means he can check his phone, swiping to refresh his texts repeatedly despite Taylor's name no longer being there. Hope used to fill him when he opened the app, even if he knew Taylor didn't text him, but over the past few days it hasn't even brushed past him. He doesn't know how to feel about that.

Disappointed by the messages, he goes to close all of the open apps except the notes app. He taps it and pulls up the beginning of another message he had yet to delete.

DEAR TAYLOR,

Do you remember when we met? I thought we were just going to hook up and you'd be gone, a quick meet up after you got off work, but then you ended up staying the night. That was unexpected. You showed up with your hair down from the ponytail you wore at work, and your clothes smelled faintly of fried fish and wine. You were exhausted from work and I felt awful for keeping you up but you sat on my couch and the conversation never stopped. Each time I finished speaking, you had a follow up question or a statement. That's not something people normally do. How could I not fall in love with that?

TO STOP his hand from shaking and to replace the sadness with anything else, he picks up his fork and shovels in casserole. It's cooled down slightly but is still hot enough to make him regret eating so quickly. The burning successfully distracts him from crying over Taylor. He takes a sip of wine with his phone hand because it forces him to set his phone down. When he does, Lydia looks away from him. He appreciates that.

"I suppose you're going to have fun music?" Chris says awkwardly, trying to insert himself into the conversation; another distraction.

Kyle welcomes him gladly into the conversation, diving into their list of 'no' and 'yes' music, and their list of music that one approves of but the other doesn't, which Kyle says will end up being a 'yes' for the ones he suggested. Chris laughs at that, knowing how stubborn Austin can be. Lydia smiles at Chris's moment of happiness. He appreciates that.

When they're done eating, Lydia offers to clean up. She tops off Chris's wine glasses but tells Kyle he's cut off so he can drive home in an hour, much to his chagrin. He twirls his empty wine glass on its base and stares longingly at Chris's.

"What are we doing for your 30th?" Kyle asks.

Lydia groans and Chris grows rigid.

"Something small," he says. "I don't want anything as big as Austin's. I would avoid it if I knew that Austin would let me."

"You can't just ignore it," Lydia says. "We'd at least go out to dinner if we weren't going to have a party."

"Don't I have to be ok with a party before you throw a party?" Chris says.

"Not if we don't give you a choice," Lydia says. "We'll keep it small."

"It's in July, right? It'll be nice and warm! We can do something in our backyard and swim in the lake and have a campfire at the end. Only invite a few people, do a cookout. How does that sound?"

"Do I have to be sung 'happy birthday' to?"

"Of course, you idiot," Lydia says.

She divides up the casserole into multiple containers for her and Kyle to take home, then wraps the rest for Chris's work lunch. Chris appreciates that.

"Fine, but do it at night so people can't see me," he says.

"You really don't want to turn 30," Kyle says. "Why?"

Chris shakes his head and sighs, his finger trailing the rim of his wine glass.

"There's just...stigmas and...things will change when I turn 30."

"Like what?" Kyle asks.

Chris is annoyed at being prodded but Kyle isn't close enough to 30 yet. He's only 27, the baby. Lydia, however, gives a sigh but continues picking up dinner and washing dishes.

"I don't know, stuff," Chris says.

Kyle gives a short chuckle. "Austin's been 30 for a few months and nothing has changed. I mean, I guess me moving in with him changed and the engagement is new, but he's still stubborn as hell. He still cares about everyone as deeply as he did before."

"But that's just it," Chris says. "Look at what has changed. He turned 30 and bam, engagement, boyfriend moves in. No, I didn't mean anything bad about you with that. I mean, look at all the permanent adult things he's doing. He's got so much responsibility and commitment now."

"Is that so bad?" Kyle asks. "He's still your best friend. Do you think you won't be his best friend when you turn 30?"

"What? No. I don't know. I guess I don't know what it'll come with."

Kyle leans back in his chair and rests his legs on the bar stool Lydia vacated. The sink runs behind Chris as she washes dishes, though Lydia's attention is divided between cleaning and listening.

"It's just another day, turning 30," Lydia says. "It comes with the same thing that comes with turning 29 or 28 or 27. The only difference is the numbers."

Chris's finger stops running along his wine glass rim and he hands it to Lydia to wash. She takes a large sip of the wine before dumping it down the drain.

"Why don't you let Keith out?" she says. "It's been a while since he's gone out."

Chris gladly takes the exit from the conversation. Would 30 really be the same as 29?

∾

AFTER THEY LEAVE AROUND 10PM, he's in his car, driving through neighborhoods with the music on as background noise. His car's motor roars like a herd of elephants when he doesn't want anyone to know he's there. He turns off his car's display and shuts off the headlights. He crawls between streetlights, the darkness between them a comfort as he nears his destination. Being in between street lights means he is hidden.

The last traces of an early night rain dry off the pavement in foggy drifting clouds. The temperature is just cool enough that the small puddles haven't evaporated. Splashing through one resounds into his car like a tsunami demolishing the shore. He hopes he doesn't leave devastation behind him, but in the dark, he can't see anything even if he did look behind him. He's terrified to look behind him, but life has been like that lately. He wishes he could turn around and see everything clearly, but he's afraid of what that means.

He'd be lying to say he doesn't have memorized the sharpness of the neighborhood turns, the potholes he swerves left to avoid or right to straddle, and the distance from one stop sign to the next. Each street name is as engraved in his mind as colors or how to write letters, and each house color is an image ingrained in his memory as clearly as every detail of his own apartment, like he's lived here forever. Even in the dark, it's all as clear as if the sun were shining midday.

Tonight isn't bright. It is mostly cloudy and the few glimpses of the moon are short. It is the type of night where you hope it is dark enough to hide you. The 5 miles between his apartment and Taylor's house feels like the long way when he's taken the same path every night for weeks. Will it ever end?

All nights start the same: seeing a friend, or sitting on the couch with Keith with a tv show on in the background, or a 3 hour call from his parents. Regardless of which starts his night, a stimulus triggers something each time: the loneliness when the friend leaves, or Keith shifting away from him, or an image in a show, or a line from one of his parents. He lets Keith out, telling his dog that he's only going to step outside briefly and then they'll be back on the couch. Keith saunters back to the couch, but Chris gets in his car, his keys already in his hands when he takes Keith out.

It is amazing how many different routes can lead to the same destination. When his gut wrenches and he can't stop crying and thinking about what would have happened had he not deleted her number being in the car and driving toward the outskirts and neighborhoods of Burlington is the best option he has. It fulfills a need that he can't figure out another way to nullify, and it satisfies the need to be seen even if nobody can see him as he drives through the dark. Sometimes, the quick drive by her house feels as brief as her passing through his life, where she doesn't even offer him a minor glance.

Turning onto her streets brings a rush similar to arriving at a party where everyone is there except the person you were hoping would show up. You're disappointed that one person isn't there but not surprised, which doesn't help the sadness lessen. Once on her street, his engine sounds louder and his headlights look like their high beams have been turned on. Driveways are mostly empty as all the cars are in garages, though porches are decorated with furniture and he knows the lawns are full of kids' toys. A few risky trips during the day when he suspects Taylor is working showed him that.

Her house comes and goes in a flash quicker than a thought. Every time he passes it, he tries glancing at it, tries looking into the windows, hoping to see her walking across the room or sitting on the couch. He's afraid if he looks at her house, she'll be able to see into his car and will come after him, yelling about stalking her and she'll demand that he leave her alone. Being told to leave her alone would destroy him more than her lack of answering ever did.

Her car is in the driveway, pulled in and half hidden by the tree next to it. Hers is one of the few single-garage houses on the street, which he's thankful for because he can always see if she's home. Seeing her car is a small confirmation of something about her, something solid that he can know when everything else is concealed from him, when nothing about her is any of his business anymore. Accepting *that* is perhaps the hardest part of everything. How can someone be everything you know one day and the next not supposed to matter at all?

Just like she did, her house passes in a heartbeat.

In his rear view, her house is a blob in the dark that could be any of the houses behind him to the untrained eye, but to someone who desperately needs to hear something from her, know that she's happy in some small way, he knows exactly which blob is hers. He knows how long it takes to drive from her house to the end of her street where he has to turn and can't see her house in his rearview: less than a heartbeat. If it took longer, he's not sure he could make it each time without breaking down and stopping in the middle of the road.

Later at home, he's comforted knowing that he'll be back tomorrow night. The thought crosses his mind as he climbs into bed and opens the note app one last time for the day.

TAYLOR,

I'm not sure what to say. There's so much I want to say, but I know you won't read most of this. I guess I'll put the most important things first and leave the rest for you if you decide to read it all the way through.

First, I need you to understand why I like you so much. There aren't many people I can touch and feel comfortable touching. I don't like touching people because of one time at a work party. Sometimes it's difficult for me to want to hold a girl's hand on a date because I just imagine it being dirty and I have to wash my hand immediately after. I see most people and see filth covering their body.

I never felt that way with you. The first night you came over and talked to me, and we slept together, I didn't want to let go. I didn't wake up in the morning and feel like I needed to wash my hands. I didn't feel like I needed to mop all of my floors after you left or change all of my sheets or vacuum my couch. That was normally the first thing I'd do after someone left. I've never felt clean like when I touched you. You're the first person in a long time...maybe that's part of why I like you so much. You make me feel safe and comfortable like very few other people can. Maybe I'm afraid I won't find someone who can do that for me again.

CHRIS REREADS WHAT HE WROTE, then deletes the note. How many notes is that deleted? Tears come. He wants to wipe down his phone.

19

CHANGE

Summer's heat wallops Burlington, forcing the city's inhabitants to sprint between air conditioned buildings or else walk with shirts dyed with large dark patches of sweat. The short walk to work makes Chris appear as if he had just taken a shower. Even the animals refrain from venturing out of shady areas or eating. Stopping for a coffee is preposterous with the line extending into the blaze of the morning sun. He has a keurig in his office; that would do.

AC soothes his burning skin as he breaks through the Bank's doors, the elation he felt when he held Taylor - no, he can't compare things to her. Besides, nothing could match what that felt like, nothing could rival being the key to someone's happiness but not being allowed to give them that. Despite the coolness, he sweats in the elevator up to his 6th floor office. His reflection in the overly shiny elevator walls is his only company, staring back at him with judgment deeper than the shame he bears for falling in love with a married woman. No, it's not his fault, it's hers for dragging him along. No, that doesn't matter anymore. Move on.

His office door is closed as soon as he's through it. Some

days, he arrives at work without a thought about Taylor, buys a coffee and greets everyone who walks in without a glimmer of her in his mind, while other days he isn't sure how he managed to wake up with a heart that still knew how to beat. Every day he hopes he won't cry. Some days he sheds only a few tears.

A month is simultaneously a lifetime and a breath in and out. May 7 is a scar on his emotions that will never fully heal, but it has faded with time and distance. Whenever he fails to keep thoughts of Taylor at bay, the scar itches and sears deeper into him. A scalding shower and staring at the wall in the dark for hours does nothing. Every day he is more desperate to tear off the scar, which he can never do. Trying every day wears him out. Memories and progress often do that.

Grumbling from overuse yesterday, the keurig roars as it heats up water and then gurgles as it pours out a cup. When the cup is filled, Chris replaces it with another and preps the keurig to make a second. He sits at one of the new chairs, regretting it and every decision he's made over the last year. Not fighting the promotion, ordering these ugly and uncomfortable chairs, falling in love with Taylor.

His closed door would be an oddity to everyone, so he opens it as the first shoes announce the arrival of his staff. To hide his face, he stares out the windows, sipping his coffee while holding a folder in his lap to give the appearance of working calmly. It hides a dark and wailing void of emptiness. Hiding a truckload of sadness from an entire staff isn't the walk in a park everyone makes it out to be: he bites his lip constantly, hoping the pain would distract him from crying, and he slows and deepens his breathing to control his emotions. Leaders can't show weakness.

The situation that led to her memory's visit today was a slip up that he should have avoided, but he was running a few minutes late. After he finished tightening his tie and removed a small fleck of dirt from his shoe, he popped into his bathroom while Keith took his last opportunity outside for 8 hours. Chris opened a bathroom cupboard and froze as his eyes fell on the canisters of cologne that Taylor said were her favorite. He hadn't touched them since he hid them behind some toilet paper rolls when he found out that was why she showered each morning. He had no other place to put them but also couldn't throw them away. Nostalgia holds onto flakes of what was good, even when the flakes are slowly dusting into nothing.

After seeing the canisters, Taylor gripped his mind in a repeating film reel: nuzzling her face into his chest and taking in deep breaths, her compliment every time she came over on his cologne that was her favorite, her sneaking out of his bed to wash the smell of him away so her husband wouldn't suspect anything. A tear drips into his coffee, so he moves the mug away from his face, which is for the best as the coffee-scented steam wets his face and leaves the scent on him all day. It's a smell that would make him different from what Taylor likes. He moves the mug a little farther away.

A rap on his door disturbs his self-pity. Keith would give the door the appropriate level of annoyed glare if he were here, but he's not, so Chris sets the mug on the small conference table, wipes his face clear of steam and tears, and spins in the chair. Lydia strolls across the office, not a betrayal of hesitation in each step.

"This is the only place to get good coffee," she says.

Lydia closes the door once she's in his office. Chris is annoyed that she's using the second cup he loaded in the keurig. She never brings her own mug; Chris wonders if she owns a mug.

"Morning to you, too," he says.

"What are you doing sitting here all alone this early?" She scans him. "That's when the thoughts get you." She looks out of the windows. "I'll never get over these fancy offices with their full wall windows. I'm not sure if I could get used to having that much window. Cleaning it must be a pain. They're also too easy for a murderer to break through. At the same time, they're useful to escape after killing someone, though they'd leave quite a mess."

"Please don't murder me."

"Not yet. You have a keurig, and one that works. You're safe for now. These things don't come around every damn day. Besides, like I said, too much of a mess with this...situation." She waves her hand at the windows. "There's cleaner ways to murder someone."

"If you ever wonder why you're still single, maybe take a look at all those serial killer documentaries that are in your Netflix 'watched' queue."

She fumbles in the mini fridge for creamer as she flips the bird over her shoulder. Chris smiles - the first he has all morning - and resumes sipping his coffee at the conference table. Rather than stare at the bright green leaves reflecting the morning sun, blowing in the disgustingly hot breeze to create a rolling ocean of green, he watches Lydia across his office finish making her coffee.

"When are you going to get stir sticks," she says. "A keurig and a mini fridge that only has creamer in it, yet no stir sticks. Maybe use some of your money to buy some."

"Or you could bring your own stir sticks, and a mug."

She carries the prepared coffee across his office and sits next to him, swiveling to look out the large windows.

"Don't make me an accomplice in this over-extravagant office while the rest of us have to share a 3 year old keurig that is questionable whether it'll heat the water at all. How's your morning going?"

Chris turns to join her in staring out the window. Talking to Lydia is smooth, like gliding across ice, swaying back and forth without a care and knowing you won't fall. The comfort rivals Austin's.

"It's morning," he says after a sip of coffee.

"What triggered it this morning?"

Chris gently swirls the contents of his mug in a circle.

"Just some old memories left for dead that I didn't realize I still had in my apartment."

"How are you doing?"

He sighs and tries to find something outside the window to point out, some distraction from this conversation, but Lydia never lets things distract her when she's focused. If she wanted her question answered, she would ask again whether he changed the subject or not. She lived through enough of men's shit to know how to stay focused.

He shrugs.

It will never be like Taylor's shrug, so careless but full of concern. Chris still marvels at how she fit two conflicting things into everything she did: carelessness and concern into her shrugs, confidence but desperate loneliness in her embrace, him and her husband in her heart. That's *if* Chris even mattered enough to be considered more than a toy she used when she was lonely. He doubts it.

"Sounds like an awful start to a morning," Lydia says, "though the sun shining through these fucking windows strong enough to give you a sun tan is also a pretty great way to start a day."

Chris smiles and takes a large gulp of his coffee. His morning will be eaten by meetings and his afternoon will be digested by distilling what was said in the meetings into information his team needs to know or data to plan his team's next moves. Neither will be difficult, but both will be arduous. He's thankful he can handle his job in his sleep, if the dreams of Taylor would vacate center stage long enough. Most nights they nag at him like his greatest desire being teased in front of him but always just out of his reach, a mirage that vanishes when it's inches from his fingertips.

Lydia says nothing as he makes himself a second cup of coffee. With her here, he doesn't feel tired, nor the need to drink it, but having a warm beverage with a best friend is a pastime he's found he rather enjoys the older he gets. That sounds dirty - "the older I get" - but he lets it pass without giving it much thought. He enjoys coffee with friends, he enjoys conversations with friends. Regardless of age, he can admit what he likes. One of those things being Taylor. Her memory is taking its time to fade. He thought more of it would be gone after a month, but some memories are too deep.

"How did you move past those men?" he asks when he's back at the table with her.

"Move past them." she repeats.

He isn't sure if she's repeating what he said to make sure she understood him or if she's talking to herself, so he lets her sentence hang between them.

"That's such an odd phrase," she says, "'move past them.' I don't think people really understand that phrase." She drinks her tan-mostly-creamer coffee, which contrasts with Chris's straight black coffee. "There's never a 'getting past' someone or something. It's more you learn how to not let them control you anymore, how to not think about it daily. You learn how to accept that those things were at one time a large part of your life, and you can't let go of the feeling they gave you, but you do learn how to not let it control you." She nods to herself, as if Chris isn't in the room. "Yeah, I've learned how to live with those things in my life. They'll always be a part of my life. You grow from the shitty stuff, and learn to live with it so it doesn't bother you."

"How do you get to the point of not letting it bother you?" Chris asks quietly. "How do you learn to live with it?"

"You realize you're stronger than you thought. And then you realize that those moments and your past don't define you." She pauses. "It isn't easy."

She looks at him for the first time since she started monologuing. He returns his gaze out the window as if he hadn't been praying some advice she had to offer would be the key that frees him from the prison of thinking about Taylor and regretting every day his decision to delete her number. He finds nothing of substance in her sentiments. With a sigh, he drinks the too-hot coffee but doesn't react; Taylor distracts him from the pain.

He isn't sure how he'll get past moments that are mountains whose peaks stretch into the clouds with no hope of seeing the top, how he'll forget nights where Taylor stretched her legs over his under the blanket, or nights where she pulled him closer than anyone before because she thought he could save her. He's not sure if he'll get over not knowing what she needed saving from, not knowing why he was important to her - if he ever was - for almost a year.

"Maybe I could get used to an office like this one day," Lydia says to no one.

"I didn't think I would," Chris says, also to no one.

They sit with their own thoughts and their own conversations, continuing to answer each other without hearing the other. They sit content as the sun rises higher and the area of Chris's office it illuminates shrinks, moving to only shine on a tiny area in front of the windows.

A knock on his door interrupts their siloed thoughts. Chris says to come in.

Kelly's head peaks through the door.

"Are you ready to head up to Devon's? Hi Lydia."

"Hey," Lydia says to no one, still engrossed by the view and the sun.

"Yeah," Chris says while holding in a sigh that still manages to squeak through.

He waves goodbye to Lydia in the hall, who is still lost in her thoughts. He and Kelly proceed down the hall and around a corner. Cubicles are occupied and emitting their melody that too closely resembles the one from his old cubicle, almost as if every sound and sight from the 3rd floor was copy-pasted to the 6th. Even the sterile smell of fresh packets of paper and the faint scent of freshly opened computer equipment permeates the air.

"How's your week going?" Kelly asks in her usual friendly conversational way to remove the quiet between them.

"It's a week. I'll be happier when this morning is done and I can just stay in my office."

Kelly laughs. He's never noticed how her hair bobs as she laughs and bounces on her shoulders.

"Surely all the meetings aren't that unbearable. After all, you get to spend the next hour with Devon and me. What a wonderful way to start a morning."

Chris glances sideways and Kelly laughs again.

"How do we have this meeting every week but we never seem to be done talking about stuff?"

"Welcome to middle management," Kelly says. "It could be worse. You could be stuck in a large conference room with the entire board for a full day, listening to them drone about numbers that are way above our pay grade."

They stop outside Devon's office, where there's a sign stating all meetings will be in the conference room on the 4th floor. Kelly laughs at Chris.

"Well, irony seems to be laughing at us today. Stairs or elevator?"

"Stairs," Chris groans. "You'd think she could've sent an email before we walked around the floor."

"You're in such a rush to start this meeting," Kelly says. "Just smile for once."

For reasons Chris doesn't understand, that does actually make him smile, which in turn enhances Kelly's morning cheeriness. She pulls the tablet she carries tighter to her chest as he holds the stairwell door open for her. He likes how she whispers a 'thank you' as she passes, her hair barely covering her face but hiding enough of it to tug at Chris's curiosity.

Their footsteps echo down the stairwell as loudly as Chris's disinterest in this meeting. Kelly walks in front of him, her pantsuit fitting her confidence better than any skirt or dress could. It adds to her beauty in a way he never sees in other women, like how an extra dash of color in a painting draws your eye to it every time.

A third pair of footsteps greet them in the stairwell. Harris turns the landing of the stairwell coming upstairs, a half-finished bagel in one hand and crumpled papers in the other. They hadn't spoken since Chris left him at the bar over a month ago, since the night he deleted Taylor's number. Harris hadn't made an effort to reach out, either, which makes forgetting him easier. He wishes forgetting Taylor were so easy. Kelly waves to Harris but says nothing. Chris doesn't know how much she knows, but he's thankful she doesn't engage Harris.

By the time Chris looks at Harris, he's already diverted his eyes and focused on his bagel. Chris's eyes leave Harris and focus on the wall ahead, on the back of Kelly's head, on his lost friendship; relief fills him rather than guilt or longing for it back. Harris pivots his body as he passes Chris in the stairwell, giving extra space to pass without risking bumping into each other. Chris turns the landing as Harris climbs another flight, his footsteps disappearing in the stairwell. Chris doesn't breathe relief because he has nothing to be relieved for; it's just over. Why can't everything end that easily?

On the 4th floor Kelly and Chris enter a smaller conference room he hasn't been in before. While the table has 6 seats, he doubts that many people would be comfortable in such a tight space, and he questions how anyone is supposed to maneuver in this matchbox with that many chairs. Devon's materials are spread across one end of the table, binders and a laptop and a tablet sprawled in front of her like a commander's workstation, not much different than her office.

"Good, you got my door sign," she says when Chris and Kelly struggle around the chairs and table, their backs scraping along the wall. "There's a leak in a pipe running above my office so I moved here to stay dry."

"Who built this room?" Kelly asks.

"It felt like a waste to take over a larger room just for us so I booked this for the day. No keurig, though."

Kelly sets up her tablet while Chris opens his laptop, both at the opposite end as Devon because there is no space closer. Devon searches for something on one laptop before moving to the tablet, muttering to herself when she finds what she's looking for.

"We have a mid-year report due in a few weeks," she says. "I have a list of information I need from both of you. The board wants to see progress toward our division's goals and numbers. Since this is all of our first times doing a mid-year report, we'll get through it together."

Chris does a double-take being reminded that Devon has been in her position less than a year. He's back at that end of summer party on the yacht where Marissa planted the roots of the promotion that Devon ended up with, where he met Taylor and a one night turned into 8 months, and those 8 months turned into 1 month (so far) of simultaneously wishing the 8 months had continued forever and had never occurred. It was all a waste of his time, but he couldn't let either go, like conflicting feelings of love and hate for someone who under-stands you but hurt you.

"There's supposedly a simple form to complete," Devon continues, "that isn't simple. I just shared it with both of you. If you pull it up, we can walk through it together."

"This sounds like needless paperwork higher ups want that will mean nothing in reality," Chris says.

Devon doesn't miss a beat. "We all know how much you despise admin work but it's the structure we have to work within and it's what we have to deal with. So the first box..."

Chris opens the file and reads through it with Devon and Kelly, listening to Kelly's questions but not really caring much to understand the form as in depth as she does. The form turns to vertical lines like a barcode as he scrolls through the document. Kelly's questions and Devon's answers pass through him like wasted breaths as an hour ticks past.

Fighting every administrative duty he deems a waste of time - which is all of them - is Chris's goal. He's tired of admin forcing others to complete inconsequential reports just to make admin feel bigger about themselves. He respects Devon for listening to all of his criticism and suffering through all of his attitude. He suspects she wraps it all in a ball that she buries in what must by now be a vast canyon of things he's said that she's forgotten about. Some days, Chris says things to see what will be Devon's breaking point, what will get him fired so he can return to not having to deal with admin bullshit. He wants his life back.

He isn't sure what that means. He does arrive a half hour earlier to make sure he's there before his staff, and he stays until the last leaves, which is often a few minutes earlier than their shift, and there have been rare nighttime events or meetings, but the rest of his time has remained untouched. The increased salary is something he would miss, but not having to worry about hiring and firing people, not having to worry about making sure he's setting a good example for his staff; those things he would be ok with losing, but the salary...maybe he'd be fine with losing that, too, if it meant his life would be his again. His savings are enough to buy a house. No, that's something adults do. One more way this promotion is forcing him to grow up when he wants to enjoy his 20s and desperately wants them to stay forever.

"I thought that would take two hours but that was quicker than I thought," Devon says.

"Since we have extra time, can we talk about upgrading the team's equipment?" Kelly asks.

Devon leans back in her chair, the first time all meeting she hasn't been leaning over her tablet like it's a coveted item she's protecting. She nods.

"We have updated laptops and new tablets but most of our employees are working on machines that are nearly 3 years old. Our staff was given the rejects from other departments. I think all of our team's computers were pulled from storage and hastily serviced and turned around. They're starting to lag and can't process some of the new applications."

"That'll be a huge chunk of money to replace everyone's computers," Devon says with her arms crossed. "I'm not sure the board will approve that."

"What if we write up a report about what we need and justifications?" Chris asks, plastering looks of surprise on both women's faces. "We can't keep expecting our teams to grow if we're working on machines years behind where our competitors are."

Devon stares between the two of them from behind her folded arms.

"Write it up and send it to me by the end of the week," Devon says. "If you both feel that passionately about this, then

I'll take it to the board and fight for it. There's going to be a lot of push back. That's a lot of money."

Devon relaxes as Chris nods, forgetting the fighting words she prepared for when Chris started talking. They wrap up one more item. Hours later, Chris leaves first.

The 4th floor hallway is of course empty except for its lone patron - the secretary across from the elevators. Chris waves as he passes her and the elevator pings open. Marissa walks out and beams when she sees Chris.

"How are you doing?" she asks, not caring that she's shattering the quiet of the floor.

The secretary raises an eyebrow but keeps her eyes on her computer screen.

"I'm well," Chris says. His throat catches as he debates if he wants to get into a longer conversation with her, then decides it's for the best. "Can I talk to you for a minute?"

"Of course," Marissa says. She motions down the hallway toward a lounge that serves no real purpose but none-the-less exists. "I love having a plot at the Community Garden. The people are so nice. I wish I had joined it years ago."

"I'm glad you like it," Chris says, breaking into a small smile. "I've only been a handful of times but we had such a large number of volunteers this year that I haven't had to go as often."

"We should meet up there sometimes so I can show you what I'm growing. There's nothing there yet, obviously. I haven't had a garden since I was a child at home. Reliving this part of my upbringing is wonderful."

The wall of windows displaying the Burlington landscape makes the lounge a mirror of Chris's office. The lounge overlooks Church Street and the pedestrians strolling along it, the children running along it with their parents trailing behind, enjoying their first week off after the school year ended. Peddlers in the street attract small crowds that toss a few bills to the street performers. Chris likes this view as much as his mountain view.

Marissa folds one leg over the other once she's settled into a chair, choosing one that has another across from it for Chris. While her relaxed position dismantles the wall of her board member title, her pulled back shoulders and stern gaze remind Chris who he is sitting with. He wonders briefly what he's doing asking Marissa to talk, as if he is anything important in the Bank that a board member should take time out of their day to talk to him.

"What did you want to chat about?" Marissa asks.

Chris regrets asking to talk with Marissa as her gaze settles all of her attention on him. He doesn't even want to be a supervisor, so why is he wasting his time advocating to a board member? He breathes in deeply; Kelly once told him that helps her when she feels in over her head.

"We were just having a meeting and brought up a proposal we're going to write to submit to the board."

"And you want me to make sure the board approves it."

Her question-turned-statement unnerves Chris, so he dives into defending the ask.

"We're asking our employees to work with outdated equipment and it's making our division fall behind our competitors and morale goes down when we don't keep up with current best practices and equipment and we can't run the programs we need and-"

Marissa holds up a hand with a laugh, stopping Chris midsentence.

"I was the first board member that wanted to promote you a year ago, and I was the one who pushed to have you promoted to your current position."

Anger wells within Chris now that the source of his forced promotion admits it.

"But I trust your decisions completely within your role and division."

The anger settles. Marissa continues.

"If you say that you need something, I will do everything I can to have the board vote on a motion and get you what you need. As soon as the proposal is submitted, I'll start working to make sure it passes."

Relief and an elation he didn't expect replaces the anger. He is prepared to ramble for an hour about all the benefits that updating his team's technology would bring. Not needing to use any of his prepared defenses and having someone support him without question unbalances him.

"Thank you," he manages through his confusion.

"Of course." Marissa stands. "I assume that's all you wanted. Now, I'm going to head to another meeting. I look forward to seeing your proposal."

"Thank you again," Chris says when Marrisa is near the lounge door.

She waves back at him and leaves him alone in the lounge. He swivels in the chair with a sense of accomplishment he wishes didn't settle so hard on him. Her confidence in him, willing to support him without an explanation from him, provides the first relief he's felt while being a supervisor. He can advocate for all of the things he needed when he was just a staff member. And he can get it for them. Maybe he is ok with the promotion.

Crawling out of bed means facing what he's been dreading for the past 30 years, confronting what he's avoided mentioning or thinking about since he turned 29 a year ago. Keith is nowhere to be seen. Now that the big three-oh has arrived he doesn't want to check his phone to see what texts and calls he's already missed and he doesn't want to check his socials to see what horrific memes about turning 30 will beat him down and pin him like a helpless worm under a rock. He took today off to avoid seeing people, to avoid the humiliation of turning 30. Maybe if he can avoid everything today, he'll stay 29 for one more day.

Dimness coats his room, not a crack of light brighter than a dead flashlight peering around his curtains. He unlocks his phone and braces his eyes against its light: 6:29. With a groan, he rolls across his bed and pulls a pillow over his head, his phone lost among the tangle of sheets. The one day he's taken off since getting his forced promotion and his body can't let him enjoy it. If he can will it strongly enough, maybe he can stretch the morning into an eternity where he doesn't have to face 30.

Rolling back and forth across his bed like a sailor tossed by

the restless sea around him, Chris's slow waking is interrupted
when his alarm sounds a minute later, disturbing the quiet of
his apartment like shattering glass. He searches blindly for his
phone across his bed, digging for it between the blankets and
cursing himself for forgetting to turn off his daily routines.
Turning 30 while lying alone in bed with nobody to say 'happy
birthday' to him, nobody to start his birthday with a smile, isn't
how he imagined turning 30 would be. He pulls the sheets
toward him, scrunching and untucking them. What does order
matter when his life is nothing like he thought it would be at 30?
Where is Taylor today? Does she even know it's his birthday?
Did she ever know his birthday?

A part of him wants to cry but a part of him is tired from
crying; so tired. He wants to get over Taylor. There, he said it. He
wants to get over Taylor. He doesn't want to have an impulse to
hope every message he receives is from her, doesn't want to go to
sleep wishing she was with him fitting like a lock and key. He
wants to be done with her. But that is *so* difficult.

He suddenly breathes less ragged admitting it to himself. His
chest is burdened by the same unseen weight it has been since
he met Taylor, but it isn't as heavy and his eyes don't water.
Instead, the pit in him aches, but not with sadness. He isn't sure
what feeling is there, but it doesn't control him. He can manage
the pit.

Keith's paws push the edge of his bed down. Chris rolls over
into his phone, which he jabs at to turn off the alarm. Keith
stares at, his ears hanging low and his eyes staring expectantly at
Chris.

"Well there's a sight I'm happy to see," Chris says.

Keith shakes his head, indicating he isn't happy to see Chris,
he's here out of necessity.. He drops his paws from the bed. He
moves toward the door and nudges it open with his snout, then
stares out of it.

"God damn, can't you let me sleep in for a few minutes on my birthday?"

Keith glares back at Chris with a look displaying how short his patience with his owner is this morning. Chris nods in defeat and climbs out of bed - leaving his phone - and lets Keith out. Chris walks with Keith down the steps and regrets it at the bottom. The July day is already muggy, though partial clouds provide brief reprives from the sun. Keith seems to not care as he wades across the lawn until after he pees and needs to walk back across the nearly sun-covered lawn. He stares at Chris expectantly, as if Chris could make the sun disappear. Dropping his head in defeat, Keith sulks through the sun, giving Chris a disapproving glare.

Chris stays at the base of the stairs as Keith climbs them and goes back into the apartment. In his shirt and shorts, the morning feels comfortable, even in the mugginess, the common weather phenomena for a July birthday. His fingers squeeze unconsciously, desiring a coffee mug. The sun rises slightly so the buildings around Chris's apartment stop providing shade. Chris wishes he could sit outside and enjoy a cup of coffee before getting ready for the day, but his apartment isn't suited for that. He thinks of the small pile of money he's been able to save since his promotion, of the house it could be a deposit on, then moves on. He can't handle two large life moments on the same day.

Keith is sprawled in front of the AC unit, which hums loudly and provides enough cool air to make the space comfortable, despite the poorly insulated walls. Chris laughs and goes back to bed. He pulls out his phone and begins scrolling through the midnight and early morning birthday wishes. Most are from the few colleagues he doesn't mind seeing outside of work, two are from college friends he distantly stays in contact with, and the last two are from his parents and sister.

One message has no name associated with the number; it's just a string of 10 numbers that he doesn't recognize. He sits up in bed, his heart pounding from the first excitement he's felt on his 30th birthday. The first words he can read without opening it are the same as every other message: "Happy 30th Birthday..." His finger hesitates over the message thread. Pressing it meant potentially undoing the past two months, could drag him right back where he was the night with Harris at O'Hanney's when he decided to delete Taylor's number, to that night sleeping on the kitchen floor with Keith because he had no will to live.

He tosses his phone on his bed like it's a red hot coal that burns his hand. It settles with the screen face up, the dot next to the unread message burning his eyes as much as the phone did his hand. In the AC, his body burns hotter than it had while outside in the mugginess. His head swirls and his vision goes blurry. He wishes Keith were here now, but that damn dog wouldn't move from the AC until he had to pee again.

Disaster sits a few feet away on his bed. Does 30 mean going back to what he used to have, if he had anything? Or does 30 mean deleting that message and ignoring that he received it at all? What if it's not even Taylor's number and his pulse is increasing to the verge of deadly for no reason? He breathes and closes his eyes. That's what Lydia said about getting past moments like these.

It helps to an extent, but not enough. He peeks with every breath in and his fingers twitch to leap at the phone with every exhale. His pulse slows a little, though his body shivers as the sweat he's now drenched in is passed over by waves of cold air. The hairs on his arm stand up and when he raises his hand to reach for the phone, his entire arm shakes. It takes every ounce of control he has to stop shaking like he was standing on a fault line during an earthquake. Were he not experiencing it, he would have thought an exorcism was happening.

Like lifting a porcelain doll prepared to shatter if his fingers moved too quickly across it, he lifts the phone. The dot next to the unread message blinds him but he presses it anyway. Immediately, he feels bile ready to come up and his abdomen feels like a fist collided with it. If the world tilted seconds before, now it is a spinning ride at a carnival moving too fast.

"Happy 30th Birthday -Ron" the message says. Chris exhales as he drops his phone on the bed, not caring if it was a porcelain doll he dared not drop seconds before. For all he cares, his phone could disappear into a void and never bother him again. He falls forward on the bed and slams his fists into his mattress, their collision muffled. The mattress sends a rattle back through Chris's arms in retaliation for his abuse. Chris wishes the retaliation would throw him against the wall and knock him out. Then he wouldn't have to wonder about nameless numbers, hoping she was contacting him.

Relief, that is what fills the pit in him. It doesn't remove the wondering if she'll text him or the dread over unknown numbers contacting him, but it takes away the tears and prevents exhaustive crying from occurring. He breathes deeply. It wasn't so bad getting past that first nameless number. He can do this, even if he doesn't want to.

An hour passes with him tossing around the bed, the sheets tangling his legs and arms like mummy wrappings and his phone disappearing into the depths of the entanglement. He doesn't care when it rings, doesn't care who's calling or what they want. Beneath the blankets, his phone is muffled, making him wish there were a hundred blankets to make the sound disappear entirely. Only two calls come in, one probably from Austin and one probably from his brother, both trying to reach him before anyone else.

"Fuck today," he mumbles.

Pulling together the small will he has after the let down of the nameless number not being Taylor, he climbs from bed for the second time and makes a cup of coffee and a bagel. He doesn't feel like eating but he doesn't feel like staying in his apartment.

"I hope you're ready for a hike, bud," he says to Keith after he's downed half his coffee.

Keith's ear perks but quickly relaxes again. His tail doesn't wag but he turns his nose closer to the AC, his look of disgust growing as Chris runs back into his bedroom and scrambles through his comforter, looking for his phone. A clatter tells him he flung it to the floor. Not caring how his apartment looks today, he tosses the comforter on his bed and grabs his phone from the floor. No new messages from unknown numbers. He sighs relief.

North of Burlington, a half hour past Austin's house, is a state park settled on the banks of Lake Champlain. Swimming holes line the state park, with some already claimed by early risers who plan to spend the day diving from the short cliffs. Pavilions scattered around the park are reserved for midday parties and cookouts that remind Chris too much of a birthday party. He walks Keith in large arcs around them, hiding them behind patches of trees.

On a lake trail that is more roots and rocks than a dirt trail, he unhooks Keith's leash. The dog doesn't move once free; he stares at Chris with a look asking when they'd be returning to the apartment and the AC.

"Can't you do this for me for my birthday?" Chris asks.

Keith sighs and looks up the trail with a look of dread for how far he'd have to walk in this mugginess. He scratches behind an ear before setting off at a pace so slow an elderly person with a walker could move quicker, but Chris doesn't mind. In the woods, he has an excuse to shut off his phone. He really just wants to spend time with Keith, ignoring everything in life. Though his dog constantly judges Chris for making him walk in this heat, Keith never verbalizes anything, and that is peace.

Lake Champlain reflects the sun too brightly, sending constant flashes of jarring light at Chris's eyes. He slides sunglasses over his face and stays just a step behind Keith, letting the dog set the pace; that is the only way to keep Keith sold on the hike. The small lake breeze is enough while they walk in partial shade to keep them cool, though Keith visits the water's edge numerous times for large laps of water. At the first picnic table, the dog trots to it and lays down, then expectantly looks at Chris to sit at the table and rest, as if Keith lying down is all in thoughtfulness so Chris can take a break. Chris's shirt sticks to his body as he bends to sit and the wooden bench offers no comfort from the tiring muggy heat. Keith resonates those feelings as he rolls his eyes at Chris's groan as he sits.

"Shut up, I'm not old," Chris says. "Being out here means we can avoid seeing people and I can keep my phone away."

Keith ignores him and lays his head on his paws to stare across the lake, the patch of shade around the picnic table serving them both well. Chris wants to stay there all day, enjoying the serenity of being alone on the lake, living in the world he wants to live in with things the way he wants it. As long as he stays here, he can pretend that he won't have to say goodbye to 29 indefinitely.

He asked Taylor multiple times to go hiking with him. She mentioned that she enjoyed hiking, so his asks were an attempt to see her outside of his apartment, out in the world and not hidden behind four walls. Her excuse was always either she was tired from work or she didn't bring the right hiking shoes or she didn't feel like doing physical activity. Each time, she met his eyes with a wide, terrified stare and a shake of her head, as if she saw a monster behind him that was asking her to publicly betray everyone she loved. If only Chris had known in the beginning how true that was.

He goes to wipe away a tear but it's just sweat. Tears used to come for many reasons: brief moments when he thought about Taylor and how she fit so perfectly with him in his apartment, when he wondered if they would fit as well together outside of his apartment, or because he'll never know the answer to that. He's not sure if he's happy or sad about that. Not crying over this baffles him, but reinvigorates him on the muggy day, like freedom has been granted to him after a too-long battle. He thinks about what Austin said: time and love are healers.

An hour later, the sun has moved enough that the shade only half covers the picnic table and the temperature feels like it's risen from hellish hot to hell on fire hot. Keith agrees and gives Chris a look that tells him he's ready to go back to the AC.

"Me, too, bud." Chris stands and Keith follows, his tail wagging for the first time since starting the hike. "Come on. Let's stop and get some ice cream on the way home. You've earned it."

Keith's tail wags wildly for a few seconds before he grows too hot and resigns himself to perking up his ears, enough of a sign to show Chris how excited he is. Boats disturb the tree's quiet rustling as they bounce across the lake. A few fishermen with wide brimmed hats float along the shore, their poles' strings dragging behind them slowly.

On their way back to the car, Chris and Keith pass couples and a few families hiking, as well as a group of people just a few years younger than him. Most wave and try to pat Keith as they pass, but the dog is having none of it. He just wants to be lying down again with a stomach full of ice cream and the AC cooling him. Chris wonders how all of these young people are able to be out and hiking. They must all be entry level at their jobs, no responsibilities to be in an office and slaving at whatever menial tasks they're assigned. He envies their freedom; guilt has prickled him since he woke up on his day off. He hates this feeling.

"I think we're going to need a large ice cream for the trip home," Chris says.

Keith's tail wags again. Chris is shocked his dog has put so much effort into relaying his happiness twice in the same day.

∼

"YOU SURE DID CHOOSE a hot day to be born," Lydia says, donning large sunglasses with a mixed drink in her hand. "It's too sticky out here to sit comfortably and play cards and Austin won't let us sit inside to play. How the hell am I supposed to take these peoples' money?"

"Maybe enjoy other people and don't play poker?" Kyle asks.

Since his engagement to Austin, he's taken to always holding things with his ring hand, often tapping the ring every few minutes against his glass so everyone notices it. Austin picked a plain ring blacker than an underground cave when looking at it from a distance, though up close an inlaid strip of light blue - Kyle's favorite color - that runs the circumference of the ring along the middle becomes noticeable. Inside is inscribed a message but Chris doesn't know what it says; Austin keeps that private. Chris exhales happily for the first time since waking up; Kyle is a better 4th for their group than Harris ever was.

Though the crowd is smaller than Austin's birthday a few months ago, the attendance hovers around 20, which is more people than Chris wanted to celebrate his 30th with but less than Austin would have invited had Chris not insisted on keeping the gathering smaller. Chairs are set up around the fire pit and a food table is set up on the deck. Beer coolers rest at the base of the deck, now half empty. Most everyone has moved their chairs beneath the shade of the trees, while a few brave suntanners set up camp on the shore where Austin's backyard smooths to flat rocks that Lake Champlain gently laps against, the lake shimmering the sun at the sunbathers. Chris sits beneath one of the trees with Lydia, Kyle, and a coworker more concerned with finishing his share of beer.

The party started with a late cookout and has otherwise consisted of only drinks and small talk with all of the guests. Chris knows at some point that Austin will bring out a cake and make Chris the center of attention with a song. He hopes that by the time that happens, he's drunk enough not to care, though the beer isn't as refreshing as he hoped it would be and he struggles to want to drink it. Nothing would be refreshing, though, when he periodically checks his phone, wondering if at some point he had told *her* his birthday and if she would remember it. He doubts both, but maybe...

Austin drags a chair from the sun to under the tree, a beer sweating over his hand in rivulets. His tank top sticks to his body as he sits, and the face he wears once sitting reveals how much of a struggle it is to walk through the sun on this hot, muggy day.

"Firing up the grill was the worst idea I've had all year," he says.

"I appreciate you cooking for all of us," Chris says.

"Every damn year your birthday is deathly hot," Lydia says. "I don't know what you do to always get the perfect sunny and hot day for your birthday."

"It's almost too hot," Chris says.

"We could go inside to play cards in the AC," Lydia offers.

Austin looks at her so she folds her arms.

"I'm glad you planned it starting at dinner," Chris says, "and we're all thankful you live right on the lake. Though I'm not really sure we need a campfire tonight."

Austin shrugs. Chris wonders if Taylor has texted him, but he doesn't hang on the thought like the lifeline that it's been for him in the past. With his three closest friends around, it suddenly doesn't matter as much.

"I woke up early to cut that wood," Austin says. "We're having a fire whether it's hot as balls or not."

"If balls are always this hot then I'm glad I don't have any," Lydia says.

She spreads her legs wide and leans her head back and closes her eyes. Her beer is on the ground within reach of her fingers. Chris thought she might stick to the chair if she stayed like that for too long.

"You should've seen him cutting wood earlier," Kyle says, "talk about a turn on."

"It's hot enough, don't go having a heat stroke," Lydia says without opening her eyes.

Chris laughs with the group as Austin and their coworker dive into a conversation about Austin's back deck and potentially expanding it enough to build a fire pit on. Since arriving, he's waited for the other foot of the party to drop, for the feeling of 30 to wallop him and strip away his youth, his energy, his personality. Someone sliding the back door open sounds like an announcement for 30 to arrive while the clicking pop of a beer opening resembles life deflating.

Each moment comes and goes but nothing changes: he doesn't feel more tired, he doesn't think any differently, and nobody demands anything different of him. He holds his beer prepared to smash it on 30 when it appears. If 30 would surprise him, then he'd be prepared to surprise it back to fight it off. He may have been forced into administration and he may be on the verge of having enough savings to buy a house and he may spend more nights at home with his friends than in a bar with drunk strangers, but that doesn't mean he's old. Turning 30 would put a number to all of that, and *that* terrifies him.

"We don't all need a massive house that could fit two or three kids," Lydia says. "Your house is too much. I just want a place that is comfortable and enough room for *maybe* one child, *maybe*."

"Eh, pay the price or buy it twice," Austins says. "I'd rather buy a too-big house that we can downsize later than have to buy another new house in 5 or 10 years if kids were to come along."

"Kid*s*?" Kyle emphasizes the 's.' "When did that 's' get added?"

"Oh, it's just the beer talking," Austins says quickly. "Regardless of a *kid*, I'd still rather have a bigger house to downsize later. Unless I just turn all of the extra bedrooms into my extra rooms."

"Whoa, you already have an office, what else do you need?" Kyle asks. "I need an extra room, too."

"The closet is more than big enough for all of your clothes," Austin says.

"Not for just that," Kyle says with nothing else to follow up, but then adds, with lackluster confidence, "I also want a video game room."

"A whole room just for video games?" Austin says incredulously.

"Think about how perfect it'll be for when we have a kid and we can bond with the kid!" Kyle says.

"Don't use the kid argument on me when I'm half drunk," Austin says shyly, though his attitude turns.

Chris smiles as Kyle reaches out a hand, which Austin grabs, despite the sweatiness drenching both of them. If Kyle was ok with being engaged to someone a few years older than him, then maybe Chris could handle 30. The thought makes him laugh and Lydia turns her head as if to ask what is funny, but Chris just shrugs and watches his best friend holding his fiance's hand.

Party-goers join their group and then split to form their own groups as the night goes on. Chris doesn't drink enough to get drunk, but he drinks enough to feel comfortable talking to everyone at the party and to no longer care about turning 30, or at least to not let his mind rest on his age for more than a second before he thinks about something else. Many people don't even bring up his birthday beyond wishing him a happy birthday. Most people just want to talk about tomorrow's baseball game between the Yankees and the Blue Jays or the best recently discovered park within an hours drive to go hiking in or one of their weekend trips up to Montreal and all of the places they demand that everyone else visit. Work isn't brought up once, and Chris smiles at that. If this is what 30 year-olds talk about, maybe turning 30 will be ok.

Nighttime sweeps the yard without bringing much relief from the mugginess. As the sun disappears behind the mountains across Lake Champlain, everyone watches from their chairs. Austin and Chris start working on the fire, or more Austin builds the fire and Chris stands with his empty beer, watching Austin and handing him the lighter and tearing up an old newspaper for more kindling when Austin asks for it. Flames slowly catch from paper to wood, creating a whirlwind of smoke that Chris steps back from. Austin continues to build up the flame as Chris tries to drink from his beer before he remembers it's empty. Austin waves him away as two people pull chairs up to the fire.

Chris gladly takes the opportunity to go inside to the bathroom. Before going back outside to grab another beer, he stands at the sliding doors and stares past the string lights lining the deck to the dot of light that is the fire his friends sit around. His phone is an anchor in his pocket that roots him inside, his smartwatch an iron chain and ball that refuses to let him take a step forward. He's barely looked at either since arriving at the party, but they've slowed him down more than the deadly muggy heat ever could.

He pulls his phone out of his pocket. The empty screen flashes on when he lifts it up. He breathes deeply. *I want this to end,* he thinks. He sets his phone face down on the table next to the sliding doors. His hand shakes as he pries his fingers off his phone. Releasing it is removing an essential organ from his body, but his lungs work better as his hand moves away from the phone.

Next, he unclasps his watch and sets it next to his phone. Letting go of his watch is easier than his phone. Both devices' screens shut off. After he inhales with the first breath that feels fresh in almost a year, he exhales a sigh. He places a hand on the door but his eyes remain on his phone and watch. *Let it go,* he thinks. He sighs again as a lightness pierces him. *This is what you want.*

He slides open the patio door and nearly stumbles into Kelly, who's searching the beer cooler for a brand she likes, though this late the pickings are slim. She stands and smiles at him, the effect of alcohol barely showing in her movements and speech.

"Happy Birthday! I wondered when I'd get you alone to wish you that."

"Thanks," Chris says with more genuineness than he has with anyone else at the party. "Have you been at the party since it started? I didn't see you earlier."

"No, I had another thing this afternoon." She gives up looking for a beer she likes and lets the cooler slam shut. "It was boring but someone had to do it. How has the party been?"

"It's been nice," Chris says, looking at the now blazing fire and shadowy outlines of his friends around it. "Austin did a really great job with it, like always. I'm sure he's happier having done it himself than with his birthday when we took over his house."

"He has an amazing place," Kelly says. "I'm always shocked

when I come over. Did you want a beer?" She steps aside to give him full access to the beer cooler.

"Yeah, aren't you going to have one?" he asks.

"Nothing left that I like," Kelly says. "I've already had one so I don't need another. I need to drive home in an hour."

Chris picks a beer from the cooler and begins a slow crawl to the fire with Kelly, neither rushing to join the large circle of shadows around the blaze. Somebody passes them and waves at the duo. Chris isn't sure anymore how to start a conversation one-on-one with a woman. Taylor always prompted everything, offered topics and led the discussion. She spoiled him that way but he's not sure if he misses it.

Despite not knowing where to start, Kelly next to him feels comfortable, like Taylor always did. He wonders if touching Kelly's hand would feel as clean as touching Taylor's, if he could open up to Kelly as comfortably as he could to Taylor. As thoughts of taking that jump cross his mind, his heartbeat quickens and flashes of stacks of blue message unreplied to paint his vision. What if Kelly is just like that? He pulls into himself and leaves the rest of the walk to the fire in silence.

Two empty chairs are left around the fire, separated by a handful of people. Kelly waits for Chris to say something but he waves with his arm bent at an awkward angle and his beer tips slightly so a splash crashes to the ground. Kelly smiles at him and wishes him another happy birthday before going to the other vacant chair. He damns himself for letting that moment go.

Once he's sitting, someone lets out a deep "Haaaaaapppppppyyyy" from the porch. The crowd turns to look through the dark and sees a shape outlined by the porch light carrying a large rectangle toward the fire, faint flickers on top of the rectangle glowing in front of the black shape. The crowd joins in singing happy birthday and Chris surprises himself by smiling as Austin sets the overly large cake on his lap, the 30 candles adding to the fire's glow.

Nobody sings in sync and everyone's different pitches mesh into a horrible chorus that would be shamed by even the worst singer on the planet, but Chris enjoys every second of the awful song. Everyone around him maintains their energy despite being a few beers deep and nobody expects anything more of him than to just enjoy the moment and blow out all the candles. When he fails to do that in one breath, a few people throw jabs at him, but even those surprisingly make him laugh. He forgets what he thought turning 30 would be like and instead waves like a spotlighted prince to everyone around him, offering them his own chorus of thank you.

Austin takes the cake away and has Kyle come help him cut and serve it. Chris gets the first piece, though he eats it slowly as a friend from the community garden strikes up conversation about joining a tennis league together and sorting through details that neither would remember in the morning. When that conversation is done, his friend on his other side strikes up a conversation about football this fall and their team's chances of winning the superbowl, though Chris is overcome by a serene sensation that puts him in a listening mood as his friend goes on and on.

Halfway through their conversation, Chris scans the crowd and fire. Most of the faces are half hidden in shadows from the flickering fire and the others are turned toward each other, deep in conversation so half their faces are completely hidden. Empty beers rest at everyone's feet and from a short distance away the shore of Lake Champlain sets a background rhythm of slapping the large boulders. He sinks into his chair and his mind stops racing as his body melds with the chair. Tomorrow he has to remember to thank Austin for hosting.

Two hours later, Chris has waved goodbye to the last person, leaving only himself, Kyle, and Lydia around the fire as Austin comes back from the house after seeing the last person out, always the decorous host. He slides a chair next to Kyle so they can hold hands and Kyle can lean his head on Austin's shoulder, the late time and the alcohol finally taking their toll on him. Lydia raises the last bit of her beer to them and then to Chris.

"Happy birthday, Chris," Austin says quietly.

"Thanks." Chris says.

The embers of the near-extinguished fire give off barely enough of a glow to see a foot away from the pit. Everyone's faces are entirely in the dark and the sound of the embers crackle to extinguish themselves, mixing with the lake. Chris could sit like that all night, with those three keeping him company and the stars just visible above the Burlington lights.

Nobody says anything for a while. Lydia stares absently at the fire, lost in her own train of thoughts that are a secret to everyone but her. Kyle leans against Austin and has one hand in Austin's while his other hand is on Austin's upper arm, a finger gently stroking it. His eyes are closed but Austin's are open. For a moment, his and Chris's eyes meet. The moment passes quickly, like the last 30 years of Chris's life have, gone before either of them knew three decades had passed. Austin adjusts in his chair and Kyle's hand tightens on Austin's arm.

Chris folds his hands on his stomach and closes his eyes. Wisps of smoke puff up, the wind every few minutes wafting a pocket toward him that smells of ash. The few-too-many beers he had leaves him undisturbed as smoke passes over him. He forgot about his phone after setting it down. He forgot about Taylor, even if just for the night. He can do this. With his best friends around, he can do this. The warm breeze takes away any worry he had when the day began.

If this is 30, Chris thinks it might not be so bad after all.

21

THE BOSS

August rolling to a close and summer preparing to transition to Autumn saddens Chris as he stares out his large window wall, admiring the plump green leaves on the distant mountains. In a few months, it will all be a painter's palette of reds, oranges, yellows, and purple, swirling together on the mountainside, and then a month after that everything will be brown and dead, waiting to be buried in snow. A cooler walk to work will be appreciated but a less lush view will dampen his mood.

A ping on his computer swirls him back to his monitor, where his secretary's message says one of the board members is there to see him. Chris tells his secretary to send in the board member. He relaxes back in his chair and spins to stare out the window again. A nearly-drained cup of coffee is cold on his desk, staining the inside of the white ceramic. His open office door lets the typing, clicking, and chatter from his team's cubicles drift in. They're surely worse than the rustling trees and distant lake lapping on the shore outside, but they're noises that he doesn't hate hearing anymore. He arrived a little later than normal today, and the two people that were here before him stared in awe that they beat him. Chris knows they'll get used to it just like he's getting used to 30.

Papers and folders he brought to his last meeting are thrown carelessly on the small round table. He handed them out to everyone while he spoke, the dual motions now natural like walking. The papers contain numbers and charts that Chris doesn't care about, but they take him no extra effort to print. He has enough spare time in his role to do mundane tasks like that. He'll recycle the packets and wonder what the point is when everything should be digital, and how long he'll have to continue printing shit until the board is forced to use tablets rather than paper that rustles and interrupts Chris's presentation.

A gentle rap on his door disturbs him from his gazing and pondering out of the window. He swivels back as Marissa walks the few paces across his office to the chair opposite him, which she gracefully sits in as if she's a monarch that floats through spaces. Even when hurrying him through the 4th floor or rambling about the garden or any number of other times they've talked, Marissa holds herself regally, yet she's the only board member Chris is comfortable chatting with.

"That was quite the presentation," Marissa says.

"Thank you," Chris says with a smile. Accepting compliments on his work has gotten easier in recent weeks. "What did the board think of my proposal?"

"We'll meet later this week to discuss it and the other proposals brought before us," Marissa says. "*You* are what I want to talk about today, though."

Chris raises an eyebrow, though the anxiety that infected his blood a year ago when someone at work said that to him doesn't arrive. Now his muscles relax and his back straightens.

"Hopefully it's not to fire me because of my presentation."

Marissa chuckles in a light way, her body barely moving, though the joy spreads across her face.

"No, no, no, nothing like that. There are two opportunities opening up at the Bank that you are a great candidate for. Since you declined my offer a year ago, I think now is a good time for me to offer something else. You've grown into your role quite well recently. You have impressed a few members of the board, especially after this morning's presentation. We have a new offer."

Without answering, he looks down at his hands, his fingers intertwined and slowly rolling around each other. Everything in his office suddenly becomes a glaring projection that hurts his eyes: his windows are a spotlight that blinds him and his keurig is a beacon that makes his eyes water. He notices Marissa had closed his office door when she walked in. The space between himself and Marissa extends to a chasm.

The side walkway of the yacht flashes in his mind, Marissa and Devon standing on either side of him, the railing doing nothing to prevent small splashes of the water from hitting his pants as the yacht navigates Lake Champlain. Memories of the anxiety growing in him during their conversation unsettles his stomach and Devon's unreadable glance unnerves him. Their conversation on the 4th floor shortly after that when Marissa offered him the promotion comes back next. He didn't know what to say yet he knew exactly what to say. He was too nervous to say any of it.

Overtaking all of those memories is meeting Taylor a year ago this week. Their initial brief conversation led to months of lies followed by months of hating himself. He isn't sure if that phase is over yet. Most days it is and not a thought about her passes his mind. He thinks he's forgiven himself for falling into her lies. Other days, he can't help but check his phone. Old habits are hard to break, though those moments come infrequently.

Sweat gathers on him and he doesn't know what to say as memories of Taylor consume him: deleting her number, crying on the floor, Keith comforting him until Austin arrived. Nearly 4 months - or is it 5 - without contact and he feels her hold still clinging desperately to him, or maybe it's his own hope he feels still grasping for something that never existed. He understands what Lydia said about never getting over it but learning how to live with it. He's mostly learned to live with it. Mostly.

"What is the position?" Chris asks slowly, uncertain what he's going to say until it's all out. He isn't sure that was what he wanted to say.

Marissa's body relaxing mirror's Chris's body relaxing, the relief pouring from her like water from a burst balloon. She clears her throat before answering, the shock too obvious to conceal.

"Two of our directors are leaving. One has a job at a new institution while the other has accepted a different position within the Bank. I think you'd be wonderful at managing the small business department. They also need a refresh to keep up with the times. You have the knowledge and are part of the group of young people that know what today's small businesses need. You would be perfect for this position."

"That's a quick jump for me," Chris says. "I've been in this position for just over six months. I'm surprised others at the Bank would be so willing to move me so quickly and have to replace me."

"Devon recommended you for this," Marissa says.

His shock must rival the shock on Marissa's face when Chris doesn't immediately turn her offer down. A knowing and friendly smile creeps onto her face. She doesn't move as she waits for Chris to respond, her patience expandice.

"I'm...surprised," Chris says. "Did she say anything else when she recommended me?"

"Not really. Just that she thinks you'd be successful in that role and that she puts all of her confidence behind your appointment to the position. If you want it."

Chris diverts his eyes because he can't look at Marissa without worrying, being excited, feeling guilty, and questioning everything she just said. He glances around his office and the comfortable place he's made it into with new furniture, the few pictures he's brought in of himself, Austin, Kyle, and Lydia, and the multiple fun coffee mugs he uses as decoration and to drink from on those too-common days when two cups of coffee just won't do. How much would it feel like starting over in a new office on a new floor with a new team, or would he be allowed to bring his office to his new department?

"The Bank also wants to move that department onto this floor, so you would keep your office," Marissa says when she notices Chris looking around.

He stares at her dubiously, expecting her to reveal some piece of missing information she's conveniently leaving out until he answers. Marissa waits patiently with her legs crossed and her hands resting on her upper knee while she lets the chair take all of her weight. They stare at each other without speaking for a minute, both taking in the other and weighing what the other might say.

A year ago, Chris would have sat and stared at her until she spoke, would have blown up with assumptions that are untrue. He expects multiple caveats to follow her offer, to turn what sounds like a great opportunity into a nightmare compared to his current position. A year ago, he would have immediately said no, then tried to close a non-existent door to his cubicle. A year ago, he was looking for any way to fend off change, like a gladiator fighting back hundreds of enemies. A year goes by in a flash that leaves bruises that are replaced by growth.

"I'm surprised," he says again.

Marissa smiles, though there is no conniving behind it.

"The Bank is not perfect. There are things we're always learning, such as how to keep exceptional employees and how to adapt. After our job offer to you a year ago, we realized what is important to you and what we were doing that was possibly not ideal for anyone. We would like you to lead the small business department."

"Is this going to be another situation where I'm forced into it without any choice?" He doesn't care that anger coats his voice.

Marissa looks down as her smile fades.

"I am sorry for doing that," she says, a tinge of regret in her voice. "I pushed for that because I thought that was what you needed to take the next step. I shouldn't have forced you into a position which you did not want. That was unfair toward you and not a practice that the Bank, nor I, want to continue. This transition will be entirely your decision. We do have a second person to ask if you say no."

He isn't sure how to take her apology. An apology doesn't undo forcing him into a new position he didn't want, doesn't give back the extra hour each day he arrived early and stayed late, doesn't compensate him for the small facets of his previous life that he surrendered to his new role. He hated her for all of that and more when he started his current position. He is surprised when her apology lifts a weight he isn't aware could be lifted so easily. He smiles at her in the same genuine way she's held her smile since entering his office.

"Thank you for that," he says, then he hesitates before continuing. "I have a request."

"Does that mean you accept the offer?"

Chris nods.

Five minutes later, Marissa shakes his hand and leaves his office, the air lighter for him to breathe. She starts up the hallway in one direction while he goes the other with a fresh coffee in his hands. Marissa has a position that she's used twice now to help him. He didn't realize until today that his current position means he now has the same ability as her to help people, if to a lesser degree.

Some of the cubicles are empty. His team isn't large enough to fill all of the empty spaces, which he is happy for since his small business team will be able to move up here. Though the carpet muffles his steps, some of his employees still glance up as he passes their cubicles and wave, one even calling for him to come back so they can chat briefly. After Chris approves the request, he stays to carry on a conversation about a new restaurant on Church Street that he wants to try, maybe for a happy hour with everyone. The employee is all too happy to encourage that, and sends messages to their coworkers when Chris walks away. Being the boss feels good.

If he keeps walking, he'll pass Kelly's office. It's still early in the morning, so she's probably downstairs in the third floor lounge area, hacking away at her laptop while looking at a different view than what Chris sees from his window, even though both face the same direction. He considers going downstairs to join her, though what would he say? He no longer has a reason to be on that floor, not since he stopped talking to Harris.

Around a corner he enters the first cubicle on his left. Will waves when he sees Chris. Thick old manuals are under Will's monitors to raise them to a comfortable height, a consequence of being over six feet tall. Will's office is decorated with pictures of a newborn and his wife, though those are nearly buried in memorabilia of the Rams football team. Will was another selected by Devon to join the team, and he did so happily. He and his wife were in the process of building a house and they needed the raise. Will also desired to one day be on the admin team, a goal he's told Chris about many times when they were at an equal level

"Hey," Will says after a large swallow of coffee. "How are you?"

"I'm fine. Mind if I join you for coffee?"

Will's surprise is well hidden behind another sip of coffee that stops his face from showing any reaction. He nods and pulls his chair slightly to the right so his monitors aren't separating him and Chris.

"I'm still baffled by how disorganized your desk is yet how efficient you are," Chris says with a small laugh in his voice.

"It works." He shrugs. "I'm good at organizing chaos, I guess."

Chris misses shrugs.

"I'm surprised you're out walking around this early," Will continues. "Usually you're pretty busy all morning. When I walked in I thought I saw that board member, Marissa, on our floor."

"She and I are friends, to a degree," Chris says.

Will's eyes widen but he doesn't let his surprise stay long. People in positions like Chris's sometimes have connections.

"Did she just come for a quick visit or was there more to her visit?" Will asks.

"Oh, she wanted to discuss gardening and how to help things grow," Chris says.

Will lets out a laugh. "Never did I think a board member would visit someone in their office here to talk about gardening. I guess the board are normal people after all."

"Better people than I think we may give them credit for," Chris says. "She came to me with news of a promotion."

Will's surprise couldn't be hidden by his mug this time.

"You're leaving?"

Chris nods. "Though I recommend who should lead this department."

Will's posture hardens but he manages to not let any more surprise show than has already leaked. Memories of when Marissa first offered a promotion a year ago flood back to Chris: his own rigidity, though for different reasons than Will's. He'll accept the promotion without hesitation, unlike Chris. He wishes he were as excited a year ago as Will is undoubtedly today. He wonders how things might have been different if he had accepted rather than fought back.

"You'd be a great leader for the team," Chris says. "You're well qualified and are probably only second to me in your understanding of how this department functions and what we're working toward. I asked Marissa if I could recommend my replacement and she said she'll talk to the board. As long as they approve you, and as long as you want this position, it's yours."

Will nearly skyrockets out of his seat, but he manages to hold himself still and retain some semblance of calm, though his body shakes from excitement, the coffee in his mug vibrating. Chris can't contain his smirk at Will's elation.

"Of course!" he says a little loudly, though the tapping of keyboards and the mild murmurs around his cubicle would make his slight outburst just another sound. "What-what do I have to do? Is there an application?"

Chris shakes his head. "The Bank likes to promote within if they can. People change positions at this level so frequently that promoting with departments like this is straightforward and simple. I'll let Marissa know that you accepted and she'll bring your name before the board to be voted on."

"I can't believe this is happening. Thank you so much."

"Of course! You're going to do amazing in the role. Plus you'll get an office with a door."

Will slumps back in his chair. "Now *that* makes any promotion worth taking."

They laugh like they had back on the third floor, like they had before Will was taken by Devon to join this team and Chris was eventually forced to join it, before one was a rung up from the other. Chris misses these small interactions, these small bonding opportunities that are often suppressed by titles or lack of time. Will had been hired just after Chris and the two bonded over adjusting to the job. Now, they'll bond over adjusting to their new roles.

"I have to go. I'll keep you updated as I hear more from Marissa."

He stands with his coffee nearly empty. Will stands with him, one hand steadying him on the desk. Chris is jealous of Will's excitement.

"Seriously, thank you, Chris. This means a lot to me."

Chris nods and smiles, then leaves the cubicle. He's certain Will pulled out his phone as soon as he was gone to call his wife, sure he'll soar on this high all day. The office air feels a little lighter, even if the new offer Marissa had for him tethered him slightly.

Instead of circling back around and passing his office again, he continues along the outer walkway and passes Kelly's office. The door is shut, though a glow illuminates the doorframe. That could be from a light in her office or the natural light that the enormous windows pours into the space. She usually leaves her office open, so he assumes she is on the third floor. He debates on heading down there to see her rather than attend his last visit of the morning, but this is a visit his churning stomach will only be settled by once it's over.

Turning another corner, the door to Devon's office comes into view. There is nothing special about it, though the faint glow on the floor from the light inside pours out, creating an unease as Chris approaches it. The unease isn't fearfulness; it's the general unease that finds him whenever he needs to visit Devon's office. She's never been threatening or mean toward him, but her office still gives him that feeling he can't shake, like the fluttering in your stomach when you are about to crest the top of a roller coaster hill to dive down on the other side, except he doesn't know what to expect when he reaches the peak.

A few offshoots into the cubicle farm invite him to avoid her office. They promise him relief from the uneasy feeling. Avoiding her office today would just put off the conversation he knows they'll have regardless. If they weren't going to be working in the same division on the same floor still, he might have avoided visiting her office. Too many pieces fit together that not visiting her office would be disrespectful, and he knows he's given her enough of that over the last year. Saying that to himself is like stabbing himself in the gut.

He doesn't need to knock when he's in the doorway; Devon is at her desk and glances up when his shadow fills the space. Her desk is empty but her face has the weariness of someone who spent the last few hours reading through hundreds of documents on their computer and needs to translate them into language the board could understand. Chris had been there before, once a month, in his current role. Sharing that torture has grown their bond, even if Chris doesn't acknowledge it.

"Please save me from this," she says.

Chris enters and closes the door as Devon stands and stretches, then goes to the keurig, her eyes briefly noticing the closed door.

"New cup?"

"Of course," he says.

The machine is quiet as it heats up water.

"Did we have a meeting that I'm supposed to be in?" she asks.

Chris sits in the chair opposite her desk, a hand raised.

"No, no, I just wanted to come chat."

Devon's eyebrow raises. Her office is decorated to be both impressive and comfortable with its muted pictures hanging on the walls and furniture that is more expensive than anything Chris has in his apartment, but is at the same time the most comfortable he's sat in. Without wearing a suit coat every day, her pulled back shoulders and erect posture make Chris feel shorter and make his words feel as if they carry less weight, are simply letters strung together on a loose string threatening to snap if he tugs at either end even a little. Her gaze holds him like lasers finding their prey but her words never carried the death that a laser would. Despite all of her appearance, with the door closed and just her and Chris inside her office, her shoulders relax slightly and her body isn't tight like she's ready to enter boss mode in an instant.

"It's still rather early for you to be wandering the halls," Devon says, "and you're visiting my office. I'm not sure how to feel about this."

Her voice conceals a tinge of sharpness underneath the softness, something she's never been able to let go of while at work, even in situations where she didn't need to be ready to bite back. Old habits are hard to break.

"It's just that kind of day," Chris says. "It seems a lot is not like we thought it was."

Devon pours a cup of coffee for herself and sets it on her desk, then takes Chris's near-empty mug and fills it. Her minifridge is full of creamer but when talking to each other, they both know straight black coffee is the only way they can manage. While the keurig starts to pour his cup, Devon leans on the counter and folds her arms.

"It's been a rough few months, please don't tell me you're

going to quit," Devon says. "You've finally gotten your part of the department to where it needs to be."

"I appreciate the compliment," Chris says, which makes Devon raise another eyebrow.

"A 'thank you,' too? Wow, this sure is an odd day."

She hands him his full cup of coffee and turns off the keurig so it doesn't gurgle while they talk. She sits behind her desk and for the first time during one of their talks, leans back in her chair. She balances the cup on her lap while steadying it with her hand, the steam rolling over her fingers.

Chris sighs, and in that sigh, releases a year of anger he's held toward Devon, a year of wanting to say so much but not knowing the right time or place to say it, a year of holding onto pride he now realizes didn't matter. Devon doesn't say anything as Chris lifts his eyes and takes a breath that feels fresh for the first time in a year. Letting go of old habits is invigorating.

"Thank you," Chris starts.

It surprises both himself and Devon, evidenced by the look of shock on both their faces.

"It has been a rough year for some of us. When you and Marissa approached me on the yacht, I wasn't sure what to think. I had such an image in my mind of what the promotion would mean, of what life would be like, of what turning 30 meant and what this promotion at work would solidify of that. I ran from the promotion because I thought that was the best way I could run from having my life upended. I blamed you for it.

"Then this job was forced on me. Either take it or be fired. I obviously stayed because I needed to and I hated you more for it. How dare you force me into a position I don't want to accept? That is no way to treat coworkers. I resolved myself to do whatever I could to make your life more difficult, resolved to be as cold to you at work as possible while still being civil so we could do our jobs. Damn, how I hated you for what you pushed on me."

"Chris, I-"

"Just listen." He sighs, but Devon doesn't speak. "Then I started working in this position and I turned 30. I learned a lot about my perceptions, whether they were right or wrong. I've realized a lot over the past few weeks, the past few months. I still am angry with you for forcing me into this role. It's not something I wanted, and having someone else make your choices is not how I wanted the next parts of my life to be decided. Who wants to have their life decided by someone else, especially their work life?

"This morning, Marissa visited me and told me about the new department head position. Immediately, I tensed and feared that the same thing that happened to me to get my current position would happen with this new position. I was prepared to fight Marissa and was at the point of being ready to quit. But I decided to try to listen to her without preconceptions. We talked and she told me of the position and I saw it differently than I saw the situation a year ago.

"She also said that you recommended me for the position and advocated quite strongly for me. It hit me this morning that you probably also advocated for me as strongly with my current role. A lot has happened to me this past year and I like to think that I've learned some things. One thing I've learned is that I can accept these opportunities and that my life doesn't have to change in the drastic ways I imagined. I also learned that sometimes having someone else believe in you when you might not believe in yourself is a blessing I didn't realize I had. I learned a lot when I turned 30. And each day that my 20s grow further away, I learn a little more. I may never be able to say 'hello' to my 20s again, but I'm ready to say 'hello' to new opportunities.

"So I'd like to say thank you. And I want to say that I'm sorry.

I shouldn't have treated you like I did over the past year. I'm still partly angry with you, but I am sorry that I reacted in the way I did. I really do appreciate the support over the past year."

He sips his coffee to denote the end of his monologue, and as a way to stop himself from rambling more. Devon sits in silence while he speaks, the steam slowly dissipating from her coffee. She also sips her coffee when he finishes.

"I appreciate that," she finally says. "There is no need to apologize. If there is, then it should be from me to you for forcing this on you. I am sorry as well. But I am happy you've seen your value and capabilities."

A brief silence settles that Chris breaks.

"So...can we start over with this promotion? My office will still be on this floor, so I won't be going anywhere. I'd appreciate having something like a weekly morning coffee since I'll be learning how to manage a larger department. Your guidance would be appreciated."

Devon smiles. "Of course.You can have your secretary contact mine to set it up."

Chris's laugh breaks the tense air between them. Letting loose in that way reminds him of when he and Devon first started at the Bank almost a decade ago and used to go out to bars to laugh, or when they pulled small pranks on each other over their cubicle walls. Having that relaxed atmosphere with her again is something he doesn't want to forfeit any longer.

A half hour later he's in his office with the door closed. He pulls a chair over to the window to sit parallel with it, staring at the mountains outside of Burlington, at the green ocean before him like it was earlier that morning. How different it looks now. The green is richer but no longer shines, and patches of brown like drops of paint are scattered about. He can't handle any more coffee, any more bitter as he stares out the window.

His phone is on his desk, face down, with the silencer on. He still wears his watch, but he no longer jumps when it vibrates or wishes it were on his wrist when he removes it momentarily to shower or when sleeping. Now, it's simply something he wears to not have to carry around his phone every minute while at work.

One year ago last week was the yacht work party. One year ago last week he saw her waitressing. One year ago last week was the last first time they slept together and the first time he realized how perfectly she fit with him, like a key in a lock. He hasn't thought about her like that for a few weeks. The thought didn't leave easily, like a dying patient hanging on for days after being taken off of life support, or a plant refusing to let its last green leaf fall after being forgotten about for a month. When that thought of Taylor did leave, it left scratches on him, but it *left*. The void grows slightly with each passing day. Something else he will never say 'hello' to.

Some days the thoughts return, an itch he wants to scratch until it leaves him alone forever, but he can't attack the itch and expect it to be gone. Instead, he persists through it and waits for it to wane, which it eventually does if he busies himself with something else or fixes his mind on another thought. Sometimes, the thought doesn't leave no matter how hard he tries. A lifetime of memories can be deleted on a phone in an instant, but that lifetime of memories with someone will remain with you forever. One day, he'll be able to fully live with them without them bothering him. Lydia does that, and he knows he can one day, too. At least he hopes he can.

22

INFINITE VOID

A utumn arrives in full force, painting the mountains surrounding Burlington with its usual palette of warm colors to contrast with the blue sky reflecting on Lake Champlain. Accompanying the color change are hay bales and pumpkins along Church Street and a slew of spooky, fall-themed drinks at his favorite coffee stop on the way to work. The need for a jacket to cut out some of the cold doesn't shorten the line winding into Church Street, causing passersby to weave around it or awkwardly excuse themselves as they push between two people.

Having known for years that at 7:50 the line starts to grow, Chris arrives either just before the rush or just after. This morning, Chris arrives a few minutes before and is now sitting at one of the black metal tables on the small roped off patio. He's alone at his table, while the other tables are filled with duos and one seats a trio of college-aged girls. Chris doesn't miss that age anymore.

Opened to a news article about yesterday's closing business trends on Wall Street, his phone is in one hand while the other is wrapped around the coffee cup adorned in pumpkins and ghosts. October is always a toss up, making the last few days of 60 degree weather a blessing that Burlingtonians appreciate. Some of his team would have already arrived at work, but it's Friday, and Chris wants to take it slow. His outfit of jeans and a sweater would surprise everyone at work.

Two people pass and wave at him. He waves back and continues to read the article. His news thread has transitioned from local news that repeated the same city business or crime stories to a thread of business articles. He still peruses the local news once a day, but a quick change of topics has freshened up his news app and offered a compliment to his job and his life, the latter of which has benefitted from following market trends for his retirement. 30 and caring about retirement. At least he isn't worrying about balding.

With a sigh and a stretch, he drops his phone into his jacket pocket and takes another long sip of his coffee. The remaining half will last him until he's in his office and makes a fresh cup. The line diminishes as the minutes tick past 8 and people have to rush to work. Now, the line is contained inside the coffee shop and the tables around Chris are filled with new patrons. He decides it's about time he got to his office, so he saunters up the street and drains his coffee before he's two storefronts away from the coffee shop. Oh well.

Street vendors roll their carts onto Church Street and the homeless from the night before slowly wake up as more foot traffic stomps past. Shop owners flip closed signs to open signs and the first break of the sun over the building's roofs appears on the brick walkway. A few people emerge from doors between storefronts that lead to apartments above the stores, neighbors Chris hadn't met since he started rushing to work. Now, he waves to a few and they wave back, bringing repetitiveness but

comfort to his walk to work. Chris had always wondered what
he missed by rushing through the street to work every morning,
what happened after he arrived at work in the rest of the world.

After a fresh cup of coffee is made, he makes some rounds
through the cubicles. His new team is huddled in 7 cubicles
directly outside of his office. Twice a week, he tries to stop in
each cubicle at some point and talk to each person. Half of his
reasoning is for when he's struggling to get motivated that early,
while the other part of it is because he doesn't want anyone to
feel like they were another cog whose life doesn't matter outside
of work. He resolved to know more about his employees as
people than soldiers of a corporation.

Conversations with his employees come as easily as tying his
shoes. His employees are as happy to dive into conversations
with him as he is with them; a distraction is a distraction,
regardless of position. Devoting time to the conversations made
his employees more comfortable talking to him during meetings
and they shared ideas more than he remembers sharing them
with Devon. Awkwardness becomes less frequent the more he
asks his employees about anything other than work. Meetings
often turn from an hour of repeating material they don't need
repeated to talking about their lives. Chris isn't sure if it's all
effective to do as a supervisor, but his department is still deliver-
ing, so he decides it works well enough.

Back in his office, he stares out the window at the Autumn
mountainside. His mornings also often started with a trek downstairs to the 3rd floor where Kelly usually hangs out to do work.
Given their date tonight, he isn't sure if he should go talk to her
today or wait to see her tonight. Both feel like odd options, but
avoiding her until their date feels like the better option so they
have more to talk about.

Nerves wreck him as he thinks about tonight. It's only
dinner, but he's never dated a coworker. Plus, he hasn't dated

anyone since Taylor. He's afraid Kelly won't be able to bring the same endless conversation out of him, won't find him as interesting, won't listen as deeply. He's afraid that if he touches her hand, he won't feel as clean as he did reaching for Taylor's hand. Tonight's date will decide a lot about where Chris is. He's not sure he's ready for that, yet.

Thinking about Taylor doesn't bring the same empty pit that it once did; now it's more of a shallow divot that reminds him it was once something deeper. He hasn't cried over her in a month, and more often than not he doesn't think every message on his phone is her. The more time that passes, the easier it is to let go of all the habits he struggled to even consider letting go of at the height of everything. More days than not, he doesn't even think about her, but she's always there as a distant thought. Lately, those thoughts don't stir any tumultuous feelings. Is this what Lydia meant by learning to live with it?

Enough of the morning is wasted, so he swivels in his chair to his desk and starts up his computer. His dual monitors illuminate and he sets to work. That shallow divot tends to stay a while, but elation from tonight fills it instead.

∾

DINNER DISHES ARE TAKEN AWAY by the server but their beers are only half empty, the second for each of them. Chris doesn't ask for the check and Kelly doesn't shift uncomfortably as he tells the server that they might have dessert so leave the tab open. That eases him as he sits back and relaxes after finishing a too-large bowl of pasta.

"I honestly can't see Keith ever hiking with you," Kelly says with a laugh. "You've got to be lying about that. He's the laziest dog I've ever met, with the worst name for a dog."

"I think his name was me foreshadowing his attitude and

giving him adequate punishment for being so lazy," Chris says with a grin. "You're right, though, it is difficult to imagine Keith walking more than to the backyard. He does it, I swear, even if it's rare."

"Well going for a hike with you sounds like a fun time, so I can see why he'd do it once in a while."

Chris blushes and twirls the beer slowly on the table. Would she actually go on a hike with him or would it be another Taylor situation? He tries to focus on the positives of tonight. They both dropped small compliments throughout dinner that made the other blush. His first compliment came out naturally and he didn't realize it was a compliment until Kelly blushed. Once she returned one, he tried to consciously say something to compliment her, but fumbled. Luckily, she laughed and complimented him back.

"Where do you normally take Keith around here?"

"There's a few flatter trails along the lake and a state park a short drive away that Keith seems to enjoy, or at least that doesn't make him lie down as soon as we get there. Or that doesn't make him glare at me as soon as we arrive."

"He seems to have an affinity for disliking you," Kelly says playfully.

Chris shrugs. "I've never met a dog with more attitude but that also has such a soft side."

"Well that seems to be a trait he acquired from his owner," Kelly says.

Every time she compliments him, he stumbles to find what to say next. Her compliments affect him differently than Taylor's. He forces Taylor from his mind; he's on a date with Kelly.

"Where do you hike?"

"I've been driving into NY with some friends to hike the 46 Peaks," Kelly says. "We've gotten about a dozen done so far."

"Yeah, Keith would never be willing to do that. I'm pretty sure his hateful glares would turn into him murdering me. And 'Man Murdered by Dog' doesn't make the best newspaper headline."

"'Man Murdered by Dog Named Keith'," Kelly adds.

Laughing with her comes more easily than getting Keith to go on a hike. She smoothly leads him through conversation and brings up new topics that keep him talking. There are slight moments of lulls, but he appreciates that they provide a moment for him to regain his thoughts and refocus on the conversation with her. His mind wavers every few minutes but he keeps bringing it back to his current situation. Taylor doesn't influence his thoughts anymore.

"Tomorrow we're going hiking locally in New Hampshire," Taylor says. "It's a small drive, but there's also a cider mill near where we're hiking."

"Oh, a cider mill? That sounds like a delicious way to end a hike. There's a few in the surrounding towns that I force Keith to visit with me. He's never happy about the car ride but when he sees where we're going, he gets excited because he knows he'll get one of the cider donuts."

"He's a spoiled puppy."

"Quite," Chris says. "New Hampshire sounds like a fun state to hike through. There's so much forest there that I imagine there's always a new park to explore."

"Yeah, we've visited a few times a year and we haven't hit the same park twice so far. We've even found random trails that we can hike on. New Hampshire is definitely an adventure."

His hand is around his beer and hers rests on the table. There is enough distance between them that to touch her hand wouldn't be an accident but an intended shift of his own. Chris debates if he should reach for her hand and brush against it, or move his hand into a position closer to her so she can move the other half if she wants to. Both options summon his anxiety about not feeling clean when they touch. In fear of that ruining the date, he tightens his hand around his beer. Taylor floats a little into his mind.

"It's getting a bit late," Kelly says.

Chris looks at his watch and surprises himself that it's nearly 8. Three hours fly by sometimes. After paying and finishing their beers, they walk out of the restaurant onto Church Street. Pumpkins decorate the street and half of the popup merchants along the brick walkway sell pumpkin flavored baked goods or hard apple cider or children's halloween costumes. The lights strung back and forth across Church Street are orange and purple, adding a glow beneath the streetlights that also reflects off the dead corn stalks lining every lamppost and other vertical object the decorators could find.

Kelly gently taps her hands onto her sides as she takes in the street with Chris. Seeing it with the sun set - the little orange and purple dots when they look up at the sky, the witch, ghost, and pumpkin decorations the shops have that light up their windows in the dark - brings them fully into Autumn mode. Chris wishes it was a tad chillier and that there was some sort of trick-o-treating event happening; the decorations seemed a waste without that, but it is still only mid-October.

"Thanks for the date," Kelly says when Chris doesn't offer anything.

"Thanks for letting me take you out," he says.

He isn't sure of what to do or say next. He keeps his hands at his side but Kelly has somehow drifted a step closer.

"Feel free to text me tomorrow," she says with a smile as innocent as any he has seen.

She moves to hug him when he makes it obvious that he is not going to move to kiss her goodnight. Chris's arms become hundred pound weights as they move to wrap around Kelly. Once they're embracing, Chris takes in a feeling of needing to wash his hands but also of not needing to. Taylor comes immediately to his mind and he's comparing her to Kelly, how he never questioned how he felt touching Taylor versus his immediate uncertainty with Kelly. They release each other.

"I-I'm not sure I can do this right now," Chris says, the words catching in his throat as he says them.

The smile leaves Kelly's face but it is replaced by confusion, not disappointment.

"It's not you," Chris says. "I'm still working on getting over something and I don't think I'm over it enough to be fair to you. Not right now. It wouldn't be fair to you if I'm still hung up on something else. But maybe in a few weeks?" His shrug brings more memories of Taylor. May 7 sticks in his mind.

Kelly's face relaxes and a slight smile returns, though it's nowhere near as happy as her previous one.

"I understand," Kelly says. "I appreciate the honesty. If you are ready to go on a second date in a few weeks, I'd be happy to go out again."

She gives him a quick peck on his cheek before she leaves. He doesn't immediately want to wash it off. But he does want to wash it off soon.

He walks Church Street alone. Kelly is somewhere behind him, though he doesn't have the heart to turn around to look to see if she's watching him leave, hoping he'll hesitate as he walks away, or if she's also turned and left, moved on from the date like it never happened. It was very real to him, though he can't face touching another person who isn't Taylor, at least not right now.

Images from that first holiday party when he drank too much flicker in his mind. Harris convinced him to get near blackout drunk and then he left Chris behind. He wandered the party alone until he ended up in the bathroom with vomit down his font and someone else's vomit down his back and splatters of urine on the wall and floor where he laid. Someone had fallen on top of him and also passed out, their bile sludging over his face. The next day he was diagnosed with a rash on his face that took 4 months to clear, and a cut he received when he fell became infected on his arm. He still has that scar. Chris's latent germophobia he overcame in high school emerged like a beast. Since then, touching anyone makes him uncomfortable.

Until Taylor came around. The smoothness of her voice, the ease at which she did nothing to pressure him and everything was his choice: he could touch Taylor without needing to dip his hands in acid, the first person he had touched in years. He'll never forget Taylor for breaking through that barrier.

Maybe one day Kelly could also pierce that barrier. But currently, she can't. When he hugged Kelly, his hands became covered in sweat and dirt and stickiness and his neck was coated with slime. He knows he'll be able to find someone else that he can touch who doesn't make him feel that, but until then, fuck, did losing Taylor hurt.

∾

KEITH LAYS on Austin's couch, stretched out so his head is on the arm while the tips of his paws touch the other arm. Every few minutes, he opens his eyes when someone at the dining room table laughs particularly loud, which happens at the end of every round of cards. Empty beers are scattered among the table with the cards, little ring marks of water making dealing difficult.

Kyle's phone is in his hand as he skips the current song playing on the speaker. When the next song starts, he sets his phone face down and rocks his head with the beat. Across from him sits Austin, who stares longingly at Kyle like a new lover watching the love of his life. Kyle winks at him and Austin blushes, the beer elevating his feelings and reactions.

Lydia sitting opposite Chris is a different story: every move he makes she glares at, the three empty beers in front of her influencing her attitude more than the ones in front of Austin.

"If you're going to fucking call a suit then don't lose the hand," she says, followed by the downing of her third beer.

She grabs another from the kitchen and asks the boys if any of them want another, which they all take, even though they still have a quarter in theirs left. She comes back with the caps still on the beers.

"If you're going to be a shitty partner then you have to open your own beer," she says, handing one to Chris.

"I couldn't let them call the suit, they're at 8 points!" Chris says. "Besides, Jack and nine, you're fine. I thought I could rely on you to at least get 1 trick."

Lydia tilts her head to glare at Chris as she sits back down, though he isn't sure that she's not about to jump across the table and strangle him. Instead, she pops the cap off her beer and drains the neck of it.

"If I wanted to be stared at like someone wanted to kill me, I would have just stayed home with Keith," Chris says.

From his position on the couch, the dog opens an eye and gives Chris a glare that matches Lydia's. She turns and nods a thanks, which the dog returns and then closes his eyes again.

"Hey, let's just have a friendly game," Kyle says. "Don't be mad at us because we're crushing you 8-3."

Lydia's glare turns to him, which makes him laugh as he deals the hand out. When he flips the top card, Lydia slams her hand on her cards and drags them off the table, scraping them the entire way. She hunches her shoulders as she stares at her hand and her eyes jump between it and the flipped card as Chris and then Austin pass. She raps her knuckles on the table, then stares solemnly over her hand at Chris and Austin as they pass again. She declares diamonds and the round starts.

"Now that's how you do it," she says when they win their third trick and everyone throws in their hand.

At her outburst, Keith opens an eye and glares at the back of her head, but decides the effort isn't worth his time so he closes his eyes again. Chris collects the cards and shuffles.

"Maybe if you played this well every hand, we wouldn't be down 8-4," he says, and immediately giggles with Austin.

Both men flinch when Lydia sets both her elbows on the table and folds her hands together, setting her head on them.

"If you two want to die tonight, keep up with that," she says. She turns to Kyle. "Do you want to be my partner after this game? These two need to learn a lesson."

"I would, but my current partner is the cutest and I don't want to lose getting to stare at him across the table," Kyle says.

Lydia mimics vomiting before drinking more of her beer.

"God, you gays are too fucking cute, you make me sick. Just deal the hand, Chris."

She gets up and ruffles through Austin's cupboards as Kyle works on changing the song again. She returns with a bag of chips and some dip. She sits and gives another death stare to Chris and Austin as she opens the bag.

"I could be at a poker game making money right now," she says, "but instead I'm here with you three about to eat my weight in Bison dip."

"And there's not a place you'd rather be," Austin says, grabbing a chip from the bag before Lydia has a chance.

She goes to smack away his hand but he retracts it before she can reach it. They laugh as Kyle opens the dip and then they all begin the next hand.

"Well, what the hell," Lydia says when Chris throws a card following suit. "A few beers and you forget how to play euchre?"

"Hey, neither of us called trump," he says. "We'll be lucky if we get two this hand."

He takes the next round but then they lose the rest of the rounds. Lydia shuffles the deck as Chris and Austin reset the score cards. Kyle gets up to pet Keith on the couch, who wags his tail with more energy than he has had for anyone else all night. Kyle climbs onto the couch and suffocates Keith beneath him as he hugs the dog, but Keith licks him and wags his tail.

"We're ready, get in here," Lydia says when she starts dealing.

Two hours later the game is broken up. Kyle is on the floor with Keith's head on his chest and a pillow beneath Kyle's head, one of his hands slowly stroking down Keith's neck. Chris marvels at how relaxed Keith appears but smiles at his dog being so relaxed and happy. Lydia has already headed upstairs, her five empty beers in front of her spot. Chris and Austin sit at the table, Austin leaning forward on it with his head resting on an arm, his beers finally working to tire him out. Chris is slouched in a chair, watching Kyle pet Keith.

"You're so lucky,' Chris says quietly. He isn't sure if Kyle is awake enough to hear.

"Thank you." Austin smirks. "He's quite amazing, isn't he?"

Chris nods, but his best friend can't see him. Chris looks around the house at what was once orderly and perfect, like a museum whose exhibits are not to be touched. Now, marks of Kyle's imperfectness mars Austin's museum: a nerdy piece from Star Wars disturbs the otherwise scenic portraits hanging around the house, the larger blanket on the back of the couch is never folded or on the back of the couch, a plant sits next to the TV, and the fridge has magnets of various Star Wars characters. Their personalities mix in the house in such a way that it looks like they had always lived together and that they mesh like a lock and a key.

Austin turns his head but sets it back down on his arm.

"How have you been?"

Chris knows what he's asking but also isn't certain he understands. It's been a few weeks since he's talked about it with anyone.

"I'm doing alright," he says. "I had a date last night."

"Oh yeah," Austin says, his eyes drooping and a yawn escaping. "Tell me about it. With Kelly, right?"

Chris nods. "It was really nice. I felt good to go on a date again. We talked a lot and I found out she hikes almost as much as I like to. She'll make a better hiking partner than Keith."

"Oh, poor puppy," Austin says. "He just wants to take it easy."

"He has the easiest life of any dog I know," Chris says, glancing up at Kyle petting him.

"So, when's the second date?" Austin asks. "The first sounds like it went really well."

Chris shrugs. No memories come back to him.

"I'm not sure if I'm ready yet. Sometimes-sometimes there are moments when I'm still caught up in other stuff. I don't want to put that on a new relationship. That's not fair to her."

Austin nods.

"It takes time."

Chris wants to say thank you but it feels random to say it. He hasn't checked his phone all night and he hasn't driven past her house in a few months. Even after his date with Kelly, the prickling of her that came when he hugged Kelly disappeared immediately.

He suddenly smiles. He is entirely content sitting at Austin's with his best friends and dog, playing cards and talking about everything that's simultaneously nothing and everything, and joking the entire time like they used to. Except, now they're grown up, and they have jobs with heavy responsibilities and engagements and a 3 that starts their age rather than a 2. He waves goodbye to his 20s forever, just like he did Taylor. There will be other hellos, but never to either of them again.

Keep Reading
www.svdbooks.com

Other books:
Count to Six

Made in the USA
Middletown, DE
10 December 2022

17990649R00209